THE ENLIGHTENMENT OF

NINA

FINDLAY

ANDREA GILLIES

Praise for Andrea Gillies' THE WHITE LIE:

"A gripping exploration of the stories families tell about themselves, myths sometimes more potent than the truth."
Financial Times

"Gillies excels in her portrait of a landscape that consumes the merely human; eats it for lunch, as it were, and has slowly, over many generations, created a family in its own image."
Helen Dunmore, *The Times*

"The prose is elegant and beautiful, and Gillies has a skill for creating both character and a sense of place... I couldn't put *The White Lie* down." For Books' Sake

"*The White Lie* is a page-turner... It is also, finally, very moving." Francine Stock, *Guardian*

"Gilles excels both at describing the landscape and at delineating those subcutaneous secrets and shared assumptions that bind families together." *Literary Review*

"A wonderfully compelling portrait of a family haunted by secrets and lies... pitch perfect on the chilling, devastating consequences of guilt." Sally Brampton

"Gillies' beautifully crafted debut combines page-turning aplomb with psychological insight... She is a tantalising story-teller, dropping in clues, vertiginous surprises and unexpected revelations." *Marie Claire*

"There's an echo of Virginia Woolf that lifts Gillies' work above the average family drama... This is an unusual, unsettling, often lovely story that plumbs the depths of what family means." *The Scotsman*

First published in 2014 by
Short Books, 3A Exmouth House, Pine Street, EC1R 0JH

10 9 8 7 6 5 4 3 2 1

A CIP catalogue record for this book
is available from the British Library.

ISBN: 978-1-78072-207-8

Cover design by Mark Ecob

Printed at CPI Group (UK) Ltd, Croydon, CR0 4YY

To friends met along the road

Chapter One

When the minibus came round the sharpest bend of the descent, trundling along on the stony dirt road, Andros crouching and peering through the windscreen in the poor light, he didn't at first see the woman standing taking photographs. Afterwards Nina surprised people by insisting on taking all the blame for the accident; she was the fool who'd stood in the middle of the hill road at dusk, pale-haired in grey clothes and very nearly invisible. It was all her fault, she said, all of it, not just this but everything, though down in the village not everybody thought the situation had been that cut and dried. She'd heard that Andros had been given a hard time by his wife and by his neighbours; poor Andros had been bombarded with questions. Why was he driving without lights? Had he been driving too fast? Why wasn't he wearing his glasses? Why had he reacted the way he'd reacted and put seven people's lives at risk?

It wasn't just the facts that mattered, but the sequence. This was something Nina had thought about a lot, by the time it came to leave the island hospital: chains of events and how they could take people in unexpected directions. On her final day she'd gone around taking last pictures of things and putting her hands on them – plants, inanimate objects, the seat outside where she'd spent so many hours – imprinting them with touch in her memory. It had become important to her, this place, not least for its beauty. There could have been nowhere more ideal for recovering from trauma. The building had been designed by an architect with a taste for the cleanly modern, a one-storey arrangement of ten white rooms that formed three sides of a square. Its wide internal corridor looked out through floor-to-ceiling windows over a courtyard garden of rocks and herbs, from which a short flight of wooden steps led down to a pebble beach.

The hospital stay had begun three weeks before. During the first 48 hours Nina revisited the collision every time she gave in to sleep, re-experiencing its shocking suddenness. Over and over she stood on the road and turned to see the boxy white vehicle bearing down on her. She hadn't seen it coming, nor heard its approach; her mind had been elsewhere. She'd been singing a song, "Cucurrucucu Paloma", one she'd listened to so often that she found she could sing it herself, even though she had no Spanish. She was enjoying that aspect, in fact: how the words had become music, like an incantation, like art in her mouth that she was making and delivering to the valley. She'd looked up the English translation before coming to Greece and had written it out in the back of her notebook.

"They say that at night he spent the dark hours crying; they say that he wasn't eating, that he had lost all appetite. They swear that the sky itself trembled in sympathy with his weeping, how he was suffering for her. Even when he was dying, he called out for her…"

It was a song that was meaningful to her and to her situation. It wasn't about her ex-husband, who'd reacted stoically to the news that she wanted a divorce, but about her ex-husband's brother, a man who had loved her and whom she had loved.

It wasn't only that she was singing. Her camera was up at her eye, being turned from landscape to portrait and back again, so as to capture silhouettes of the nestled and darkening settlement lying below, set against the metal glow of the sea. The sun went down fast on the island, and its setting was brief and fatal. *Magic might become manifest here, if a person could only be alert to it,* she'd said, in the postcard that she'd written a few minutes before. She'd been profoundly unwell by then. *An island is a world,* she wrote, *though this is an untypically perfect one; this world is a family and even its housing's democratic.* She'd wanted to read *The Tempest*; earlier that day she'd rummaged through the books on the English stall at the market, wondering if the universe might provide, but nobody takes Shakespeare on holiday. "The isle is full of noises," she'd said, on first arriving at the viewpoint, having walked the long, slow incline from the harbourside. There were swallows, bats, the occasional flying insect blundering about; human voices rising up and magnified; a tiny scooter making its bee hum on the coast road. The teenage boys liked to circumnavigate at this time of day, a journey that took less than an hour, their white lights tracking and overtaking one another. She'd taken out her camera. She'd begun to sing the song.

So, Nina wasn't paying attention to the possibility of the bus, but nor was Andros paying attention to the possibility of Nina. He was looking for goats. They could be hard to see on this, the last journey of the day down from the upper village, especially if he was running half an hour late (as he was today for trivial reasons), and he'd tried in the past to abolish this last run, but the women who tended the gardens – most assertively, his wife Olympia – had protested. After the accident, when Andros lost his nerve, they had to make the argument again. They needed to go up to the allotments, they said, and needed to get home again, and it was ludicrous to make them use their cars. Not all of them even had cars. What, were they going to have to take their cars up there and leave them in the sun all afternoon? It didn't make sense. He was just going to have to grit his teeth and carry on.

Andros was almost on top of the goat when he realised it was there, a big brown billy-goat with a defiant goat expression, rotating its jaw in chewing. An immediate decision needed to be made: there wasn't quite enough room to pass on the left – if he went that way he'd scrape along the hillside wall – but there was plenty of space at the other side, without having to venture too near to the edge and its sheer drop. He veered to the right, and that's when he saw Nina.

Unaware of the goat's role, it was hard for Nina to make sense of what was happening. The minibus was coming right at her, but in a pause that might have been catastrophic she saw Andros realise she was standing there, his eyes widening and mouth mutely cursing. Luckily they had compatible instincts: she threw herself backwards to his left as Andros veered further to the right, though their actions weren't quite enough for them to avoid one another, and so as her legs rose into the air the bus clipped her hard between knee and ankle. She felt it break, her right leg, heard the snap, the impact travelling through her cells, passing the bad news through her nervous system. Her head bounced against the road and then her back, and her vision pulsed and darkened, narrowing rapidly inside a dark border line. There was a rumble that she heard through her spine, a bang, a pause, a series of thumps and then far-off-sounding shouts. Puzzled goat faces peered down as blackness eliminated the sky, and she was unconscious until, unquantifiable minutes later, she half opened her eyes and saw Andros looking down at her, and ambulance personnel preparing to lift her, saying her name, and there was pain that returned like a whip.

Because the island's own facility had no surgical wing, Nina was taken across the bay on the boat, to Main Island and to the ugly 1970s-built hospital in the town. By the time the long, hearse-like vehicle got her over the water – by special arrangement with the ferry, which had been tied up for the day, and round winding roads to A&E, she'd begun to hallucinate. She imagined that Paolo, her husband, was there in the back of the car with her, and felt urgently that she had to explain things to him, recent events and their auto-biographical origins. He didn't respond, adopting an apparent deafness and blindness, which as she'd say later was pretty typical and meant that she kept on talking. Administered drugs began to kick in, and so by the time the hospital staff got Nina onto the examination couch she'd forgotten about the encounter with a man who shouldn't have been there.

"I don't want Paolo to know," she kept saying. "You won't tell him, will you? He's already so disappointed in me."

A second shot of morphine was offered, but Nina wanted fiercely to remain aware, to make decisions and exert control. She wanted information but recoiled from some of it. The leg was snapped jaggedly between ankle and knee like an object, though she couldn't look at it and was advised not to. She'd always thought of her bones as enmeshed, wrapped, integrated things. What had happened to her muscles, her veins? Was she at risk of bleeding to death? She vomited with fear that the surgeon would amputate, her voice full of pleading. An English-speaking doctor, worry-ingly young-looking, said, "If they offer you more anaesthetic in there, take it, because it can get quite..." he paused, looking for the word, "...noisy."

"Noisy?" she queried. "Noisy?"

Another face appeared, a tired thin-faced nurse, and a form was presented and Nina signed it, her signature unlike anything it had ever been before, big and looping and going off the edge of the page. "Please take the morphine," the young doctor said. "She will get into trouble if you don't take it." Nina consented, and just as the senior man appeared, an emperor surrounded by courtiers, felt the warm rush of it flooding her, and her eyes rolled back in her head and the pain and the fear stabilised. Things became not just manageable, but amusing. She was able to laugh at the serious things the consultant had to say about pins and screws and bones and stitches. He took her flippancy in his stride.

Two days after the operation Nina was returned to Small Island, a place that the guidebook referred to as the calf to Main Island's cow, but in terms of scale was more like the rabbit to Main Island's elephant. By now she had crutches and was expected to begin to move about, though no contact was to be made between the damaged leg and the ground; not yet. It was disconcerting not to have a cast on it.

"Why don't I have a plaster-cast?" she'd asked Dr Christos on her second day back, ensconced in her room in the cottage hospital. She'd wondered, as a tourist, what the building was for. She'd walked past it along the shore and had mistaken it for an art gallery.

"A cast is to keep things in place," he told her. "You don't need that because they've put pins inside the bone."

"Inside, inside the bone? I thought they were alongside."

"They're inside, and they keep things straight. But I can see why people would prefer a cast. It feels like a protective shell."

"Exactly. It feels wrong just to have bandages, when what's underneath…" Nina couldn't finish the thought. It was disturbing, the idea of inner scaffolding. Someone had been inside her leg, while she lay with her self in dormancy, inert and gaping and absent, and they'd pushed metal into the meat. She looked down at her leg, laid on the top sheet of the bed – it was too hot to stay under it, with this stiflingly hot limb swaddled tightly in crepe – and saw faint watery outlines of bloodstains. Dr Christos looked too.

"We'll need to change the dressing," he said.

"Can I have more morphine for that?" She was only half joking. She was beset by imaginings. But the unwrapping ritual didn't reveal the scene of carnage that she'd feared. It was clean and ordinary: ordinary, that is, aside from the long and fairly neat cut and the Frankenstein's-monster stitches. "When will I be walking?"

"Not for a while, but we need to get you mobile. It'll be difficult, exhausting, but we need to get you moving on the crutches. Little expeditions at first. We'll start with the bathroom."

"How long do you think I'll be here?"

"Depends. Once you're whizzing about confidently and we're happy with the general state of your health you can go home."

"Right." Her spirits dipped at the prospect of returning to face the music, the explanations.

"How's the head today?"

"Still a bit nauseous, still tired, but better than it was." She sank deeper into the pillow and closed her eyes.

"Then you should sleep. Your biggest fan is coming to see you later, by the way. The island priest. Brace yourself: there's been a lot of church-going and candle-lighting. You know they've put up a shrine at the scene of the drama?" The picture on his phone showed a small stone niche, about eighteen inches high, inscribed inside with the date of the accident and fitted with a painted plaster crucifix, pink and blue, one that had been finished with gold leaf. "This has been a big event for the island," he added.

Dr Christos had been there the first morning, sitting beside her bed doing paperwork. When she'd opened her eyes in the white cube of her room, its whiteness relieved only by pale-blue stripes on the windowblind, the palest possible green of the metal bed, the dark blue of the bedside chair. she saw that the chair was occupied by a man busy writing with a fountain pen, a man who hadn't yet noticed that she'd woken. The doctor had coughed and she'd stepped out of the past, scooped from a conversation with Luca, her husband's brother. They'd sat side by side in an armchair that was upholstered in pink velvet, one only just big enough for two skinny children. On his lap there'd been a vast book with a dusty green cover and gold lettering, a world atlas, and he'd had the page open at Italy, showing her where his grandfather came from. She was ten years old and felt sick with happiness; her heartbeat had drummed through her hip bone. It was bewildering to be bounced from this dream, one that felt nothing like a dream but like life lived over again, and into this alternative and dreamlike reality: the white room, the blue chair and the stranger. He was about her own age, this stranger, mid-forties at a guess, with shoulder-length black hair, some of it twisted almost into ringlets, and, when he glanced up towards the wall, tapping the pen thoughtfully against his upper lip, the kind of face that seems immediately trustworthy, though not handsome as such: his chin was small, his eyebrows outlandish and his nose had broken once. His wide mouth pressed wider into concentration as he returned to write on – whatever it was he was writing on – a piece of paper at the top of others in a file, which he'd balanced against the thigh of his raised leg, his ankle resting over his other knee. He was on the sturdy side of averagely built, wearing a faded red collarless shirt, frayed jeans and black cotton shoes that were rope-soled and flattened at the back.

He'd introduced himself as Dr Christos – his English accent was part southern British, part North American – and had gone to get coffee. "It's no trouble; I have a machine in my office. They are painting my office." He made a face. "But I prefer to sit with patients during the day, anyway. If I'm at my desk inevitably the phone rings or I'm interrupted. I look less available here." The coffee was dense and oily and she'd made an appreciative noise. "You like it?" He looked pleased, settling himself again in the blue chair, for a hospital an unusually soft and comfortable-looking chair, apparently leaving the conversation at that.

After a short while Nina said, "It looks as if you have a lot of – what are they, patient notes?"

"All the many items of paperwork that pass through the hospital. We are having a financial crisis here; you've probably heard. We no longer have a manager, so all of this joy has devolved to me."

"You speak very good English."

The compliment might have been patronising but he didn't seem to mind. "Thank you; in fact most of my life has been English-speaking. I left here as a student and spent some years in Baltimore and then Boston, in London and then the States again, and never meant to return, other than for... I forget how it goes, births and marriages and deaths; something to do with hatches."

"Hatches, matches, despatches."

"Yes! I must write that down before I forget it again." He stared at her, an intensity about him, a deliberateness of focus, something fearlessly direct, so that she found it hard to look at him. "Your notes tell me you're from Edinburgh. I haven't been but hear it's beautiful. You don't sound very Scottish."

"My father was – is – but my mother wasn't. She was Norwegian. My accent is kind of nowhere."

"And you have an Italian name."

She lifted her wrist with its hospital tag. "I noticed that I'm Nina Romano here."

"It was the name in your passport."

"I'm Nina Findlay, but my husband's name is Romano."

"I don't think I've met any Norwegians. We get a lot of Dutch and Germans who bring their tents and caravans and even their own bread and like to walk around naked."

"Dutch and German people have tried to talk to me in their own languages on the beach."

"I should have stayed in the US. I came back because my father died and my mother was ill and the years have gone by. My mother died two years ago, and I still seem to be here." He checked his phone for messages and was silent for a minute. "Also, I should warn you that they're preoccupied, the locals, about how lucky it was. The accident. There's lots of talk about whether it was luck or divine intervention."

"Lucky how?"

"They had a narrow escape."

This was undoubtedly true. It was lucky that the incident took place just at that part of the hillside in which there was a broad ledge jutting out beneath the road. That's where the minibus landed when it disappeared over the edge, having blown its front right tyre on a small pointed rock, one that afterwards would have a set of rosary beads, a *komboskini*, draped over it. Having veered away from Nina, the bus had been bumping along in loose stones just inches from the drop, and may have avoided going over the side or may not have, but the blown tyre shunted it decisively to the right, whereupon it tipped away, tilting and hesitating and then flipping over in a graceful full circle before coming to rest once more on its wheels, bouncing on its suspension and stopping dead, a mere seven feet from the precipice. After a short silence came the realisation that they were saved. Andros put his head onto the steering wheel and was sick, and the women in the back were screaming.

A church service of thanksgiving was held, its invitation ringing out from the chapel at the top of the hill, a white-painted blue-domed building with a panoramic outlook, sitting on the island's highest point as if announcing its ocean governance, while at the same time conceding its powerlessness, marking its losses with bell-ringing. Dr Christos took a note that Nina had written, and translated it in reading it out, and returned with pictures on his camera, and pointed out the people who'd been passengers.

"So they're okay, they're really all okay?"

"Scratches only and bruises. They were brought here to be checked over; nobody had to go across the water. Four stitches was the most, and nowhere near an eye." He went to the window and moved the vertical blind aside and opened the French doors, revealing a world outside that was vividly coloured: a stripe of sea, a vast zone of sky, the creams and greys of the garden, their cacti and agave and tropicals offset by the dotted colours of flowering herbs. The hot air that drifted in smelled first of rosemary and thyme, and then of warmed lavender. "We don't want you doing this kind of thing while balancing on one leg. Let Nurse Yannis do it for you."

"She does, she has – she's very kind."

"Windows open in the morning when the sun is round the back; closed and darkened for siesta in the afternoon; everything opened again until it starts to get dark. Or closed if you'd prefer it; if you'd prefer to be alone." He turned to her. "Would you? Prefer to be alone?"

"I don't know yet."

He raised the striped blind, a roller blind, from the smaller second window. "There's a mosquito net on this one, so it's the one to keep open at night. Ventilation without bugs." He took his phone out of his pocket and looked at it. "I have to go, but before I do, I meant it about working out of my office. I tend to circulate around the patients and spend time working in their company, so I'll come and do admin here for a bit of each day, unless you'd rather not. I sit with the ones who don't get visitors. Whole families troop through here for some of them, with bagfuls of food, hot lunches, bigger televisions, but some other people don't have anyone. I assume you won't be visited, unless your husband is on the way."

"Ex-husband. Soon to be ex-husband. I disgraced myself and moved out."

"Disgrace. There's something delicious about the word disgrace."

"He sent a text today, wanting to escort me home when I'm ready to go, but I told him not to. We … we parted on bad terms."

"Evidently he's forgiven you, if he wants to come to you here. What was it, this disgrace?"

"He will never forgive me. He's not the forgiving kind. No, that's wrong. He is the forgiving kind. He's just not the forgetting kind. And we've agreed that it's over." Dr Christos waited. "I was an idiot. In short. For a long time quite stupid, and then for a brief time, unhinged."

"It'd be good to hear the whole story. We're going through a tedious patch here; dull interminable diseases and endless paper-work. Lately almost everything's seemed tedious. Generally the people I sit with don't want to tell me anything interesting. Or they have Alzheimer's and accuse me of being the cousin who ruined their dry-cleaning business. Or they are – I am sorry to say this – very boring; nothing's ever happened to them. Or they have broken their necks diving off the rocks and aren't up to much. Sometimes I am even driven to working in my office." He gathered up his things. "I have to go. But I will be back, that is if you don't object to company."

Chapter Two

On the flight to Greece Nina found herself sitting beside an insurance broker, a large man and the only one on board dressed in a suit and tie, clothes that were in decidedly unsummery shades of brown. Before they strapped themselves in he gave everyone within reaching distance his business card, stretching across the seats to hand out others, piles of more than one, asking people to pass them on, and made an announcement to the wider vicinity. "Anybody want to talk about Life? Instant quotes and cover given!"

As she took the card Nina was aware that there was unimpressed muttering in the seat behind, and an ostentatious ripping of the gift into four pieces. She inserted hers into her book. "Alternatively it makes a good bookmark," her neighbour said, introducing himself as Keith. He shook Nina's hand and stowed his belongings, applied a beanbag neckrest, took two pills with a miniature of whisky and fell deeply asleep with his mouth open.

Nina lay with her head against the seatback, her book unread on her lap. Over and over she ran through the conversation she'd had with Paolo at the airport, the look on his face. She'd had to text Luca to warn him that Paolo knew, and what it was that Paolo knew, because how could Paolo not steam round there and bang on the door? She couldn't help visualising it, the standoff on the doorstep and what might be said in her absence. But perhaps nothing very much would be said. Perhaps the men would each decide never to mention it again. It was as likely an outcome as any other. She recited it to herself from time to time, the text message she'd sent to Luca as they'd prepared for takeoff, just before being told to turn off her phone. The repetition was self-critical. The situation had been urgent and rushed and it hadn't been a kind message, nor convincingly apologetic.

Just told Paolo about us, the basic fact, in rush at departures, and am now on plane. Also, important detail. It was April and

11

after I moved out. Nothing said about February, nor about April conversations. Please stick to story for my sake. For both our sakes. Sorry.

Why had she written "for both our sakes"? She shouldn't have written that. He might interpret it as some kind of a hinted threat. She'd expected him to respond straight away – Luca's phone was always kept in view – and that they'd talk more, but the reply hadn't arrived until the following day. The island signal was dodgy, but even so. Even so. sixteen hours later. It took him sixteen hours, and even then it was just an ok without even a full stop to follow it.

Ok

The journey to Greece had suffered a dispiriting start. Almost everyone Nina encountered on the way there seemed miserable and mean: there was a striking unanimity about their filthy mean moods. The taxi driver arrived ten minutes early and became irritable about Nina keeping him waiting, when the fact was that he was early. He hadn't helped with her suitcase, even though she struggled with it when a wheel came off on the pavement, nor replied to her polite chat, nor thanked her when she gave him a generous and undeserved tip. Once inside the airport, the operator at the coffee counter had reacted badly to a £20 note. "Seriously?" he'd said, holding it as if it were poisonous – and the man at Security had spoken sharply when it took time to find the plastic bag of toiletries for the scanner. The staff at the gate had made a fuss about a sandwich, like it was a second piece of luggage, and made her put it in her bag for boarding.

In the middle of the flight they'd hit an alarming pod of turbulence, one of those that feels like you've sailed into a vacuum and are dropped like a ball. The plane sank abruptly, causing gasps and shouts of fright, before bouncing along the floor of nothingness and rising steadily again. The captain made one of his smooth, chocolatey announcements, reassuring everyone that all was well and that this kind of thing was just a fact of life and perfectly safe, although perhaps unpleasant. He didn't say anything about being flirted with by extinction, but everyone else knew that's what had happened, right there in the middle of the drinks service, just as the trolley caught on one of the seats and another of the cabin crew was trying to flog scratch cards. When the flight hit a second bout of what the captain referred to as *lumps and bumps*, one that threw the plane for several minutes from side to side, a deeper silence descended while people made bargains to enjoy life more, to go freelance and buy boats. The air in the cabin became dense with resolve, while Keith slept peacefully on.

"No one ever survives a plunge into the ocean in a jet plane," Luca had said once at a family party, interrupting his wife's account of an on-board spat. He'd been chided by a member of crew for reading during the safety demonstration. "It's a total joke," he'd said to the crew member, "all this rigmarole about life jackets under your seat."

"Brother, your optimism is one of the best things about you," Paolo told him. Nina laughed because that was Nina's role. She had always been the glue that bound them. Her laughter, her interceding, had always been crucial, reminding each of them that they loved one another.

"It's absolutely safe, flying, as long as nothing goes wrong, and then you're well and truly fucked," Luca said.

He and his wife had flown to Italy on business more often than Nina and Paolo, but that particular occasion had been a social trip, to go to the party that marked the end of the wine harvest in Francesca's home village. She'd been born in London, in fact, but her parents had returned there to live for their retirement. While he was gone Luca emailed Nina every day, morning and night. Additionally there were frequent text messages. *Think I just ate horse, but have had better. Think it was the saddle. Missing you.*

Now, as the plane was chucked from side to side, Nina pondered why it was that she'd handed over her destiny so readily to this (possibly imperfectly maintained) airborne vehicle, its thin skin of metal the only thing separating them all from oblivion. It was clear from the faces around her that others were feeling the same. They were all together on a rollercoaster of coping and dread, clammy with alternating cynicism and trust.

It'd been Nina's doctor's idea that she go on holiday. It was mid-September when she travelled, and blustery and grey at home, the Christmas puddings already stacked high in supermarkets; it remained late summer on the island, though things would close up for the season very soon. In October the locals did other things: stayed at home, tended their gardens, watched DVD boxed sets and went on holidays of their own. Nina hadn't been to Small Island for 25 years, but there hadn't been much change in the interim: not in its look and layout, nor really in its culture either. It was surprising that nothing had changed, and yet what could change? Motorways and superstores were irrelevant there, and the local mood too conservative for other more optional sorts of progress. As they'd approached in the late afternoon on the little ferry, its small dominion had looked like an arid hill rising out of the sea, sticking out of the southern Aegean. It was only when they grew closer that the softer intermediate slopes became visible, the flatter sections thick with olive groves, the terracing cut for the growing of wine and the modest houses among them. Most of the shoreline was pebbly, though there were stretches of sand beach at intervals and a bigger one, a golden hundred-yard strand known as Blue Bay, a short walk from the main village. People who weren't fishermen or in tourism made a subsistence living; though there were only two settlements there were also homes perched on contrary angles of the hill, smallholdings that worked tiny parcels of land. The main village was down by the harbour in a T-shaped arrangement: a single joined-together row of houses facing out to sea, a couple of shops, a café and two tavernas, and then between the tavernas a road going back at right angles, a no-through road lined on both sides with more simple houses. A narrow band of tarmac encircled the island, most of it adjoining the shore, and a dirt road, hard and pale and loose with grit, stretched up the hill to the top village, which was really only a hamlet and wasn't quite at the top. This was the winding and precipitous route on which Nina had met the minibus and broken her leg.

She could see the shore road from the furthest corner of the hospital grounds. She could see the women waiting at the bus stop in the morning, on their way up to the allotments, and liked to go out and look at them waiting. They were the people whose lives she'd imperilled, though they seemed to be fine; nobody was limping and they were in their usual high spirits. She'd walked past them, these same six women, every day in the week before the accident; they were always together and always talking nineteen to the dozen. They were the first islanders she'd seen on her first morning, on leaving the hotel. It'd been a day full of promise and she'd breakfasted early, alone on the terrace in the fresh morning air, sitting under a roof made of wooden poles and the grapevine that bound them, the sunlight dappling and shifting through the leaves. Afterwards she'd packed spare clothes, a towel, suncream, biscuits, a bottle of water, two books and her journal into the beach bag, putting her swimsuit on under her dress. When she came out onto the street the women were standing at the bench, a rudimentary one that Andros had installed and painted yellow. There were more yellow benches at Blue Bay, at intervals along the road, and round the back of the island on its wilder rockier side. Nina hadn't taken the bus. She'd wanted to walk, to see things unfold at walking speed; she'd wanted to slow everything down: her thoughts, her heart rate, her experience of hours passing. She needed to metabolise the recent catastrophe. Besides, if she took this morning bus and was the only tourist on board she'd have to go up to the top village and down again, before being taken along to the beach. That was the scheduled route; the women would only speak up, instructing Andros to take the tourists first, if there were more than two and they liked the look of them. Nina never took the bus, but she could imagine sitting opposite them on the seat that had its back to the driver – a seat they never used themselves – and being under the silent appraisal of six pairs of very dark eyes. There was something almost tribal there, something about blood and belonging that made Nina envious. All the women wore floral dresses with aprons over them, and ankle-height wellingtons; all were small and sturdy, with soft lined faces of a similar shape, wide at the brow but with pointed chins, deep-set eyes and teeth that looked older than they did. When Nina got closer, on her first morning, the conversation loosened just enough to allow for a good look at her, and they'd tonelessly returned her call of *kalimera*. She'd taken a photograph and was seen doing so and was scowled at, a chiding finger wagged in her direction. She'd strolled on past the harbour and had sat on the wall a while to watch the boats, which had been out very early and were pulling in and tying up. The men offered her something from the catch, and she got her phrasebook out and made a hash of explaining that she had no kitchen.

"Give to Vasilios," one of them said, trying to push a pink fish, one that looked like a child's drawing of a fish, into her hands. "Vasilios cook it."

She shook her head shyly, though Vasilios would have cooked it up for her, there was no question; he'd think nothing of it. Favours were nothings here; it was one reason she'd wanted to come back. One of the other men dangled a tiny live squid in front of her. "Here: pet for you." As she walked onwards she saw him beating the thing in swift reprisal against the harbour wall.

Now the road began to bend gently to the right, until soon she was out of sight of the village and – aside from the tarmac road – in an ancient landscape, a biblical one of shepherds and sheep. It took ten minutes to walk round the slow curve of the hill, out of human contact and observation, ten minutes that were without houses, out of sight of the fishermen and not yet within sight of the beach. She walked at a faster pace, trying not to have city instincts, but then there it was, stretching ahead, Blue Bay, shaped like a mouth turned up at the corners, one backed by Mediterranean pines, and above it on the hill a cluster of white-painted houses that marked the edge of the upper village. The pine aromas released on this beach in the evening were sumptuous: it was worth walking down here just before dark to experience the scent, released as if from storage heaters, though when she and Paolo had promenaded here before dinner, 25 years earlier, the weather had been too chilly for the effect to be dramatic. When they'd stayed here they'd been the only Britons at the hotel. Most of the visitors, even now, were day trippers who came from Main Island to swim, to stroll the quaint streets and eat on a café terrace, to buy shell necklaces and postcards and venture up the hill to buy honey from a smallholding, stopping to marvel at the view, before heading back on the late-afternoon boat, quietly across the sound in failing light. Andros, minibus owner and, as he said of himself, the island's one truly entrepreneurial spirit, had thus far failed to galvanise support for his long-standing project, a three-storey hotel with 24 rooms. There was no lack of suitable plots, but he had one insurmountable problem: he couldn't get the villagers behind the plan. Most crucially, he couldn't get his wife Olympia's support, which was a pity as she happened through inheritance to be the major landowner, and besides that was also the leader of the island council.

Taverna Vasilios had much better accommodation at twice the cost of the other more basic hotel, which was across the road at the T-junction and had a bunkhouse for backpackers. At the time Nina was staying there, half of Vasilios's six rooms were taken by British people, and he'd put them together on the first floor. Next door to her were two elderly English sisters, Iris and June, who brought with them an atmosphere of period drama, in their shin-length dresses and long strings of beads, their grey hair gathered identically at the napes of long necks, and next door to them a Welsh couple, Cathy and Gareth, a professional body-builder and his athletic wife, their muscles a deeper shade of walnut every day. The other three rooms, up on the top floor, were occupied by a Belgian family, a solitary German and two mainland Greeks. She failed to catch most of their names when they were introduced. The morose Belgian couple, people Nina never saw smile, had an equally morose-looking child, who played silently with whatever toys were produced for him at the dinner table. The Greeks were easily spotted at a distance because the woman had very wide hips and the man had an extravagant moustache; they were friendly, animated early retirees and their being jovial at mealtimes earned them mutterings and rolled eyes from the Belgians. There was something about the dynamic of the group that reminded Nina of an old-fashioned detective drama and a gathering of suspects. The German, a man called Kurt who was there on his own, watched the rest of the guests with keen attention but said little. He'd come for the scuba-diving; it was Kurt who'd joined Nina in the afternoons at the island's best swimming spot, a small, deep swimming hole, greenish turquoise, accessed from an incomplete circle of flat rocks that was positioned anonymously halfway between the village and the other headland, in the other direction from Blue Bay. On her first day Kurt had nodded his greeting to Nina before lighting a driftwood fire and stripping off, unself-consciously and in plain view, and disappearing into the sea clad only in mask and flippers, flip-flopping into the water with his knees pulled high. Nina watched him surreptitiously over the top of her novel. He floated face down for a few minutes, his eyes scrutinising the seabed, before going into a sudden dive, his large pink buttocks rising abruptly upwards. A muffled thud followed and then Kurt reappeared, rising up like Titan, his sturdy thighs glistening, before emerging out of the water with a small octopus attached to a speargun. He dismembered and cooked it, crouching by the fire, and, seeing Nina watching, offered her a flame-curled, sucker-covered tentacle on the end of a skewer.

Nina had hoped that a beach holiday would put an end to her over-thinking. There wasn't any doubt that she'd over-thought herself into a corner. She craved a meditative narrowing of her life, a shrunken world of small things, in which nothing's expected other than that the smallness is fully lived in and with joy. Who used the word joy any more? She knew that joy was what she needed, in order to be cured. Joy would do what drugs couldn't. It was all very clear in her head, but the ideal of freedom and spontaneity proved illusory, very quickly illusory; she found without intending to that she'd come up with an itinerary on the first day and was to repeat it ever after. Following breakfast on the terrace there was a morning at Blue Bay, and lunch in the café on the harbourside: tepid broad beans in tomato sauce, a couscous feta salad and a small carafe of rough wine that sent her groggily into siesta. After a shower and a sleep, the air conditioning roaring, she swam at Octopus Beach, keeping out of Kurt's way, and returned to the hotel and showered again, clock-watching and waiting for the evening, reading on her bed. At 5pm she went out, and strolled around in the coolness of the late afternoon, and browsed at the gift shop, looking at the same few things over and over, and then she sat on the terrace with dinner and a bottle of wine, chatting a bit to the other residents, romanticising her life at home into something interesting and honourable, before retiring early with a book. This went on for seven days. She'd meant to set aside a couple of mornings to go to Main Island for the trips marked as Must See in the guidebook: the donkey ride to the caves to see the stalactites, the expedition up to the ruins of a monastery, the trip out to a sandy uninhabited islet to swim. They were all things she and Paolo had done on honeymoon. She'd go again on the boat to what the guidebook called the best beach in the Aegean, which was inaccessible by land, and where there was a seafood shack with tables under coconut matting umbrellas (it had been closed when they'd visited, because of the rain). She'd make Paolo laugh by making fun of herself, vis-à-vis the donkey situation, her fear of donkeys. The key thing was to self-deprecate before others could deprecate for you. She'd say how much smaller the interior of the main cave looked in good weather, and how much less sinister. When they'd visited together the place had been like a cathedral of the dark arts, rows of Gothic pillars with inky folds, great black mouths gaping at each side of them, yawning and full of odours that suggested the presence of wells and potholes and other hidden traps, the air heavy with damp and sulphur. She'd not wanted to go forward with the guide and his torch, and Paolo had satirised her fears. But they were young then and there were things they didn't realise.

The writing of happy postcards was easy enough. *This is paradise and I may never leave*: that was all that needed to be said on some of them, the words stretched across the open white field at a diagonal so as to fill it. Others got a fuller account. *My day starts with warm bread and home-made apricot jam, eaten while sitting looking at the sea, in the cool shade of a day that's going to be hot and blue, and ends with resiny white wine and reading and wonderfully cool linen sheets that somebody else ironed. Swimming, eating, taking pictures, relaxing properly into a stack of novels, socialising when I feel like it and no dishwasher in sight: can life be bettered?* It was fraudulent and necessary work. There was also the problem of what to write to Luca. She couldn't not send him a card because Paolo might read something into that. An omission could mean anything. Much better to be chummy with Luca and very clearly over things, post-obsessive and well, as she'd insisted at the airport that she was. But how to talk to him, a man she no longer wanted to talk to, a man she felt almost violent about never seeing again, whose name made her fingernails press involuntarily into her palms? Sticking to food and drink was the answer. The quality of food and drink was a constant Luca preoccupation.

Dear Luca, I'm sitting here with a pot of the best yoghurt I've ever tasted, and amazing island honey, which tastes faintly of herbs and also of brine. The wine is much better than it used to be, fruitier and fatter. You might even approve. You would have liked the swordfish that was barbecued last night. And hold the front page: there IS a point to peppers stuffed with rice. Figs and peaches: that's the trick. Like everything good, the sweet and the savoury. But perhaps sunshine and fresh air make all the difference. See you soon, Nina.

It was done. The foodie's postcard was written and done, and she was satisfied that nothing was revealed or betrayed in its writing or reading. It wasn't even personal; it wasn't friendly or unfriendly. That's what's needed now, she reflected, ordering a second bottle of wine, smiling at Vasilios as he came to light the anti-mosquito candles: a position of perfect neutrality. Neutrality and sanity. She hadn't added the line she was going to, about swimming out to the yacht that was anchored in the bay and how she'd swum right under it, as they had done together once when they were children, the two of them, while Paolo watched from the shore.

Three days would have been fine. If she'd stayed for three days she could have regarded the visit as a triumph, but by the fourth day the possibility of performance ripening into authenticity was gone, vanished in the night, and Nina woke with the old dread. She was afraid of the over-scheduled empty day and longed for the comfort of work. She wished she'd brought a manuscript with her: she worked as an editor of books, and craved her editorial language of secret symbols, for the absorption and certainties of a project-led life, and for the way that it could be allowed to take over the waking hours, running on seamlessly into the evening and obliterating doubt. That was always at least half what work had signified. Having drunk too much the night before, having lain awake until long after 2am, Nina slept in on the fourth morning, right through the 7am alarm, and when she came down to break-fast everybody else was already there.

"Ah, here she is," June and Iris said together, with open relief, as if she'd been missing and was found. The Belgians looked up at her without speaking. Kurt waved and smiled, his mouth full of bread. Cathy and Gareth asked if she was all right, Cathy's face concerned.

"I'm fine," Nina lied. "Just got too much sun yesterday, and then stayed up too late reading." She grinned round the room. "But maybe it's okay to sleep in on holiday."

Kurt was amused. "Ja, it's okay," he said.

Nina took her seat. "It's ridiculous really but I do like to get to the beach early, when things are still fresh." She didn't recognise this voice, the persona that she'd adopted here.

"And you're not even German," Kurt said.

"There's nothing like a good book." Cathy was satisfied that all was well.

Vasilios's teenage daughter, wearing skinny jeans and a midriff-baring T-shirt, her dark hair dipped pink at the ends, brought a basket of seeded rolls, a bowl of honey, a plate of goat's cheese, tomato and olives, a yellow glass bowl of chopped fruit, a blue glass bowl of yoghurt. Nina looked at the feast without appetite.

"I hope you don't mind me asking," Cathy said, "but are you all right on your own? What I mean is, if you want to join in with Gareth and me, we're off to the caves today, if you want to come. We have a hire car."

"That's nice of you," Nina said, eating a slice of cheese. "Actually I'm enjoying being alone. I've had a very busy year, and my mother died," – she heard herself saying this as if it was something recent; it continued to feel recent – "and my sister-in-law died – well, strictly speaking she was my brother-in-law's wife, but I always thought of her as that... She died, and then my husband and I separated."

"Oh no, I'm sorry, what a year you've had of it."

"And all I really want at the moment is to be on my own and just recover a bit."

"I'm often tempted to walk out on him," Cathy said, nodding towards Gareth, who looked unsurprised, "but to be honest I just can't be arsed to find somewhere else to live."

Dr Christos came into the room and said, "Penny for them."

Nina looked up from writing. "Sometimes you sound very English. More English than English, actually."

"I know. I'm Dick van Dyke." He looked in his bag. "Ah I forgot to bring it. It doesn't matter. Tomorrow. Andros is into our local mythology, and he showed me a photograph of a mosaic floor, one they've found at another island. It's from the second century. You were on it. There you were, riding a dolphin."

"There I was?"

"Long fair hair, turquoise-blue eyes, a long nose and a certain very determined expression. It was definitely you. You had armour, too. You looked like you meant business." As it happened Nina had been there, to the island of the mosaic, but she didn't tell the doctor this. He said, "Do you know about the Nereids?"

"Not really. Were they mermaids?"

"Mermaids, yes. Sea nymphs. People confuse them with sirens but they were the opposite of sirens. Sirens meant harm to men, but these sea nymphs were more like guardian angels. They lived deep in a silvery sea cavern, fifty of them with their father Nereus. They came to the aid of sailors in distress. Andros is very superstitious."

Chapter Three

Luca had always been Nina's closest friend. When he married Francesca, when they were all really young, Nina gave him something in addition to the official gift that was really from her dad, the pair of Victorian wine glasses. This second gift was wrapped in tissue paper, a tiny thing that was pressed into his hand in a coffee shop. It was a soapstone heart, about an inch across, and had belonged to her mother.

"In that case I'm doubly privileged," he said. "I loved your mother." Nina's mother had only recently died.

A few days later a padded bag arrived bearing Luca's handwriting. In those pre-email days it wasn't unusual to get letters from him. He wrote fairly often, long, rambling messages in his jagged, spidery hand – letters that covered subjects big and small, the somethings and nothings that had occurred and that he hadn't any other way of expressing, but this was the first padded bag, the first object that had ever arrived in the post. Inside there was another heart, of about the same size; one of Venetian glass, so dark blue it looked black, but with other colours suspended within it, ones visible only when you held it up to the light. There was a note, but it was only ten words long. *I thought we should exchange hearts. It seemed only fair.*

She rang him to say thank you. In those pre-internet, pre-cellphone days, phoning demanded predictability about where a person was going to be on any given day at any given hour, and Nina was inhibited about leaving messages on Luca's answerphone, which sat on his new hall table in his newly acquired hall like a sleek black brick. Nobody was at home when she called. All Nina could say, her low voice amplifying into the echoing high-ceilinged space, Francesca standing listening, was that it was nothing, and she'd try again tomorrow. Francesca scribbled Nina's wish on the memo pad and left it for Luca, and Luca called from the office the following morning.

"I have something to tell you," Nina said. "Paolo and I are

going to be married."

"Have you slept with him?"

"Yes."

"When?"

"When did you first sleep with Francesca?"

"Mind your own business!" His outrage was faked. If Nina had wanted details he'd have supplied them.

"It's possible it was the same night I first slept with Paolo."

"Oh I see. That night." He still thought it was a joke. "When can we meet?"

"Sunday lunch at your mother's."

"You're coming?"

"I'll be there and the engagement will be announced."

"No, I meant when can we meet privately?"

"You're married now, Luca. Privately might be frowned upon."

"I miss you."

"I miss you too."

"No, I mean I really, really miss you."

Luca kept the soapstone heart in the pockets of jackets, and felt it between his fingers sometimes, its familiar smoothness, its curves and indentations. Then one day he put a suit into the dry-cleaning pile and Francesca found it on a routine check.

When he came home that night and into the kitchen, she was standing holding the thing in her outstretched palm.

"A present from Nina, wishing me love in my life, wishing us love in our lives," he said, answering the unasked question.

His wife looked sceptical. "I'm surprised you didn't show it to me, then, if it was about us."

"You don't need to be worried." He dropped his bag and put his arms around her, his arms at the back of her neck, her face pressed into his chest, so tightly that she could hardly breathe. "It's you I want to be with," he said into her hair. It was copious, long, wavy, tinted auburn from its almost black.

"You danced with her more than with me, at our wedding reception. Do you know that?"

He pulled himself away. "You counted?"

"It mattered to me." Her dark eyes were filling.

He went into the hall and divested himself of coat and shoes, and Francesca followed. "But she's my sister. She's like my sister.

She's been my unofficial sister almost my whole life, since we were five years old. I've always treated her house like my house and vice versa. At our wedding – you have to understand – our wedding was also a big occasion for Nina and me. It was like a goodbye to that life."

"Luca, can you hear yourself?"

"We've always been incredibly close, twin-like, finishing each other's sentences, reading each other's minds…"

"I know. I know."

"…and now things will be different. Someone has supplanted her. You don't see how important that is to the two of us?" He went back into the kitchen and Francesca followed.

"You're in love with her; you just don't realise it." She had begun to hear it in herself: her resignation to the facts.

"Wrong, so wrong." He took a bottle of wine from the rack.

"So this heart doesn't mean much to you." She held it up between her fingers.

"It does mean a lot to me," – as he spoke he was using the corkscrew – "in so far as it's about my friendship with Nina. Nina's my sister and that's her sisterly love."

"You carry it around with you." She put it onto the countertop, which was a large slab of polished stone, glossy in their bleached-oak kitchen.

"I'd forgotten all about it. It was hidden in a pocket." His voice remained unexcited.

"Hidden. That's an interesting word."

"Oh honestly, Fran." He took glasses down from the shelf and filled them. "Forgotten about in a pocket. Very nearly drycleaned." He gave her a glass and picked up the heart. "I'll give it back to her if that's what you want."

"That isn't what I want. What I want is for her not to give you secret signals."

"This isn't a secret signal."

"Secret reassurances."

Now Luca began to gesture with the glass. "She's my sister! She's been my sister without being my biological sister my whole life!"

"She is in love with you."

"I'm giving it back. Look, I'm finding an envelope." He put his wine down and rummaged in a cupboard. "Here's an envelope.

Look, I'm putting it in the envelope and sealing it."

"Luca, calm down. Calm. You don't need to do that: you just need to sound more convincing about what it means."

"I'm calling Nina. I'm calling her. I'm going to put her on the phone to you." He picked up the phone receiver and dialled.

"Please don't. You're just trying to humiliate me now."

He put the phone down. "Well, I'm sorry. I don't know what else I can do."

Francesca didn't mention it again until some months later. It happened to be when Paolo and Nina were in Greece.

"The weather's terrible over there, for September," Luca said, as they watched the evening news. The map of Europe was uniformly grey, and there were flash floods in Athens.

Francesca's reply was unexpected. "Did you give that trinket back to Nina?"

"Yes."

"When did you?"

"Ages ago."

"So that's another one at the back of your socks."

"Oh for God's sake." He got up off the sofa and spoke from the door. "I forgot about it. All right?" He went out of the room and returned with it, one hard corner in the flimsy white envelope. "Here." He put it on the table. "Throw it away, return it, whatever you want. Your choice."

The next morning, Francesca dropped it at Nina and Paolo's flat. She was about to put it through the door when she realised that it wasn't marked with Nina's name. She didn't want Paolo opening it and wondering, so she took a pen out of her bag and wrote *Nina* on the front.

When Nina got back from honeymoon, she found the heart waiting for her. She saw that it was Francesca who had sent it back. At least she assumed so; it was a woman's writing on the envelope.

Luca rang within an hour of their return.

"Francesca dropped off the heart while we were gone," she told him.

"We should have lunch," he said. "Tomorrow. I want to hear all about it. The honeymoon, I mean. Complete with sex bits."

"Did you hear me? Francesca put the heart through my letterbox."

"I know. It doesn't matter, does it?"

"Not really, no. Not in itself, no."

When she got off the phone, Paolo said, "What heart was that? I couldn't help overhearing." She had to produce both hearts, so as to make it clear it was mutual and token and nothing.

"It was just about good wishes for married life, wishing each other love," she said.

"Commendable of you both," Paolo said. He used the voice he always used when talking about Luca and Nina.

Nina didn't tell him that she was meeting his brother the following day for a drink. They met and drank wine and caught up with one another, and then, as they parted out on the street, kissing each other on the cheek, she gave Luca the heart Francesca had returned. She said, "The one you gave me is in there too, inside the envelope."

"What? Why?"

"I didn't want it any more," she said, surprising him and walking away.

Francesca, who'd been told about the drink, went and searched through Luca's jacket pockets after dinner, and then his coat pockets, and found nothing. She looked in his bag while he was in the bath, the big leather bag she'd bought him in Italy, and found the envelope there, in a zip compartment. It had been sealed and opened and imperfectly resealed. She opened it and saw two hearts, settled together into a corner. Nina, it seemed, had answered the return of the heart with a second gift to add to the first. Nina had redoubled. Nina was emphatic. Francesca put the envelope back where she'd found it, and never brought the subject up again.

Perhaps it was only because Nina had returned the Venetian glass heart, but Luca began to telephone more than he used to. He said he wanted reassurance that she was okay. For whatever reason, it became a ritual, their daily conversation. As he'd explain later, this was his process of withdrawal, a kind of tapering-off from the patterns of the old days. He rang from the office at his dad's wine distribution business, to Nina the junior copy editor, who at that time was working in-house for an Edinburgh publisher. He did it when Paolo went out, which he did routinely at lunchtime for a stroll, eating a sandwich at the café across the road and dipping into the second-hand music shop. Nina and Luca told each other about their days, and the conversation wandered into the random and bizarre; the punning, the anecdotal and the irrelevant. It'd lead off into improvised riffs, the two of them laughing into their handsets. It's how they'd always been when they were together. When winter came and Paolo went out less often and Luca didn't feel he could call from the office, he began to ring Nina from home in the early evening, before Paolo got there – he always worked shorter hours than his brother – though he didn't like shutting the door against Francesca. Even though he would maintain later that it was absolutely, unambiguously innocent, the covertness of it bothered him.

Things became a lot easier after email and texting became a normality. Things could continue, things could even increase and develop and deepen, without actual speaking being necessary, and without being defensive about being caught behind a closed door on the landline. Once there was email there was regular email, and the inadvertent privacy of the inbox, its facilitating of the sharing of the inner life, meant that the conversation could and did drift into the strictly confidential. It was easy for the penpals to confide about issues in their respective marriages; it wasn't so easy when they were reminded, by seeing each other at family occasions, that the supposedly safe distance of the written word was really something else entirely.

In addition and long before the arrival of the domestic internet, they met sometimes for lunch. The incidence tailed off over the years: it was a regular thing before email and only intermittent after, when it became associated with drama, or with bad news. They met each time at the same small French-family-run bistro, one secreted in a Georgian back street, a ten-minute walk from each of their flats. It became their place. The tradition began two years after Nina married Paolo. It was Luca who suggested it.

"Don't you have male friends to moan to?" Nina asked him, as they sat looking at the menu on their first visit. They'd been there for fifteen minutes and Francesca's recent failings had already been listed, frankly but with warmth; the warmth was where the loyalty lay, hanging on by its finger-ends.

"I'm the only 23-year-old I know who's married. Why did we marry so young?"

"You know why."

"And so, what about Paolo?"

"Paolo's perfect. No complaints at all."

"Oh, come on. Bet he's a bit of a Svengali. He's always had a Svengali aspect. Bet he makes you watch history documentaries and David Attenborough. Bet he makes you go to museums, and puts important biographies at the side of your bed, and tries to talk about politics over breakfast, reading bits out from the newspaper. He's so like your father."

"No, he isn't. Not remotely. And I love museums."

"Please. We have not come here to praise Caesar, I trust. I was hoping for scandalous frankness."

"You first, then."

"Francesca hogs the duvet."

"Nicely done. Paolo finishes crosswords that I started."

"Francesca can't cook to save her life."

"Paolo eats toast in bed. In fact, he's constantly eating."

"Francesca spends hours on the phone to her girlfriends when I'm sitting in the TV room alone."

She was getting into the swing now. "Paolo's too quiet. And he refuses to argue with me, even if I provoke him."

"Not even for fun?"

"Not even for fun."

"Francesca is passive aggressive. It's all more in sorrow than in anger. Drives me nuts."

"Paolo never buys me flowers."

"Francesca makes me go to the theatre."

"Paolo tidies up my desk."

"Francesca tidies up my desk."

"They should have married one another."

"I'd give them six months."

It was at one of these lunches, in the week before Nina's 24th birthday, that Nina happened to ask, over fish stew, "Do you still carry my heart?"

"Yes I do, e e cummings." He looked at her seriously. "I carry it in my heart."

"Do you carry your own heart, also?"

"Yes. They're in the pockets of this jacket, right now." He glanced down, and patted them.

"Not in one pocket together?"

"No, because they jiggle together and clank and people ask what's making the noise, and then I have to lie. I'm not great at lying, though I think I might have to work at getting better."

She was going to ask what he meant by that, but didn't. That would've been in breach of the rules. Flirting was allowable as long as it wasn't allowed to become concrete. They could play at being on the brink of adultery. Both of them knew it was only a game.

Instead she grinned at him, faux-complicitly. She said, "Can I have your one back, the heart you gave me?"

"Here you go." He put the Murano glass heart on the table.

"What's this? You've had this fitting added." A twisted gold coil was clamped into one end, in the space at the top where it divided.

"It's in case you wanted to use it as jewellery." He produced a small velvet box. "There's a fine gold chain in there. An early birthday present."

Nina threaded it through and put it on, but couldn't get the fastening to work, so Luca leaned across and did it for her, his face close to her ear. She could feel his breath on her neck.

On Nina's birthday she and Paolo had people over for dinner. Francesca spotted immediately, as Nina took the flowers and the waxed-paper packet of cheese from her, that she was wearing the glass heart as a pendant. Her eye went to it and it kept returning. She noted how much of the evening was taken up by Luca and Nina talking exclusively to one another, how often their eyes met, how Nina's eyes went straight to Luca's if anything was funny or extraordinary, or if someone was wrong or dull, wanting to share their mutual recognition of wrongness or dullness. She noted that Nina and Luca came into physical contact a lot; the rough play of their childhood friendship continued, and there was poking in the ribs and shoving. Twice, Luca picked Nina up and put her down again. When Nina complained – but only to Luca, with whom ingratitude was allowed – that the cheese he'd brought was so overripe that it had achieved consciousness, Luca picked her up and put her into the larder and leaned against the door until she apologised. It had been like this always. At Luca's wedding he'd taken joking exception to her tease about the cut of his suit, its big lapels, and what she called his mafia shoes, gleeful about her own daring. He'd lifted her up and put her over his shoulder; he'd taken her out of the marquee, long and skinny in her honey-coloured bridesmaid dress, and dumped her on the already dewy lawn. She'd come back into the gathering bearing wet patches across her back and backside, her pale hair falling out of its complicated bun, and she'd stood with her hands on her hips and said, "Right, Luca Romano." Everyone around had seen the potential of the thing to descend into pranks, and how inappropriate that would be. Pranks were often mutual and ongoing. There could easily be a prosecco fight. There could be cake thrown. It wouldn't have been the first time.

"Only kidding," Nina assured the friends who had gathered to urge calm. She'd been taken off to a table, led by two hands holding hers, the hands of two kind friends, and she'd been put into a chair and plied with booze.

"No, no, no more," Luca had said, at the same time, putting his hands up as his father approached. He'd gone instead to his new wife, and had waltzed her around the room, and then they'd walked around it together hand in hand, making sure to have proper conversations with people, and all had been well.

Chapter Four

Dr Christos came into the room to show Nina a copy of the island newsletter, a stapled A4 booklet that featured the accident as front-page news.

"Oh my God. They have my picture. My passport photograph."

"I didn't think you'd mind. It's funny. You don't think it's funny?"

"Oh cheers. Hilarious. I'm sure it'll all seem hilarious eventually." She didn't like the sound of her voice and corrected herself. "So what does the headline say – is it about my being stupid?"

"The woman who almost killed seven islanders. Look at your face. I'm kidding."

"Kidding but not really kidding."

His own expression was indulgent. He began to translate the report into English for her, and as it turned out it was purely factual, merely a blow-by-blow account of what had occurred. When he'd finished he handed the newsletter over. "Keep it. Souvenir."

Two other photographs showed the scene of the accident and the damage to the minibus. "What does it really say, the headline?"

"The English Tourist Whose Leg Was Broken. That's good, isn't it? That's passive; you were a victim of circumstance as much as anyone."

"Not really. I was the one standing in the middle of the road."

"Nobody sees it that way. Well – maybe one or two zealots. Maybe just the seven people on the bus, and their families and friends. Wait, that's the whole island. On second thoughts perhaps you need an armed guard."

He smiled to himself at the wit of his own remark, and settled himself to work, getting his laptop out and his spectacle case and consulting his notes over the top of his reading glasses, their frames as dark as his eyebrows. Nina needed something to do, so she pulled the wheeled table into position across the bed and wrote a second batch of postcards, dividing each message space into two sections with a pen line. The top half was headed On Being An Arse, and described a woman standing in the path of an oncoming bus; the second half, below it, headed Silver Linings, went on to list the upsides of the broken leg: the modernist hospital right on the beach, the herb garden and meals on tap, the utter peace and freedom, the days devoted only to reading and napping. *Far better a holiday than the holiday in fact*, she wrote (and how true that was, she didn't add, and what an understatement). Smiley face; two kisses. While she was writing the last of the cards, Dr Christos went out and came back with a breakfast tray – it was still only 8.30am – one that featured a flesh-pink ceramic bowl of hard-boiled white eggs. Nina took an egg and cracked it against the table edge, and began a slow peel, imprinting in memory the impact of her browned hands on the eggshell, the tiny suction noises of its loosening. When she'd cut it lengthways in half she picked up her camera, always beside her, and took a photograph. Instagram came into her mind, and Vine, and Twitter and Facebook: places she could share her thoughts about the egg. She felt it, the old pull, but only fleetingly. There mustn't be any more of that.

Dr Christos was watching. "You're still getting it, the survivor's euphoria," he said. "I've had people photographing their breakfast before. The boy a year ago, for instance; the English boy whose back wasn't broken after all."

"Christ, what happened to him?"

"Tombstoning, he said they call it. Jumping off high cliffs into shallow water. The most stupid idea of fun imaginable."

"A peeled egg. I know it sounds mad, but there are things I want to remember, to associate."

"You were never in any danger, though, not really; not once we knew it was just your leg, just a little concussion."

"It didn't feel so straightforward at the time. Have you ever thought you were going to die?"

"No. Thankfully. I haven't even been in hospital, not as a patient. Probably it'll all happen at once. I'm sure my appendix, gall bladder, liver and prostate are just getting their ducks in a row."

She smiled at him. She liked his company. "Well, not to over-dramatise, but it felt like it was the end. Everything happening in extreme slow motion. The bus tilting and going over, and goats looking down at me from the slope. My vision going black at the edges, getting smaller – the window was getting smaller as if I was going blind. But I wasn't afraid. It was bizarrely ordinary. I thought, 'Oh well, it's goodbye to the world, and it's a pity because I really want to live'."

"That's a good thought to have."

"When I woke up the ambulanceman was lifting me at the shoulder, the driver was at my feet, and another man was looking down at me. His big fearful bear face."

"Andros. He's a good man. He went in the car with you."

"I grabbed hold of his wrist, did he tell you?"

"He told me."

"In the car – I thought I was dying so I drank it all up. I wanted to take it all in, everything I could still see, all the last things."

"What last things?"

"Just things we saw on the way. The beauty was overwhelming, the colours. There was a blue door with an angel's head knocker, pots of flowers, strong shades of red and orange, lit windows, people ambling along who had all the time in the world. The soft summer dark. Big teenage boys on small bikes. The lights of the car flashing off a big white house, one with columns and wide steps. A scruffy cat was stretched out on one of the steps, a black and white cat, which raised its head to look at us as we went by, holding up the paw it was licking. And apparently I was talking to Paolo. I thought my husband was in the ambulance." She made an embarrassed motion with her mouth, pulling it to one side.

"Don't worry. It was mostly gibberish."

"The ambulanceman pretended he couldn't hear."

"He's used to it. He didn't tell Olympia, though she worked hard on him afterwards. But he's discreet: that's part of the job. People say all kinds of things in the back of the ambulance."

"It's strange how some details stick and some don't. I don't remember the cup of green tea I drank before I went to sleep at the other hospital, no memory of that at all, though the cup was there in the morning. But I do remember the smell coming through the open window of my room: stale seawater and tanning oils. I remember looking out of the window and seeing towels hanging over balconies."

"The hospital's surrounded by blocks of flats. Holiday flats, most of them."

Even though they were acutely short of beds at Main Island hospital, there'd been resistance to sending Nina back across the water and into Dr Christos's care. It was all down to health politics, he told her: over there they had to cope with a shoddily built, tired facility, and were irritated in the extreme by the money that had flowed in from the European Union for Small Island, replacing the first aid station, converted from a boathouse, that had been in place for the previous twenty years. Before that they'd made do with the home of the island doctor, who'd been sensible enough to marry the island nurse, and people had given birth in the family's dining room, on their dining table. The boathouse had been equipped with a defibrillator, had a well-stocked pharmacy, had a side room with gas and air for pain relief in labour, and most of the residents of Main Island judged that to be more than enough.

"Now that money is in such short supply, their point about our sucking up their funding is becoming less good-humoured," Dr Christos said. "And we have trouble defending ourselves sometimes, when the only business going through here in an average week is about stitching cut feet, and dealing with sunstroke and jellyfish stings."

"So you're quite glad of my concussion."

"Thrilled. Only disappointed that more people on the bus weren't hurt." He held his hands up. "Joke. But they might actually shut us down. We might have to go to Michael Ithika again."

"Michael who?"

"Michael Ithika. I was going to be surprised you hadn't heard of him, but then why would you. He's our home-grown internet millionaire. He has a weekend house here, his own compound hidden away on the other side. You wouldn't know it even existed unless you saw it from the air."

"Is it his helicopter that I've seen coming and going?"

"It is. He lets us use it for emergencies, as long as we clean up the blood. He put up half the money for the hospital and was influential in helping to get us the rest."

"How wonderful to be able to be a philanthropist."

The doctor had an odd reaction to this. He drew himself more upright in the chair, seemed almost to shudder. "You don't like him?"

"Do I like him? Well, I admire his focus. He's been unfailingly generous to us."

"But? I sense a but."

"Everything's always come easy to Michael. I hear myself saying that and know that I'm basically jealous... though not because of the playboy lifestyle. He has a good life, genuinely enjoys his empire and does what he wants. He's distressingly anomalous to the conventional idea of the miserable rich person."

"He's a playboy?"

"Oh yes. Yes, indeed. I don't like the way he treats women, to be honest."

"How does he treat women?"

"As an endlessly replenishing supply. The guy needs to go out with an American and have his consciousness raised, stat." He smiled wryly.

Nina felt a wave of admiration. "Sounds like it."

"But I feel bad dissing him because he's got a social conscience and he uses it well."

"Were you at school together?"

"God, no. He's not even 30."

"Ah. One of those."

"There are people here who loop the two of us together, Michael and me. The people here: they get married as soon as it's legal and then they stick, no matter what. There's still a real stigma about divorce. There's even a stigma about seeing other people afterwards. Divorcees here act like widowers."

"Why would they loop the two of you together?"

"Just because I've had relationships since my marriage ended. But things that look the same aren't always the same."

"That's true."

He dipped his head low and rubbed slowly at the back of it, at the hairline, his neck and scalp. Paolo had often done the same when he was weary. "I'm tired today. I didn't get home till 2am and was called in again at six. I get rather low when I'm this knackered. Knackered. I like that word; it's a good London word." He lay back as if to have a nap, shuffling lower so that his head rested on the back of the chair, and folded his arms over the belt of his jeans. A cowboy belt, she noticed, with a big brass buckle. "Tell me a story." His voice was like that of a man on the verge of sleeping. "Tell me about Nina when she was a child."

"Only if you agree to take your turn."

"Deal. Give me Nina at twelve and Nina at eighteen."

"Nina at twelve... was long and bony and timid. She was fairer-haired than now, waist-length hair always worn in a plait. She never wore skirts if she could help it."

"A timid tomboy. I like tomboys. Did you climb trees?"

"Timid with strangers and at school but not with my friends. There was, yes, a lot of tree-climbing, haystack-climbing, stream-damming, getting dirty and wet. A lot of playing with the boys next door."

"Who were the boys next door? What happened to them?"

"My husband, my brother-in-law."

"Oh, I see, I see. Right. Carry on." His eyes were open now.

"There was a lot of bicycle riding. Between the ages of seven and twelve, I was on a bike most of the time. I was part of a gang – don't look like that, it was all completely innocent. We played in the street: the village was quiet then. There was a lot of reading – my dad was constantly buying me books – but I watched television when I came home from school until tea time, like every other pre-internet child, and did my homework afterwards. The TV wasn't often on when Dad was in the house; he didn't approve. Are you sure you want to hear all this? I ate a lot of sweets; sweets were a big thing back home, before children had computers. And board games – board games were a big thing. We'd have whole-day bouts of Monopoly. What else... I always wanted a cat but I was allergic. Eczema, asthma, sensitive. I was quite serious, I think, like my dad, though my mother jollied me out of it. I played the flute, though not very well."

"I liked that. I was entertained. Okay, my turn. Let's see. No flutes, no tennis, no TV. Bike riding yes, and running wild – I can relate to that – but the books were few and mostly borrowed. We were poor. I had to work on the farm after school and at weekends. I hung out at the beach with my friends, flirted with girls out of the sight of our parents. Had to go to church, but it was normal; everybody did. This place was one big family then, and not only in its ideas; I mean literally. We're all related somehow or other, though there were always two factions, the two villages. And then things changed. I was good at chess and was sent to the big adult tournament and won it. School realised I was an adept student and treated me differently. They found opportunities for me. I worked hard and went off the island."

"I was always terrible at chess, though my dad tried. Wrong kind of brain."

"Yes, your parents. Tell me." He shuffled down a little more, crossing his legs at the ankle.

"Loving in different ways. My dad, Robert, was an academic at the university, a history lecturer."

"Was he what he'd always wanted to be? Describe, please." He closed his eyes again.

"He was. His ambitions were fulfilled. He's tall, strong-featured, has brown and grey hair in a radical side parting, 1960s hair, my mum used to say. Grey eyes, a bit fierce-looking, not quick to smile. He's from the Western Isles, a Protestant community not unlike Mum's origins, and he has an island accent. My mother's dead but he's still alive. She was a housewife. A home-maker, as Dad always introduced her to people. She was good at making a home. A happy person, the most energetic I ever met, and public-spirited; she kept an eye on the old people and got their shopping. The whole village came to her funeral. She wanted to have a homewares import business but it never happened. When she was young she'd wanted to be an artist. Or an actress. Both impossibilities, though."

"Why so?" He opened one eye.

"Because of the family in Norway. Orthodox Lutherans, I suppose. Fairly orthodox. At any rate, no showing off was allowed. She was all set to be a primary school teacher when she met my dad."

"So, Nina at eighteen."

"At eighteen I was at university. Things changed then, as they do, and I didn't see much of her, but up till then Mum and I were very close. We liked to do the same kinds of things. I didn't have anyone else I could dress-make with, or who liked baking and photography and drawing. Even at university, it took me a while to make friends. Everyone around me was getting into booze and decadence and it wasn't really my thing. I shocked people by wanting to work hard."

"You were a nerdy wallflower. Gotcha."

"Pretty much. Shy. Useless at talking to boys."

"Other than the husband and the brother-in-law."

"Things had become complicated, though, on that front. It didn't seem possible to be friends with both any longer.

Not at the same time."

"I bet." Dr Christos was frowning at his phone.

"Is everything alright?"

"It's my daughter in Athens. Things are sometimes difficult there. Will you excuse me? I think I should call her."

"Of course, of course. Go speak to her."

He made as if to go out of the room, but then said, "Nina, will you have dinner with me before you go home?"

"Oh – I'd love to," she said, with spontaneous pleasure, perhaps just a tad too gratefully. "Thank you very much; that would be lovely." She'd added the rest, its well-manneredness, in the hopes of sounding casual.

"There's a new restaurant over there; it's outdoors and in a little cove, on the western side, and they have great sunsets. I'd love to take you. We can talk about your moving here and make a plan."

She'd told him the previous evening, during his brief goodnight visit, that she wanted to live abroad for a year and was thinking seriously about Greece. He'd become excited; he'd pulled up a chair. But notwithstanding his excitement, it wasn't a big deal. It was just dinner.

She didn't see him again until the evening, until she went out onto the terrace, slowly on her crutches, to look at the sunset over the sea, and saw him standing on the beach, his back to her, looking out across the bowl of blackening water and towards the other shore, where a hundred tiny white lights were twinkling, lights that marked invisible streets and village clusters on the hills. She was afraid he'd turn and see her there and so she returned to her room and settled herself in bed with a Jeeves & Wooster, one of only two books in English in the hospital library, but it proved impossible to concentrate. She swapped it for the novel she'd started on the plane, but found she couldn't remember who anybody was or what'd happened to them, and so it too was abandoned, tossed onto the end of the bed. The restlessness was building. Perhaps dinner wasn't just dinner at all. He'd said, "We'll make a plan." Not just a plan, but we who'd make it. It was language that nobody used with her any more. It was rain on arid ground. In some ways hope is the worst thing; whenever there's fresh hope there's also something new to lose.

Nurse Yannis came into the room, adjusted the netted window

for maximum breeze, filled Nina's water jug with more ice, emptied the waste-paper bin, taking sly glances at her all the while, and seemed to be looking for something else to do. Finally she came and sat in the blue chair, and folded her hands in her lap. They looked at one another. Nurse Yannis was probably about her own age, Nina thought. She was of average height and wiry build, discreet muscles showing in her upper arms. Her nose was bony and her mouth narrow and full, and her short brown hair, which suited her heart-shaped face, was red with henna in the artificial light.

"My sister is on the bus," she said. "She goes to the gardens."

"I'm so sorry. Is she all right?"

"It is fine. It is good for her." She looked into Nina's face for the first time. "My mother wants to thank you."

"To thank me?"

"She wants to come, to hold your hands. She has no English." She rose from the seat and sandwiched Nina's hands between her own with a steady pressure, before releasing them again and returning to sit. "That is what she wants. She will kiss your hands also. She has no English but I have taught her 'thank you'. Can I tell her you permit it?"

"Of course, if that's what she wants. But I don't understand."

"My sister is been sad. My mother is despaired. Is that the right word? It isn't right."

They were interrupted by Dr Christos, who put his head round the door and muttered something to the nurse. Sighing, she hurried out.

"Sorry," he said. "You were having a good chat. I hope you weren't getting ahead in your story."

"Not at all. She was telling me about her sister. Apparently she was one of the passengers."

He came further into the room. "She's always been a little bit lost. The sister. But there's good news: she's going to work for Michael. He wanted to know if he could do anything for anybody who was in the crash. He enjoys that, being the benefactor. Anyway, she's taken a job at his company on the mainland; not working for him directly, I'm glad to say. Not that he'd be into her. He goes for the porn-star type."

"Does this mean there will only be five women now, the women gardeners?"

"They've already recruited a replacement." He was looking at the novel on the bed. "Did you buy that at the English stall at the market?"

"No, I bought it at the airport. What made you ask that?"

"Somebody saw you, Olympia's sister, buying a book at the market on the day you were hurt. She said she saw you throwing a book away, in a bin. You seemed upset, she said. She was on the same boat back with you." Nina searched in her handbag as if looking for something, a phantom lost thing. "Was there something in the book?"

"Nothing like that."

He picked the discarded novel up and looked at the back. "Perhaps I could borrow this, when you're done. All I seem to read lately are thrillers. I only get to read in short bursts, and when I'm tired I find it hard to concentrate unless a story's very visual. What kinds of books do you work on?"

"General fiction. Usually there's a romance element somewhere, but then I think that's true of most novels being published now – even the war stories, the histories."

"It sounds like a dream job, but I suppose it might be annoying if you didn't like the book."

"I don't usually much like the books. I'm more of a nineteenth-century girl."

"Do you like Tolstoy?" He sounded hopeful.

"I love Tolstoy."

"It's going to be great when you move here. Someone who reads, who likes films. It's been lonely since my only real friend moved to the mainland last year. Did Vasilios tell you about his movie evenings in the winter in the bar? There's a projector and he shows them on the big wall."

"The wall with no pictures on it. He told me about the film nights."

"He gets uptight if people even lean on it. It has to be kept clean and white. So we have the movie club, and get-togethers, but otherwise people devise their own entertainments. The key thing on islands is to have a good home life. A good home life's the saving grace." He was looking at her now. She hadn't imagined it, not anything. He was making the same daring leap.

It was too much, talking about it openly as if it was decided. "It's not decided yet," she reminded him, and then, because he looked disappointed, "What's Christmas like here?"

"Quiet, devout, not at all Anglo. Though Michael comes at Christmas with his famous friends, pursued by photographers. The weather's not bad, sometimes windy and rainy but often bright, and only rarely really cold."

"What's the downside?"

"The downside. Well, I suppose it can seem like a long wait until the tourists come back. We go into a kind of hibernation. I get around it by spending the holidays with my other daughter in the States." His phone was ringing. "But you know, it's a very different life on an island if you have someone."

He answered his phone, and she watched him, patiently dealing with a query, sorting out someone else's problem in his slow, beautifully articulated Greek, his kind and authoritative intonations. She'd had almost six months of being alone, of feeling starkly alone and convinced that she would always be alone, but perhaps there was hope. People had second relationships; they did, and sometimes they were happier the second time. Perhaps there was going to be one more opportunity for tenderness, one more offer of a hand held in life, a warm hand held tightly in the street in the brutally disinterested world, and this was it, its genesis. It was possible. She'd classified herself as fundamentally unlovable, after everything that'd happened, but what if someone else just didn't see it? It was like an old novel, the way her mind was working now, its firm response to an opportunity, and she was taken by surprise. Surprise was the nub of it: that it might really happen, that it might happen here. It wasn't a planned response. It was odd, weird, that being surprised by your own ideas was even possible – after all, they were supposed to be intrinsically yours – but there it was, the unsolicited thought, that if he offered himself, his life, a share in his life, she might not hesitate. Being alone was too hard; it was that simple and difficult.

She picked up the newsletter again and flicked blindly through the pages, pausing to scrutinise stories as if she could read them. Gifts from the universe were rare; it would be a kind of sacrilege to squander a gifted chance. This was her mother's language, which continued to self-generate, whose seed had been planted; it was typical of a mother to read too much into one date, and one that hadn't even happened yet. It was only dinner. Only dinner and no more; a new restaurant he wanted to visit. But it was already too late for low expectations; the truth was that there was already hopefulness. It had found her again – she could feel it, its contagion, beginning to threaten all her practised sadnesses, and that was risky in itself. The sadness was a place of safety. The last thing she'd ever do was allow her heart to be broken; that had always been the golden rule. She looked at her phone, at the most recent text from Paolo, the one about the divorce settlement, and sighed. The exciting, daunting thing that had unexpectedly happened was that she was back in the arena of *what if*. Nina allowed herself to imagine, knowing it was foolish but allowing it anyway. She saw herself in glimpses in a new incarnation: the incomer who was once the doctor's patient and who stayed on and married him, the dark-haired doctor's blonde and blue-eyed wife, exotically semi-Scandinavian and long of limb, her Greek a little rusty but a woman anyone could depend on. She could throw herself into winning the love of everyone, this whole society, a help and friend to all and giver of the island's best parties.

But it was only dinner.

"What's funny?" Dr Christos, a man she didn't know, sat in front of her, closing and repocketing his phone.

"Just a funny thought." Crashing into the scenario had come the probable reality. *"Nina? Who's that?" "You know – the foreigner. The one with the limp." "The odd one, looks like a mermaid, hides in the house and doesn't talk?" "Yeah, that one."*

Her smile vanished. She saw that it wasn't her own face – introverted, socially inept, awkward Nina, awkward with everyone other than Luca – in the bits of film unspooling in her mind, but that of her mother. In a different context it could easily have been her mother's story. In any case it was all highly improbable. Dr Christos had a paler indentation around his ring finger where a wedding band had been removed, and he might be available, but so what? They'd have dinner and she'd fly home. They'd have dinner, have sex and then she'd fly home. Perhaps it was only sex that he wanted. He was busy on his laptop now, replying to email, and she looked at him working and felt the first stirring of attraction. This available man might be someone she could lust after. The right kind of intimacy, the right kind of eye contact, the right kind of conversations when they were alone: perhaps that could grow into

– she couldn't use the word, the L word, but perhaps something permanent and comforting. She looked at his capable hands, his forearms and then at his mouth. How could attraction really be made to equate to time, to understanding, to a shared life? Now that the old reliables had worked loose from their definitions and floated free, what would it mean to fall for someone again? It didn't feel as if it could be the same, or as if it was physiologically possible to replicate that falling, the falling and certainty she'd experienced once when she was young, and so it would have to be something else, a new kind of thing, something sufficient. But would she recognise it, this sufficiency, when it arrived? Now that there wasn't any choice other than to be self-determining there was a lot to be said for bypassing the whole love question and choosing, in a cool-headed way, someone who'd be good to grow old with.

Nina's thoughts were racing, moving as fast as the doctor's fingers across the keyboard, and she wondered if she was actually really well again. These thoughts about falling in love with a stranger, leaping forward from an offer of dinner to an envisaged second marriage, weren't these evidence of continuing illness? But perhaps she'd always been ill in this particular way. It might help explain a lot of what had happened. She closed her eyes against the flood. She slowed her breathing. Her mind went to things that her mother had written, in the diary that Nina had brought with her. *Perhaps romantic love is always a kind of undiagnosed madness.*

Her phone buzzed its receipt of a text message. It was another one from Paolo. *Am now coming five days earlier. All booked up. Need a holiday. Can stay out of your way if that's what you want.*

Chapter Five

The first time Paolo rang Nina at the hospital she was taken aback, not only by the way he spoke to her but that he'd called at all. His final words to her at the airport had seemed definitively final, so she'd been surprised to get his text, half an hour after sending hers informing him about the accident, saying that when it was time he'd come to Greece and get her. His telephoning, a few days later, was also unexpected. Her phone had rung out and she'd seen his name come up on the screen, and had answered with a comical braced expression, her teeth set together.

There wasn't any kind of a greeting; no hi, no hello. He launched in. "So how's the leg?" If this was how it was to be, if he was opting for a chummy kind of amnesia, then so be it. It made a kind of sense.

"The leg's still there, but I keep dreaming that it's gone," she told him. "I dream that I wake up and all that's left is a stump." Nina was aware that she sounded nervous.

"It takes a while to get over these things." Really, Paolo? How was she to answer that? Paolo pressed on. "I had coffee with your dad today. He'd just been to the cottage. He said to tell you that all's well. Your herb garden's growing fast. He wanted me to say that he hoped it was okay to take some trimmings. I said I was sure it was."

"Of course. Have you had much rain?" Yes, the weather.

"It's been monsooning. Your dad seems well. He said to tell you that he's had a breakthrough on the book. He's writing to you."

"That's good to hear, about the book. He seemed like he'd got stuck, when I was living with him. Though maybe it was because I was living with him." She felt weak. Surely they couldn't keep going like this without mentioning it?

"I bet it isn't raining in Greece," Paolo said.

"Too warm, some days. I'm longing for a swim. I can hear people on the beach."

"But it's pebbly there, isn't it?"

"How'd you know that?"

"Google."

"Ah. Google, of course." The anxiety was building, tight in her ribcage and soft in her stomach. Was she making a fool of herself in not seeing that this bland chatter was supposed to be her cue to sweep through it and apologise?

"It's been quite warm between the showers," Paolo said. "Good for your garden. Your dad might be struggling to keep on top of things."

"I told him to hire someone and that I'd pay." She sounded to herself as if she might be about to have a stroke. Her tongue felt enormous.

"Listen, I have to sign off, I'm late for a conference call. Good to hear you're okay, Nina."

"Thanks. Bye."

"I told your dad that I'd ring. He's anxious for news. Bye then." In the tone of this voice, inside this farewell, was unmistakably the sound of obligation.

When Nina left Paolo she'd lived with her dad while the legalities were completed for the buying of a house in the same village, barely a mile from her old family home. The day she got the keys and moved in, a chilly day at the end of June, Paolo had sent flowers and Nina rang her friend Susie in tears.

"What on earth's the matter?" Susie could hear Nina's voice breaking. "Paolo sent flowers. What's wrong with that?"

"He wished me a happy life ahead. A happy life, like we're not going to see one another."

"He is trying to be dignified, Nina. That's all."

"Why doesn't he feel things? He doesn't seem to feel anything about this disaster."

"Nina. I say this to you as a friend."

"What?"

"You left him. It was you who left Paolo, and without much of an explanation."

"There was an explanation. We talked it over."

"You talked incomprehensibly by all accounts. Even by your account."

"You've heard his account?"

"He thinks it's about Luca." Silence. "He said he thought

having Luca staying with the two of you would make you happy."

"He was wrong."

"He said he thought it was what you always wanted."

"He was wrong about that, too."

"I wish you'd tell me what happened."

"I will. Just not yet."

"Can I ask you a question? Was it because you and Luca had sex? I wouldn't blame you, I should add. I would've, like a shot."

"No."

"Was it so you could be with Luca, finally – did you leave so you and Luca could get together?"

"Absolutely not."

"Twenty-five years after marrying the wrong brother."

"He wasn't the wrong brother."

"Of course he was. You've always been completely smitten with one another."

"He wasn't the wrong brother. That wasn't the tragedy."

"Tragedy? What tragedy?" Silence. "Luca's moved out now, Paolo says."

"It wasn't about Luca. Luca was irrelevant." It wasn't entirely true.

"Poor Luca, being irrelevant. His wife had just died. Paolo says you made it obvious you didn't want him there, staying with you. That's outstandingly odd. It's not like you to be unkind and especially not to Luca; Luca of all people. What gives?" There was no response. "Darling. Noble silence is all very noble, but on the other hand it's a licence for gossips. The story going around is that you expected them to swap, when Francesca died: Paolo was to step aside, so that after a decent interval…"

"People can think what they like but they've got it all wrong. When I left Paolo, I didn't want to see Luca ever again. It was why I left."

"What?"

"I can't be in the same room as Luca any more."

"Not really irrelevant at all, then. To be honest I'm kind of offended. I'm offended you won't share this with me."

"I'll tell you some time. But right now what I need is distraction, and not to get messages from Paolo wishing me a happy life."

"He means well."

"But it's all part of the plan, isn't it? Kindness is part of the plan."

"What do you mean, love?"

"It's all part of the hatred."

"You worry me when you start to talk like that. I think you should see someone, your doctor. Let me make you an appointment."

"I'm absolutely fine. I'm clearer about everything now. I've never been clearer."

Meanwhile, across town, Paolo had asked Luca if they could have a talk and Luca, alarmed but possessed of a natural inscrutability, had said that of course they could. He was managing this sequence of events with aplomb; he'd adopted his preferred alternative to the truth as if it was accurate, and his mental reflexes had fallen obediently into line. It was only June; it was to be another three months before Paolo would turn up at the airport to see Nina off, three months till he'd be blind-sided by her confession of adultery, and so he had another three months left of trusting his brother. It wasn't an unalloyed trust and this may have been the prime reason for their talking often about it; Paolo was keen to soak up fresh layers and applications of Luca's practised version of things.

They were in Paolo's office, a room unchanged in 50 years but which looked far older even than that, because their father, a lover of all things British and antique, had instructed its fitting-out in a Victorian style. It was book-lined, but only with old leather books, brown and red; it was wood-panelled and waxed, decorated with rare maps, and smelled of beeswax and dust and slightly of damp. An eighteenth-century window looked out over a narrow street to other eighteenth-century windows.

Luca had brought coffee, and put both cups down on the big desk, a partners' desk inlaid with emerald green hide. He sat on its corner and looked attentive. "Go on."

"I know you said she would pass through this and then she'd be ready to come back, and that the best thing was just to let her be, to leave her alone to work through it."

"I still think that's the best policy." Luca took his phone out and looked at it, and put it on the table between them. "It isn't just you. She told me she didn't ever want to talk to me again. That's not Nina." This was a risky approach, pretending he didn't know why, but he'd decided to go flat out with whole-hearted ignorance.

"She said. It helped me not suspect you. It helped avoid the elopement scenario."

"Not that again. I don't know how many times I'm going to have to say this. There wasn't one and there isn't."

"Why isn't she talking to you?"

"Why isn't she living with you? Same reason, I suspect."

"Which is?"

"It's a mystery."

"I didn't recognise her, Luca. When she started talking about it, her unhappiness. It came out of nowhere. I was caught off guard."

"I told you. She's seemed different to me too."

"We can't just leave her in this state."

"So go round there. Take food. Take wine." He was absolutely confident that Nina would never say a word. Putting the two of them together in a room didn't actually feel remotely risky. "What did you say, in the note with the flowers?"

"I wished her happiness in her new home. I kept it simple."

"It's all very perplexing."

"Why was she so weird about your staying with us? That was completely out of character. She's always wanted you around. She's craved you. Let's be honest about it; it was a craving, being around you. But then suddenly she can't tolerate you being in the flat. She said she couldn't eat any more bread that you'd made us. It was actually bizarre."

"She's unwell. It will pass."

"I'm worried."

Luca came over to where Paolo was sitting, in his father's old chair, and put his hand on his brother's shoulder, but was aware of Paolo's struggling to keep composure, and withdrew. He sat down again on the edge of the desk and folded his arms and looked at the floor as if it interested him. "Have you spoken to her?"

"Yesterday. I rang to see if she needed help with the move."

"Don't get distracted by sentimentality."

"What?"

"What was her answer, when you offered?"

"She seemed offended. She said that of all the things I could have said to her, in our first conversation since April, asking if I could help with the move was the last thing she expected."

"Well, I can sort of see her point."

"But she'd made me promise not to bring it up. She said she

needed space to think. She asked me not to ring, or visit or write."

"You shouldn't have rung her, then, strictly speaking."

"I wanted to know if she needed help moving in."

"I can hear Francesca tutting at you. Help with moving in sounded like help with moving out."

"Francesca's still talking?"

"She's still talking. I don't see her as much now. I kept seeing her, the first few weeks. Just glimpses. I think I told you."

"You told me, but tell me again."

"I'd see her leaving the room. That very last moment, when you're not sure if you just saw someone walking out of another door. I was visited at random times, sitting watching telly or in the middle of the night, but just by her perfume, cucumbery and musky at the same time. The last time I saw her she was on the sofa, when I came into the sitting room after work. Just for the briefest flash. There, and then not there. Doing the sudoku in the *Times*, pen in her mouth and her face all frowny. Her little hands. She was perfect, you know. Not just beautiful, though that counts for a lot. She was so tolerant of all my terrible shit."

"Indeed." Paolo was looking at his phone.

"Message?"

"Not from Nina."

"Is it ever from Nina?"

Paolo began to walk around the room, slowly around the partners' desk. "It's the same thing that keeps bugging me. What was it? What was it about Francesca's passing that set her off, that made her ill?"

"I couldn't tell you." Luca had phrased it so it was literally true. "But it seemed like it brought on a new bout of grief about her mother."

"That was the thing that floored me. She decided that I was like her father, too much like him."

"You are, you're very like him. It's why she married you."

"Thanks for saying so. I hadn't heard that before, other than for the previous 999 times."

"Welcome."

"She got it into her head that I was going to reject her, like her father rejected her mother, because I was secretly miserable and bored and masking it all in being a workaholic, and that I was ripe for an affair and she couldn't bear it to happen and was leaving before it could. That's pretty much it in a nutshell."

"You really have honed that nutshell."

"I've had lots of time to hone it."

"So what's the plan?"

"Why doesn't she want to see you any more, Luca?"

"I can't make sense of it either."

"That's the bit I don't get. Why didn't she turn to you, in this crisis? She's always turned to you."

"She said it was time for that to come to an end, that it was disloyal to you. I told you."

"Is there something else, some other reason? Why would she say this to you about never wanting to see you again, and why would she tell me she didn't think we were in love, and…"

"I think she's unwell."

"…and yet still worry about disloyalty? You can see where I'm going with this, though. Let's be frank for once." Paolo reseated himself.

"What do you mean, frank? And what do you mean by 'for once'?" Luca stood up and put his hands on the hips of his chalk-stripe jeans. Paolo looked down at Luca's polished brown Chelsea boots, and up at his white shirt, silk jacket, grey and tan striped scarf. He thought, *It isn't any wonder that people think he's gay.* He glanced down at his usual dark-blue suit, the blue striped tie, and was aware of their dullness. A lack of imagination seemed to have become an issue. The two men were, in their own different ways, both showing signs of their age, though neither had much grey to speak of, nor much that had affected them facially, beyond crow's feet around the eyes. Their body shapes were just as ever – Luca slim and lithe and Paolo broad and strong. Luca was taller than average, and Paolo four inches taller than him. It had occurred to Paolo on several occasions over the years that if it came to it, he could take his brother easily and snap his neck.

"Paolo?" Paolo had gone vague. Paolo was staring at Luca's shoes. "Hello?"

"I just need you to be frank with me. Nina's departure, her state of mind – I'm not sleeping well."

Poor Paolo. Luca saw that he needed something. He'd begun to feel intensely sorry for him. "She said she needed to be loved more than she loved. She'd lost that confidence."

"And so had I."

"It worked for Francesca and me. We took turns loving the other most. You and Nina have never really grasped this nettle."

"What's the nettle?"

Luca didn't say, "Drifting, the drifting." There were different kinds of things he couldn't say. Instead he said, "She needed me to love her more than you did. I mean, to look as if I did. Actual love is neither here nor there."

"And you think that's what you did?"

"She came to a decision, when Fran died. I don't know why. It was just time, after a long time. That's the best I can do for a summing-up."

"Is it really, though?"

Luca looked hurt. "Whatever else you think, it was consistent. She decided that a) she wasn't going to see me any more, and that b) she wasn't going to see you any more either. It would always be both of us at once. You do see that."

"That's interesting. Was that inadvertent?"

"What?"

"You listed yourself first. You were A and I was B. Is that how it was?"

"How can it have been? You're talking paranoid nonsense again."

"She needs someone to love her unconditionally."

"And you couldn't do unconditional any more."

"It was fine until she said she didn't think we were in love. That was humiliating. Do you think there's somebody else?"

"How could there be?"

"She said it would be better for her not to see me or talk to me again. Out of nowhere. It's unimaginable."

"I know. Listen, while we're discussing things, there's something I need to talk to you about. About the future. About mine."

At the airport, standing looking for her paperwork, Nina had been taken aback suddenly to realise that Paolo was in the crowd, his familiar shape, his familiar face, intent on finding her. He'd said, "I had to come." He'd moved closer, so as to stand six feet in front of her, and she'd moved aside from the throng and then they'd both moved further aside so as to be out of people's way. Paolo looked sad. "I talked to my brother again. I know there's something. He's being evasive and he's never evasive."

She'd blurted it. "We slept together. Luca. Me."

She said it looking into his eyes, because cowardice had always been an issue and she was determined that it wasn't any longer going to be. It was time to take things on and face them squarely.

Paolo was at first stunned and then unsurprised. He didn't speak initially, but he adjusted his stance, moving his feet wider apart as if unsteady, and he dropped the carrier bag he was holding, which, she saw, had magazines in it that he'd intended to give her for the flight. He stared at her and there was a long exchange of eye contact, the seconds ticking by. He'd already shown on previous days that he was the kind of person who grows silent when angry. Shock had already given way to an unbearable contempt. She had to look away, and was aware that she was crying, long dribbles of tears, and it was when he saw her tears that he spoke.

"When?"

"I'm sorry."

"When?"

She wished that she hadn't used the euphemism. Slept. They hadn't slept. She should have used a far more brutal and appropriate word.

"Nina? When was this?"

She'd told the lie about the timing of it. There hadn't seemed to be any choice. It didn't feel like a choice. "It was after I moved out, and it wasn't really anything. It was once."

Paolo was sallow. "I knew it, I knew it."

"It was the wrong turn. I'm fine now and it's all over, the whole illusion; I promise you. I promise you." Why was she pleading?

Paolo didn't seem to have heard. "I knew it," he said again.

"You didn't. Even I didn't." She'd never felt less coherent.

"You're in love with him; have always been." He said it more to himself than to her, as if chiding himself for being too trusting.

"It was more like – it was like addiction." She saw Paolo wincing; she was wincing herself.

"That's just a synonym though, isn't it, Nina."

"But it's over now. Finished, all of it. I promise you."

They were standing in the zone that was just before Security, where people queued to have their boarding cards scanned. People around them pretended they couldn't see them, the couple who were standing aside; they pretended they couldn't hear the conversation. But they smiled at each other as they talked, these strangers, speaking to one another in a way designed to mask their listening in. Such drama, going on in this cramped institutional space, couldn't help but verge on the absurd.

Nina said, "I need to go through."

Paolo said, "I wish you hadn't told me." She gathered her things together and he watched her. He said it again. "I wish you hadn't told me."

"I'm sorry."

"How are we going to do this, now?" He began to sound angry. She'd begun to walk away. "I'll never forgive you, Nina," he said, loud enough for everyone to stare, for people to begin to stifle laughter. "I didn't think this was really over. But it's over, isn't it? Over and done with and this is goodbye." Her face was hot with shame. As she went through, she heard his raised voice saying, "It's goodbye, Nina. Next time I talk to you I won't really be talking to you, because I won't really be there."

Chapter Six

Triangles are stable things, mathematically stable but sometimes misleadingly so. We could do away with the triangle and place Nina and Luca and Paolo at points in a circle, each of them holding the hands of the other two, though the idea of a triangle, with its corners, its pauses and reversals, is better suited to the three of them. Perhaps it was always complicated, though very little of this embedded complexity showed up in the photographs that Anna took, hundreds of them, of Nina and the boys who lived next door. For reasons Nina would only understand much later, her mother always took it for granted that Nina would marry one of the Romano boys. At night, stroking Nina's hair until she slept, Anna told Nina stories about her life as if it were an old folktale. *There were once two brothers, tall dark and handsome brothers who loved each other with absolute love, and who as boys met a girl called Nina, as fair as they were dark, whose pale hair and pale-blue eyes marked her as a fairy creature.* "Which of the brothers would win the fairy girl?" she'd ask. The outcomes weren't always the same, but the versions in which she married the handsomer, more confident brother usually ended less than well.

Because she had no children of her own, Nina always kept pictures of her own childhood with her. Herself and Luca and Paolo as children: these were her children. In the photo that sat at the front of the picture slot in her wallet, a print in Kodacolor taken on a big flat beach, she and Luca were eight and Paolo a taller, robust-looking ten-year-old, his eyes watchful and his smile guarded. He was physically distinct from the other two, with a soft belly, large thighs, the beginnings of a double chin, dimensions that didn't much change in later life other than to be firmed up by the hours he spent at a city swimming pool. Even as a child his expression was unlike that of the others; there was something about Paolo even at ten that was wearily human. Anna said he was an old soul.

Luca and Nina, on the other hand, looked like immortals, like sprites. They had similar bodies, then, similar long, bony limbs, prominent knees and elbows, angular faces and wide smiles, eyes that shared and escalated mischief. The beach photograph at the front of the slot was the picture Nina showed Dr Christos, one that illustrated the circle. The one she didn't show him illustrated the triangle. It was hidden at the back of the compartment, one of her and Luca at fifteen and Paolo at seventeen, photographed in the garden. Nina was in the middle and had looped a skinny arm around each boy's neck. Her white-blonde hair was in two thin plaits that wound around the crown of her head like some Nordic girl goddess.

That was the day it started: the triangle's official beginning. By then everything was in flux. Paolo didn't look any longer a willing part of things; he was standing right next to Nina but looked as if he was already pulling away from her even as the picture was being taken. This separateness had begun in the summer holidays: Paolo had been unavailable, having found other things to do and other people to do them with. Now, at the start of the October half-term, his not wanting to spend time with Nina and Luca was obvious. He'd begun to tire of the pranks and silliness of his brother, and Nina's enthusiastic, uncritical aiding and abetting. He'd curl his lip a certain way, when Luca was being lunatic and Nina his devoted accomplice, and look into the middle distance, wishing himself elsewhere. That afternoon had been a case in point. After they'd had their picture taken, summoned into the garden and put into the old pose, Luca and Nina went to the Findlays' sofa and listened to *Dark Side of the Moon*, an album of Nina's mother's, one that her father had deemed barbaric; the barbarians, he said, were long past the gate and were trampling through the rose beds. Paolo had declined an invitation to join in. Instead he'd followed Anna into the kitchen, glad of a chance to talk about his dilemma (whether to go to university or not), but then she'd had to go out and so he'd wandered into the sitting room, still holding his coffee cup and with the stance of a spectator. Luca was lying with his head on Nina's corduroy-clad thigh – it was a proper autumn day and they were all in cords and sweaters in mud and heather colours – playing a game of their own devising that was called Alternatives. One person declared a theme and then, after the others narrowed it down, had to come up with a funny alternative to the lyric they were listening to. Paolo wasn't keen on playing; he wasn't as quick-witted as the others and his brother could be scornful.

It was Nina's go. "Jobs. Professions."

"Weavers," Luca said straight away.

Nina began to laugh. She was laughing even before she could spit it out. "Dark side of the loom!"

She and Luca both found this hysterically funny. Paolo didn't. It was a small thing, the kind of thing that could create alliances and also destroy them. Luca, laughing and bouncing the back of his skull uncomfortably on Nina's leg, had been tipped off it and rolled forward. She'd tried to save him and the two of them had gone over the edge of the couch and onto a lambswool rug. Their limbs had become entangled. They took their time disentangling them.

"For God's sake," Paolo said. "You're so bloody childish."

"And what should we be, middle-aged like you?" Luca countered, looking up at him, his legs wrapped around Nina's hips. Nina should have said something. Paolo was her friend. She was always the glue that bound them. "Personally I plan to be childish for a long, long time."

"In which case, have a nice life," Paolo told him, sounding more peevish than he meant to.

"What, you think our parents are a good advert for growing up?" Luca said, sitting straighter. "They're miserable and bored and that's why they fight all the time."

"They don't fight all the time," Nina objected, though the truth was that they fought a lot. It was, as Anna explained to Robert, the reason the boys were at their house and on their sofa so often, and not at home.

Paolo put his hands in his two front pockets. "Just grow up a bit, little brother," he said. "It gets a little tedious, all this, and a bit embarrassing."

"What does?" Nina asked. She didn't get it.

"Fuck off," Luca told him.

"The cavorting, the flirting," Paolo said. "And now I'm off to play tennis. Bye."

Thanks to the positioning and the screening of ancient trees, the two families occupied a private corner in the village, and so

Giulio and Maria Romano's screaming matches were muffled from most neighbours, while at the same time being broadcast right into the Findlays' garden. The Findlay place, built on a plot that had been a scruffy car workshop in the '60s, occupied a corner at the convergence of two quiet Victorian roads. Their wide, flat-faced two-storey house, built in 1971, was the first modern building in an otherwise ubiquitously nineteenth-century locale, and was something of a talking point. When they first moved in, Anna would find locals at the door wondering if they could have a wee look; wasn't this open-plan layout going to be awfully expensive to heat?

Anna had been dismayed by the apparent disintegration of the threesome in the summer holidays, but was philosophical. It would just be a phase, she said to Nina. She'd acknowledged the change in front of the boys, that day, when she'd opened the door in the fence and asked them to come for a photograph. She must at least have her annual photograph, she said. The door, made out of a modified hinged panel with a bolt on both sides, was one that the two fathers had made together when the children were small and went back and forth. The parents had gone back and forth, too. There were frequent get-togethers on weekend summer evenings over wine, usually at Giulio's invitation (he worked in wine; there was always wine). Maria joined in but she was unmistakably just a little less keen to socialise, trying to keep the visits to a fixed schedule and openly averse to their dragging on too long. She didn't like the neighbours, and particularly not Anna, but it was also a kind of self-knowledge: when she and Giulio drank too much there'd inevitably be bickering that could tip into open warfare. She'd object to the length of Giulio's anecdotes. He would call her a joyless nag. She might say that he'd had enough to drink. He'd say that it wasn't any wonder that he drank. She'd say that she wasn't going to be chastised in front of their friends. He'd say that was rich coming from her. Later, many years later, Nina would see *Who's Afraid of Virginia Woolf* on television, sitting cuddled up with Luca on a night that Paolo was away, and she'd say, "Do Liz and Richard remind you of anyone?" and Luca, wincing, would say, "So much so that it feels almost like one of my own memories."

"So that's your parents," she'd said. "I wonder who'd play mine."

Luca had considered the question. "Max von Sydow and Daryl Hannah." They'd laughed because it was true. They'd laughed some more imagining the four having dinner together. The imaginary dialogue that came out of the initial riff had spiralled into a routine that was added to intermittently for weeks.

Having made his terse farewell, Paolo left the Findlays' sitting room, stomping off through the front door and banging it behind him. Through the large glass window that dominated the front of the building, nine-paned like a noughts-and-crosses board, they saw him stride past, his mouth set into irritation. Luca and Nina watched in silence, then caught each other's eye and laughed again, Luca pressing his lips together and blowing a laughter raspberry through them, the kind done in the presence of pomposity.

He stopped quite suddenly and looked pained. "Jesus, he's turning into such a wanker."

He and Nina made Marmite toast and tea and took them outside, to the wooden seat behind the shed at the end of the garden. It was a south-facing corner and the day seemed almost warm there, out of the wind. No sooner had Nina sat down and put her hands on the edge of the bench, wrapping the ends of her fingers underneath, than she squawked in pain and withdrew. "Splinter. Fucking splinter." Luca had taught her how to swear, though she only exercised her new talent in his presence. "Bollocks. Fucking hurts." The fingertip looked instantly as if it were infected, puffing and pinking.

Luca had taken a packet of Marlboro and a lighter out of his jacket pocket, having told Nina that he was going to teach her how to smoke. He put the cigarettes back and said, "Here, let me look." They peered at the index finger together. "It's gone right in. Hold it steady; I'm going to get it out."

"No, no, don't; it'll hurt." She was flinching, screwing her face up. "I'll go find Mum; she takes them out with a hot needle."

"A hot needle sounds a lot worse. Hold still." He squeezed at the injury from both sides with the tips of his thumbs until the end of the splinter popped up, and then grasped it and pulled. "There's a tiny bit left; let me suck at it."

Nina was already doing that, sucking at the wound and then peering at it, squinting. She felt a thrill of disquiet at Luca's suggestion. "All gone I think. It's bleeding, though."

Luca produced a clean tissue, winding it around the finger and tucking in. the end. A blood spot seeped red from within, spreading and then ceasing. "That should do it," he said. "Might need a plaster later."

"Thank you." She put out her good hand. It was a thanking gesture, brushed against his ribs.

What happened next happened in a rush. Luca took hold of the hand and pulled her towards him, adjusting his balance on the bench, and then he was kissing her. They kissed softly and then harder and moved closer to one another. He put his arms around her lower back and now his tongue found hers; she put her arms around him and pressed her breasts into his chest and he made a small noise, a soft grunt, something out of his throat like a small admission of relief. Immediately after this there was a new noise, one they both recognised: the door from the kitchen opening and closing. Nina's eyes widened as she realised that it was her mother approaching, her feet on the paved path; she moved back and Luca moved back further, pushing away from her and turning rapidly to face forward. They'd only just extricated themselves when Anna appeared, barefoot and wearing a red shirt dress with buttons that stopped short of the knee, revealing long smooth legs that still bore traces of summer. She had wet laundry in a blue basket balanced against her hip. The washing line was attached to the shed at one end, and at the other to a rusting pole that Robert had planted in the hedge for the purpose.

"What are you two up to?" She'd dropped the basket and was beginning to hang the clothes. She didn't mean anything particular by it, but Luca had already sprung to his feet.

"I'm going in now; see you," he said. Anna turned to Nina while holding a shirt, offering an enquiring look, but said nothing, returning to the task, and Luca went through the door in the fence and disappeared.

Disappeared was the apt word. He didn't look Nina in the eye for almost three years. Instead, he began spending a lot of time alone, or with new friends, new faces in the garden that Nina realised were really old faces, boys she'd been at primary school with, like Andy Stevenson, who looked like a young farmer. Luca was busy with projects and mystifyingly apparently cheerful. As for Nina, she was thought to be ill; her parents worried about her paleness and lack of sleep, her poor appetite, her inability to sit still. It affected her schoolwork. She'd study a little while or read, she'd listen to music or go to the hobby room to her mother's sewing machine, but it wasn't long before she was back at the window, to see if she could see him. Sometimes he'd be alone in his garden, kicking leaves or hitting a tennis ball repetitively against the wall. He'd sit on the swing – Nina's bedroom gave a grandstand view of it – with his feet in the dirt patch that had been worn beneath, moving himself back and forth with his shoes trailing. When it was fine she'd see him reading in the hammock, one that Giulio had strung between two silver birches, with successive trilogy paperbacks of *The Lord of the Rings*. Sometimes he'd look up, a quick disguised look upwards, and if he saw her he'd go inside. It was clear that he didn't want to know her any more. Their friend-ship was over. Unable to believe that it was over, Nina persisted, for a few disheartening weeks, in asking if he fancied doing stuff – a nostalgic bike ride, a trip to the cinema? "I'm busy," he'd say, frowning at some fixed third point, as if she ought to have known, as if they'd already been over this. It was like the kissing was her fault somehow, as if she'd let him down.

What is it that makes us fall in love with someone? A list of attrib-utes is a useless thing in answering. Plenty of people have those same attributes and we don't love them. There are people we dislike who have those same attributes. Tick the boxes, retrospec-tively, that mark the qualities of the person who was loved, and there may even be things we'd never tolerate again. The intan-gibles at work are things as unreliable as weather, forces that go beyond thinking and deciding, all of them convincingly perma-nent but proven by other examples of love to be as transitory as fog, as sunshine. On what basis had she done her choosing? In the hospital Nina wrote pages and pages on the whole slippery idea of the basis. Was it really something as embarrassingly superficial as the look of somebody, the way they spoke, their absolute faith in themselves? Luca and Paolo were both solidly good-looking, though Paolo was a lot more solid than his brother. There wasn't any doubt that Luca was the more conventionally handsome; Paolo's nose was longer, his mouth narrower, his eyes deeper set. But it couldn't be that. If Luca and Paolo had swapped bodies it would still have been Luca. It could only have been down to a shared wit, a way of thinking; recognition of a companion mind. Perhaps it was simply instinctive, one of those rapid sub-verbal assessments that stick; attraction is happy to betray all rationality. As someone once said – possibly a prose stylist at Hallmark Cards – the heart wants what the heart wants. We can stage all the neurological interventions we like: it wants what it wants. There are things that take place in closed session, deep in the interfaces between mind and will, deep under the crust of the known self, where the playing-out of heart goes blindly on. Sometimes the whole thing is utterly baffling afterwards. Nina continued, in her hospital bed, to puzzle over events in her notebooks. *Was his cruelty, his inconstancy, a part of it? Did his being in a way dangerous, his approval hard to win, make his love worth more than Paolo's – or is it all just more evidence of my own lack, lack piled upon lack, in being dazzled by unpredictability and disdaining constancy?* She paused, pen poised, and added *It's such a dismal fucking cliché among womankind.*

If Nina had a tendency to drift into prose that was Jane-Austenish (lack upon lack, dazzled, disdaining, constancy, it all seemed fairly Austen to her, reading back, though admittedly the final line was firmly modern), then this was in keeping with Anna's preoccupation with Nina making a good marriage. When Nina was seventeen, in the second year of Luca's great silence, and Paolo seemed interested in her, Anna was unsentimental about what Nina should do: in short, bag Paolo – who at that time was all set to be sole heir to the wine business – and step away from Luca, who was determined at that point to be a poet. Associating Anna's advice with dull materialism, Nina found it easier to dismiss. The deed was already done. Hers and Luca's souls had exchanged, silently and invisibly, their potent hormonal business cards. Not that you'd have known it, looking in from the outside. From the outside there was scant evidence of anything other than indifference, though because of the timing of it his abandonment looked ordinary, even inevitable, to others. To the surrounding adults it looked more like a sudden growing-up, a sudden leap forward of maturity. Almost simultaneously with Anna's advice to Nina, Luca decided that he was giving up on being a writer and would try for law, and started to study harder. He began to take sports more seriously, joined the athletics club at school and played competitive tennis. He became quite suddenly taller and filled out across the shoulders, and began to attract female attention. Throughout all of this Nina was ignored.

That's how things stood when she went to university, to Glasgow to study literature. Luca stayed home – having given up first on poetry and then on law – to join his brother at his father's wine distribution business. He was busy being a new broom, accusing Paolo of conservatism, wanting radical shake-ups even in the staff kitchen. Nina saw Luca that Christmas at her mother's annual party, watching from across the room as he busied himself being lively in the presence of others. She watched how other girls talked to him. There was a lot of fluidity in her character that she could direct in ways Luca would approve of, if she could only be sure what those things were. She began to read her mother's self-help books, looking for answers.

"It's a mistake to accept that the person you think you are is the person you are for ever," Anna had told her. "A person is a work of art and can be remade in different ways."

Her dad scoffed at this. Robert disapproved of the writing of books and also the reading of them. He was disdainful of the idea of self-improvement, dismissive of what he called the inward-looking gaze, calling it the unhelpful offspring of the cult of individualism (this was how he talked), something that enforced a tendency to self-absorption. "What people who think they're depressed need is to do community work, to help other people," he'd say lugubriously. "Let them visit the poor, and help the elderly, and put other people first." He encouraged Anna to be a local volunteer, and she said that she found it uplifting. Robert had rarely been irritable with her – theirs was a marriage almost entirely without arguments – but he was openly intolerant of her self-help phase, and openly relieved when it was over and she gave the books away to a church hall sale.

Nina hung onto one of the books and kept it with her sports equipment in a long zipped bag. The chapter on love was especially well thumbed. It talked about identifying a mate, and Nina recognised that she'd identified Luca early. Although, was identification the right word? It didn't seem so during the long days on the island, as her shin bone knitted slowly back together. All her hidden self had offered up was notification that something irrevocable had taken place, something that manifested itself as possessiveness.

Even at fifteen, she'd owned Luca. She owned the way his shirt sat on his shoulders, the bulge of shoulder blades at the back and then concave between them, the way that he turned up his sleeves, unbuttoning the cuffs and folding them to the elbows. There was something about his forearms that drew her; when the two families ate together she'd look discreetly at them and at his hands as he broke bread. She knew the curves and outlines of his neck and spine and the backs of his legs, the shape of his feet, their bones and planes, the scattering of dark hair on his toes, the way his toenails flared upwards and how very short he cut them, so that the end of the toe bulged out afterwards; she knew the particular, individual system of muscles around his knees. She noticed small changes made to his hairline, and to his smell; his skin had a smell like but unlike his brother's. She mapped and knew his physical self like a learned and recited poem.

The facts were the facts. Luca had decided two things in the same year, the year of the beginnings of ownership: firstly that he would kiss her and secondly that the kiss was a mistake. There wasn't any other interpretation possible. He couldn't any longer even acknowledge her. So it was beyond surprising, when Nina came back for the long vacation at the end of her first university year, to find that Luca was there in the garden with her parents, waiting with them for her arrival. He'd brought samples of the new wines he'd been credited with sourcing in Italy, and was doing a little showing-off. That was okay. It was allowable; Nina's parents showed it in their faces, their finding it endearing that he should want to impress them, though some of the things he said were things they already knew, talking them through wine regions and varieties as if they were beginners. Nina had arrived quietly, letting herself into the house, and watched unseen from the kitchen window for a minute or two before opening the door to the outside, breaking the spell of Luca's monologue. She was grabbed and hugged and kissed by her mother. "It's so good to have you home, I can't tell you." Anna inhaled deeply at her daughter's neck. "I'm so glad you're home."

"Wine, Nina?" Luca asked, as if things between them were normal.

"No thanks; travel headache." She went back into the kitchen for water, watching them as she ran the tap colder. They were sitting at the metal patio set, the bistro set, so-called, on the uncomfortable white metal chairs. She saw Luca drape one arm over the back of the fourth chair – the vacant one that awaited her. When she returned she insisted on standing, leaning against the fence and saying that she'd been sitting too long.

"So, how are you?" Luca was smiling at her as if they were friends, as if none of it had happened. "How's university life? Do you like living in Glasgow? And how long are you back for? For the whole summer, I hope. Do you have a summer job?"

"It's good, thanks. I do. I'm here till September. And yes, wait-ressing in town."

"Well, that's systematic. And are you well?"

"I'm very well." The briskness was sufficient to earn a raised eyebrow from Anna, and Nina adjusted her tone. "How's Paolo doing – how's he liking London? He wrote to me and I meant to reply but then I didn't get round to it." Paolo had gone to London to work for a national wine shop chain.

"Paolo's fine," his brother said. "Fine, fine, dull as ever, fine."

"Luca, that's mean," Anna protested.

Luca just laughed. He poured more wine into the glasses, Nina's included, ignoring her protests about the headache.

He came into the Findlays' house the following day without knocking, just like he used to. Nina came into the sitting room and found him there. He'd made himself at home on the couch, having taken a pile of books from the shelves; he'd helped himself to snacks and put records on, just as he used to. Nina came into the room, thinking she was alone at home, and found him there: Luca, a Genesis LP, a Martin Amis, a sandwich.

"Making yourself at home, I see."

"This is bloody good ham. Can I make you one?" He didn't look up.

"Why are you here?" She was in the right, so why did she have to sound as if she wasn't?

"What do you mean?" It was as if he genuinely didn't know. "Your mother said I could come whenever I need to get away. I needed to get away. Am I bothering you?"

"Not at all." The insincerity was blistering. She sat beside him and picked up a magazine. Her hands were shaking. Her stomach churned. She needed to be offhand, but her chilliness with him was doomed. He paid no attention to her attempted coolness, refusing to acknowledge her coolness until her coolness was defeated; this was crucially the thing that Luca always did and Paolo didn't.

He said, "So how are you really? Are you seeing anyone? I've been going out with Susie; you've probably heard."

"I heard that you dumped her."

"She's going to be a success as a lawyer. That's all I'm prepared to say. It isn't a compliment. I'm getting another sandwich; can I get you one?" He went into the kitchen.

"No, thanks. I've got one last essay to finish; I'd better go finish it." She went to her room and sat on her bed and wondered what to do next. There was no essay. She was trapped in her room. What was she going to do?

"Nina." He'd come up the stairs in his sock feet. His head had appeared round the door.

She reached for the book by the bed, the dilapidated Byron, and he saw her do so and knew everything. He took the book off her and put it down and took off his shoes and lay on her bed on his back, and opened his arm and said "Snuggle time," and was absolutely unemotive about it, as if addressing the ceiling, and she complied, going and lying beside him and resting her head on his shoulder. He turned and kissed her softly on the lips and said, "That's better." After a while he said, "What shall we do with the summer? The summer: that's too big a concept. What shall we do tomorrow? Let's get on a train and go visit somewhere we've never been."

"I'm starting work tomorrow afternoon," she told him.

Luca just pulled her in closer. The tightness of the hug was a way of saying the unsayable. It was an apology. It couldn't be anything else. Nina didn't bring up the hiatus or her own confusion about it. She was too relieved to say anything. She wasn't impressed with herself about this, but on the other hand the relief of it was above every other feeling.

The following Saturday Maria and Giulio came round for a drink for Anna's birthday, and sat at the outdoor table and drank more of Luca's new wine. Luca and Nina lay on the grass together on a tartan rug, looking private and conspiratorial, and Giulio began to talk about the two of them as if they were a couple, though he did so under his breath so that they couldn't hear, whispering that he foresaw an announcement. None of the other three had anything to say to this, but each of their faces had its own reaction. Anna's was cheerful scepticism, her eyebrows raised, smiling. Robert's was openly aghast. Maria's was directed at her husband, and could have killed a smaller mammal.

Until Nina went back to Glasgow, and when they weren't working, Luca and Nina spent a lot of time together, through June and July and August, and then half of September. On fine weekends they'd lounge in Nina's garden, reading and dozing and listening to Anna's battery-operated radio. The days were long and lazy and nothing much happened or was even said, though from time to time one of them shared bits from a book, or instigated idle chatter or a tease. Mostly they were verbal teases. "You've been immensely boring today; you're the most boring person I've ever met." "I'm not the one who mentioned photosynthesis twice over breakfast." "You're worse; you take books of logarithms on holiday."

He kissed her sometimes, on the mouth, closed-lipped though sometimes for a long moment, with a constant firm pressure, what he called a Hollywood kiss, one from the golden age of film. He kissed her chastely, and held her hand, and put his arm around her often. Were they boyfriend and girlfriend, or not? She dreaded anybody asking. It seemed more like a regression than anything; they'd returned to the sibling patterns of childhood. That August at Giulio's sixtieth, standing in the Romanos' kitchen, Nina said the pâté was too salty and Luca pretended he'd made it and was offended and swooped, rugby-tackling her from the side so that both of them fell onto the linoleum. Other guests had moved swiftly out of range.

"Hey! Be careful there, you two. Glasses. Holding glasses here. Take it outside."

"What are they like?" another guest asked rhetorically. "Like deranged giant kittens."

"I foresee an announcement," Giulio said, looking happy.

There were no question marks, nor irony, but there were question marks and irony afterwards for Nina, alone in her bedroom, turning to bury her face in the pillow so as to laugh. The need to make asses of themselves in public was mutual, circumventing even the stern disapproval of her father. There was hope and fear and self-consciousness afterwards, but above all else there was certainty, absolute certainty, that this was the beginning of her and Luca's life story, their life-long story.

The day after the party, finding they both had hangovers, Luca decided that they should play garden badminton. Paolo, who was catching the morning train, came to say goodbye as they were fixing the net. Luca had retrieved its mouldering end from inside the hedge and was carrying it across to attach it to a hook on the wooden fence at the other side.

"I'm off, then," Paolo said.

"Bye." Luca wasn't looking at him. He busied himself with knotting the ties.

"Great to talk to you, as ever." Paolo left without saying anything further.

Nina said, "Why do you have to treat him like that?"

Luca looked confused. "He talks to me like that too. All the time. Just not in front of you."

Nina hit the shuttlecock really hard, serving like gunfire. Luca smashed it back and she lobbed it, and he lobbed it higher and further in return, and Nina backed and backed and blundered into the rockery, twisting her foot and sinking to the grass with a shout. Luca was straight there, dropping his racquet and ducking under the net and running to her.

"Don't move, don't move, let me look at it first." He removed her tennis shoe with tender care, Nina wincing and shrieking, and hoisted her foot onto his leg just above the knee. His hands stroked over her instep, over the ball of her foot, lightly and gently flexing her toes. "It isn't anything much, I don't think," he said, "but we need to get it up and get some ice on it pronto."

It turned out that Paolo was still there. He was standing in the kitchen eating toast, when Luca carried Nina back into the house, staggering under her supposed weight and demanding she eat less chocolate. He followed the two of them into the sitting room and watched as Luca ministered to the foot. Luca got Nina settled, her leg propped on a cushion, and fetched frozen peas for the swelling.

Paolo hovered. "The swelling's a good sign – it means it's probably not broken."

Luca's expression was withering. "What do you know about broken ankles? Zero; less than zero. The swelling's a good sign, indeed. I don't think Nina thinks the swelling's a good sign."

Paolo went to an armchair and took another of the cushions and put it against his stomach and wrapped his arms tight around it. "I love your feet," he said. Luca turned to stare at him. "No, really," Paolo continued. "They're elegant. My toes are like five fat prawns in a box, but yours are – look how thin the stems of your toes are, the little pads at the end."

"It's because she's a girl, Paolo," Luca said. "And you're not, most of the time."

Paolo blushed. He never had the answer until afterwards. He got up and left the room, and then a few minutes later left the house with his bag over his shoulder, following his dad out to the car for a lift to the railway station. There was a note for Nina on the kitchen counter. *Hope your foot's okay. It's been good to see you. Come and visit me in London one weekend.*

There was no doubt that Paolo was the nicer brother. Always kind. Even-tempered. Reliable. Loyal. But it hadn't been any use.

Chapter Seven

"You mentioned that you've been here before," Dr Christos said, as they sat having breakfast together. Olive oil had dripped onto the notes that sat beneath the plate, and Nina pointed it out, and he began blotting the paper with a napkin.

"Paolo and I came here on our honeymoon, 25 years ago this month."

"Twenty-five years ago. 25 years ago – I must have been a student then. I must have been here. I came home from the States for the summers. That's right, I was here. I was working the summer for Vasilios."

"Really? You were here that September? Or had you gone back by then? We arrived on the eighth."

"Ah no. I had to be back at the university at the end of August. We just missed each other. Wait – was that the wet summer? That's what they call it here."

"It rained almost all of the time."

"The freak wet summer. You were here on honeymoon then? That was really bad luck."

"It seemed like an omen." Dr Christos gathered the plates and put them on the table, and opened the French windows. "It hasn't changed much, the island," Nina added.

"It hasn't. That's its blessing and its curse. As they say." He went to the corner and turned on the room fan. "Air con's broken down today." It spluttered into life and rotated its metal sunflower face, first this way and then that. "The people don't change either. I don't know in what year the people here stopped changing: we talk about it sometimes at home. With my sister and her family, I mean. I live alone now."

He got the Scrabble board out and set it up. They played board games now, in the second week: Scrabble and backgammon and chess, at odd intervals during the day, starting a round at breakfast and finishing by nightfall.

"Do you like it, living alone?"

"Not really. Look at that: it's all consonants. But my wife didn't want to live with me any more. One day she said she'd had enough of my bad moods and irregular hours and my only doing the laundry every five years. She lives opposite her dad, in the houses up at the end of the no-through road, and I see her almost every day. So."

Nina put the first word down. VARIANT.

"You used all your letters." He sounded almost accusing.

"Sorry. It was what I had given to me." She wrote down the score. "In my case it was me that did the leaving, but that was only technically as he wanted me to go, and it was pretty much the same with my parents."

"I feel as if we might need a bottle of whisky for this conversation. Whisky's depressingly expensive here, though I can produce wine. My sister's husband has the vineyard, the one you can see from the beach."

"It's the wine that Vasilios serves."

He put down a word, and she followed with another, better one.

"It is. You'll have tasted it. I can bring some in after hours, when I'm no longer your doctor, and we can sit on the patio and get toasted; toast your survival, I mean."

"Is that allowed? The drinking, I mean."

"I'm the one who does the allowing, though we hide the liquor when the humourless people come calling." He inclined his head towards the window. "Quarterly inspections hoping to catch us out. And I have to say, it's also how it felt in my marriage. Audits and reports and failure to meet standards." He put down QUEST with the Q on the triple, and his face confirmed that honour had been saved.

He shook the tiles in their bag. "The thing with relationships is that talking's neither here nor there, and when it's wrong it's wrong. As soon as we know that, we should acknowledge it and move on. Surely." She put I – O – N onto the end of QUEST. "Is that allowed? I don't think you've changed the root of the word. You can't go making plurals and changing verbs into nouns. But I'll allow it just this once. My letters are terrible." He frowned at his board. "Women always want reasons; they want to go for a long walk, but sometimes it's better if people don't talk things over. Go with the instinct; the instinct's usually right. And then don't look back – that's absolutely the key thing."

"My husband would agree with you. My ex-husband. I don't know what to call him any more. He drew the line in the sand and stepped over it, and on the other side there were lots of single women who'd formed a queue. My dad says he's dating, out having dinner and looking a lot happier."

Dr Christos put down DRAB. "I know, but it's all I have. This doesn't always seem like a game of skill. Anyway. It's just a game." He got out fresh tiles. "I wish my ex would fall in love again. My life would be a hell of a lot easier."

Nina had her word prepared and Dr Christos followed immediately with EXIT, the X on a double.

"How can it be better not to talk things over?" she asked him. "The end of a marriage is a big thing in anybody's life."

"I don't think it follows" he told her. She laid down APHID above EXIT so that she also made EH, XI and ID. She had to show him the booklet with its list of acceptable two-letter words. "For Christ's sake," he said. "You're way too good at this. I diagnose too much Scrabble in your life. And no, I don't think it follows. Few people can do justice to their decisions when asked about them. Language is an inadequate thing for feelings."

"But you have to make an attempt at it, at least."

"A decision comes at the end of a long sequence of thoughts. A person's already talked it over a long time in his head." He looked at his tiles glumly. "All these useless four-letter words. I can't put CHAT down, not after ID, the ID incident."

"It doesn't matter. Put CHAT down if that's what you have. As you say, it's the luck of the draw." She watched as he put CHAT on the board and garnered nine points. "But you have to give reasons, surely. You can't not give reasons."

"I don't know if that helps. In our case it made things worse." Dr Christos looked at his phone. "I have to go; I'm late for a meeting. I'll bring work back with me. You mustn't distract me this afternoon."

When he returned, after lunch, the aroma of coffee preceding him in the corridor and the sound of his flattened espadrilles flapping, he said, "I know what I said but please distract me: this is turning into a crap of a day."

"Do you want to carry on with the game?"

"Let's do that later. I may need to eat a dictionary first. I'm actually really tired. I'll close my eyes for a bit and listen. Tell me something. Tell me something new."

He sat himself down in the armchair, his red jeans and gaudy Hawaiian shirt super-real against the white of the wall, and rested an elbow on the chair arm and rested his head in his hand.

Nina said, "I had a sort of a breakdown. Before coming here."

Dr Christos opened his eyes and closed them again. He didn't look especially surprised. "Go on. If you want to say more."

"What happened was fairly straightforward: my sister-in-law Francesca died in February, and for various complicated reasons I became depressed."

"Various straightforward complicated reasons. What did she die of?"

"Breast cancer. She was 45."

"What were the complicated reasons?"

"Francesca died and it was very distressing, and everybody fell apart. Even me, which surprised everyone because I'm a cold fish." She grimaced.

"Surely not."

"My mother-in-law's phrase, because I'm reserved. Normally, yes, reserved, though I can see that might be hard to believe. And then Paolo wanted to talk to me about my being a misery. I was surprised because I thought that was him. We had a conversation about love. I didn't think we were in it and he didn't argue. So I moved out and went back to the village, really a suburb now, where I grew up, and then I went a bit nuts, and got pills, and felt better, and my doctor said I needed a proper holiday, so here I am."

The doctor's eyes were closed. It made confiding easy. It was comforting for Nina to be able to do this summarising and hear it the way it ought to have been, its loose ends all tied.

"Was that the disgrace?" he asked.

"No, there was more. I'll come to that." She settled herself flatter on the bed. She could feel her heartbeat slowing.

"When you say breakdown – how did it start?"

"Are you going to take notes – have you gone into doctor mode on me?"

"Not at all. Sorry. Just very nosy."

"It started with a cauliflower. Of all things. Paolo came to the cottage to see how I was settling in. He'd brought wine and a pair of small chickens that were ready to cook. I forget what they're called; there's a word for the little ones; they come in pairs and you eat one each. I've never liked them because it's like eating babies. Anyway. He said he would roast them. I didn't want that. It seemed like a big deal." She focused hard on the window blind, which was bobbing in the room fan's breeze. "I wasn't well. But you see, why did I have to eat chicken with a man I had recently told I didn't love? It's always been other people who decide what's kind and what's rude. I've never been one of the deciders."

"Was it true about not loving him any more?"

"I don't know."

"How could you not know?"

"You say that as if it's always been clear to you, who you love and who you don't."

"Shouldn't that be 'whom'?"

"I tend to pretend I don't know that, in conversation. It's so doggedly formal. Course, if I was editing you it'd be different. Paolo didn't like my editing him. He didn't like the way I'd done the food shopping, either. Why was it any of his business?"

Before she could stop him he'd opened the fridge, saying, "Dear God, what's all this?" The ready meals were stacked in two piles of three, and on the upper shelf smaller cartons, of rice, couscous, prepared side dishes, sat alongside tubs of hummus, salsa, prepared garlic and chilli.

"I haven't felt like cooking."

He pulled out one of the meal boxes so as to be able to read the label. "Cumberland sausage with parmesan mash."

"I haven't felt like cooking."

Paolo found a roasting dish, washed his hands, salted the birds, and then – taking a knife from the rack on the wall and a board from behind the bread bin – chopped onions and garlic cloves and added them to the tin. He rummaged in the fruit bowl, and sliced a lemon up and added the pieces. "There. As easy as those terrible cook-chill things."

"I know. Why are you treating me as if I don't know?"

He'd turned up the radio, and steamed the potatoes and boiled some green beans and they'd eaten lunch and talked about nothing, about world events.

Then he'd said, "Does the chef get a cup of coffee?" and he'd hung around, sitting on her sofa with his feet on the table, reading her weekend newspapers with faked raptness as if he hadn't already read them at home. He mentioned, on leaving, that he'd left her a cauliflower that he'd bought at the farmers' market, and some good cheese for the sauce.

Her father had found her later that afternoon, sitting on the kitchen floor, a destroyed cauliflower around her, bits of floret clutched in balled fists. She'd smashed it over and over, its cauliflower brain. He'd driven her to the village surgery, 150 yards, as Nina felt too dizzy to walk it. The doctor was grave and kind and elderly, technically long past retirement age; she'd been the family GP for a long time. Nina thought of her as another mother. She was Dr Macfarlane but Nina had long since been urged to call her Alison.

"So what happened today?" Alison asked.

"Paolo brought me a cauliflower. I've never liked cauliflower. He was the one who liked it."

It seemed as if her thoughts and preferences would always be tangled up with his, conjoined like Siamese twins, and she wasn't wholly confident that her own would survive if surgically detached. Cooking was part of the problem, Nina told her; cooking was something too associated with the past and with domestic expectation. Chopping vegetables seemed too much like an act of faith in the future. Nina wondered if that's how her father had seen things: he hadn't cooked after Anna moved out, other than for the Sunday joint of beef, which sat under foil in the fridge for the rest of the week, awaiting slicing. Cooking, he said, was for people who didn't have much else to do. Time was precious. He had 10,000 more books to read than years to read them in, and beans on toast and fruit from the bowl was a perfectly good dinner, thank you. He didn't need to make a salad of the fruit and add elderflower cordial and mint and whatnot.

"It's not going to be for ever," Nina said. "It's just that I need to go through a period of food not mattering. Much more time is freed up for curling on the sofa in a ball."

"Tell me more about the curling up," Alison said, picking up her pen. It was an ordinary day in the despair business.

"It hasn't settled yet, the swinging pendulum," Nina told her.

"Though sometimes I can feel it, the pendulum, striking hard at my inner walls."

"I don't understand what you mean. What's the pendulum?"

"Sometimes it seems as if I caught a virus a long time ago." She'd felt it there, waiting deep inside her cells, waiting to be tickled back into life. "That's what I've come to you about. I think I have a virus."

"What are the symptoms?"

"Over-excitement and then feeling dead. A virus in my brain, that's what it might be."

"It sounds rather like it might be a kind of depression."

"I'm not depressed. I just have to change and I'm too tired."

"I wonder if you should have a chat with a friend of mine. She's a psychiatrist at the hospital."

"You mean the mental hospital?"

"She's a friend of mine, and it's just where she works. She's a good listener, and she will have more time." She looked at Nina over the top of silver-framed glasses. "It's entirely up to you. I think it might help and wouldn't hurt, but you don't have to go."

"I think I'm ill. I don't think it's depression," Nina said.

"Darling, it's the same thing. Your mother said exactly the same words to me once, and I reacted with those same words then."

"My mother? My mother didn't suffer from depression."

"Everyone does from time to time. It's completely routine human stuff. Shall I give my colleague a ring and get you an appointment?"

Nina went home and looked at mental health forums online. One person had described their illness as a dark wood. He was always aware of its presence, its dark edges, he said; it was important to keep your back to it and focus on the landscape in front of you. Nina thought about this on the plane, after the second lot of turbulence, when the aircraft swung side to side and it felt as if the wings would break off. She'd had ultimate clarity then and was full of resolutions. Better to go through the wood than to avoid it. I'm going in there with matches in my pocket, she thought, and I'm going to make a fire, and I'm going to stop worrying about all of it, wholesale and entire. Take it or leave it: I'm making a fire. It was only on the fifth day of the holiday, coming down again to the same breakfast, the prospect of the same day laid out before her on the blue checked tablecloth, that she realised that her fire-starting abilities had left her.

When Dr Christos brought the breakfast he'd also brought flowers, mauve and yellow flowers that grew on the hill, placing them on her bedside table in a jam jar, and when he went off to do the ward rounds (as he called it, though there weren't really wards), Nina drew them, their delicate small faces set among spiky leaves, a rough sketch in her notebook, noting the date underneath. If something was going to begin, perhaps it had already begun; perhaps it began with the flowers. It felt as if he was presenting to her a door left slightly ajar. All she might need to do was push. She thought about living here. What would life with Dr Christos be like? She saw the two of them as if from the ceiling, curled naked in white cotton on a spring morning. He was telling her a bad Greek joke and she was laughing. The vision panned out to show his big wooden bed, the stove whispering in the corner. Now she saw the house from the sky, with chilli peppers drying on the steps, and towels, two sandy pairs of shoes; over the little tarmac road the sea was dazzling and the shoreline skimmed by light. Gradually and steadily the details inked themselves in. When she'd contemplated living here, it was love that had been missing from the plan. She smiled at the little piece of film she saw of their island wedding, the two of them standing under the tree in the square, the whole community gathered around them. It was what he needed: he wasn't hesitant about reaching out. All she had to do was smile back, to encourage him a little. It might be unexpectedly in her reach. Lightness. Tolerance. An unsuspected deep attachment. Permanence. What had permanence been with Paolo? A deep unthinking lassitude. What would permanence have been with Luca? He would have reinvented it every day. It would have been volatile; it might not have lasted. There had to be something else, some third option, an arrival somewhere at once fixed and evolving, and perhaps this was it. Perhaps in Greece, with a new life that was genuinely new, she could begin to do as her mother had done and become a practitioner of gratitude. She could hear her dead mother's voice telling her that she was one of the privileged of the earth and ought to damn well realise it and stop being so idiotic. It's what Anna had said when Nina was down.

She'd told the other hotel guests about her plan to live on the island. "I can work anywhere there are pencils," she'd said. "...Well – pencils and a postal service and broadband," and this expanded list was accurate, though even now in the digital age most of Nina's projects were still presented to her on paper. She'd seen Andros's brother delivering letters, and imagined him at her door with one of a succession of big padded bags. She'd have one of the little white houses that faced the sea, at least at first, while having something built, and she'd swim before starting work. She saw that her hair was wet as she took out the manuscript, encircled in its rubber band, its fat pile of paper densely peopled with words. Those fresh storylines and societies would keep her from feeling confined here. Perhaps in addition she'd write a book about her life on the island; the accident and the way she met her second husband would both be gifts to an opening chapter. The small blue flame of her self-regard sparked and caught, when she thought of this plausible life.

"Why this island?" Cathy had asked, unable to disguise her opinion that it would be a mistake.

"I came here on honeymoon and so I suppose I'm drawn to somewhere I was so happy," Nina told her. "But I can see that it might not be practical."

"You couldn't really work here, though, could you?" Cathy said. "Not really. And you'd miss Sainsbury's after the novelty wore off. You'd miss people. Don't get me wrong, the Greeks are lovely, but they're not the same, are they?"

Nina picked up her notebook. *The thing I love about the plan is that its simplicity and luxury are all the opposite to how they are at home.* The simplicity would be in the material facts, their few possessions. The luxury would be in the backdrop, the sunshine, the seafront location, and most importantly in the stretching-out of time. There'd be the opportunity to be properly alive. There would be four summer dresses; there'd only be a need for four. There'd be local leather sandals and a big plain hat and straw baskets for visiting the street market. She'd have an allotment up in the top village, and join the women gardeners on the minibus. The seven of them, six alike and one startlingly different, would stand together at the bus bench and scrutinise outsiders. Her Greek would be good by the second spring. She'd be able to build a new house: Dr Christos didn't know, yet, about the money her mother had left her. She'd be able to have something built that would celebrate the newness, not just of the life but of love and of hope. Imagine if there could be faith in the future; imagine if the future was genuinely going to be better than the past. There could be 40 years of happiness to come. She began to make sketches in her notebook. The house she wanted had a lot in common with the island hospital: a courtyard house, single storey with large airy rooms, and French windows leading into a central garden that'd be planted with aridity-loving shrubs. There'd be a swimming pool that looked like a black pond, its water cleaned in cunning modern ways, with a miniature waterfall and hidden pump. She'd have an annexe for bed and breakfast. Paying guests were vital, not just for the income but for the approval: they'd reflect the beauty of her life right back at her, every day. Dr Christos – she realised that she didn't even know his first name, grinning at this absurdity – would come and go, busy, happy, pretending to be disenchanted with a job he loved and amused by stories about the visitors. There'd be seats for the guests to take their coffee out among the flowers and bees, and all around the inner three sides of the building there'd be a veranda, with stout wooden pillars made of a hard Asian wood and terracotta tiles underfoot. Indoors there'd be simple furniture, simple and expensive and unshowy: good fabrics, pale colours, nice pictures, a lot of books, a lot of music, perhaps a piano by the window. Nina saw herself out watering her pots in the evening, wearing a white linen tunic and trousers, her hair tousled and full of salt, her bare brown feet encrusted with sand. She looked absolutely content, this woman, and young for her age. Her new husband was sitting on the veranda with the newspaper and with wine. He was saying, "Let me cook tonight; I was given some fish today." He was saying, "Did you bring artichokes down from the garden, my love?"

Everything had gone disastrously wrong by the sixth morning of the holiday. There didn't seem anything to do but the same things she'd done the day before. She began to be frightened; there ought to be other things to do, other things to imagine, so why couldn't she imagine them? She went along to Blue Bay, stopping to take photographs that were identical to ones she had already, of the morning sea, the boats arriving back in the harbour, the fishermen's blue trousers and bent backs. At the beach she made camp in a shady patch under a pine tree, swam for a few minutes and tried to read while drying off, and swam a second time and returned to the tree and lay with one eye open, watching the other tourists. This was the best part of the day, but it was over by noon. By then she didn't any longer want to be on holiday or here or alone; by noon she felt stunted by misery, her heart wrapped tight and all her responses and thoughts blunted. She ate warm white beans and tomatoes at the café, drank a small carafe of wine and went back to her room for a siesta, but sleep wouldn't come, so she lay looking at the square of bright blue sky, and at the small agile lizard on her bedroom wall, which was darting and then standing as if in a trance. She watched her alarm clock, longing for it to be time for a swim at Octopus Beach, but was bored by her visit there and didn't stay long. After an early shower, clad in fresh evening clothes and aware of time's slow creeping, she went to the shop and bought two leather belts, jewellery made of polished blue and green pebbles, brightly dyed wallets for the children of friends and a series of boxes covered in tiny glued shells that Vasilios's daughter had made. Then, having deposited her finds in the room, she went down for dinner and ate squid rings and fries and salad, and tried to look absorbed in her book.

"Nina, didn't you hear me?" She looked up and saw Cathy's face. "Will you come on a boat trip with us tomorrow? We're sailing off to see a ruin and taking a packed lunch." Cathy could see that Nina didn't want to. "Please come," she urged. "Kurt is coming with us and he's going to feel like a big German gooseberry otherwise. Aren't you, Kurt?" Kurt turned down his mouth and nodded. It wasn't possible to refuse.

So on the morning of day seven, Nina went on a boat trip. Kurt seemed to think they were on a date, moving closer so that their thighs touched, putting his arm along the back of her neck and resting it on the metal rail. He said, "How is such a beautiful woman single?" He kept turning to look at her profile as if something additional wasn't being said that needed to be said, but which he continued all morning not to say. After 90 minutes of sailing time they arrived at a tiny uninhabited island which had the remains of a villa on it, roofless, its windswept columns snapped and eroded. Only remnants of walls marked out lost rooms; a weatherproofed display board offered drawings that illustrated how grand it had all once been. The archaeologists had only recently left, and so as a tourist attraction the place was brand new, so new that it wasn't yet listed in guidebooks. The most exciting thing there, the thing that would draw people, was the surviving patch of a mosaic floor. It was the mosaic Andros would recognise her in, the one of the Nereid with the long fair hair and turquoise eyes, armoured and riding a dolphin. It wasn't Nina as she was now, but as she'd been in her twenties and stupidly sure of everything. Nina stood in front of the explanatory board but couldn't seem to take in the English written on it. She felt obscurely angry, couldn't eat the picnic, and paced about on the shore until the boat was ready to return, with Kurt trailing after her. Cathy, sitting opposite on the journey back, held Gareth's hand throughout, and whenever Nina caught her eye Cathy winked at her. When they disembarked Kurt put his arm around Nina's waist and Cathy said, "Ooh, what's this, a holiday romance?" Nina pulled herself free and ran all the way back to her room, and stayed there till she heard everyone else going down to dinner, then went elsewhere to eat. On the eighth day, the day of the accident, she said no to Cathy's offer of a cycle ride, and went to Main Island alone.

Chapter Eight

When Nina left the doctor's surgery and her father had
driven her home, and she'd insisted she was fine and that
he should go, taking the sweeping brush from him and cleaning
up the cauliflower fragments, Nina went into her sitting room
and was engulfed in darkness. It was still early, a summer evening
and bright outside; no lamps were lit indoors, so it wasn't the
electricity playing up, doing that odd swooping, though it was
exactly as if the daylight had been dimmed with a switch and then
undimmed. It wasn't a subtle thing, but a dramatic darkening,
pausing like a held breath before letting go and allowing the light
to return. Nina's reaction was immediate: she picked up her bag
and her coat and locked up the house and went and spent the
night at her father's.

"Have you ever seen a ghost?" she asked Dr Christos, as he
handed over a dense, sticky rectangle of baklava. Nurse Yannis
had turned 50 and there was cake for everyone. His fingers brushed
against hers.

"No such thing as ghosts. Oddities of light, of perception,
absolutely. Hallucinations, sometimes. What did you think you
saw?"

"When I moved into the cottage there were peculiar things.
Sudden cold spots. Shadows that seemed to be moving. Noises."

"How old was this house?"

"Seventeenth century, the oldest bit."

"Buildings of that age shift and creak."

"Believe me I'm as sceptical as you are."

"I doubt that very much," he said, straight-faced.

"Funny," she said, acknowledging the joke. "Paolo agrees with
you that it was the old house settling. There had never been central
heating, for instance. I got heating installed and he thought that
was enough to explain the noises. But there were other things.
Objects not where I'd left them."

"Stress plays tricks with the memory." He went out of the

room and wheeled in the shredder and dispensed with a pile of unwanted paperwork, making paper tagliatelle of shreds, pink and yellow and green. It was briefly noisy in the stillness. "Sorry for this. If you would prefer I will return to my office." He looked at her. "Do you like having me here?"

"I do," she said, allowing her smile to be intimate and finding, in his own smile, his own eyes, that the intimacy was returned. They'd swapped, in some small way, a confession of mutual attraction for one another.

The nurse came into the room, and Nina wished her a happy birthday and said the baklava was the best she'd ever eaten, and Nurse Yannis thanked her, before saying something in Greek that was evidently pointed, raising her eyebrows at the doctor. He sounded contrite, but when she'd gone he said, "It's not like we're understaffed. We're ridiculously overstaffed, in fact." He went out into the corridor. "And it's not as if I'm not working in here!" he yelled after her in English, before reappearing looking rattled. "She refuses to accept that I'm working when I'm with a patient. It's obvious that I'm working. I'm working as hard as I need to. Why work harder? This is something we really have trouble with. She goes around inventing tasks so as not to have a moment of relaxation. Makes no sense to me. But she's always been that way. Stubborn as hell."

"You've known each other a long time, then."

"We were at school together. Friend of my sister's."

"Old friends, then."

"Pain in the arse. So, have you done your exercises?"

"Not as such. No."

"Do them, while I make a call. I'll bring lunch back, and we'll go and sit outside. We need to get you out of this room and into the good sea air. While we're eating you can tell me more about your ghost."

When Nina agreed to buy the cottage she'd agreed to the asking price and paid in cash, using the money her mother left her, though her father winced at the news that she'd not bothered to haggle, saying it was a mistake to start a battle with a white flag. It was her father she'd taken to see the cottage. Robert had said, "Nina, isn't this the place Luca was talking about buying?"

and she'd said she didn't know, although she did know. Luca had been to see it and had decided against. For years he'd talked, in the way of people at no risk ever of having to put their words into practice, about having a country life, a kitchen garden and hens, and when Francesca died he'd said he thought that a chicken house was the way forward, though it was a certainty that had only lasted two days. He continued to live in the marital home, in the middle of an immaculate residential district at the heart of the city, and had soily ingredients delivered in a weekly box. A vegetable plot was one of Nina's few fixed plans, but her father had dismissed the idea as impractical. "It's a lot more work than you think," he said, casting an experienced eye over the mossy lawn, the thickets of rhododendron and thistle that had taken their chance while the house lay empty, but he'd liked the paved front patch, with its alpines and its cottage borders. When she took him round to the back he'd taken out a notebook and had begun to make lists of all the work that was needed. Everything was overgrown, feral, rampant; diseased crab apple trees sagged with parasite climbers and lichen, and the walls of old stone were cracked and bulging, their pointing reduced to dust. Nina couldn't bring herself to tell him that she didn't intend to change anything. They went inside, where several centuries had made their presence felt and rubbed alongside each other in peaceful disharmony. There were seventeenth-century proportions, eighteenth-century shutters, Victorian cupboards, 1920s plumbing, 1950s improvements and 1970s formica. Her father tapped and stamped, looked under carpets and sucked through his teeth.

"You've already agreed to buy – legally sewn up?" he said eventually.

"Yes."

"Then I think it's fine."

It had started the first morning. Nina said goodbye to the man with the van who'd delivered her boxes, her few bits of furniture, and was standing at the sitting room window looking out into the back garden. The glass was dirty, the view blurred by cobwebs, and it was so quiet that she could hear her own breathing. Into this steady rhythm of air taken in and expelled there came another noise, a soft click from upstairs as if someone had shut a door very carefully, a click and a creak of floorboards. The carefulness of it, as if not wanting to be heard, was what made the hairs stand up on her arms. She'd gone up there, and just as she got a clear view down the corridor, thought she saw a white cat cross the hall into her bedroom. Nina checked everywhere, behind curtains and in cupboards and under beds, just in case a cat had got in during the move. There was no cat. She went downstairs and sat in one of the armchairs by the fire, and began to feel unwell.

"Unwell how?" Dr Christos was fiddling with the patio awning to create a deeper shade.

"It was like a bad hangover but I hadn't been drinking."

"Probably a virus, or just old dust."

"I lay on the sofa and slept for a while. Then something woke me up. It was a shout. My name was shouted. Nina! Like a warning."

"Perhaps you were warning yourself."

"Myself?"

"Ghosts don't exist, so why are you seeing a ghost? That's the interesting question. I used to see my dog sometimes, last year after he died, but it wasn't really my dog."

"It wasn't just seeing; I could smell smoke."

Dr Christos looked as if he'd expected this. "Hallucinations can be multi-sensory. What happened next?"

"I put my coat on and went out into the garden and walked around it for a while. And I remember thinking that Miss Plowman spent a lot of time out there, this tiny figure, swamped by her tweed trousers and big ugly cardigans and a man's fishing hat. She was out there in all weathers; maybe she didn't like the atmosphere either."

"Who's Miss Plowman?"

"She was the previous owner. She lived there for a hundred years."

"A hundred years! Seriously?"

"She was born there and lived there all her life, and died two days before her 101st birthday. Then the cottage was empty for eighteen months. Nobody wanted it. I had the chance to buy lots of her old possessions, her furniture, and most of it was very nice so I agreed. But I began to associate her tables, her chairs, with the bad feeling in the house. I slept on the sofa sometimes and then I'd get annoyed with myself, and spend time upstairs and crash about and sing, trying to dominate the space. But I was spooked. Once I got frightened while I was having a bath."

"What happened?"

"It's a nice bathroom. It has alternating black and white tiles and there are tropical fish on the black ones – it's unchanged since the '20s. There's a really big deep bath with long-stemmed silver taps. So, I ran the hot water, got in and washed my hair, and as I was doing it, my eyes half open, I thought I saw someone."

"Someone who?" His face was openly doubtful.

"It doesn't matter."

"I'm sorry. Go on. I'm interested."

"There was masses of steam and it was like it was gathering, into a shape, like a person." She stopped there in describing it, but it had become denser in the corner by the door, spinning the fog into muscle and bone. Limbs became more distinct, a neck, an elongated head, a deep grey crevice where eyes might be. "I got out of the bath and opened the window and it dispersed. It wasn't anything."

Nina had been prey to specific, private fears, though others in the vicinity would have said immediately that it was Miss Plowman's ghost. Miss Plowman was still notorious in the neighbourhood. When Nina was young the children of the village had referred to her as the witch, a name picked up from their parents, in some cases even their grandparents. She'd long had a reputation for being fierce and humourless. There had been an ongoing feud one summer with children who sat on her low front wall on warm evenings – Nina among them – and things had escalated, with parents getting involved, banging on her door. Apparently her language could be pretty spectacular. Perhaps angry Miss Plowman had left her indelible trace, all that misdirected bad energy. It would have been a relief to catch a proper glimpse of the entity, and to see that it had a human form, and to see that it was only Miss Plowman.

"Did you see it again, your steam ghost?"

"No. But I saw my mother. When I cleared the condensation. In the mirror, in my own face." It was a relief to change the subject.

"Only because you look alike."

Nina had seen Anna looking back at her, as she had been during the last year of her life, separated from Nina's father and living alone. It was the expression in her eyes that startled her; Anna's soul had shone out through her eyes, like some people's do. But where was that soul now? Not gone, surely; not ended. Nina liked to think of it blown like a dandelion clock, seeding across the world in new and unexpected places. She'd asked that her ashes be scattered on the roses at the house, roses she'd planted and had tended for fifteen years. "Next year you'll find me there, redder than red," she'd written, and Robert had cried when he read that in her will. Perhaps that was the point, the intended reaction; sentimentality is a powerful toxin, after all, a fine biological weapon. It wasn't possible to deny the request and nor was it possible to avoid the metaphor, which would grow in his garden ever after. Nina had visited the rose beds on the first anniversary of her death, but it had rained hard the previous day and the blooms were sodden, flattened, browning and becoming mush. She remembered words of her mother's when Granny had died. Surely so much love as that could only feed the world of spirit in which it was laid to rest. Love that was so absolute: surely that couldn't be extinguished? Apparently it could. Apparently love was entirely extinguishable.

"Also there were clunkings, like shoes being dropped on the wood floor in my bedroom, that I heard from downstairs. And then I was pushed when I was sleeping. I woke up early one morning feeling like I'd been pushed hard in my back. I was sleeping on my side. I surged forward. I could feel her hand on my back."

"Her? You thought it was Miss Plowman?" Now he looked perturbed.

"No. Its hand. But of course it wasn't a hand." At the time she'd known it was a hand, and whose hand it was. Nina was haunted; she knew this. She'd been afraid, on the holiday, fearful that it was a personal haunting and would always be with her, and wasn't just confined to the house.

"When I sat up in bed the wardrobe doors were both open, and I always closed them at bedtime. My Norwegian grandmother made me afraid of open wardrobe doors."

She'd also said that if there was a ghost you'd most likely see it reflected in a mirror and standing behind you, or at the very edge of your vision when you were looking at something else. Were you aware of what was standing at the edge of your peripheral vision?

"Old houses move and doors move with them."

"Paolo said the same."

"The reason the cottage feels cold and damp," Paolo said on his second visit, "is because it is cold and damp." He was comfortable talking about the house; they'd talked of little else. "It was built on a gradient and the back garden is higher than the front – you must have noticed that. It occupies an earth hollow, with soil banked up against the back wall. Hence dampness and the armies of woodlice."

"The damp doesn't help."

"It's not that it doesn't help, Nina; it's the reason. You could get the earth dug out and drainage put in at the back; that would make a huge difference." Her father had said the same. They pressed in on her from both sides, these men and their pronouncements. In any case there wouldn't be visits from Paolo any more.

After he'd left and she'd put the books away and hung the picture – things of hers he'd brought round that she'd left behind – it came to Nina that she was setting up in anticipation of a solitary life. Like Miss Plowman, she might never come up with a good reason to live anywhere else than here for the rest of her days, and die alone at 100 years old and be found by the postman. It wasn't just that. Miss Plowman had been reclusive, friendless, near sociopathic, and Nina had a foretaste of a possible old age. All she'd seemed able to do lately was push people away. She craved people and then couldn't tolerate them. Was that how it had started, the extreme loneliness of poor Miss Plowman? Her kitchen drawers had been left unemptied after the sale and the dresser had yielded its treasures: yellowing piles of recipes cut from newspapers, tobacco tins of buttons, scrapbooks of gardening records, and four cards from when she'd turned 100, one of them from Anna and none of their messages convincingly warm. Nina's father confirmed that Miss Plowman had never been married, had never had a boyfriend as far as anyone knew, and was not well liked. *Miss Plowman was not well liked* – what a terrible legacy, what words for a tombstone.

She'd suffered a stroke and had been found on the kitchen floor, having already been dead for 48 hours. What must it be like to have nobody, no one at all? It didn't bear thinking about. She'd lived alone and slept here in the very same mirrored 1930s French bed that Nina slept in now, the same other than for the new mattress. If Nina had been Miss Plowman, at 46 she wasn't even halfway through her life; there'd be 55 years of living alone. She was standing in the bathroom cleaning her face with cotton wool as this occurred to her. She'd developed, she thought, a disappointed look, and since the disaster, her personal disaster, had also begun abruptly to age. A grid of creases had appeared under her eyes, and marionette lines that led down from her cheeks to her chin, and when she looked more closely at her hairline, grey strands were obvious in the blonde. There wasn't any doubt that in terms of – what was that hideous phrase? Sexual capital – in terms of sexual capital she was already over the hill, essentially finished and over, prompting desire in no one ever again. The thought provoked a slow stir-up of fear, like the bottom of a pond agitated by a stick. Her mind clogged with silt and her pulse began to race, speeding forward unchecked, thumping harder and faster as if it might break free of its clock. She took hold of the sink with both hands and felt violently sick and leaned forward. Couldn't she go back? Too late, too late, the summit was passed and she was on the road down, all opportunities wasted. Three men, three men in her life had spoken to her about wastefulness and about not paying attention; they'd seen what she hadn't seen and it had all gone by. Nina began to feel as if it was hard to breathe. There was pressure on her chest as if she was far under water, too deep to prevent a final deep ingress of liquids where air should be, flooding all the little daisies in her lungs. She was going to die, not in 55 years but right now. Her phone was in her bathrobe pocket; she leaned against the wall and slid down to sit on the floor and rang the surgery, the top of her head tingling, her arms heavy, but it was too late, after hours, so once the answerphone chimed in she rang Dr Macfarlane at home. Alison had soothed her fears. No, it didn't sound anything like a stroke. Could she make that appointment now, with the friend at the clinic? Nina agreed that she could.

"And after that, what I prescribe is the holiday you talked about."

"I was sure that I was dying," Nina said.

"Of course you're dying, we're all dying," Alison had consoled her. "But not now. This is just anxiety. Take the holiday."

Dr Christos said "Your phone's ringing. It's flashing at any rate."

"I had it set to silent. It's Paolo." Nina picked it up and said hello. She smiled at the doctor as she did so.

Paolo's voice said, "Just tell me one thing absolutely honestly – are you in love with Luca?"

"Hold on a second."

"Absolutely honestly: is it Luca that you want?" He wasn't ever going to stop this. He wasn't ever going to be convinced. "There's nothing to lose now, in being honest," he said. "Do me the honour of being honest with me."

Nina said, "I can't talk now; my doctor's here," but Dr Christos was already leaving, saying he'd be back, and Paolo overheard her saying goodbye.

He said, "So answer the question."

"It's like I said at the airport. I was trying to tell the truth. It was something else. Like an addiction."

"Addiction is an odd word to use."

"Is it?"

"So you're distinguishing between love and infatuation, and felt neither for me."

"I didn't say that. Where did that come from? Have you just called me to be angry with me?"

"I want to know if I should be talking to my brother, or if I'm a gullible fool."

She lost it for a moment, the tight control. "I'm pissed off with him, too."

"Pissed off why?"

Why had she said that? "Just because of all this mess." The tight control was exhausting her.

"I know it was Luca who initiated it. He told me."

"You've had the conversation, then." Her voice sounded very small.

"I get it. I see how it happened. You'd moved out and were mildly deranged. He was grieving and withdrawn and nobody knew what to do for him."

"I'm sorry."

"But why did your sleeping together make him worse? Why did you become so ill afterwards, and why are you both so much better now? Just tell me. Tell me again. You're not with Luca. You're not with him in some hidden way that'll come to light when you come back?"

"I don't even want to run into him again. Run over him, maybe." What was she saying? This conversation could very easily career off the road it absolutely had to remain on.

"Why do you say that? Did he behave badly? He didn't…

I mean, I hope he wasn't…"

"What?"

"Nothing, it doesn't matter."

"What do you mean?"

"His account is pretty anodyne. You were both depressed, you comforted each other. And then… then decided it must never happen again and it was all fine, but – hang on, how does this bit fit into the story – never spoke to one another again, either." Nina didn't have an answer and Paolo continued. "Things are squared here. If that's really how it was. I do need to know where I stand with him and I'm counting on you to be frank."

"There's nothing else to tell."

"To be honest I've wanted you to have an affair for a long time."

"You haven't. Don't do that."

"Just to get it over with, the inevitable. So I could hate him officially and we could move away, after however many bloody decades it's been with the two of you and your mating dance. I had nights when I went out in the car and shouted and punched the steering wheel."

"I'm sorry."

"Stop! Stop saying how sorry you are. This has destroyed us. We're destroyed and it can never be mended. I don't want to talk about it any more. You know what the worst of it is, Nina? Luca and I are strangers now; I don't trust him and I can't talk to him. What do you have to say to that? Sorry. Sorry." He'd mimicked her low voice. "Sorry – that's all you have for me, isn't it? Why am I even calling you? This isn't helping. I'll see you when I get to Greece." He hung up the phone.

Dr Christos came into the room looking cheerful, and stopped in his tracks. "What's the matter?"

"Bad call. Bad phone call."

"Who with?"

Nina was aware of her need for approval, but didn't approve of her need at all. She managed to stop herself. "It's fine. It's all fine."

"You look so anxious."

This, though, she could risk being frank about. "I'm always anxious. I'm becoming bored with my anxiety."

He dropped a stack of paperwork onto the table and settled himself in the chair. "Always? Why always?"

"It started when my parents separated. If you want to know the real beginnings of it."

"Your parents divorced? I'm sorry. It's very hard for children."

"They didn't divorce. They separated when I was nineteen and then my mother died a year later. Heart failure."

"You've been anxious since you were nineteen years old? That's a long time."

"Not continually anxious, but predisposed to it, I suppose. Luca, my brother-in-law, was my boyfriend, sort of my boyfriend, at the time. He proposed to me the night my mother died, and I said no. I thought we were too young and that was the end of that. He married someone else six months later. He married Francesca, and I married Paolo the following year, and we were all happy, I thought, the four of us."

"The four of you?"

"Happy and good friends."

"But. I feel there is a but."

"My husband always thought that really I was in love with his brother, and when Francesca died it made him afraid. I went quiet and withdrew, when Luca came to live with us, and that made him more afraid. He couldn't explain it, you see."

"And were you? In love with Luca?"

"I don't know if I've ever been in love. I used to think I had. I knew what it meant. But now I really don't."

"Oh, come on."

"What's it mean if it comes to an end in the course of one conversation? What if someone says to you that they don't think you were ever in love?"

"People use the word to punish other people as well as seduce them. They don't always mean it. It doesn't matter though, not really, whether you can use the word or not. It's not the word that matters. It's how you behave."

"You don't think the word matters, the use of the word? The other person using it? Really?"

"Listen, whether people use the word or don't, it's very simple: they'll stay with you or they won't. In the meantime it's a peace-keeping word. That's why people are constantly asking for it. My wife used to. She needed me to look into her eyes at the same time. It said to her, 'It isn't going to be today, the day I leave you.' That's all that it could mean."

Chapter Nine

When Nina and Paolo were together Sundays were often difficult, not only because they were committed, by long years
of precedent, to go to lunch at Maria's, but because of what always
happened afterwards. Invariably Nina was restless at home on a
Sunday evening. She'd flit between books, start and abandon work,
go out for head-clearing walks, put on a film and then stare out of
the window, her hands moving against each other, fingers finding
skin and stroking there. She said it was the classic Sunday blues.

Sometimes Paolo made the mistake of remarking that his
Mondays were more to be dreaded than hers. What could she say
to him? She loved her job. All she dreaded about the working week
was Paolo's being brought low by it. "I know you work harder
than me," she'd concede. It seemed important to be emphatic in
keeping conceding this. It was incontestable that Paolo worked
very long hours. He had to: once Giulio died, the year Paolo
turned 30, the business was basically down to him, and as the
years rolled on it operated on tighter and tighter margins. Its
engine was constant maintenance, constant vigilance, which was
something Luca never really seemed to get. At least, he acted as
if he didn't get it. Luca worked a principled seven-hour day on
the basis of work–life balance, leaving his brother to pick up
the slack, and if he was challenged about it he'd maintain that
Paolo's approach was inefficient, even obsessive. Once, jokingly,
Francesca had said that his overworking must be Nina-avoidance,
though she hadn't been quite so blunt as that; the joke had been
about Paolo avoiding her cooking by eating at his desk, though in
fact he only did that very seldom. Paolo was overworked – that
much was incontrovertible. He'd be tired at the weekend and then
he'd go back to the office at 8am on Monday and wouldn't much
be seen for the following five days, other than to come home late
and fall asleep in front of *Newsnight*. It was the weekends that
were at first contentious. He'd generally be found in his home
office on a Saturday morning, and also on a Sunday night, and it

was a situation that couldn't be helped. They'd had that argument once and it wasn't repeated. Saturday afternoons, though, were designated as couple time. He and Nina would go out into the city together; they'd do the shopping and come home to read the papers, with music playing (über-gloomy German lieder, as Luca put it); they'd cook and eat and watch films. It was, in retrospect, all highly and repetitively scheduled, with little oxygen let into its habitualness. There wasn't much in the way of lingering eye contact, little in the way of daring to be purposeless and alone.

The usual pattern on a Sunday, after a Saturday night DVD double bill and way too much to drink, was that Nina and Paolo would sleep in, do chores, and be at Maria's by midday. They wouldn't often be home again till 4pm or even later. Things got stretched, and everybody knew the reason. Nina and Luca found it hard to say goodbye to one another after the lunch; their weekly reunion had a quality to it that was like something long-delayed. Paolo and Francesca would hear about things neither had mentioned, that had been saved up, and also things they'd heard about in brief, that were extended and reframed into comedy. There was also teasing. There were occasions in the early days when Paolo imagined that he could join in with this, do teasing of his own and make cracks to his wife about Luca dependency. They were always a disaster, these attempts. They fell like iron snowflakes, like hailstorms of ball-bearings.

Once, in the tenth year of the marriage, Paolo was startled to discover that Nina and Luca were holding hands at the lunch table. This wasn't something he could pretend not to know. He hadn't ever had cause to drum up a hierarchy of betrayal, but just for that minute, right then, hand holding at a family occasion seemed far worse than meeting in secret. Something had to be done; he knew he couldn't just go home with nothing said, festering and menaced by fear, so as they left their mother's house he took hold of his brother's arm to signal that he wanted a word. Nina and Francesca had gone ahead and were standing in the garden looking at the newly opening tulips; after Giulio died Robert had put dozens of bulbs in as a gift, and this was their first flowering. Maria was putting dishes away noisily in her kitchen. It was safe to speak up. Francesca could be heard saying that she'd always lived in city flats and had never had a garden. Paolo paused his brother in Maria's porch, doors open indoors and out, among the pink pelargoniums that grew there on shelves.

"Can I ask you please, not to," he said. He had to be formal. He didn't trust himself to be calm.

"Not to what?" Luca didn't seem to know.

Paolo turned so that his back was to the women. "Nina's hand." It was hard to say it in a whole sentence. His practised look of resignation was misleading.

"It was Nina."

"Doesn't matter who it was. Don't." Luca was surprised by the forcefulness. Paolo was always unfailingly polite.

"She was the one who held mine," Luca said quietly, glancing at his wife. Francesca was now talking about her Italian relatives, who worked in the fields and loathed even the idea of gardening.

"Don't."

"It doesn't mean anything. But no. Not again."

"There are other people here who'd misinterpret it." That was the gallant approach to issuing a warning. Paolo was always conscious of the gallantry in things, or lack of it.

"I know." Luca didn't acknowledge that he'd been warned.

Paolo could feel his reasonableness, his famed reasonableness, beginning to fray. "Don't do this."

"There isn't a this," Luca told him.

He managed to lower his voice, "Don't treat me like an idiot."

"I'm serious. Let me tell you what it is. You're never demonstrative. You're more like Robert than she realised you'd be."

Francesca turned to them. "Enough conspiring, boys," she said. "It's time to go home."

When Luca arrived at the company offices the following morning, Paolo asked if he could have a word, and a few minutes later Luca came into his room holding his pen in one hand and an order book in the other. Luca's not really having the time for idle chat was indicated. "Paolo."

"What did you mean, more like Robert than she realised I'd be?"

Luca closed the door. "Brother, I love you; more than I could ever love a woman. But you are not a demonstrative person; you never have been."

"Demonstrative." He seemed to weigh the word.

"You were never the one who was physical with Nina. Can you remember ever touching her – and no, Anna's photographs don't count – before you kissed her at my wedding? I think not." He tapped the pen against the book. "Had you ever had so much to drink in your life? No. Don't look like that; it isn't a criticism. Some people are not tactile, and you are one of the not-tactile people. Nina and I have always been physical with one another."

"So what you're saying is that sex wouldn't mean anything either."

The bitterness of this took Luca by surprise. "Paolo. What on earth."

"I'm just seeking clarification."

Luca put down the things that he was holding. "Listen to me, listen. I am not in love with Nina. I am never going to be in love with Nina. Nina is my sister."

"I know, I know."

"My unofficial sister that I never had. A loved person, loved to bits in every other way than romantically."

Paolo knew this. He knew that Luca wasn't going to use his power to take Nina from him. He didn't allow himself to add a second thought, following on, which was that to Luca it was only possession of the power that mattered. He didn't allow himself to dwell on that, because thoughts go on the record, even there in the deeps, and might rise to the surface and be real. Things we don't allow ourselves even to think come out of our mouths in arguments.

He'd made a decision early in life about how to act on his certainty. He could have confronted them both – Luca, Nina, – and destroyed it, the triangle. He could have made their love guilty, furtive; he could have brought the subject of others' suffering into it, spelling out the ramifications, and made it impossible; he could have run far away and married someone else, his own Francesca, and didn't feel as if he ever got the credit for not doing any of these things. He'd always loved Nina unconditionally and that was enough for him. There wasn't anything she could have done to diminish his love, and so she had a power over him that he sometimes resented. He knew he was liked, respected, approved of, adored, and in the context of adult sexual bonding, in the context of a long-term and loyal mating, wasn't adored the same as loved? The trouble was that it wasn't. Only loved was loved and the L word had to be used. There wasn't any alternative. There were no synonyms. It was love or nothing, and if Nina didn't love him he couldn't see any alternative but to divorce. He had his own timetable of the inevitability, of its countdown: he would have pinpointed the beginning of the end as a moment during the summer before, during the Romano clan's annual family holiday by the sea, when, very late one night, Nina had been discovered kissing Luca. It was the only time Francesca ever broke her silence; Francesca had gone to Paolo in tears. She'd interrupted them, she said, in the kitchen. It was hard to take, she'd said. Paolo hadn't gone to Luca about it, because Francesca had begged him not to and had made him promise. It was all to do with the illness, she said. Luca had been acting weirdly ever since Francesca's cancer diagnosis; he'd been odd at the office, he'd been odd with clients, he'd been odd at the Sunday lunches. He'd been badly affected by it and by things being uncertain, and allowances needed to be made.

On the first evening after this holiday, having spent a day at the office without Luca around (Luca and the rest were still away, though Nina had also come home), having brooded all day at work about the kiss, what it might have looked like in the holiday house kitchen and how poor Francesca was affected by it – driven even to confiding in him, which wasn't usual at all – Paolo went home earlier than usual and with an armful of roses. As Nina took them from him he put his arm rather awkwardly around her neck to pull her face close to his. His displays of affection were always awkward.

"I missed you today," he said.

"I missed you too, but I got lots of work done." She smiled at him. It was what he used to say to her when they were first married.

"Do you want to do something?" he asked, as if it had just occurred to him. "Go out somewhere? Why don't we eat out? Be wild and eat out on a Wednesday night?"

She held his hand as they walked along the streets to the restaurant, and he returned her pressure equally, his fingers clasped round hers. She asked him about his day and he described it and she reciprocated, and then they got to the place and were seated and talked about the menu.

"I think we should push the boat out and have the forbidden

dishes with the big supplements." He waggled his eyebrows.

"What, the steak with the £4 supplement? That's an outrageous idea."

"We're not the kinds of idiots who order the £14 set menu and then spend £15 on supplements." She knew that he was going to do just that. It was as if Luca was there in his chair, a kind of possession. "So let's see. The scallops starter, the posher steak, the fancier sauce, the extras. Though I've never seen the point of scallops and black pudding. Black pudding is crazy with scallops – it kills them dead."

"Hopefully they're dead already." The pig that wants to be eaten came to mind, from *Hitchhiker's Guide to the Galaxy*, but that was a conversational detour she could only have made with his brother.

"We'll order only according to price," Paolo said. "The most expensive wine on the menu. I've always wondered why it's so great, that white burgundy."

"Let's find out what's beyond the label."

"If anything."

"If anything." She reached out her hand and put it over his, but he needed it to turn the page.

"It's my sad duty to report that there isn't a pudding with a supplement." His voice was comically sombre.

She turned her own page. "What, no custard tax?"

"No custard at all, in fact. This place is going to the dogs."

"Well, at least it's not going to the birds." She looked at him hopefully. Luca would have been right on it. Bird's Custard.

Paolo said, "I think the panna cotta is bought in. Certainly the sauce, from what I remember."

Nina said, equally factually, "It was way too red to be actual strawberries."

"It tasted like cheesecake topping, the deep-frozen kind. It undermines one's faith in the rest of it. I'd have more respect for them if they did cheese and a baked apple. That's what I'd do if I owned the place."

"I know." She gave him the fond look that reassured him his repetitions were endearing, but at the same time she knew that Paolo brought up this subject when his confidence was running aground. "You and Luca have been talking about opening a bistro for I don't know how many years. Do you think it will ever happen?"

"Didn't take you long to bring Luca into the conversation."

"I'm not allowed to mention Luca?"

Paolo's smile morphed into doubt. "Course you are. Any time. But that's the point. It'd be nice if you chose not to. In restaurants, for instance."

They ate the bread and oil. Paolo continued to look at the menu, making comments on the wine list; the Italian section was woefully out of date. When the scallops came, and they'd eaten some, Nina said, "You were right about the black pudding. I wonder why it's a thing." She did something that ordinarily Paolo did, and instituted a topic: they talked about great meals they'd had on holiday, and not so great meals. Afterwards they walked home separately, together on the pavement and side by side, and each with their hands in their pockets.

In bed, wanting to make amends in the dark, Nina got slowly and silently on top of Paolo, who always went to sleep facing downwards, his head to the side. Sometimes he slept right at the edge of the bed with his nose clear of the mattress, and it was difficult not to see a correlation between days when he made that choice and episodes that had made him feel undermined. Nina always felt bad about his being undermined. She took off her pyjama T-shirt and then, naked, raised his as high as it would go, edging it up until it strained against his shoulders and armpits. She lowered herself onto the small of his back and forced her hands under his chest. She was expecting him to say he was tired but instead he said, "That's lovely."

Encouraged, she wriggled down the bed a little and put her hands between his thighs, which were full and firm and warm and delicately hairy, and stroked inwards and upwards. Paolo turned over and took off his own T-shirt, and she removed his shorts – he consented, lifting himself – and then, positioning herself astride, she leaned down and kissed him.

He said, "I'm sorry I was such an arse about Luca."

"It doesn't matter." He didn't have the slightest sign of an erection and so she was talking about both not mattering. She wanted him to know that neither mattered, that nothing did. She ran her hands over his belly and he supported, with a cupped palm, the knee that was about to slip off the side. She said, "I'll tell you what it is. It's just that we find the same things funny. That's all it's ever been."

"I don't think Francesca likes it. I think she minds more than me."

"What makes you say that?" Nina shifted her weight so that she sat further back, resting her hands on her own thighs.

"Are you saying that you're surprised?" His tone was unfortunate, unintended.

Nina got off the bed. "I'm thirsty," she said, beginning to walk towards the door in the half-dark. "I found that red dehydrating. Do you want some water?"

"No thanks, I'm fine." Paolo turned over, putting his hands beneath his head, and when she got back he was asleep.

The next morning he'd already gone to the office when she woke and it was after eight when he got home again, looking washed out. He hadn't slept well, he said. The white burgundy followed by a Côtes du Rhône with the beef: that was a mistake, he said, broadcasting the remark over his shoulder as he hung up his jacket, put his shoes in the rack under the hall table and went to the bathroom. When he came out his disembodied voice said, "Actually I thought I might go for a swim; want to join me?"

She spoke to the door. "I won't if you don't mind. I feel like I have a cold coming on."

"Okay – well, I'll see you later." She heard him putting his shoes back on, the scrape as they were taken once more from the rack. "Oh! Dinner! I forgot to ask."

"It's a ham salad," she said, calling back to him, blindly from the sofa, where she had a manuscript propped on cushions. "It'll keep."

"You go ahead and eat," he said. "No point waiting for me."

She ate in front of a film she'd seen before, barely noticing it. Something was wrong, but what? Paolo came back just as the end credits were rolling and went straight into the bathroom and showered. Nina waited and when he emerged went to him and kissed him and put her hand on the edge of the towel by his navel, but Paolo hung firmly onto it at both sides. "You're not going to get your way with me that easily, you hussy," he said.

She left him to dress and then she heard him in the kitchen, whistling as he got the salad plate out of the fridge and removed the foil from it, admiring the slaws she'd made, his favourite potato salad dressing, the scent of a home-boiled ham. She heard him opening wine and the radio going on, and her anxiety tightened its lacing. *This is stupid*, she said to herself. *Since when did a trip to a swimming pool come loaded with such threat? It was a swim. He's home and he's whistling.*

After he'd eaten Paolo came into the room in his pyjamas and a big red sweater. He was holding his briefcase.

"Do you have to work?"

"Yup. But then when do I not? It's like that for some of us."

"What do you mean by that?"

"Nothing at all. I'd better get on with it. Big meeting tomorrow and there's something wrong with the figures." He settled himself cross-legged at the other end of the sofa. "Music would be nice," he said, without looking up. Nina complied, putting on the Bach Cello Sonatas, the Pablo Casals recording that he loved. "Any chance of a coffee?"

"Too late, isn't it?"

"Too late?" His eyes betrayed a moment of alarm.

"For coffee. It's not going to help with the insomnia."

"Tea would be good in that case." And then, as Nina went out of the room, "I saw Francesca at the pool."

Nina came in again. "Francesca?"

"She was there for a swim." He flicked through the papers. "We swam together. That is okay, I hope."

"Course it's okay. I was just surprised."

Paolo went up to bed before her, saying unnecessarily that he was over-tired, and was gone when she woke.

The next day, Nina rang Luca at the office.

"Luca. Me. Is it safe?"

"Nobody here but us chickens."

"Did you know that Francesca went swimming last night and met Paolo at the pool?"

"Francesca? No. She didn't go swimming. We had people over."

When Paolo got home, Nina said, "Why did you say you'd seen Francesca at the pool?"

Paolo looked as if she'd walked right into his trap. "How do you know that I didn't?"

"Luca mentioned that they'd had people over."

"When did you see Luca?"

"He rang earlier, worried about you working so hard."

"Well, that's ironic. You wouldn't mind, though, if Francesca and I had something we did together? Like going swimming. Or learning salsa? She's keen and I'm keen and you're not keen."

"Salsa? But – but Paolo, you never dance. Not even at your own wedding, despite my pleading with you to dance."

"I think it might be time to learn. Do you object?"

"No." No-but, no-but. Surely he must hear the but.

"Excellent. I'll go and call her."

Later, when Nina was quiet, Paolo asked her what was wrong. "It's nothing," she said. "Just thinking."

"You're not completely happy about the dancing plan."

"She jumped at it. She sounded... I could hear her from right over here."

"Luca doesn't want to learn either. What's wrong with it?"

"Nothing. It's just that we don't do that much together outside the flat."

"It's held on a Thursday night. Why don't you and Luca do something?"

"Paolo. What are you doing?"

"I'm not doing anything. You and Luca like to do things I don't like. Why don't you two go to the cinema? I can't sit still that long and Francesca says she gets fidgety too."

"I might have a few people over and play cards. Poker nights. Cigars. Pizzas. Beer."

"Well, that sounds marvellous."

"It will be."

Paolo jabbed one finger in her ribs. "Poker," he said. "I might be good at that."

"You might."

"Do I have to go dancing? I hate dancing."

"You have arranged it, I think you'll find."

He put his hand to his forehead. "Oh God. I'm going to have to call Francesca back. She'll think we're both mad."

"She thinks that already," Nina said, feeling safe again.

Chapter Ten

Autumn was coming and day on day the light seemed to be yellower, saturating the garden with richer-looking colours. The sea shimmered so brightly that it was hard to look at.

"It's so beautiful here," Nina said, as she did every day, going to the chair that Dr Christos was holding in place. He'd already been there for some time, sitting at a table with a desk-top calculator.

He looked at the view as if it didn't often occur to him to look. "It is. It's very fine." He stood up and gathered his things together. "I'm supposed to be somewhere, but George here is the person to tell if you have a problem, a pain, or need something." He gestured to a man sitting at a table further along, a man of about 70, bald but for a grey monk's tonsure and stiff grey moustache, who was dressed in striped blue pyjamas and a blue robe edged in red.

"What's George going to do?" she whispered. He looked far frailer than she did. He was bent over a newspaper, his nose wrinkled up so as to keep his glasses in place.

"He has a mobile phone in his pocket, always, don't you George?" When he didn't respond Dr Christos said something to him in Greek and in answer he raised his thumb without looking up. "George has my number and he will call if you need me. He calls me a lot. We talk more on the phone than in person." George put his thumb up again and turned it decisively down. "Hah!" Dr Christos said. There was a possibility that he was wary of George and humouring him.

When Dr Christos had gone, Nina attempted to catch George's eye. "Thanks!" she called across the garden. "Efharisto!" George looked up at her and furrowed his brow. He took his phone out of his pocket and appeared to offer to dial. "No, no – it's okay. No need for Dr Christos." She shook her head and waved her hands at the same time, and he put his phone back and gave her one last look, as if identifying a time-waster. Nina moved to one of the shaded sunloungers and got her book out, the other English remnant left at the hospital by a previous patient. It was a Swedish thriller and full of twilight and blizzards and menace, the perfect antidote to an Aegean idyll.

When Dr Christos returned he pointed out that Nina's phone was blinking receipt of a text message. It wasn't Luca. Every day she hoped it was Luca with a proper explanation, an apology. She felt the sourness of repeated disappointment. "My dad," she said, pressing the button. Why was she announcing the names of people who contacted her, as if she needed to account for herself? "Apparently it's snowing at home. That's decided it. I'll move here and do bed and breakfast."

He'd opened a folder and was distracted by it, lifting out the top sheet so as to re-read what was written there. "It's not good news for one of our guests. Crap. I don't know. Some people just can't get a break. But why tell her today? Why tell her at all, come to that? She's so old. It's not going to make her happier."

"But she has a right to know her own bad news," Nina said. "Surely."

"I don't agree." He took his laptop out of his bag. "Happiness is way more important than the notional truth."

"The notional truth?" She expected him to laugh at himself but he didn't. Was that one of the things? She was trying not to list them, but there had to be things. When you took such a big step forward, there were bound to be small steps back. But how many?

"I'm very glad about the decision." She looked confused and so he clarified. "The decision about moving here."

"Paolo will also be glad. My living abroad was his idea. He thought it would be good for me. It makes me deeply miserable when he talks like that."

"Why so?"

"Because he talks to me as if I'm just an old friend, like someone he doesn't need to see very often and can keep up with on Facebook. Not that Paolo uses Facebook. I can't even imagine Paolo using Facebook."

"Why not?"

"Because... Why not... because I suppose there's something about him, like my dad, that's old world. Paolo's a reluctant user of technology. He's pen and ink. He's stayed pen and ink while the whole rest of the office, the rest of the world has become computer-operated. Luca more or less lives on his phone and his iPad. Paolo has email but that's about all, and his assistant does most of that. Not because he's incompetent with it, but he just doesn't want to live there, in that culture, I suppose. He holds onto the old culture. He writes letters and sends them through the post. He buys old books and won't have a Kindle. He doesn't really use the internet. He's like a one-man campaign. Paolo, alone in his fort, surrounded by progress he doesn't want and completely outnumbered."

"You sound fond of him."

"I am. I'm very fond of him. But we're not going to be reconciled."

Dr Christos clicked his biro on and off, and on and off and on again. "So let's get this straight. You don't want him, but you want him to want you."

"It's not that. It's just that he's got used to not being married to me too quickly, like it never really amounted to anything much. Are you all right?"

"Too much wine last night. I need aspirin." He rummaged in his bag and found some. She wanted to know who it was he'd got drunk with, but decided against asking.

"Almost kills me, when he talks to me like that. But with my job, I can live pretty much anywhere. It's been whispering to me, the grass is greener thing, sending junk mail from faraway places into my brain. *You could live here. You could live there.* It has to be the best decision I ever made."

"What, bigger than marriage?"

"I'm 46 years old. I might only be halfway through my life. Aside from my mother people in my family have tended to live to be very old, well into their nineties. I got myself in a stew, thinking that if I was going to be alone, then it'd need to be a fantastic place to live, friendly but anonymous enough, busy but peaceful enough, city but country enough. I've decided to abandon the shortlist and just come here."

"So, you'll do bed and breakfast and give up editing."

"I wouldn't give up editing. I need to work and I love to work. Why wouldn't I work?"

"There's no need to be defensive." Dr Christos looked at his phone messages and clicked through them.

"Paolo always said I didn't need to. Didn't need to – it's always struck me as a weird expression. To have the luxury of interesting work is one thing, but not working at all seems anything but a luxury to me." The doctor wasn't really listening. "Francesca never had a job, not after she married, and it was always a stupid old-fashioned thing about the two of them, Luca and Paolo, that it was a source of pride if a wife didn't. They didn't really take the life of the wife into account. To be honest it frightened me, Luca's saying his wife would never work."

He looked up from texting. "Luca said this? When?"

"He was engaged to Francesca. They wanted the same things. They assumed they'd have lots of children and then they couldn't. But it frightened me that it wouldn't occur to him that he was blithely signing a woman up to a lifetime without achievement, like it was purely a matter of prestige for himself."

"Achievement outside her domestic achievements," Dr Christos interjected. He began to make notes on the second sheet.

Somewhere at the back of her mind Nina found that the list had begun, and was writing itself, the list of negatives. It was one she intended to ignore. The idea of the perfect match, the soulmate, had proved disastrous, after all. A partnership with some incompatibility in it was as good an idea about the future as any other; perhaps the best. They'd call it "spark" and it would keep things lively. She said, "I suppose it's different if you have children. I gave up work when I was pregnant. I had eclampsia. Toxaemia, they used to call it; a better, more descriptive word."

"I'm sorry, Nina." Look at his face, his kind face. It didn't matter if he could be pompous, a bit of a dinosaur. He was open, open-hearted. They didn't have to agree about everything. She and Paolo hadn't.

"Some people were confident that working was the reason for my getting ill, implying I'd put the baby at risk, that I'd killed the baby. My mother-in-law, for instance. I said to her that it was hard to imagine how lying on a sofa reading could be to blame. Paolo mis-sold the job to her as reading books, when we got engaged, and she never really saw it differently. She was in two minds. It was womanly and effete, the job, so that was a plus, but on the other hand, pointless and easy to sacrifice."

"You love your work."

"I like being good at it."

"Perhaps more than being married."

"What makes you say that?"

"It's just a point of view."

"You don't approve of women having careers?" The list was adding to itself in a slow italic.

"Of course I do. Absolutely I do. I'm not my father. He didn't even approve of my having one."

"There was an assumption that I wouldn't work after I had the baby, that I'd have better things to do than work."

"But – you would have had better things to do. Maybe we should stay clear of this. Did you keep trying, to get pregnant, I mean?"

"I couldn't go through it again."

"I'm so sorry."

"Luca was wonderful to me. Luca was wonderful. Paolo was hurt and absent and Luca was there."

Luca was the first of the Romanos to come to the house. He came gravely and kindly, bearing flowers, cake, art books. He said, "Let's not speak about it," and held her close, which was what she needed: everybody else had wanted to talk, had wanted glib assurances that they'd "try again". He made her tea and toast and put the radio on and sat holding her hand. He'd been to a talk about Caravaggio and leafed through a book of his paintings, telling her what he'd discovered. When she was tired and closed her eyes he read aloud to her from *Sense and Sensibility*, which lay open on the coffee table. Nina had always found solace in Eleanor and Marianne.

The day after Luca's visit Maria and Francesca turned up, each of them carrying a heavy bag. They'd brought meals for the next four days, chicken and beef dishes they'd made together and had sealed in cartons they'd found at a kitchenware shop. Nina's gratitude was waved away. It was nothing. Families looked after each other, Maria said, shrugging. Francesca had gone to the newsagent and bought a bagful of media distraction: the *Telegraph* and the *Guardian*, *Marie Claire* and *National Geographic*, *Private Eye* and *Good Housekeeping*.

"We really have no idea what kind of thing you like," she said. "So I hope this covers it. You're such a serious person. Intellectual, I mean. Not like me, who didn't even finish school."

Nina said, "Educated shouldn't be confused with bright." She'd meant to pay a compliment.

"I didn't say I wasn't bright," Francesca said, slapping the magazines onto the table.

Anna had always been clear that it was best not to share your fears and weaknesses. She'd said exactly that when Nina was seventeen and Luca was distant. They'd been icing a chocolate cake together. "These things pass," she'd said. "But the people you confide in will never forget it, what you said when you were low: they'll fix it for ever as a truth about you, when it's only a truth about that moment." It had been hard to contribute to these conversations. "People know their own complexity very well, but invariably they try to simplify other people. They can't help it."

So Nina had never confessed – other than to Luca, who could take it – just how unhappy she was after her miscarriage. Paolo didn't know that she'd found herself following women with babies around the city. She'd always tried to keep her failings from him – though that also meant that there was a void, in which she couldn't be positive and (unable to be negative) wasn't anything, was apparently a blank. Paolo always took it badly if she was unhappy, thus proving Anna absolutely right. It was Luca who heard all about it. He'd hugged her and said nothing; his grip on her had been tighter. She'd told him how, pausing outside a department store changing room, she'd stroked the misshapen head of a tiny newborn still sleeping off his birth journey, passing a forefinger over his pulsing fontanelle. She knew he was a he, because he was colour-coded in a variety of blue clothes and linens and had plastic cars strung on his pram toy. He'd looked very like her own lost boy, who'd died before he could live, delivered perfect and lifeless as if he'd changed his mind. Nina bent her own head close to the tiny face, taking in its scents and its whispering rapid breaths, and had inhaled deeply. The woman had emerged from the changing cubicle and, seeing Nina, had shoved the clothes, the hangers, hurriedly onto a rack, wheeling the buggy vigorously away from danger.

Nina picked up another paperback she'd brought with her, one from which protruded a Sistine Chapel bookmark. Inside she was confronted by a page with a squashed mosquito close to the fold, and a blotch of sun oil that had blurred an irregular patch of words. It was the page she'd been at on the day she'd broken her leg and she closed it again, unable entirely to defuse the memory. This book would have to be disposed of.

She said, "I've been thinking I might go and spend some time in Norway. Even if I moved here –"

"If?" Dr Christos jumped right in. "You're still thinking about it? Quite right. These things take time. Actually no, to hell with that. Just do the mad thing and agree."

"When, in all probability I move here," – she paused to make a "there you go" face – "I could go to Norway for July and August, when it's too hot for me in Greece. It never bothered me much but now I'm impatient to go. It's been 30 – no, 32 – years since I was there. Mum never went back once her parents had died. I call them her parents but really they were her grandparents, and old even when I was small. Their weekday flat was rented – which was usual for Oslo – but they owned a summer house by a lake, one we used to visit every year. It was a modest, ramshackle house. They had money, but they lived modestly on principle."

It was an old wooden house and right on the shore, in a small community of other wooden houses; it was absolutely quiet, there, with the lake in front and the forest stretching behind. The house had been rented out since Anna died, but recently the tenants had given up the lease and Nina found she was keen to visit. Anna had also inherited a substantial amount of money, it turned out, and when she died it was both house and windfall that passed to Nina. When Anna's will was found, the size of the cash inheritance was really surprising; even Robert hadn't known it was so much. Anna hadn't told him the truth about it. He'd thought it was a little nest egg put aside for a deposit for a flat, for Nina when she left university. It had been an accidental fortune, because without really meaning to, Grandpa had made a lot of money. He was given shares in the furniture company when he first joined, to make up for low wages, and it was a small concern then, just three of them, three carpenters hand-making lovely carved things, but then it was a huge success; it became a factory in the end, churning out machine-made tables for a chain of shops. He kept working there, even though he hated what it had become. Anna told Nina that it was a Norwegian thing, and hard to explain, but it was unacceptable among the family and his friends and neighbours not to work. They didn't even move house, and if they hadn't bought a new car you would never have seen any difference in their lives. She said it was all to do with Janteloven. Jante law: the pressure to be the same as everyone else, not to be different, not to contradict the norms; fundamentally, not to show off.

"Why on principle, what was the principle?"

"They were embarrassed by the money. And so they had a freedom they never used. And in turn it was the same with Mum. She could have gone off and done something interesting, instead of mouldering away in that horrible rented flat. Someone else's flat. Interesting thing, masochism, isn't it? She was punishing herself."

"Punishing herself – why?"

"She felt she must have deserved to be rejected by my father, somehow. I can't explain it to you because I don't really understand it either. Seems completely fucked up to me. Sorry for the language."

"I don't mind the language. I don't think it suits you, though."

"Doesn't suit me how?" She thought she knew the answer, but wanted to hear it.

He looked at his watch. "I have to go do rounds and then I have meetings, over there." He nodded towards Main Island. "I'll come by again later."

When he'd gone Nina picked up her journal, turned to a clean page, smoothed her hand along the crease, and wrote *Dr Christos doesn't like women to say fuck.*

The afternoon went very slowly. She had a brief conversation with George about shipwrecks (there'd been two notable finds in the bay), a chat translated and chaired by Nurse Yannis, who afterwards ordered her to go in for a siesta and followed her into the room to darken the windows. They talked about the progress of the leg, and about shoes; Nurse Yannis wore shoes in pretty colours that she bought by mail order – tangerine-coloured moccasins today – and blushed sweetly when Nina admired them. After that there was an interminable three hours in which nothing happened but the rhythmical fluttering of the roller blind in an onshore breeze. Nina tired of reading, her mind wandering, and she couldn't focus on anything else, on writing or planning. She lay and watched the blind moving. She longed for work, a working

day at a table, with a coffee pot and an omelette, and logs crack-
ling in the woodburner. She longed for a Scottish summer day.

Dinner arrived, a pink fish and a green salad, and shortly after
that Dr Christos, but he didn't stay long. He reported, under ques-
tioning, that the crossing to the island had been ordinary, the bus
to the town crowded and hot, and the town crowded and hot too.
The meeting had gone fine. He didn't elaborate. He asked how she
was and looked at the chart, and then he left, saying only, "See you
tomorrow." It was as if they had argued but had to work together.
It was as if they were at a conversational staging post on the route
back from sulking to being at ease again with one another. She
reviewed their last conversation. It couldn't have been *fucked up*
that did it, could it? Surely not. He hadn't been able to use the
word *feminine*, if it was *feminine* he was thinking and not saying.
Had *fucked up* been some kind of a let-down? It didn't matter.
But it did matter. Things mattered now that didn't used to. Charm
mattered more than ever, here in the onset of – what should she
call it? – of diminished allure. A woman whose skin is beginning
to line and sag, whose hair is beginning to thin and to grey, she
needs self-confidence if she is still to be noticed by men, if she's
still to have romantic potential. She needs charisma; she needs
unyielding self-belief, and it needs to show, in her eyes and in the
way she speaks, and in her posture, an expectation of being loved.
Nina wrote these thoughts down in her notebook, noting the echo
from a speech of Caroline Bingley's in *Pride and Prejudice*, but
couldn't think what to write next. She started doodling: first the
lake house with the shore in front, before sketching in the woods
that lay behind, and then she put the notebook down again feeling
deeply dissatisfied. There was some unidentifiable blockage. What
was the blockage? She felt nervous, on edge.

Nurse Yannis came back into Nina's room and asked if she'd like
a cup of coffee. Nina said eagerly that she'd love one, thank you,
and the nurse went out into the corridor and pushed the trolley in.
She handed her a plate with a cake on it, a slab cake dotted with
island berries, dark-red berries that had leaked their juices into
the sponge.

"My sister, she makes this cake and sends it," she said.

"Your sister!" Nina exclaimed. "How is your sister?"

"She is well."

They ate cake and drank coffee.

"You speak very good English," Nina said, looking for a topic.

"I learn at school," Nurse Yannis told her. "And I speak it here. It is not fantastic. I talk in now all the time."

"The present tense."

"I suppose."

"I have no Greek at all so the present tense is great for me. I'm the same in Italian. I can't do the past and future and stick to the present all the time."

The nurse's response to this surprised her. "Nina, I need to say to you… about Christos. He is a little bit in love with you."

Nina kept it together. "He's just friendly. Have you known him a long time?" she asked, though she already knew the answer.

"We are at school. His sister is my friend. You know he is married?"

"I thought he was divorced."

"They live different, in different houses. But married."

"He is just a friend," Nina said.

"I am glad." Nurse Yannis looked down at her feet. "Because he is not safe."

"Safe?" The nurse put Nina's cup and plate onto the trolley and made as if to push it back out of the room. "Please – wait – please say more. What do you mean, not safe?"

Nurse Yannis paused at the door. "He loves his wife."

Panicking slightly, she said, "But you used the word 'safe'. Is it safe that you mean?"

The nurse came back in and leaned over the back of the chair. "I don't talk more about Christos. But safe is not the word. I mean only, he loves his wife."

Nina had to get off this line of enquiry. "You knew him when he was a boy."

"Yes. His sister I like very much." The emphasis on "sister" was intended.

"What was it like, the island when you were children?"

Nurse Yannis shrugged. "It is just the same. We have no electricity but just the same. No cars but just the same. Not many tourists. But the same."

"Was it a happy island? It seems like a happy place to me. People seem happy here." She felt the dull inner thud of fatuousness.

"They are the same like everywhere." Nurse Yannis was unmistakably bored.

"But it was a happy childhood? Lots of swimming and freedom?"

"Yes, yes."

Nina had run out of questions. She looked stupidly at the nurse's face. Finally Nurse Yannis took up the conversational baton. "And you, you are a happy child?"

"I was. I was a happy child."

"Lots of swimming and freedom?"

"Lots of freedom. Not a lot of swimming, other than at the city pool, which had too much chlorine in it. It's not usually warm enough to swim outside in Scotland, though we tried on our holidays, at the seaside house we used to go to every year. Do I speak too fast?"

"I understand."

"My village has changed a lot since I was young. I've moved there again and it is very different. When I was a child we played tennis in the street, and skipped in a big skipping rope, a jump rope. We spent a lot of time on bicycles. You know the word bicycle?"

"Of course."

"Sorry." There didn't seem to be any way of talking to Nurse Yannis without looking and sounding like an idiot.

On the long summer evenings preceding the holiday Nina had walked around the village each evening at dusk and had seen children go by on their bikes, in single file and in safety helmets, exuding anxiety about the traffic, shouting to each other what was safe to attempt and what wasn't. In the 1970s they'd spread out across the streets as they cycled, and cars had kept their distance, unexcited by the raggedness of their road manners. They had been five, a tight unit: Nina, Paolo and Luca, plus Becky and Andy, a group that was known as the Old Village Gang, a gang intermittently in playful war with another group of five who lived on the other side of the high street, in the new houses. It wasn't ever a Montagues and Capulets level of conflict, although hard fallen apples were thrown, on one heated occasion, illicitly in somebody's orchard, and Andy had suffered a bruised cheekbone and a bloodshot eye. Nina had taken him home and

Anna had ministered to his injuries, clucking and applying a poultice. She'd poured and offered a glass of apple juice, keeping a straight face, watching to see if he got the joke. Mostly it was harmless fun, and considered perfectly normal. Children were expected to play in the street, to be seen and to be noisy, to congregate and to share ownership of public spaces, which weren't yet sealed off and designated, issuing their conditional welcome. Children hung around on street corners and conspired, and set things alight that didn't really burn, and swung from municipal trees and played tennis in the road, and played on other people's fields and built dens at beauty spots. It was all routine child activity then, but now inhabits a lost world.

When Nurse Yannis had gone Nina wrote this paragraph down, about how childhood had changed, and felt the pang she felt sometimes, the one that heralded the lack of a daughter to hand her world on to. She wrote another paragraph. *It isn't just love that's handed down, and the genetic inheritance, and tics and habits of mind. There are other necessary things. Regret. Melancholy. An understanding of loss. It's begun to mean something to me, not to have anyone to pass these things on to.*

Nurse Yannis came back into the room, interrupting her. "Letter for you," she said.

The handwriting was Luca's. Nina hauled herself up into a more upright position on the bed, swiftly with both arms, pulling uncomfortably at her leg, her shoulder muscles, and tore at the envelope with shaking hands. A single large piece of paper, a good paper, thick and textured, had been folded into three. She opened it out and gulped its contents down, skimming to the end and the signing-off. Then, her heart pounding, she read it again, paying attention to each line.

Dear Nina. The handwriting was terrible. Luca lived permanently at one keyboard or another. Having to decipher ambiguous words to make sense of some of it made the adrenaline course around her system all the harder.

Paolo wanted me to write to you to say some of the things I said to him, but they are things you and I have said to one another already and don't need repeating here. Please destroy this after reading. Neither of us wants this on the record. I know that Paolo is coming for you, so when you tell him that you received this, you

*can also tell him that it was an apology to you for how things got
so out of hand after Francesca's death.*

*I agree that it was April, that it happened, and after you moved
out. That was the basis of the conversation Paolo and I have
already had. I'm never going to tell him about February. I think
we should spare him that. He is dogged, dogg-éd, in many ways,
good and bad, and he'd worry that February led to March. I told
him sincerely how it was: that it was once and a mistake, and that
it was all about my own grief and your comforting me. They were
kindness and comfort that went wrong and can't be put right.
So here it is, the big decision. I've made the decision I knew was
coming. I'm moving to Italy. Probably not for good, but for now
and until it feels like time to come back. There's a job there to do
and I can do it well and have a sort of a new life, and I'm in need
of that. I'll be in Rome when you return. Perhaps we can email,
but can I ask you not to contact me until you know that you're
in love with Paolo. If that doesn't happen, please don't email. It
won't work between us, the three of us, until the two of you are
together again. But you knew that already. This much we have
learned.*

*I'm not sure whether to add this or not, but I'm tired and so
I'm going to risk it. If our conversation resumes it must never
return to the things we said and wrote to each other at around
the time that you moved out. Nothing could be distilled out of
that other than for things neither of us wants to revisit. I hope I'm
making sense. I'm not absolutely confident of that. Castigate me
about it, when you write. If you write, tell me the trivial things
that have always been the most important.*

*I hope the leg's making steady progress and that you'll be pole-
vaulting again before too long. Paolo has kept me informed of the
basics, the updates, and I hope that will continue. I miss you. I
miss our old friendship. You have always been my sister, which is
why so much of this has been so weird.*

Luca

There was no mention of it, the unforgivable thing. No apology.
Instead there was an ink dot beneath his name, where perhaps
he was going to write a postscript and then didn't. Or where,
perhaps, he was going to add a kiss before changing his mind.

Chapter Eleven

It wasn't until the engagement party given for Luca and Francesca that Nina first met her. This wasn't neglect on Nina's part: it was the first time anyone in the family had met her, since she'd only arrived from Rome that afternoon. Years later, at one of their lunches, when Luca complained that Francesca didn't read and wasn't interested in painting or history or ideas, Nina had asked him, taking care to pick a convivial moment, why he'd proposed to someone he'd only known a month.

"What's the time got to do with it?" He seemed to be serious. "These things are instinctive. You know straight away."

She laughed, inviting him to join her, but he looked if anything more solemn. "She was prepared to take a risk," he said, solemnly.

"So you said in the letter. She stepped out of the plane trusting you'd given her a parachute."

"I asked the question and she said yes, even though it might have been a joke. It was a joke, until she answered. She passed the test."

"It was a test? One I'd failed, then."

"I knew I needed daring and spontaneity in my life," he said, not looking at Nina but aware that he'd criticised her, nonetheless.

Now that Francesca was dead, after a battle with cancer that seemed for a while to have been won, Nina was deeply ashamed of herself for never having liked her. She'd not cut enough slack for a person who was going to die young. There could never be enough slack cut for a person who was going to die young. Not treating someone who was going to find themselves in that predicament with the reverence, the tolerance, the empathy that was warranted, was always an issue after they were gone. All those last occasions, last interactions, that should have been loving and sincere, that should have meant something definite. It was a situation that mourned its own lack of clairvoyance.

Clairvoyance was topical. Dr Christos imagined he was being

clairvoyant right now, but like Susie he'd got it all the wrong way round. "You left Paolo because Francesca had died, to signal to Luca that you were ready to be with him. Yes?"

"No. The last time I spoke to Luca I told him I would never speak to him again. That was the day I left Paolo."

"I thought you fell in love."

"What makes you say that?"

"I thought there was a disgrace."

"We slept together. Luca and me. That's inaccurate, in fact. There wasn't any sleeping."

"When was this?"

"It was in April. Before I moved out. Though Paolo thinks it was a couple of weeks after."

"He knows. How does he know?"

"I told him at the airport. I lied about the timing."

"For understandable reasons. Lying gets an unfairly bad press. There are often good reasons to lie."

"I feel terrible. But Paolo would be destroyed if he knew it was before we separated." She had a new thought. "I keep forgetting that you're going to meet him."

"You can trust me; don't worry."

"Luca was in a state after I left."

"Because he thought…"

"Luca assumed, like you did, that I was signalling that it was our chance to be together."

"So let me get this straight. Francesca died in February. In April you made love with Luca. Then you fell out with him. Oh I see – I see now. Luca was horrified that it was just sex; he thought it was building up to something. Then you left Paolo because you realised that you didn't love Paolo either. You saw that you didn't really love anyone."

"I said to Paolo that he was ripe for an affair, but really it was me. It was obvious that it was me. This is starting to sound like a soap opera."

"It's because the soaps are accurate."

"Paolo thought that I was in love with his brother, when we married, but Paolo was the one who was in love with someone else. Though he'd deny that if you asked him."

"What? Paolo was in love with someone else? You haven't said anything about this. Who was it?"

"It doesn't matter any more."

Luca and Francesca's engagement party took place in Maria's house, in the sitting room that opened into the dining room through double doors that had been wedged open. The house was crammed with dark-wood furniture brought over long ago from home (Maria still referred to Italy as home), dark furniture and prints of Tuscan scenery in gilt frames. Everybody was there who should have been, other than Anna, who had died. There were people who hadn't seen Nina since her mother's death, which had happened mere weeks earlier, and who took the chance to offer their condolences. Nina hadn't wanted to come, not least because she knew she'd bring bereavement with her. She felt like the angel of death at the marriage feast, and so once she'd circulated, briefly and politely, she sat in a corner nursing a drink, watching as the engaged couple were taken round the relatives. Francesca's unselfconscious laughter rang out again and again. She was quick to laugh, unmistakably elated, and why not – even Nina had agreed that this event should bring to a final close the period of mourning, although a little of its melancholy was revived, as one person after another came up to say how sorry they were about Anna. Francesca, meanwhile, had put lively Italian music into the cassette deck and was encouraging the whole gathering to dance. (She wasn't to know why it was that the evening had a melan-choly aspect. Luca hadn't explained.) She'd taken on the role of hostess, because Maria was very evidently over-tired. Francesca didn't mind: she said it was an ideal way to meet people, and took the job seriously, moving around the room attending to the needs of all, fetching drinks and finding lumbar-supporting cushions for Giulio's elderly relatives, who were so frail and old as to be papery, like animations of bones. Over and over Nina heard the story being told of the whirlwind romance that had taken place.

At just after 9pm, as she was about to make her excuses and go, Paolo arrived from the train station, walking into the room in a dark-blue suit, a pale-blue shirt open at the collar, smelling of fresh antiperspirant applied over sweat, and was greeted with general acclaim. "Here he is, the London Romano!" his father cried out, clasping him around the neck. Paolo was used to Giulio's emotional response to reunions and took being clasped and kissed in his stride. He left his rucksack by the door and went round and said hello to everyone, starting with his mother, who was sitting to Nina's left and who introduced him at length to Francesca, before proceeding clockwise around the room so that he came to Nina last. Recently, someone had said to him, "Touch the woman you love, lightly and briefly, when you're talking." His hand glanced against Nina's thigh as he came to rest in the vacant chair beside her. That same someone had said, "When you look into the face of the woman you love, think how you feel about her as you are speaking." When he said he was glad to see her and she turned to meet his eyes there was such an intensity to his expression, such soulfulness, that Nina was floored. She moved back in her chair as if she'd been physically pushed there. What had happened to Paolo? She'd never seen Paolo like this. He looked at her as if they shared a secret, as if they were secretly and illicitly in love.

Aware of her reaction, Paolo turned his attention to the wine. "This is drinking so well," he said to the glass. He looked across the room to where his father was standing, and raised the glass of red up. "It's drinking like twice the price, three times the price," he said, shouting above the din of chatter. Giulio, gratified, raised his own glass in return. Paolo's gaze returned to Nina's profile. "I haven't seen you in ages. I was hoping you'd come down and visit."

She couldn't look at him. "I'm sorry," she said, still looking at Giulio. "It's been a tough few weeks. I wasn't prepared for how delayed it would be, the grieving."

"You must miss her every day. I miss her too. And I must admit..."

"What must you admit?" The words escaped her before she could stop them.

He blushed. He must know what she meant. "Just that it's odd being back here, and having a social occasion without. You know. Without your mother. That presence. Things seem flat, don't they." He didn't seem able to call her Anna any more.

Francesca came across to them holding a plate of chocolate-covered strawberries and offered Nina one. "I'm sorry I haven't had the chance to talk to you properly," she said. "I've heard so much about you and all of it very good, obviously."

Nina thanked her and welcomed her to the family. She said, "Luca's obviously besotted," and Paolo acknowledged the handsomeness of this gesture by brushing his hand against her leg again.

"Luca thinks of you as his sister," Francesca continued. "So we're going to be more than friends, I hope."

"It's true, you're right; Nina is our sister," Paolo told her. "At least, she's Luca's. I'm not sure I'd classify her as mine."

"Ouch." Francesca had misunderstood, and looked from one face to the other as if the joke was about to be elaborated on.

Nina had registered a strong and sour wine aroma coming from Paolo's direction when he spoke, not the high-achieving new red but another that lay beneath it, an under-achieving one. *He was drinking before he got here,* she thought. *He drank wine on the train.* It was true. He'd drunk a whole bottle of an astringent Bordeaux, for courage.

"You were positively joined at the hip when you were children, I hear, the three of you," Francesca said. She had nice teeth, even and white, and terracotta-coloured lips, full lips and soft. Much about her was soft, in fact: her black wavy hair, which fell in a silky S to her shoulder, the expression in her large and very dark eyes, and the bloom of her skin, which was caramel-tinted, an olive skin that had seen some sun and glowed with a vanilla-scented lotion. Her face was confident and mobile, the look on it constantly changing, mapping her changing thoughts and feelings, and she fidgeted as she stood, moving her arms as she spoke, adjusting her stance and running her hands over her own lower back and hips. She wasn't thin like Nina. She was ample, curvaceous, luscious. When she laughed her abundant bosom shook and rippled at the top of her dress.

"Look at the two of us," she said, putting a butterscotch-coloured arm next to Nina's near-white one. "We really couldn't be more different."

There wasn't any way back, only forward.

Paolo and Nina's engagement party, held a few weeks later in that same room, was a more formal, less relaxing event. There wasn't any mystery about that different atmosphere: Maria Romano didn't like Nina. She would say afterwards, chastised by Paolo, that she hadn't treated Nina any differently to Francesca, that she'd given Francesca just the same kind of advice about starting married life on the right footing.

"Not in public," he'd reminded her. "Not in the middle of the room in the middle of the party."

The trouble had all been kicked off by Nina's admission that she didn't want a church wedding. Maria was deeply upset by this decision. Think of all the people coming from Italy! It was unfortunate that Paolo, in the interests of handling his mother, didn't say straight away that he agreed with Nina about the registry office. Instead, he framed it as a desire to give Nina what she wanted. He thought that was reasonable, he said (reasonable was a very Paolo sort of a word). It was Nina's day.

When Maria took Nina on, each of them standing with a salmon pinwheel sandwich and glass of fizz, Paolo stood on the sidelines pretending to listen to the people he was talking to but half watching the two of them, like a bodyguard who knows he might have to intervene. Afterwards, he insisted that his mother ring Nina to apologise, which she had done with good grace. All she wanted, she said, was for everybody to have the best possible, most memorable day, and for the photographs to be wonderful – but of course it was Nina's affair, she added, as if that was self-evidently untrue. Francesca and Luca were there with Nina when Maria rang, and so when she came off the phone Nina was asked to recount the whole conversation.

"It's such a shame." Francesca rubbed consolingly at Nina's upper arm. "It's such a pity that the wedding's becoming such an ordeal."

"Francesca," Luca said neutrally.

Nina looked from him to his wife. "Who said it was an ordeal?"

"You're becoming more and more stressed," Francesca told her. "Fighting the family isn't going to make you happier. Wouldn't it be easier just to say yes? You are becoming a Catholic, aren't you?"

"No, I'm an atheist."

"But Maria thinks you are. She thinks you are having instruction."

"Atheism is a bit of a stumbling block."

"You lied to Maria. That's terrible."

"Paolo, not me. He wanted to keep her happy till after the ceremony. I agree, I think it was a mistake. But there isn't much I can do about what Paolo says to her."

Luca looked up from his newspaper. "He's such a milksop."

"You don't want to have it in your mother's church?" Francesca looked as if she might know why not. Most things had been explained to her, by this stage.

"I don't want to have it in any church," Nina told her.

"But a church wedding's a real wedding. It's so much nicer, the day you'll have, the dress, the ceremonial. The registry office is pretty dire. Have you been inside it?"

"It doesn't matter," Luca said, quartering his paper so he'd have a hand free for the coffee cup. "It's all about the party afterwards."

"I just think she'd be happier," Francesca persisted.

"Happiness isn't the issue," Nina said.

"Happiness ought to be the issue." Francesca turned to grimace at Luca.

"I'm perfectly happy, thanks."

"A word of advice: Maria doesn't understand reserve. She likes straight talking. She and I have had our moments."

"And how," Luca agreed.

"I like straight talking too," Nina protested.

"That's true, actually," Luca said. "That's how she got into this mess."

"I do know Maria, you know," Nina reminded her. "I've known her all my life."

"You're saying that the fact I've known her for less time makes my insight less valuable?"

"She isn't saying that." Luca's voice was sharper.

"I know that you've never got on." Francesca looked sympathetic.

Nina heard herself gasp. "We've always got on fine. What did she say?" The humiliation was like a hot knife.

"Can you see yourself from the outside?" Francesca asked. "Can you look at the situation and wonder why Nina doesn't just have it in the Catholic church and make everybody happy?"

"Francesca. I'm technically a Protestant, but actually an atheist. My Catholic future husband is also an atheist and would prefer not to have a Catholic wedding. You're saying – what – that I should become a Catholic solely for my mother-in-law's sake? Seriously, you think becoming a Catholic isn't that big a deal?"

Luca shook out his newspaper to its full broadsheet size, and disappeared behind it, other than for his hands at its edges.

"Here is my suggestion," Francesca said. "A registry office wedding and then a blessing by the priest to please the Italian contingent."

"You say 'Italian contingent' like that doesn't include you."

"I was born in Greenwich. That's in London. And look, they're coming a long way and some of them really can't afford it."

Luca's newspaper said, "I think Nina should do what she likes."

Francesca was vexed by this. "But what about Paolo? He's not happy about it either."

This was surprising news to Nina. "What? What makes you say that?"

"He doesn't seem happy about it to me. That's all."

"But Paolo agrees! He doesn't want a church wedding and a big fuss."

"Right on," Luca said.

"Francesca tells me that you don't much like my mother," Paolo said later, walking with Nina to the pub. "Not that I'd blame you."

"Your mother's lovely," Nina said carefully, "but she's also used to having things her own way."

"And so are you."

"And so am I." She agreed because agreement with a mild reproof is attractive in a person. It was what Anna said, that it's undignified to disagree with criticism and shows a lack of confidence. *It doesn't matter, it doesn't matter*, Nina said to herself. But it did matter.

"I have news," Paolo said. "…that possibly you're not going to like. Francesca has interceded with Mum."

"What? Interceded how?"

"She's explained you to her." Paolo seemed to be amused. "She promised her that they'd take her to Rome."

Nina stopped walking, an appalled look on her face. "I don't want to go to the pub. I'm going back." She turned in the street and began walking the other way. "We need to talk to your mother."

Giulio was at the office, and they'd only missed Luca and Francesca by ten minutes, Maria said, calling through the hatch from the sitting room. It made her twitchy to have other people in her kitchen; she'd do as instructed and stay put, but then she'd direct all the news, all the questions, through the hatch in a rush, so that by the time they sat down together Maria was all out of conversation. Nina could see her face looking through the tea-tray-sized hole and when she caught her eye Maria reminded her to rinse the pot with boiling water first. Maria wouldn't drink tea that hadn't been made in a warmed pot. She could detect an unwarmed pot.

"She knows how to do it, Mama," Paolo said irritably. He and Nina made the tea, sourced and plated up the digestives, washed and assembled the china that was for best, dusty on the dresser shelf, and took the tray through.

Paolo set it carefully down on the ugly table that had been his granny's once, and that was known among the family as the Heirloom. "So, what did Francesca say to you?"

"They are taking me to Rome," she said inconsequentially. She broke a biscuit in half. "I don't wish to discuss the wedding." She looked critically at the tray. "No tea plates, Paolo." Paolo went obediently to the kitchen. When he'd gone through the door Maria said, "Please, you must stop flirting so much with Luca. It isn't proper."

Nina could feel herself flushing. "I don't flirt with Luca. Luca's one of my oldest friends. We're friends."

"He's married now and he doesn't have friends. Not female ones. It isn't right."

"That really isn't fair."

"And you shouldn't have behaved the way you did at his wedding."

"That's just ridiculous. You're being ridiculous." Nina was aware of sounding shrill.

Nothing further was said until Paolo came back into the room. He'd heard some of it. "What on earth's going on?"

Nina was aware that it wasn't how her mother would have handled things. Anna's priority in dealing with anyone at all was that she was loved and admired at the end of the conversation. Maria reached into her handbag, the one that was beige patent leather, found a handkerchief and clicked the bag shut. She dabbed at her eyes and Paolo put his arms around her and said ,"Don't be so dramatic about everything; everything's fine." He didn't sound absolutely sure, though.

"Maria likes to make situations," Francesca said, on the Sunday after this at lunch. "But she has a good heart. Try to put up with us a little."

No matter how many times Nina rehearsed it in her mind

afterwards, she couldn't make Paolo see that "try to put up with us a little" was a put-down. She brought it up unhappily on the way home. "It says that I'm the outsider and she's on the inside," she argued.

"She's married to Luca, she's close to Maria, she's Italian – of course she's on the inside," he said placidly.

"Paolo. Paolo." Her heart beat wildly. The top of her head ached. "You did it too. You just did it too. You place me on the outside."

"It doesn't matter," he said. "I'd be on the outside too if I could."

The registry office skirt suit was made of a heavy raw silk and was cream with white trims. The buttoned fitted jacket had a big soft collar, and the wide skirt, billowing over net petticoats, was tightly belted and ballerina length, so that the whole effect was very like an old Dior design, an outfit in an Audrey Hepburn photograph that was also a postcard Nina kept by her bed. Anna had made the suit, though Nina only found it after she died, in her mother's flat on the top of the wardrobe, inside a suitcase labelled with her name. Under the layers of tissue there were also cream silk stockings, white shoes, a little hat with white netting that she could lift so as to be kissed. It was strange and wonderful to wear the clothes, as if Anna was also there at the ceremony, there in the fabric, the seams and hems. In the end the day passed well and Maria was brave, even stopping to admire the flower arrangements at the registry office, though she was also overheard saying that she didn't find Nina very bridal.

After they'd eaten three courses in the marquee in her father's garden, and had danced to the jazz trio and had cut cake, Nina found that the waistband had become a bit too tight for sitting down in comfort, which was a pity because quite a bit of sitting had to be done, in the Daimler that Robert had booked to take the newlyweds to the airport, and then on the evening flight to London. They were to spend a night there in a swanky hotel booked by Giulio, ready for the early-morning journey to Greece. Nina was preoccupied on the London flight, uncomfortable in the skirt suit and casting sly sideways glances at Paolo, wondering if he too was thinking about why things had become awkward between the two of them. It was hard to account for, their formality with one another. She adored Paolo and he adored her and everything should have been rosy. They'd been friends all their lives, were deeply bonded, were all set for a comfortable life, and they'd already had successful, enjoyable sex. What else was there? What on earth was wrong? She struggled to make sense of it. She was nervous about the honeymoon, too, because of having to make sure that it was unequivocally happy – it felt as if this responsibility was hers – in a place where there was nothing to do but to be honeymooners, where everyone would know they were honeymooners. She was quiet, the following morning, as they soared out of the sunshine of London, into the cloud cover of mainland Europe and onwards into the unseasonal rainy weather of the Aegean. She'd slept badly – Paolo insisted on cuddling up in bed, had tracked her across the sheet in his sleep, and he was large and fleshy and made her overheat. Both of them were tired, because of the wedding and having risen very early, so they caught up with some rest as they flew, which meant that Nina was able to close her eyes and go over things. It was baffling to her, what it might be that was wrong. Didn't she want to be married to Paolo? Yes. She did. She had meant it when she said yes. Did she really, privately, long to be married to Luca? No. She didn't. She had meant it when she said no. It was the right order of things, to be married to the friend, a man who loved her sincerely, and to have Luca there in the vicinity. Luca was never going to love her as Paolo did and the pattern of things felt right. Anna would have approved it. So what was the problem? Even the geography of the problem was unclear.

Anna had said, "Put yourself into a situation in which you gain things that can never be lost." Nina remembered the day vividly; she'd recently begun her last year at school and they'd been stencilling in the downstairs bathroom, ready for Christmas, even though it was only October. The subject of Paolo had started the conversation off; Anna didn't miss an opportunity to speak up in favour of him. "He's one of those people you'll never lose," Anna said. "Those people are rare. You only realise it when you get older. He'd be loyal to you your whole life."

"Maybe." It was all Nina could offer. She never felt adequate during these discussions.

"But in fact, that which can never really be lost – they're the things that are only real in your head. That's why music and art are important."

"And reading."

"And reading. I can't read fiction any more. But music and art – they are the true art-forms, the purest. They're expressions of a personality that aren't limited to that person, or to the facts, you see, and that's unlike a novel. Music and art, they can be about me and yet they're universal at the same time."

"I find lots of that in novels, too."

"The point is, your head is your place of safety," Anna said, looking as if this was important advice, "and you can be different there. You can continue to be yourself there in absolute freedom." Nina hadn't known how to respond. "You can love whomsoever you like, think what you like and these are your truths and no one can sabotage them." These are your truths: they were words from one of the self-help books. "It's why I think journal-keeping is vital. Write in it every day. It ensures that you keep track of yourself, and return to her."

You can love whomsoever you like? All Nina could do was resort to the facts. "Did you love someone else before you met Dad?" Or after; or after; she didn't dare use the words, but even thinking them made her lose concentration on the task, letting the mylar stencil slip and messing up the line. One of the mistletoe sprigs was wonky even now, on the ceiling above the bathroom window. She came down the stepladder.

"I didn't love your dad when I married him," her mother said, standing back and looking as if she knew this would cause a sensation. "I really liked him, don't get me wrong. Real love is something that grows over time. It's not 'falling in love', which is something altogether different." Nina stopped what she was doing. "I'm just trying to protect you," her mother continued. "It's never straightforward. But you see, when you're young and lovely, you can have just about anyone you want and it's so easy to make the wrong decision. If you decide against Paolo, you'll find that when you go out into the world after university, or even while at university, chances are that you'll become infatuated, obsessive, over someone you barely even know. You'll fall in love, whatever that means."

"Whatever that means?"

"The trouble with falling in love is that it's not a conscious thing, it's not a decision. It's a decision made for you, and isn't always good for you."

"Who makes the decision? I don't understand."

"Something inside you that's out of your control. I don't know if that's even really you, not in any meaningful sense. It's the one acceptable example of the subconscious really taking absolute charge of us, and nobody really questions it." Anna's latest self-help book had been based in neurology; she'd begun looking for titles that Robert would have more respect for. She began to climb up the stepladder. "It's a strange thing, falling in love, and to be honest not something I'd recommend."

"Was there somebody before Dad?" Or after; or after. She couldn't say it, the name on her tongue.

"Oh yes, of course." Anna had smiled, remembering. She'd put her hand to her brow as if to regulate her thoughts. "I was twenty and he was dazzling. He made me ill with longing. But I didn't want to be ill. I wanted to be in control. It was all too dangerous. I wasn't going to hand over control of my happiness to someone else." She started to put the masking tape around the holly stencil. "The point is that you think you'll only love once, or one person at a time. Isn't always so."

"You can't be in love with more than one person at once." Nina found that she'd got acrylic gold paint on her jeans and dabbed at it. Anna threw her a wet sponge.

"That's just a tradition. Oh no, now I've shocked you again. All I'm saying is, don't make the mistake of thinking that there's only one right person for everybody, the other half of a divided self, all that baloney." When she said baloney it was with a Norwegian accent. "The truth is there are lots of men out there you could be happy with. All I'm saying is, don't get hung up on one as the love of your life. It doesn't really work that way. People meet second loves of their lives, and sometimes third. Sometimes the third turns out to be the first, the important one. Strictly in terms of your safety, if you want to have that intense feeling it's best to have it for someone you will never marry."

"Courtly love; it's courtly love," Nina said.

"But look. We're supposed to be doing this and the paint dries really fast. Come on, we need to get this finished." They resumed work and then Anna said, "Talking of which, how are you getting on with *The Faerie Queen*? And the Wyatt?"

"I like the Wyatt," Nina told her. "I've only read bits of the Spenser, though. It's absolutely huge."

"You could do English at the university." Anna was wistful. "I longed to do that, when I was your age. Imagine it, reading novels and poems all day and sitting in lectures hearing what they mean, and writing your own ideas about them. Sounds heaven. Spenser is on the first-year syllabus here. I had a look. That's why I bought it for you."

"At the university here?"

"You'd be able to live at home," Anna said. "Think of the money you'd save. You could have a car, some spare cash to go out. You could bring your friends back here any time. Dad and I would make ourselves scarce."

Anna might have diagnosed Nina's problems as springing from not doing honour to the present. It was the way she spoke some-times, and if people noticed she'd explain that she learned a lot of her English idiom from nineteenth-century novels. She'd done a lot of reading before she was married, every summer in her teens, all summer long at the lake house, one after another.

"I live in the present too, I hope," Dr Christos said. "It's some-thing we should all aspire to. Don't you think? You don't think so?"

"I can't even imagine that," Nina said. "When I've monitored myself, what I think about, where my mind roams and dwells –"

"Really – where your mind roams and dwells?"

"My mother. That's how she used to speak."

"Sorry. Go on."

"I find myself in the past and in the future, going from one to the other and back. I use the past to speculate forward. I'm barely in the present at all."

"Isn't that just another way of saying that you're a worrier?"

"I suppose. Even here. Especially here. The holiday was supposed to be all about living in the day, making the most of each minute of it; really savouring life. My mother could have pulled it off. She spent a lot of time reminding me to be present, *in the room*, as she'd say. 'Be in the room, Nina.' And I suppose when I was small I was really good at it. Less so later."

"It didn't work, then. The plan. Coming to Greece and not being anxious?"

"I found it hard even to notice Greece. I took hundreds of photographs so that I could see it afterwards."

"You said that you felt drawn to return because you'd been so happy here on honeymoon."

"I didn't say that to you."

"You did, you said you wanted to return to somewhere you'd been so happy."

"No – I said that to Cathy. At the hotel."

"That's right; it was Cathy."

"When did Cathy tell you this?"

"While you were off getting your leg done. This is a small place. News travels fast in villages, and islands are even worse."

The first day of the honeymoon was okay, because everything was new. It was cloudy and puddly and only just warm, but they took advantage of the temperature to be active: they took the bus round the island and hired bikes from Andros and walked along the beach, and it was fine because it was all new. On the second day it was cooler, the clouds lower and greyer, and Paolo suggested that they take the boat to Main Island. He'd read in the guidebook that there were caves worth visiting. They could do that, do some shopping, look at the old church, have a nice lunch, visit the museum: what did she think? She said that it sounded like a very good plan, and it was; it was a good plan, but at the same time obscurely disappointing. Why must the day be so busy, so crammed?

"We can get the early boat back if you don't feel up to it. But come on, we need to get a move on if we're to get the morning ferry."

What was I so afraid of? What do I continue to be afraid of? she asked herself later. It felt already like the marriage survived from minute to minute only because Nina was making a vast effort to keep it going, an exhausting constant feat of concentration that wasn't dissimilar to the one that she'd enact 25 years later, on the plane when the turbulence hit. The day had gone well, though it had rained during the donkey ride up to the caves. Nina had been wary of the donkeys. She'd been bitten by one on a beach holiday when she was small, and she'd been thrown off a horse when she was ten. It had taken ages to muster the courage to get on the donkey, and Paolo had been impatient with her.

On the third and fourth days it rained constantly, and they ended up spending most of the time in the taverna, in the bar and in their room, going from one to the other and back. There wasn't any heating, they didn't have sweaters and the rain had brought a chill along with it, so they ended up reading in bed for most of each afternoon. On the fifth day it was sunny in the morning, so they went to Blue Bay, but Paolo was bored by the beach and had run out of things to read. By the time they'd had lunch it had begun to rain again, so they played backgammon in the bar and drank Greek brandy. The following day the sky was blue, albeit with a procession of clouds, and so they took a boat trip around uninhabited islands and swam, despite the Scottish temperature, in a churned-up and gritty sea. It began to rain while they were swimming and rained all that night, and continued at intervals for the final two days. They spent their last afternoon in the town on Main Island, running between shops as the rain pelted down.

On the day Nina moved out Paolo had said that she hadn't really seemed present to him, when they were in Greece on honeymoon. Other things, other disappointments were cited, as if he'd compiled a list of long-ago infractions, as if the list had silently accrued ready for the possibility of this moment's coming to pass. This old view of an old episode, or perhaps new view of it, had shocked her, not just in its having lain in wait but in its being unanswerable. As she was packing a bag, he'd listed them one after another, the ways in which she'd failed him. He'd appeared unconcerned about her leaving. He'd stood aside and let her leave. He'd said, "Off you go, then, if that's what you want." He hadn't looked her in the eye. He'd picked up a book and, still looking at it, had asked if she needed a lift. He'd said, when she'd called the cab and put her luggage by the door, that he was relieved that the day had come that had been so long in coming.

Chapter Twelve

Nina paused in doing her exercises. "I've been trying to chat to Nurse Yannis; I asked what it was like here when she was a child but she wasn't very forthcoming."

"No, in general she isn't," Dr Christos said.

"I'm not sure she likes me very much." The truth was that the nurse's lack of interest in becoming friends was putting her off moving to the island. Perhaps she wasn't going to be accepted, loved, a part of things. Perhaps she wasn't going to be asked to join the women gardeners.

"It's not that she doesn't like you. She's like it with everyone."

"Can I stop this now because I can't do any more. Please."

"You can stop if you like. Have one skinny leg and see if I care."

"I'll do some more later."

"They all say that. The island hasn't changed much on the surface. The gift shop, the internet... that's about it. The internet's made a huge difference."

"I bet. The whole world opens up. All those museums, for a start; all that music. All those online newspapers."

"I was thinking more of the porn. That's made a big difference to the shepherd's life. He can sit under a tree with his tablet and with 3G. Sorted."

"Shit."

"I think you might have a bit of an idealised view of us. What do you think people talk about? It's not Socrates and the leader in the *New York Times*. I was at my aunt's last night and the talk at the table was all about the problem with pests in the crop, a lot of gossip about the usual people, the war with the neighbour over his dog and the fight at the council."

"What's the fight about?"

"Ithika wants to build a five-star resort, over at his side. It's completely divided them. The incomers won't allow any change and some of the locals agree. Others have developed a healthy respect for cash, and also for celebrities, which is a shame. Andros is pissed off too; he's been trying to get a hotel going for years."

"It's like that anywhere, though."

"These small isolated communities, they almost verge on the cannibalistic. You need to know this about us before you move here. There's so little that's really going on that we start to eat ourselves. Everyone thinks they know everything about everyone else. The bitching is endless; it's mostly male bitching, I should add. Sometimes I think I couldn't stand another winter."

"You sound quite jaded."

"I am, I'm quite jaded. Sorry. I'm over-tired. But it's being on your own that makes it wearying. The thing with all places like this is to be with someone, to have a good home life, to have your own team, your own support. It's all pretty good if you have that." He glanced at her. She thought, *I'm being considered for this, for being his home life.* She wanted to laugh at the absurdity of it, and because of her own gratitude. "But it's the same as ever," he continued. "It hasn't changed. It was the same when I was young. A friend of mine at school was gay and the homophobia was fricking terrifying."

"Wasn't it happy, your childhood?"

"It was fine. I suppose. We didn't spend a lot of time with our parents. There wasn't any Scrabble. They worked long hours on the farm – we had the only really sizeable island farm, on the land that's now the allotments, and also the land that's now the vineyard."

"Why did you sell up? If you don't mind me asking."

"I don't mind you asking anything. Ask away." He looked at his watch. "I haven't had breakfast. You didn't eat this morning, I'm told. Back in a jiffy. I love that word. Jiffy." He went out and in a few minutes was back with two glass dessert dishes in which berries and granola had been added to thick yoghurt. He talked as he stirred them together. "My dad sold the farm when I went to medical school, so you see, unusually, my becoming a doctor was disappointing. I was a disappointment to my father. He managed to stay disappointed with me a long time, and died still disappointed. But I was a medical student and – what's that English expression? Full of myself. I was full of myself and stubborn."

"Do you regret it now?"

"I regret my dad being so upset for so long. I still feel bad about that. I could probably have found a way to hang on to it, the farm, tenanted it out. It could have been different but I didn't see that it could be done differently. It was a hard life, you see, when I was a boy. A subsistence life. There wasn't any spare money. Getting new shoes was always a big deal."

"It sounds like the life that my grandparents' parents led, in Norway. I never met them but I heard the stories and that was a similar set-up."

"Well, there you go. The life my parents led was very like the lives of older generations in other parts of Europe. We were backward here in almost every way."

"I thought my childhood was absolutely ordinary until quite recently, its happiness, but it wasn't at all ordinary. In any case I've had to revise it, my memory of it. It seemed happy at the time, though I'm not sure a happy childhood does us a service, later on. We go into life with high expectations, and then –"

He interrupted her. "I love it that you talk like that."

"Like what?"

"You're one of those people, the kind of people who say everything, who dare say anything, like friends I used to have in the States. You talk about your life, you have ideas about it. It's not usual to do that here. It's a relief to be with someone who sees the overview, who sees connections. It's been lonely since my friend Jason left. He'd been in the States too, and tried to come home to live but it just didn't work, so he went back. I've been feeling pretty isolated since then."

"I've been lonely too."

"I'll get us coffee." He went out of the room, humming, and was back with the tray a few minutes later, handing a cup across the table. "So how did your parents meet?"

"My mother came to Edinburgh on holiday with two friends, and they got talking in a theatre. Mum was 22 and Dad 27."

Anna had got separated from her friends at the interval – they'd gone downstairs to the bar they'd had a drink in before the show, not realising there was also a bar upstairs. She bought them drinks and waited – they'd gone to the ladies' room first – but then they didn't come back. Robert was there with his godparents, and came to her rescue; he'd noticed the other two girls going down the stairs. Impulsively, after chatting outside after the performance, he asked for her address, saying he might be coming to Norway for a conference. He wrote to her, and they became penpals. People had penpals then. They met again the following year, when Robert went to Oslo, saying he was visiting the university – which was true, although the university didn't know that he was. They married six months later over in Lewis, the island of Lewis, in the church where his father was the minister. Nina was born two years after their meeting in Oslo, almost to the day. On Nina's first birthday Anna was presented with drawings of a modern house designed by a Norwegian architect. They moved in when Nina was five, so that she could go to a country school in the green outskirts of the city.

"Do you have a picture of this Norwegian Scottish house?"

"Not with me. Hundreds at home. My mother took hundreds. Every time she repainted, added something – it was all documented. She really loved it, every inch of it."

"And your dad still lives there?"

"He still lives there, though he rattles around and it makes him sad. It drags him down. He doesn't realise how it affects his mood. I keep telling him he ought to move."

"He still misses her."

"He was the one who wanted a divorce."

"That doesn't mean he doesn't miss her. Doesn't mean he doesn't have regrets."

"If he did he'd never admit to them. But I see it in him sometimes: guilt. Not directly, but he can be short-tempered, which isn't like him. He gives a little and then there's a flat refusal to discuss it."

"What's he guilty about?"

"Falling out of love."

"Well," Dr Christos said. "Nothing can really be done about that."

"Is that what you think?"

"Of course. Don't you? Nothing can be done about falling in, and nothing can be done about falling out again."

"I used to think that, but now I'm not sure. I'm not sure about the terms. Anyway, who am I to say?"

The house was a big flat rectangle, and passers-by could see, through the vast nine-paned window, an interior that glowed in waxed pitch-pine fittings, with a room-height white enamelled stove in one corner and substantial wooden stairs going up to a gallery. The walls were grey and the picture frames white. The low-slung modular furnishings were all in pale colours; tall vases of naked twigs were decorated in Christmas tree lights – all of this utterly alien to village culture in the 1970s – and on the wall opposite the window there was a blue and green abstract with ad hoc upright metallic lines at its centre, that Anna always said made her think of her summer home, the lake and the sprawling birch forest.

Anna's real mother never married and lived elsewhere and had to work long hours: this was the official story of why she was raised by her grandparents, though the prime reason may have been that she'd looked too much like her mother's married ex-boyfriend. He'd turned up sometimes on Anna's birthday with elaborate gifts, but the trouble was that he didn't always turn up and there wasn't any way of knowing if he would or not, because his name was never mentioned. Anna said that she remembered several of her birthdays as days of nausea, of false hope. But she had said this to the teenage Nina with a bright-eyed philosophical look, shrugging as she spoke about it.

"It must have been hard," Nina said.

"Everyone has something about their lives which is hard." She looked thoughtful. "But this is all in the past, and the past should be shrugged off. I'm serious about this: this is the best advice I'll ever give you, so listen. It's vital to live in the present. Live now. Not in everything that's gone wrong; not in tomorrow and what that might be like. Neither of those days really exists."

"They feel like they exist, though."

"If you don't live in the present, right now, then it doesn't exist either. You end up with three non-existent ideas of time, all three of them."

Dr Christos was doing his daily work session in Nina's room, busy replying to email, and Nina, who was writing her journal, found herself watching him working. She wanted to tell him everything, the whole story. She felt as if she was coming up onto a beach after a long swim. She could take this oblique route into telling him about Luca; she needed to tell somebody what had happened and there wasn't anyone else she could tell. She would begin with her mother. She said, "Do you find yourself thinking about things your parents said when you were younger? My mother's been on my mind a lot lately; things she said to me."

Dr Christos considered. "I can't remember anything my mother ever said to me. Other than for the day-to-day and things I had to do."

She told him what her mother had said about time. "Don't you think that a determination to live in the present might also be a refusal to have feelings about things?" As she was speaking an elderly lady in a floor-length pink dressing gown came into the room. Dr Christos took her hand and led her out again, speaking soothingly, and they went off down the corridor together.

Nina went out into the garden, to the steps that led to the shore, and watched an old couple walking along at the edge of the water, a man and a woman, both rangy, leathery, bare-chested, light-haired northern Europeans. They couldn't have been further from Anna's grandparents' style, which had been buttoned-up and conventional, though not joylessly so. Anna was very different from the people who'd parented her, although some things from her childhood had stuck fast. She'd turned over a big section of the plot to a vegetable garden, and had made clothes for herself and for Nina: skirts with appliqué, with strips of ribbon and velvet at the hem; bright summer dresses with big pockets. She was always looking for ways to save, a natural saver, taking absolute delight in the numbers rising in her blue savings book, despite the money, despite the half a million pounds secretly accruing interest in the bank.

When the grandparents visited Edinburgh – which they managed only once, already well into their eighties – Mormor (the Norwegian name specifically for a maternal grandmother) had tutted her disapproval of the size of the new house, the cost of heating its open-plan spaces, the heat loss that was inevitable through such great showy windows, though she approved of all the wood inside and the tall stove. She liked the many old things bought at low cost from sales and junk shops, the recycling of old quilts, all the second-hand kitchenware. Anna had taken pleasure in touring the house and showing her what she called the Finds: the 50p colander; the antique linens bought for £2 a bundle, though she'd spared her the sums spent on other things – the astronomical amounts (Mormor would have thought) for light fittings, sofas and mattresses. Mormor would have keeled over.

When Dr Christos came out to join her and their conversation resumed, she told him about the Norwegian visitors and about the finds. "Your mother would have fitted in well here," he said. He began typing again and Nina looked at him, imagining his face if Anna were to walk into the room, his reaction to her. He'd be taken up and swept along, as all men were, as all men had been. Anna had been a man-magnet, and Nina, though she looked near identical, just hadn't been, not really; not in the same way. There had been some quality about Anna when she talked to a man, an absolute focus on them, inviting eye contact; it had also been about the use of her mouth and her awareness of its movements, her own obvious awareness of her body, fiddling with her hair as she spoke and that way she had of rubbing her shins, her knee-caps, when seated. The radiant smile, everything in her alive, alive; even in her forties everything about her radiating youth. Nina imagined Dr Christos after a half-hour of chat with Anna Olsen Findlay, his eyes glassy, his face obedient, his whole demeanour lost and craven.

She said, "It's fashionable now in the UK to have what they call vintage – you know the word vintage? – but it was considered a bit weird then, to have second-hand things. Paolo's mother was snide about it, though never to my mother's face." Then she added, "Mum knew, though, that she was privately snide, and referred to it once. She could be a bit tactless, sometimes. She didn't get on that well with other women." She thought, *And here I go, trying to talk a man out of being a little bit in love with someone who's dead*. It wasn't the first time she'd done it.

Dr Christos, oblivious, replied, "We can't buy clothes or furniture without crossing the water, and so if someone gets bored with a chair or a coat, they swap it. Sometimes they get the original thing back after a dozen swaps. It's the kind of thing we do to cheer ourselves up in the winter. Andros takes the seats out of the minibus and we move things around."

She'd been dying to ask and now she did. "What does your house look like? I must have walked past it every day on the way to the beach."

"It's small, painted white, with a blue door and red flowers on the window ledge. Like every other house, in fact."

"What's it like inside?"

He looked up from working. "Very simple. There's a tiled floor, four chairs and a table. Also, highly controversially, white sofas from the mainland. That caused some excitement – my white sofas arriving on a lorry from Athens. But I also have cupboards that were my family's, ones that came from the farm and that nobody wanted. There's not much else to tell. It's one big room with two bedrooms above. I have a good kitchen and a summer kitchen at the back, an outdoor one for the summer, leading out to a small garden. We grow a lot of our own food; the local shopping's limited, as you know."

"You're right, my mother would have fitted in well. She was a housewife in a very 1970s style, a practitioner of crafts. It was all about the furnishing and bettering of the home, in low-cost labour-intensive ways, at least once she met her friend Sheila, who was even more into it. The house tracked my mother's life. That's why it was so hard to leave; it was part of her and she was part of it. When she left, she was bleeding and it was bleeding."

"Nina. Are you alright?"

"I'm melancholy today, thinking about things I don't often allow myself to think about. I'm never sure if sharing a problem, a bad memory, is a good idea or not. My mother always said that a problem shared is a problem doubled."

In April, the day she'd left Paolo, Nina had intended to go to a hotel; she wanted to be in an anonymous environment and to be spared having to relate to people, but when she got into the back of the cab, asked by the driver where she wanted to go, it came to her that what she really wanted was to be in her childhood bedroom and in her childhood bed. She had two suitcases and a laptop and an envelope of old photographs: these had been the priorities. Coincidentally, aside from the laptop, this was just how Anna had left Robert, in a cab with two small suitcases and a bag of photograph albums. Robert was taken aback by his daughter's arrival on his doorstep, but he acclimatised quickly, convinced the separation wouldn't stick, that it was just a row that would be resolved in the morning. He and Nina sat in the dark nursing glasses of whisky, the only light in the room emanating from the lit stove in the corner, steadily emitting its sweet chestnut wood smell. She didn't want to talk about what had happened with Paolo, Nina said. She asked if they could talk about her mother.

"What is it you want to talk about?" Robert's voice was softer than usual. He didn't like it when Nina was upset. She'd arrived at the house weeping and in a state, alarming the taxi driver.

"You and Mum. It was good, wasn't it, when I was young? It was good for most of my childhood. It wasn't all a lie."

"It wasn't all a lie." Her father swirled the amber liquid, attempting the slowest possible swirling, slowly round the crystal tumbler.

"I remember your nights out, on Saturdays when I was little. You seemed happy then."

His concentration intensified, as he sent the whisky into reverse, counter-clockwise, before answering. "We were. We were very happy then."

When Dr Christos was called away, leaving her in the garden, Nina took up her crutches and went to a lounger in the shade. One of the old ladies – the same one who'd wandered into her room, an IV needle fixed into the back of her hand with tape, her hair set in soft silver curls and her pink dressing gown lavishly embroidered – came and sat in the adjoining chair and read a book, having first said hello and attempted a little conversation, to which the only response was "Sorry, no Greek", words spoken with an accompanying guilty shrug. It wasn't the first time this had happened, nor the first time that Nina had apologised; perhaps the old lady had memory problems. She had scaly legs and yellowed thickened toenails, but beautifully manicured fingernails, the same glossy pink as her robe. They smiled at each other, in the way that their attempts always culminated, and then she went back to her book, which seemed to be about a series of grisly murders, judging by the cover art. Nina looked up at the awning above her, its yellow and white stripes. She looked beyond it, into the dense chalk blue, in which aeroplanes had drawn faded white trails, and gave up all her senses to remembering. There was a dress of midnight-blue velvet, Anna's favourite over many winters – a dress with a neckline trimmed in blue-black satin. Velvet and then satin: Nina could still feel the transition under her fingertips. She could still call it up at will, the scent, her mother's scent, the warm mother-liness of skin, the smell of hairspray supporting the chignon, and Anna's pale hair in the near-dark, as she brought her face close to Nina's, her blue eyes very close to her own. "Now you be good for the sitter."

"I will."

"A promise is a serious thing. Do you promise?"

"I promise."

"You're not going to keep getting out of bed and bothering her, are you?"

"I'm not." Even now, the smell of toasting cheese sandwiches reminded Nina of insubordination.

"We're going to the golf club to eat prawns in pink sauce and steak with onion rings, and then I'm going to dance the night away and get indigestion."

"But you'll be back in the morning."

"I'll be back long before the morning; it's just that you'll be asleep when we get home. If you're not, you can come and get in if you want, and cuddle up."

What safety had there been since then? There hadn't been safety since then.

She and the babysitter had watched television, though the sitter had always turned it off when the car came into the drive with its warning white lights. Robert was vocal on the subject of there being a hundred better things to do than sit in front of the tellybox, though when he was away Anna and Nina had TV binges and laughed at the badness of the bad. On those evenings that Robert wasn't in his study working, Nina would find her parents sitting together in their usual way, at right angles on the G-plan sofa, the big L-shaped sofa that occupied a corner. There was always music playing and Robert would always be reading, though Anna would interrupt him from time to time, and they'd pull themselves upright to sip at the wine; there was always wine, sent from next door in limitless supply. Nina could hear the audio of their evening from her bedroom, if her door was left ajar: her room was off the galleried landing that looked over the double-height sitting room, and their voices rose and dispersed like smoke, a drowsy nocturnal hum that was love and home and sanctuary.

Sometimes she'd go onto the landing, unseen behind the wooden balustrade, and watch them, glimpses of them, hearing her father's pessimistic remarks about the world, its dark future, and Anna trying to counteract them. Robert had a tendency to be gloomy and withdrawn, but Anna, never; she was the antidote, always, and she'd be as inventive with him as she was with her child. Nina had come into the sitting room once and found her mother washing her father's feet in a basin. These acts of grooming were mutual, which seemed at odds with her father's usual daytime austerity; there was another, unsuspected aspect to her father, something she struggled to square. He'd volunteer to wash Anna's hair when she went to have a bath, and he'd brush it out for her at bedtime. She kept it long because Robert liked it.

If Robert was in one of his intense work cycles he'd come out of his study for dinner and then return. There wasn't any arguing with work: the rest of the household had to curl itself against its polished stone monolith. It was the basis of everything, he'd remind them: there wasn't any house or food on the table without his job and there wouldn't be a job without the right kind of atmosphere to work in at home. It was just how it was and hard to argue with, but it also meant that Anna spent a lot of time alone. Nina remembered coming out of her bedroom once when she was small, sleepless at midnight, and seeing her mother sitting upright on the sofa with her toes braced against the edge of the coffee table, staring into space. Robert must have been in the study, but his music was on the record player – usually it was Schubert, Dvorak or Richard Strauss; Anna had won the battle to keep Wagner out of the evening rotation. Nina had gone and got on her lap and asked if she was all right. She'd had intuitions then, which had passed out of her at puberty, her old alertness to nuance replaced by the inward-looking gaze.

"I'm very good indeed," Anna said. "I'm a happy person and so are you, but sometimes I think about sad things. Not for very long. But sad things need to be thought about sometimes."

"What kind of sad things?"

"Oh, you know. When people die. That kind of thing."

"So what was it, Dad?" Nina asked him, the night she arrived on his doorstep. "You seemed happy. There were no signs whatever of unhappiness."

"Well, the same could be said of you and Paolo," he'd said, looking almost triumphant.

She didn't rise. "Explain it to me."

"It's hard to explain it to you."

"Try."

"It's not about reasons, Nina. It was never about reasons. It was about feelings. It was what I felt."

Nina stared at him, at his profile, unable to see a way forward in what she had hoped would be a final and frank heart-to-heart. How could he continue to wear that sweater, the Guernsey fishing sweater knitted from a dark-blue wool, the one that had gone at the elbows and that Anna had patched for him once, long ago; she could still see the tiny neat stitches around the suede. How could he continue to associate himself with those stitches, all that painstakingly stitched love?

Dr Christos appeared. "Lazy, lazy Nina. Get up. Come on. We need to get your blood moving. We're going to walk around the grounds, one circuit only. You need someone with you, so I'll come." He helped her get into position on the crutches, making swift passes of his palm across her upper back, his hands settling briefly on her shoulders, and followed closely behind down the side path, into a world of enveloping heat and glare. When they got to the main entrance, the electronic glass door, Nina felt utterly drained, light-headed, and had to sit down at the hospital bus stop, on the yellow bench. Dr Christos sat beside her looking at his phone. Across the road the hill rose steeply, and goats could be seen clustered halfway up. Nina put her hand to her forehead, shading her eyes, the better to see them. She thought she could see it, the goat that had featured in the accident. She stood up. "I'm going back indoors. I'm feeling a bit woozy."

"Let me help you. It's very hot today."

Nina took one step and said, "I've got to sit down again."

He put one arm around her, binding her tightly, and the other onto the left crutch. "Give me this and put your arm around my shoulder. We mustn't have you falling."

Back they went in slow progress around the hospital building. Once she was settled Dr Christos made her drink the tepid water from the jug, and took her blood pressure and pulse, his fingertips soft on her wrist. He said, on leaving the room, "I'll be back again soon to check up on you."

Nina was just drifting off to sleep when her phone rang and it was Paolo. "Right," he said without preamble. "Is there anything you want me to bring from the cottage?"

"To bring?"

"Nothing you need? I'm going over to see your dad and I'll be driving right past. He's fine too, before you ask. He's invited me for dinner."

"Because you're flying tomorrow and it will save on cooking and cleaning time."

"Exactly so."

"If you have room in your bag, could you bring me the stuff that I left behind on my bedroom chair? A pink and white dress, dark-pink cardigan, blue trousers and shirt."

"Consider it done. Let me just write that down." After a pause he said, "Also, I need to tell you something. I'm seeing someone. Karen. Outside of the office, I mean."

"Karen your assistant?" Karen was an attractive 30-year-old Australian with short red hair.

"Your dad wrote to you about it but I gather it got posted late."

"Karen, really." Her heart palpitated, but it was just the surprise. It was, as Dr Christos had said, entirely to be expected, a continuing possessiveness that didn't really mean anything. It was just possessiveness, and having to come to terms with being replaceable. She said, "Are we getting all the hard stuff out of the way on the phone before you arrive?"

"It doesn't seem like there's much privacy there."

"I'm sure Dr Christos will keep his distance while you're around. He's already said as much. Look, you have to understand this: he's been great and he's given me lots of his time. I've been really alone here. I arrived with four books and there are two other English-language books in the hospital. The television is all Greek to me. The days are very long."

"You should have said; I could have sent books. Still, all that time. You could be working."

"I haven't felt well enough to concentrate, not until the last few days."

"You could have been writing your memoirs. Have you been telling the doctor your life story?"

"Not really. A bit. Highlights."

"He knows all about it, then."

"Some. The bare bones of it, the thing that happened in the spring. The disgrace: he calls it the disgrace. He's moral, a moral person. A churchgoer." What was she saying now? It seemed like this was already spooling out of control.

Perhaps Paolo saw this. He'd always changed the subject if he thought she was lying. He said, "So I'll see you the day after tomorrow. You can go back to chatting to your handsome doctor now."

"How do you know that he's handsome?"

"Google, obviously. Google has the answer to all questions."

When Paolo rang off, Nina had a nap, and then when she woke Dr Christos was there in the blue chair, with paperwork and the calculator. He said, "Balancing our budget would take a miracle of some kind."

"You need someone like Paolo."

"Paolo's an accountant?"

"Among other things. He's good with money. He can persuade it to bend to his will."

"That indeed is a gift I do not have," Dr Christos said. "Perhaps I should employ him."

"I don't think you could afford him."

"You sound proud of him when you talk about money."

"Ouch."

"Just an observation. I apologise. So when did you and Paolo get together?"

"At Luca's wedding."

He gave her a wide-eyed look. "Wow. Really. And what did Luca think of that?"

"He seemed to approve. But it had already become a huge tangle: what Luca felt, what I felt, what both of us really felt, how that corresponded or didn't to how we behaved. It's continued to be a huge tangle."

"Will you tell me, who it was that you thought Paolo was really in love with when he married you?"

"My mother. Paolo was in love with my mother."

Chapter Thirteen

It wasn't even as if the evidence amounted to much. It's a peculiarly human failing, the leap to conclusions; it must have an evolutionary purpose. Perhaps the point is to hurry things along and to introduce into every human life a frolicsome element of carnage. There wasn't anything like carnage, in this case, but there was yearning. For him, perhaps first love. For her – who knew for sure? – perhaps not the last.

Paolo and Anna had always known each other, but when Nina was seventeen she'd seen Paolo begin to look at her mother in a different way. She told Dr Christos that she could remember the day she first noticed it. It was an afternoon in early summer, and also, in a way, Paolo and Nina's first date, though of an outstandingly casual sort. (There wouldn't be another one for over three years). Paolo came to tell Nina that he was going to the cinema and to ask if she'd like to tag along. It was a film she'd told him that she wanted to see, just trying to make conversation. More and more, Nina found herself devising lists of things to talk about before seeing him: where he'd been, his tennis, what he was reading, how work was going. It was always very different with Luca. Nina and Luca, if put together in a room, would talk nineteen to the dozen – "Turn their keys and set them down and watch them go," as Anna said once – though that wasn't true in this particular year. Two years on from the kiss in the garden, Luca's silence had built and built, as if silence could intensify its nothingness, and Nina was at the apex of misery. A key part of her unhappiness was that Luca didn't appear to be suffering any ill effects at all. He'd swivelled away and was seen to be paying enthusiastic attention elsewhere, to a life that was merely otherwise. So, Luca was in his silent phase, and Paolo, in his socially awkward way, had become attentive.

The doorbell rang, on that warm afternoon, and Nina, who was lying on her bed with a book, did what she'd always done and crawled out onto the gallery, crouching at one of the gaps between the planks of the balustrade so as to observe unseen. She always hoped that it'd be Luca, though it never was. The doorbell rang a second time and she heard her mother, busy making a casserole, shout that she was coming. Anna opened the door to find Paolo there, standing on the step of the porch, tall and dark and broad-shouldered in a red plaid shirt and putty-coloured chinos, his hands in his pockets. He had grown to six foot four. He was experimenting with a stubbly beard. He was nineteen and looked 25. Nina didn't go down immediately. Sometimes she'd keep very still so as not to make a sound, when Paolo was on the doorstep asking if she was in. Anna knew not to push it, if Nina didn't answer when she called her. She'd say Nina must have gone out; she knew what Nina's silence meant. Though Nina didn't always hide: sometimes she'd invite him in and make a pot of tea and put on music of her father's, earning his polite thanks, and watch him do a crossword and chip in a bit. She could hand him a newspaper and pick up a magazine; she'd done it before and he didn't seem to mind. She might do that today. She was feeling low and that had made her bored; she was bored almost beyond endurance. Sitting with Paolo listening to sad German songs would be better than lying on her bed feeling sorry for herself.

She was going to stand up and make herself known, but when Anna opened the door Nina saw it in Paolo's face, his infatuation. He wouldn't even have noticed her. His infatuation was absolutely obvious.

"Mrs Findlay, hello, how are you?" Christ. He was blushing.

"I'm very well, thank you for asking, but I'm afraid Nina isn't here. I think she's gone to play tennis, Paolo, but she won't be long. She's never late for dinner." Paolo smiled. It was a two-families joke, Nina's appetite. "Do you want to come in and wait a while?"

Paolo said something that Nina couldn't catch, and then the conversation continued at a whisper. Anna was looking down at her feet and Paolo was doing the same. They were lightly tanned, her toenails painted the usual shell pink; Anna never wore shoes or slippers or even socks indoors, and not always out in the village either. Her bare and blackened soles were locally scandalous. Paolo said something, evidently something funny, and Anna laughed and it seemed like a private moment, a slow laugh that bore a trace of its private beginnings. They continued to talk as if what they said had to be concealed from eavesdroppers. Why else would he dip his head so conspiratorially, his hands on his hips? Why else would she echo the posture so she could reply? There were, suddenly, no innocent reasons. Nina was finding it harder to breathe quietly.

Anna was wearing the yellow dress with the halter neck. She was still using her clothes from ten years before, and still had that old era's habits, persisting into the 1980s. She was braless in the dress – in fact, rarely wore a bra at all; Maria had been heard to snipe that she had no use nor need of one. She'd used the word bony about her neighbour, and also the word boyish.

Giulio had taken issue with this description once. "Hardly boyish," he'd said. "She has a tiny waist."

"Skinny legs," Maria countered.

"Skinny maybe, but shapely," Giulio had said, absolutely unaware of the thin ice where he was walking.

Anna had been doing some gardening. Her shoulders and arms were golden and she'd rubbed in a jasmine-scented cream. Her white-blonde hair was up in a hastily gathered knot, bits of it falling at her ears. She was 42 years old and looked far younger, though not quite young enough to be Nina. She was Nina down the road, in years to come, an experienced and worldly Nina, a more obviously feminine Nina, a possible Nina, a version of Nina that men were going to like: one who wore dresses and showed skin and looked men in the eye and was quick to laugh, and facilitated conversations that made men feel good about themselves. There was little wonder that women disliked her. There was little wonder that Paolo found himself drawn.

Paolo followed her into the kitchen, which led off from the sitting room down a double step to Nina's left. Nina went down the stairs, stealthily in stocking feet. The voices were audible now.

She heard her mother say, "Well, that's the thing about Luca, isn't it?"

She heard Paolo say, "I have to agree, even though he's my brother." His formal way of talking grated. Luca made fun of it and aped him.

Nina went down the steps into the kitchen, startling them both. Her mother's hand held onto the waist of Paolo's jeans at the back, and she let go and stepped away, a swift balletic sidestep. A small hairslide had fallen out and she replaced it by one ear. "Darling!" The way she said the word it was possible she was horrified. "I thought you were off playing tennis. I thought you had court time until" – she looked at her watch – "until ten minutes ago. Paolo wants to take you to the cinema, the early showing."

Nina said, "Is Luca going?"

Paolo looked at Anna when he answered. "He saw it yesterday. He says it's good."

"I don't know. I've just got going with something. I'd better finish." Nina was about to sit her final school exams.

"Okay then. Never mind."

"What a shame," Anna said. "But you could do it tomorrow, surely."

Paolo looked hopefully at her. "Why don't you come with me, in that case? Seeing as Nina doesn't want to."

"I could come, I suppose," Nina said. "I do want to see it."

"You should come with us," Paolo told her mother.

"Thanks, but I don't think that would be the thing. Robert's home soon in any case."

Nina looked at her watch. "Are we going for the 6.30?"

"Yes. Plenty of time."

Anna couldn't help but cast a maternal eye over Nina's clothes, swiftly top to bottom. She said, "Perhaps you'd better change."

Nina looked down at herself, at black jeans that had worn grey at the knees, a rock band T-shirt that she'd bought at a market, and big red socks that she'd taken to wearing turned over the tops of chunky laced boots. Nina had thought she looked good. She'd seen in the long cheval mirror that morning a girl who looked quirky and interesting, her eyes smokily made up with a kohl pencil, her waist-long hair crimped by sleeping uncomfortably in plaits after washing. She'd left the two front plaits in, fastened by ironic pink gingham ribbons.

"Do I need to change?" she asked Paolo.

"Not at all," he said. "I'm going like this. It's only the Odeon."

She was nervous and foolish in the car, aware of the eczema flare-up on her fingers, her long thin fingers, hiding them between her thighs. She asked inane questions about the various levers and buttons. She said, "It's very clever to be able to drive," and he'd barely humoured her, just directed aimless smiles vaguely towards the passenger side as he concentrated on junctions and roundabouts. She'd stopped exclaiming and he'd not filled the quiet with remarks of his own. She'd looked surreptitiously at his convex belly in the red shirt, his big hands on the steering wheel; his hands were identical to Luca's. She brought her mother into the conversation in the cinema queue, twice, and he'd not picked up the thread either time, but had looked seriously ahead as if still driving. They watched the film, which was embarrassingly erotic at points, and hadn't said much on the way home. He'd looked relieved when she said goodnight and went up the path to her door.

Anna was waiting in the kitchen, her face lit up with expectation. "So?"

"The film was good. Nice. It was fine."

"Just fine? Only nice? No second date arranged?"

"It wasn't a date."

Paolo had gone in to find his mother waiting for him in the hall, grim-faced in the gloom, her arms folded under her bosom. She didn't say anything, not until Paolo had dropped his keys on the table and groaned. Not until Paolo had banged his head against the heel of his hand and said, "Paolo, Paolo, Paolo Romano," in a voice that was openly despairing. She'd said, "I kept your supper warm." She'd followed him into the kitchen and dished up the cutlet and mash, and watched him eat. Eventually, as he rinsed the plate, his back to her, she'd asked, "And how's the Findlay girl?"

"Nina," Paolo corrected.

"How's Nina?" Maria spoke the name as if it was preposterous.

"Nina's fine. Nina's lovely actually. She sends her warm regards."

A few weeks later the Findlays and Romanos went out together for the evening, to an open-air concert in the gardens of a country house in honour of Maria's birthday. Her favourite tenor was to be the special guest. Their two cars went in tandem, southwards out of the city and down increasingly rural roads, into gently hilly countryside that was dotted with pretty villages and ancient woods. The event took place in the grounds of an Edwardian mansion, on a stage built at the far side of a lake so that the end of show fireworks would duplicate in the water. Everyone was dressed up, but it wasn't a warm evening, so most people were wearing coats over their good clothes. Over Anna's navy-blue silk dress she wore a fuchsia-pink shawl that was almost a blanket. Nina was self-conscious and awkward in a long black skirt and white lace shirt of her mother's, and was grateful to be able to wear a baggy black sweater of her dad's over the top. She'd bought a trilby at Oxfam and wore it low, pushed down to her eyebrows. She was wearing joke earrings – they were tiny plastic toilet rolls – and postbox-red lipstick. She didn't say anything to anyone all evening.

The two families spent some time pondering where to sit. It had rained a couple of days before this, so their first choice of spot proved to seep damply through their picnic rugs and into their clothes, arriving with a sudden Oh. "Oh! This is wet, I'm getting wet." Eventually after experimentation they opted for a grassy hillock, which had a flattish section before the small hill rose bumpily again.

"It's also going to be excellent for an unimpeded view," Paolo told them, having gone ahead.

"An unimpeded view is important," Luca agreed, his mouth twitching.

It was time to unpack the picnic bags. Paolo said that he'd do it but Luca was already on the case, lifting out chicken legs and antipasti from tupperware into bowls. Paolo said he'd see to the wine, filling two buckets with ice from a flask, and Luca began to pass round the plates and napkins, raising his hand against offers of assistance. Paolo took the plastic glasses out of the shopping bag, one of his mother's with a noisy zip, and was about to hand them round when Luca muscled in, taking them from him, saying, "Perhaps you should give Mrs Findlay a hand." There wasn't any doubt that this prompted a look, an exchange of looks between the brothers – audacious on one side but promising death by a thousand cuts on the other.

Paolo said, "Mrs Findlay, can I assist you with that?" He looked utterly miserable.

"No, no, it's fine," Anna replied. "Nina will help." It was Anna's back that spoke; she remained turned away and spoke from over her shoulder. It was obvious to Nina why this was: her mother needed to be so brisk because she'd picked up that Luca was beginning to be mischievous. There was always a risk that Luca's mischief might escalate. Perhaps in addition Luca knew something that Nina didn't.

Anna said "Come on, Nina; chop chop, spit spot," and Nina came to her aid, lifting out a spiced ham from its wrappings. They'd also brought whole prawns and pickled sliced cucumbers and a potato and dill salad. Everything was laid out now and ready and looking enticing, prompting a jokey attempt by the people sitting next to them to trade sandwiches and beer. Lights and sounds and movement began to be seen and heard from across the lake, as the technical crew busied themselves on the stage.

The two bottles of fizz were drunk quickly, and now that it was time to open the white wine Luca realised he hadn't packed the corkscrew. He said it had got lost somehow and began irritably emptying the bags. Paolo produced his key fob and its miniature device, holding out his other hand for the bottles to be passed to him. When Luca tried to snatch hold of the keyring Paolo held his arm up out of reach. "Just pass the bottles over," he said, with studied sweetness. Their mother brought the skirmish to a halt. "Luca." It was all Maria needed to say. "Oh," she added. "Giulio has the corkscrew. He put it in his bag. Where is his bag? He is wearing his bag. Of course he is. Is anything done right if Maria doesn't do it herself? No, it isn't." She looked around. "Paolo, go and get the corkscrew from your father." Paolo got to his feet and set off across the grass.

Robert and Giulio were under the trees to one side of the park, having gone off at the first opportunity to stretch their legs, which meant in short to have a cigarette. The whole party watched as Paolo went over to the men, and spoke to them, and kept speaking to them. Nothing seemed to be happening.

"It could be hours," Luca said, picking up a piece of ham and a slice of Anna's brown bread.

Maria slapped the back of his hand. "Not until everyone's at table." She continued watching as they stood talking, saying, "Paolo's a lovely boy but he has absolutely no natural authority." Meanwhile the musicians had begun filing onto the stage, the men in dinner suits and bow ties and the women in long black dresses. Maria stood up and signalled to Giulio, and the threesome began to walk back, albeit slowly and in a way that communicated that really they were too engrossed to be bothered with eating, or music. "You're so bloody selfish," Maria told Giulio when he got within earshot. "It's supposed to be my night, remember. You're not even going to sit with me, are you?" He didn't answer her. He sat beside Robert and kept talking as if nothing had interrupted them.

Paolo took up the serving spoons and said, "Right, let's get organised. Anna – some tomato salad?" It was the first time anyone had heard him call her Anna. He reached his arm out towards her for her plate, but instead Anna gave her hand to him. She wasn't thinking what she was doing, as she'd say to Robert afterwards in the car. She'd been talking to Maria, who occupied a deckchair, and wasn't thinking what she was doing.

"No – your plate please," Paolo corrected.

"Oh!" Anna exclaimed, laughing and withdrawing. "I am such a silly billy." Paolo put a little of everything on her plate and when she took it from him she said, "Thank you, darling." Nina's heart lost its footing for a moment, until she'd reassured herself that her mother called everybody darling.

When Paolo took his own plate and went and sat down beside Anna, his hand landed over the top of hers, just as if he'd misjudged the space, and Anna lifted her index finger and passed it over the back of his hand, twice side to side, *tick tock*, as if she were brushing an insect away. There wasn't anything else that could be, nothing, other than an endearment, a stolen moment in a crowded room. The other moment they shared was less private. After they'd eaten, when the intermission came, Luca set a trend by taking a cushion from the pile they'd brought and going further up the slope, lying so that his head was resting on it and his feet were downhill. Nina went and lay beside him, although he didn't react as if she had, and Anna followed suit, going to sit straight-backed next to Nina. "Come on, Paolo," she said, patting the grass beside her. "So comfortable, and a brilliant view."

"Unimpeded," Luca added.

Paolo complied, holding a cushion and a glass of wine as he sat down, which was over-ambitious. He crossed his legs and tried to lower himself and lost his balance and landed askew, going down onto one elbow, his head falling onto Anna's lap. "Oh well, look, here's a nice surprise," she said, putting her hands delicately around his dark mop of hair, looking down at his face and smiling. It had been a few significant seconds before he pulled himself up and out of the way.

Dr Christos looked expectant. "Yes? So what happened next?"

"Nothing. At least, I didn't see anything else."

"I'm becoming confused. You seem to be giving me one reason

after another for not marrying Paolo."

"My mother's death made Luca impossible."

"How was that?"

"She didn't like him. But I was surprised to find it was a once-only offer. And I was really surprised when he seemed keen that I marry his brother."

"What was he like at your wedding?"

"He ignored me at the reception, quite pointedly ignored me, until we were about to leave for the airport, cheerfully looking in the other direction the whole day. But then... then he kissed me. In the bathroom. I went in there and he followed."

"Why did you do that?"

"It was goodbye. The last time."

"But you'd just married his brother."

"It didn't feel like a contradiction. I didn't want to take my clothes off. I didn't want to take his clothes off. I just wanted to keep talking."

"It wasn't talking, though, was it?"

"It was just kissing. That isn't adultery. It's just kissing."

"Of course it's adultery."

"It seemed harmless at the time. It made a dull life a lot more exciting."

"Poor Paolo. The dull husband."

"No. You misunderstand. It wasn't about anyone else's dullness. It was all about mine. I struggle with boredom, you see. I struggle not to be bored with a good life. Always have. I'm so very much not like my mother."

"Why not marry Luca, then, and avoid boredom?"

"But what if Luca and I had been dull together? What if it had all worn off, our thing, whatever you want to label it – what if he'd had a fling? What if, even worse, he started having lunch with another woman, and what if he kept his phone in view all the time, hoping she'd text him?" She flicked through the novel she was holding as if the answer lay inside. "When we got back from honeymoon we had a flat-warming party. Luca kept his distance until the end, until I went and fetched Francesca's coat. He followed me into the room and said he hoped that Paolo and I would be happy. I said we were already, very, blissfully. I remember the words. 'We are already, very, blissfully.' He looked absolutely stricken. I wanted to put my arms around him."

"What a mess."

"You say that, but the truth was that I was cheered up. He needed me the same way I needed him. It was something that passed between us. I was also his someone to run to. We had something that would never fail us. We thought so, anyway. It didn't work out that way."

"You and Paolo: you were happy? At your happiest – were you happy?"

"I thought so. I thought I did a really good job of being married. But Paolo says not."

"I'm sorry. That's hard."

"I find it difficult to judge now, but I thought we were fine. I thought the way we were together, how we lived together, how we talked to each other, what we did, how we were when – well ,anyway, I thought it was all how it was for everyone. But Paolo surprised me, when we broke up. He said that Luca had always been in the way."

"How could that have surprised you?"

"It did. It surprised me very much. Because Paolo was in on it. They were all in on it. Luca and me: we were the basis to two happy marriages. Don't you see? We weren't the hindrance. We were the basis."

"How did you and Paolo get together? You said it was at Luca's wedding. Were you making a point?"

"It wasn't Luca; it was another date a few days before that did it. I wanted to take someone to the wedding and that's the only reason I said yes when this boy asked me out."

"Who was he?"

"An old schoolfriend. But I didn't take him to the wedding in the end. We had one date. He was good company, talkative, into politics, actually incredibly boring about the politics, but we knew each other well and it should have been easy. We went to the pub and I began to feel panicky. I didn't know how to behave, how to talk. He held my hand and I stared at it because it was so odd. It wasn't a Romano hand. When he kissed me his tongue was cold and slimy and tasted of tobacco. When I saw Paolo at the wedding, the way he looked at me: I knew."

The door was open. All she needed was to push it a little. All it took was to go up close to him and to look up at him, into his eyes, until he bent and kissed her.

"He was waiting for a sign."

"He was. And in fact, I'd been giving him signs for months. Since Luca got engaged. When Mum died, I changed, you see. I became a different person."

"In what way different?"

"In almost every way. It was time to change."

When Anna died Nina had begun to dress as her mother had done, in fact, for a while had worn her mother's old clothes, her 1970s dresses, and that transformation had made all the difference. It had turned Luca off and Paolo on. Luca had been openly appalled, at the engagement party, to see how like Anna Nina looked, her hair up the same way and wearing one of the old frocks. It was good to give up the faded black jeans and the walking boots and repel him: she needed to assert her independence from his approval. Like so many things in life, it was all about timing. Timing, and femininity and smiling and legs.

"If you dress like a boy Paolo will treat you like a boy," her mother had said, when Nina got back from the cinema that time, the day of the yellow sundress.

"I don't mind that; I'm not interested in Paolo," Nina told her.

"You should be. He would make a good husband. He's a lovely boy, and much more suitable than Luca."

"More suitable?" she'd said, aghast.

"You laugh at me but marriage is a contract. That's something you children overlook. It's important to think about what your life will be like, what it will be like over decades and also hour to hour."

"Mum. I'm not going to marry for ten years at the least and probably never."

"It's your life," her mother said. She'd say it in a singsong voice, giving the word *life* two syllables.

"And anyway, what makes you say that Luca is unsuitable? Not that I'm interested in Luca."

"Luca is only exciting because – well, basically because he's mean. He's mean, Nina, and a bully."

"You don't know him at all," Nina said.

Chapter Fourteen

The day that Anna died was the first time Nina and Luca slept together.

Nobody else knew or would ever know: so Luca said, though that turned out not to be true. Nina had never told anyone. She woke alone in her mother's flat with two kinds of grief: one that had become part of her, that ran in her blood and was ineradicable, and one that was really an anger, to which it seemed there might be a solution and an end. Anna's passing had changed her for ever. She lived in this now, inside the loss of her mother; she'd remain unborn inside her death for the rest of her life. The problem of Luca was of a different kind. Luca was, in a way, the more immediate problem. She'd offended him, and he'd left at 2am without saying goodbye.

They'd lain together in Anna's spare bed, in the room Anna had furnished and prepared for Nina, but which Nina had never used. This was something else to feel guilty about. Once Luca left she slept in the sleigh bed her mother had bought her, in cornflower-blue linens, newly unpacketed and smelling faintly of dye, their creases still evident. Anna had added touches that made it look as if Nina had been there already, as if she lived there: framed posters from recent exhibitions and a white bathrobe, nineteenth-century novels stacked in the bookcase, and beads and scarves hung across the mirror. Nina dozed and had bad dreams, and so when it began to get greyly light, a cool chill dawn, she rose and put on the bathrobe and looked out of the window at the city roofscape, which was becoming steadily more three-dimensional. She went through to the kitchen and boiled her mother's kettle, and then emptied the boiled water out and refilled it and boiled it again. She opened the wrapping of the rye bread her mother ate, and looked at the cut end of it, and rewrapped it and boiled two eggs instead, and ate them with salt, and drank tea, opening the new carton of milk and disposing of the opened one, and all the time crying noiselessly in a way that was more inconvenient than anything, because it was ceaseless and itchy and dripping. She took the next tissue from the box on the dresser and found she couldn't use it, and had to use the one beneath.

The flat, a Victorian top-floor with coombed ceilings, was a rental that Anna had taken unfurnished, and though she hadn't been able to paint the landlord's magnolia walls, she'd bought vividly coloured furniture, pea green and sky blue and Indian pink, and striped rugs, and curtains made of sari fabric. She'd installed gold buddhas and Australian art, African masks and artefacts from all over the world that were like stand-in souvenirs of all the places she'd never been. Robert hated to travel and had only been enthusiastic about desolate Highland scenery and the conquering of hills. She'd hung pictures of Nina that she'd had enlarged to A3, some of which featured Luca and Paolo, on beaches and in gardens. She'd said, "It's wonderful to be able to do these things without feeling that I need permission."

After breakfast Nina returned to her mother's bedroom and stood a few minutes at the threshold looking in. It was done out in monotones, in contrast to the rest of the flat, with dove-grey linen curtains, a room-sized grey and white rug and, across the four-poster, a white bed canopy that Anna had made from junk shop sheets and lace. Nina got into the bed and drew the top blanket, one of thick mole-grey velvet, up over her ears. She put one hand questingly under first one pillow and then the other and found Anna's nightdress, which was long, with a heavy fluidity of satin drape that was a steelier grey in colour, and held it to her face, feeling its silkiness and enjoying its human scent, her mother's scent, the jasmine body lotion and just a hint of odour at the armpits of the thing. She saw that on the top of the chest of drawers there were purple silk pyjamas, put there in readiness for the nightdress going in the wash. Nina felt herself caught in a disappeared human event, suspended inside one of her mother's last thoughts, one of her last anticipated actions; changing the nightwear for an evening that wouldn't come. She got out of the bed, went to the wardrobe and slid it open and saw that it was sparsely filled: some things on hangers, the rest in neat piles on open shelves and not a dress among them. Anna hadn't brought her old clothes; she had lived in trousers and tunic sets made by a home-based dressmaker originally from Pakistan, a widow who had moved into the house at the other side of the Romanos. Why had she used Maria's neighbour, and gone all the way there on a bus? Nina had wondered if it was a way of saying that she wasn't afraid. Robert would say later that he hadn't seen her go by, not once.

When she'd looked in her mother's wardrobe Nina wanted urgently to leave, though locking up her flat seemed like a terrible thing to do, like shutting in a child, callously ignoring her pleas and leaving her. She went down the three gloomy flights of hard stairs, through the green halls, each with their ironwork banister, past the maroon-painted Victorian front doors of strangers, each with their brass nameplates, umbrella stands, doormats, their faint remnant cooking aromas, and went out onto the street and hailed a taxi. The driver had the heating on full blast, and so by the time she got to her dad's house she was sweating and felt toxic, her organs unclean, her pores emitting an uncleanness that was the result of sleeplessness and upset and alcohol. She and Luca had drunk a bottle of prosecco, and then a bottle of Montepulciano d'Abruzzo, a Romano & Sons bottle they'd found in Anna's kitchen. There was a note from Paolo sitting at the bottom of the box. *Hope you enjoy*, it said, and underneath that, *with love from Paolo*. Paolo, it turned out, had kept her mother supplied with wine. By the time Nina got out of the cab she was keenly aware not only of a general toxicity but of Luca's smell, mixed in with her own, and was grateful her father wasn't there. He'd gone to the university. He'd warned her already that that was where he'd be. He'd said that only work was going to make him feel better.

Luca's arrival the previous evening had begun with a phone call. He'd heard from Maria, when he got home from the office, that Anna had died unexpectedly that afternoon, and phoned the house next door, hoping Nina would be there. Robert had answered and Luca had expressed his sorrow, in a rather ungainly, unprepared way, and then Robert had volunteered the information that Nina had insisted on staying over at the flat. Luca rang her there and told her he was coming over with a cheesecake and a bottle of fizz. Nina had protested: she couldn't eat cheesecake, she couldn't drink. Her mother had died. Her mother had only just been taken from the flat, like an object, like garbage, in a black bin bag disguised as a coffin. Luca said that no, on the contrary, prosecco was just the thing. They were going to celebrate Anna, her life, in just the way that Anna had when Mormor died. It had made a big impression on the Romano family, Anna's insistence on a death being a celebration of life. So he'd arrived, and they'd hugged, and they'd drunk a lot of wine. They'd got drunk and then he'd kissed her. He'd said, "I know what it is that both of us needs."

Neither had any real idea what they were doing. This made Nina self-conscious and clumsy, but Luca became very grave, as if following unseen instructions. It was unfortunate that this in turn made Nina giggly. Luca had told her to shush.

"Shhh," he said. "Don't think, don't talk; concentrate on touch and sensation." He climbed naked off the bed and got down on both knees and said he just wanted to look at her, and she became aware of the look that had taken charge of her face, the sceptical, embarrassed look. He ran one hand over her near thigh and hip and onto her stomach and crossed over a nervous frontier of some kind, and Nina went into spasm as if she'd been tickled, and laughed and drew away.

He'd said, "You need to relax."

"You're telling me to relax?" She sat up and drew up her knees to her chest and pulled the sheet over herself and rested her forearms on it. Nothing now could be seen of her other than from the shoulder up. "Luca, my mother died today. She died. Here in this building. In the next room."

"Let me take you somewhere else than that."

"Somewhere else?" Nina's own voice was stridently practical.

Luca stopped the stroking abruptly. He looked disappointed in her. "Nina. Don't you want this?"

"I'm really hungry." She didn't want her first sexual experience to be here, and not on this night, but there wasn't any way of telling him that, not now. What she wanted was another kind of physical attention: to have her back stroked and her hair played with. What she wanted was toast. She wanted him to put his clothes on and go and make her some. She hadn't been able to face the cheesecake.

"We'll eat afterwards," Luca said, moving in and pushing her gently back onto the bed and setting the sheet aside.

The thing she'd imagined would be momentous was brief and unarousing, a quick exertion in her passive body, Luca not meeting her eyes as he moved, his face fascinatingly vacant. Nina kept it to herself, the brevity of it and how impersonal it had been.

In any case it had been fine: Luca held her very tightly afterwards, saying he was sorry about Anna and that he'd miss her. "It hasn't sunk in yet that she's gone."

"Gone," Nina said, as if it were a word new to her. "Oh no, no. I'm not going to see her again. I'm not going to see her face again. This is goodbye. Not even goodbye. I couldn't even say goodbye to her." She'd cried and cried.

"We had sex twice, and both times it was because someone we loved had died," Nina said, taking coffee from Dr Christos. The cup wasn't quite inside the saucer's indentation and almost slipped off as it was passed across the bed.

"Had sex. I don't like this 'had sex'. It's so unromantic."

"What do you prefer? Made love? We made love." In retrospect that was far too romantic a phrase. "Then when I stopped crying, Luca proposed. He said I needed someone to take care of me. He said he wanted to. He said, 'Will you marry me, Nina, and love me the whole of my life?' He looked as if he meant it."

"And you said no."

"I said no. And I'm afraid that I laughed."

"Ouch."

"It was shock. It was the surprise of it that made me laugh. I wasn't laughing at him, as he insists that I did. Anyway. Yes, I offended him. He got dressed and he left. Recently when we talked it was obvious that he still minded. He said, 'You laughed at me, when I asked you to marry me.' He still minded. I said, 'My mother had died; she'd just died', but that didn't seem to make a difference. Laughing was the unforgivable thing. I reminded him that he hadn't even come to the funeral; he'd sent flowers from Italy, suddenly finding he was needed in the Roman office."

"That must've hurt."

"He said it was my fault. He said that I'd made him very low, but that Italy had worked its magic on him. I was straight in there. I said, 'And Francesca, she worked her magic on you, too.' Depressing, how people talk to one another, isn't it?"

Arriving that morning in the cab from her mother's flat, her mother's key still enclosed in her fist, Nina saw the family house and its contents differently, as if she was visiting it a long time later, as if months had passed since the death and not eighteen hours.

Once she'd showered and dressed, once Luca's persistent scent and wetness had been removed, she went into what had been her parents' room. She needed to know how different it would feel to be in there. The door was locked but the key was still in it, ready to turn, and it was noticeably chillier inside than in the rest of the house; Robert had turned off the radiator when Anna left, and had moved into the spare bedroom and its single bed. In a way that was undefinable the room smelled of Nina's childhood. Perhaps it was to do with manufacturing, something as prosaic as that, the old ingredients of paints, carpets, toiletries and fabric conditioners. She looked at herself in the cheval mirror, at the tall skinny twenty-year-old with the bags under her eyes, hung-over and no longer a virgin and exhausted by crying. The girl who was her – and simultaneously not – was wearing dark jeans and a sky-blue American college sweatshirt, the red socks and a pair of red DMs. The clothes were wrong, now; somehow since the day before they'd become startlingly wrong. She opened the wardrobe door and was confronted with a row of Anna's dresses. Anna was dead; everything in every moment repeated this impossible thing in her brain. Not only that, but Luca wasn't going to be hers. That too was over, for reasons no one else would have understood. In any case, for the time being it was something she felt nothing about. She couldn't, she couldn't; it wasn't possible to have all these feelings at once. She took out a Liberty print dress, a shirt dress her mother had made from a purple and blue floral fabric, and took her clothes off and put it on, and put her hair up, pulling down strands to sit by her ears, and rubbed baby oil into her arms and shins, and smeared vaseline on her lips and eyelashes. There she was, reflected back at herself, a hybrid Anna-Nina, near identical to the Anna of the early photographs.

Photographs. There were photographs here that Anna had said she no longer wanted. Nina cast an eye over the bookcases and didn't see the albums, which were bound in a dark-red leather; she pulled the chair from the dressing table and swept her arm across the top of the wardrobe and found nothing. Nor were they in the drawers of the bed – the divan bed Anna had hated but that she'd bought for Robert because of his back. She stood surveying the room, then returned to her mother's wardrobe, opening its pine doors and pushing her hands between the coats so as to open up a space, and there they were, stacked on the bottom beside a jumble of shoes. She pulled three of them out, took them into the sitting room and settled herself in the elbow of the sofa.

The first one she opened was entirely of trees, garden trees and village trees in black silhouettes and in close-up. To have amassed a whole album of pictures of trees... it was almost too much. The tree studies had only been possible because of Anna's absolute confidence; her safety, her illusory safety. The trees made Nina cry again. She said aloud, "Oh, Mum", as she turned over the pages. They were more upsetting, the tree pictures, than the last family album, chronicling the final holiday, its pages of views and sights and buildings and lunches. It had been Anna's camera and so there were few pictures of her and Robert together, but plenty of Nina and her dad, doing holiday things in holiday backdrops. It was Anna's first visit to France, somewhere she'd longed to go. Robert had organised it as a surprise. They'd spent a week in a villa near Nice, before travelling west, a chunk of the Midi at a time, past vineyards and canals, past salt-flats and hilltop castles, over the Pyrenees and into Spain. Nina studied the photographs closely, but couldn't see any of them written there, the things that her father later said he'd felt. Why had he organised the trip? He hadn't needed to. It was an odd thing to do in the circumstances. Perhaps guilt was at the root of it, guilty even before the fatal thing had been said, wanting to give material compensation in advance to a woman he no longer loved.

Nina took some of the photographs from the third collection with her to Greece. They'd been fixed to the pages with glued-on corners and had been easy to take out. She'd put them into a manilla envelope and had them now, some held in a pile in her hands and the rest scattered onto the white sheet. This album had been dedicated to Grandpa and Mormor's summer home, somewhere that Robert never visited; he'd use Nina and Anna's absence to get on with work undisturbed. The lakeside setting was quietly spectacular, though the house itself was properly rudimentary, with a basement at the damp ground level and plank stairs going up to a wide veranda. Inside was tardis-like, seeming far bigger than it looked from the front, its main room fitted with two curtained box beds in niches. Nina always said she had fantastically happy memories of being there, each summer with her mother, and that was true when she was ten, but at fourteen she'd been bored after the second week and had itched to get back to Paolo and Luca.

The older photographs, the black and white ones, were of Anna just before she met Robert, Anna at 22 at the lake house in a swimsuit. The swimming costume had its own moulded pointy breasts, and Anna's small waist had been accentuated by its belted style. She sat with her legs to one side, revealing long brown tapering thighs, one hand up, laughingly protesting to the camera operator, and the other holding onto her floppy-brimmed hat. There were pictures of Grandpa and Mormor, too: Grandpa Sven had a ship's captain's beard and smoked a pipe, the constant drift of smoke narrowing his eyes into sea-blue slits, and had distinctively calloused, gnarly hands with enlarged knuckles. His being frustrated creatively at the furniture business was the reason that the lake cabin had become an ongoing DIY project. Over the years he'd refurbished and remodelled it, installing its panelling, its carved beds and window frames, its built-in storage, its beautifully dove-tailed dining set, and Anna had photographed his improvements. Nina saw her mother with the camera, barefoot in shorts and a bikini top, her smooth tanned back. She smelled her sun-warmed, lake-silty skin, and now, out of nowhere, she saw her turn to look at her.

"Why did Anna leave the Norwegian pictures in the wardrobe?" Dr Christos asked. "Surely they were precious to her."

"It's a good question," Nina said. "Sometimes I worry that it was because the album upset her. As if it reminded her of a time in which she was about to make a bad decision."

"Marrying your father was a bad decision?"

Nina didn't answer. She ran her forefinger over a close-up shot of Mormor, whose real name had been Kristjana, whose dad had been Icelandic and who was as short as Sven was tall. Traces of her were seen in Anna's long nose and wide cheekbones and little chin, but she'd had dark almond eyes, and brown hair that even in her youth was striped with bands of wiry grey. She'd been photographed at the desk by the window, in the act of writing a letter, and Nina found that she was beginning to imagine herself at the lake, working. She was beginning to look in that direction, at possibility, at the open road and the sun shining down on it. There wasn't any reason why she shouldn't go back and forth as she wished. These days her main duty at the publishing house (one

she didn't often mention because it was embarrassing to admit to)
was as a re-writer, reworking poorly written books that had been
produced by people with good ideas but no talent for expressing
them. Other than for fitting in with the publisher's schedule she
had no obligations to be anywhere at any given time. She could
have a semi-detached sort of a love on her Greek island, something sensible and lovely, and come and go; she could spend part
of the year in Norway and have people to stay; the people she
loved could come and go in drifts. She saw, in her mind's eye, Dr
Christos coming up the wooden steps, barefoot with bits of wood
he'd found for the stove. Evidently she could imagine him there,
for there he was, like his visit was already a memory.

After-dinner coffee had been a mistake. Nina was still awake at
1am, the whole hospital hushed, aside from one of the old ladies,
who talked in her sleep. She rearranged her pillows, wincing as the
twisting prompted fresh pain, and lay back, listening to the noises
coming in from outside: the soothing percussive zizz of cicadas, the
occasional voice magnified from elsewhere, a motorbike echoey
on the hill road. The smaller window was open, its mosquito-
netting frame in place. They'd had nets at the lake house, also, so
as to keep the insects out. All the July days they'd spent at the lake
had merged into one, a single remembered summer made from
condensing all the summers. The visits had come to an end when
Nina was fourteen, the year that she was openly bored, although
the boredom wasn't the reason it had been the last visit. Anna and
Nina had only been back in Edinburgh a few weeks when Grandpa
Sven died. They had gone to the funeral together – Robert was
excused – in head-to-toe black, Anna in a fitted suit and a hat with
a veil like Jackie Kennedy. Mormor seemed, in the month since
they'd last seen her, to have become someone much more elderly
and frail. When they returned home Anna said that she'd have to
do a lot more visiting from now on, a plan Robert wasn't keen
on, saying they should bring her to Edinburgh, to a good nursing
home. But it didn't matter in the end. Kristjana only survived her
husband by one autumn, and then at Christmas she too was gone.

Two of the photographs had become stuck in the envelope. Here
was Anna at a wedding in a green silk dress, the one with the
Chinese collar, her hair pinned and twisted in a complicated up-do,
and here she was pictured at a dance in a gold off-the-shoulder

number. It occurred to Nina that she'd never seen a picture of her mother in which she wasn't smiling. Anna had always kept the household buoyant. Had she known that Robert might fall out of love with her if her buoyancy faltered? Even if she had, she couldn't have foreseen the catastrophe that would come when Nina went to university. Lately, Nina had come to feel at one with her mother on this question of jollity. She had felt, her whole married life, that she carried the mood of the marriage in herself, at once dictating and embodying it. If Nina was withdrawn Paolo took his cue and was more so, and the whole house took on a dreary aspect, the food like ashes in their mouths. Luca was different, the opposite, and it was a thing about him that she'd always cherished. Luca upped his own jollity and raised the morale. He would have said, "Come on, droopy face, we're going out for dinner." He would have found a funny film; he would have taken off his sock and talked to her via a hand-puppet; he would have made a chocolate fondue; he would have instituted a thumb war; he would have insisted she dance with him; he would have been physically overpowering, dragging her off the sofa and rolling her across the rug, persisting until she smiled into his eyes and their bond was re-established. That's how Luca was, and they were all things he'd done with his sister-in-law already, at family get-togethers and on holidays. Paolo had never done any of them. Paolo seemed to expect Nina to provide; she was depended on as the source of fun and lightness in his life, as if Nina was really Anna all over again. This had been clear to Nina when she moved out, that Paolo had married her thinking he was marrying Anna, and that it had been a mistake. He'd referred, in the last conversation in their marital kitchen, to the trouble he'd had with her depressions. He was dragged down, he said, and he didn't want to be dragged down.

Nurse Yannis came in to see Nina, scowling. "Your light is still on," she said. "You must turn it off and sleep." She cast a practised eye around the room and was gone again without saying goodnight. Her initial friendliness seemed to have petered out, and nor had her mother come to the hospital to kiss Nina's hands; it hadn't been mentioned again. Had Nina annoyed or offended the nurse in some way? She turned off her light and lay blinking in the dark. She saw herself at eight years old, curled up with her mother, giggling and tickling with feathers they'd found in the garden, ignoring Robert's warnings that they were probably diseased. They'd made and then eaten a whole lemon cake, a cake intended for when he got home, eating it with their fingers, the topcoat of lemon syrup crusty with unabsorbed sugar. They'd made crumbs over a hilariously wide radius of the house, unable to explain how some had got onto the stairs, and had laughed helplessly. These were the kind of things Nina remembered, and though she knew that her repertoire of quotable days was actually small and repetitive, she'd made a decision not to let new information discolour it all, not to let doubt seep in and instigate its slow rot. Her childhood must remain intact. She could still say, without risk of secret self-contradiction, that most of it had been absolutely happy – her heart swelled with good memories – and that was enough. There were many things to be nostalgic about, though Luca wasn't one of them. Not any more.

When Nina arrived to take Anna out to lunch the last time – though she hadn't known it would be the last – her mother had been stitching by hand, having left her machine behind. The radio was on and she hadn't heard the door; Nina, who'd let herself in, surprised her by appearing in front of her, and Anna had knocked her sewing box onto the rug. They'd searched and searched and were confident they'd found all of the pins, but one had been missed. It had stuck in Luca's foot, at 2am on the night after she died, when he was dressing and looking for his shoes. It had gone in deep and it had hurt him. Remembering this, lying sleepless in the island hospital, it was hard not to see it as a warning.

Chapter Fifteen

Nina looked at her watch for the fifth time.

"What time are you expecting him?" Dr Christos asked, as if he didn't already know.

"About three. The boat gets in just before three."

"It's going to be fine."

"Of course." Nina found she was patting the sheet. She was sitting on top of the bed, dressed in white trousers and a thigh-length white smock, and long stone necklaces in sea blues and sea greens that she'd bought at the gift shop. Her arms were brown against the white.

"It's bound to be tricky." He took her hand in a doctorly way. "The last time you saw him, you told him you'd slept with his brother. That's bound to be a little bit awkward."

The moment for minimising had come. She said, "It'll be fine. It's not like we haven't talked about it. We might not even discuss it. He needs a holiday; he'll pop in every day to see how I am and it won't even be mentioned, because it isn't appropriate here."

"That's possible."

"But the other possibility is that he's come to thrash it out, that it's all he'll want to talk about. Maybe that's why he came five days early. Oh God."

Dr Christos went and looked out into the garden, and then returned. "Have you given any more thought to my suggestion?"

"I can't think about that now."

"This is the best time to decide. Looking forward is your best defence."

"When are the rentals available from?"

It looked to him as if the decision was being made right then, in real time. "November the 1st."

"Okay. At least, I'll give it some serious thought." Nina took a deep breath. "Also there's something I want to tell you. Before Paolo gets here. Something Paolo mustn't know." If she was going to live here, she had to tell him the rest.

Dr Christos looked at his phone. "My meeting's been delayed. "We have time."

"Where to start. When I came here, to Greece, I mean, it was clear that everything terrible that'd happened was my fault."

"You're too hard on yourself," he interjected.

"I haven't been hard on myself though, that's the trouble. I thought I was right about everything. I thought I understood everything. And then when I nearly died – "

"You didn't really, you know. Nearly die. But go on."

"There are things I decided never to tell. Self-protective, I thought. I'm getting better; I'm so much better, but a lot of that has been about getting it back in place, the self-protection. Do you understand?"

"Of course. It's what happens when people get better." He smiled at her. "They reacquire their old inhibitions."

They looked at one another.

"I've been talking to you for – how long has it been? I've lost track. Weeks. But there are things I haven't dared tell you." Her voice became uneven, and he looped his arm around her neck and pulled her closer to him.

He said, "This will pass." His face remained close to hers. "I'm going to get you a brandy from the crisis cupboard. The bottle we keep for accidental deaths."

When he'd returned with it, Nina said, "The thing is, I've always kept Paolo at a distance, and then when Francesca died, even more at a distance."

"Why was her passing so important?"

She didn't address this. "When I pushed Paolo away he only went a short way, and then he waited. There were other people I pushed away who stayed away, people who proved to be easily deterred. Close friends, people I'd always thought were friends. I told myself I was happier not having to deal with people, but I wasn't happier."

"Well, if it's any consolation, I have so been there, as my American child would say."

Nina wiped her eyes and blew her nose. "Where does your American child live?"

"In Baltimore, where she was born. One of the girls identifies as American and the other's Greek and they never see each other."

"That's a shame. They Skype, though, I imagine."

"They don't. They don't really email either. They manage to misunderstand each other even by email. You know – you could have borrowed a laptop and had email and the internet. It would have been a lot less boring. Nurse Yannis said she'd offered and you didn't want it."

"Thank you. She's right, I don't want it, not yet. It's hard to explain, but inside a computer… that feels like somewhere Luca is, where Luca lives, that's still about Luca and me. That's how it feels right now – I'm just telling you how it feels – to the extent that even the physical equipment, the laptop, even my phone – it's as if it's all his territory, our territory, part of an old way of life. I'll figure it out but for now I need to stay away."

"It's addictive. I've had whole weekends that have disappeared, not even getting out of bed."

"I'm afraid of it at the moment, like I won't be able to stop myself from reconnecting with him if I return to the old haunts. That it won't even be something I choose."

"I understand that."

"I want to want different things."

Dr Christos looked down at the suitcase, which lay spread open on the floor. Some shoes were in it and some clothes; three of the four books and some of the souvenirs, stowed away in their floral paper bags. "Are you packing?"

"Not yet. Just having a sort-out and making sure everything fits. Nurse Yannis has been helping as it's difficult to reach down."

"Has she… has she said anything more to you?"

"About what?"

"Just about anything."

"Not a word. Why?"

"No reason. You could always leave things with me, for when you come back."

"I'm counting on Paolo to have room in his bag. He'll come with six shirts and a razor."

"Just say, won't you, if you want to stay a few more days. There isn't any rush."

"Don't you need the bed?"

"Quite the opposite. We've kept inventing reasons for you not to be discharged. We've massively exaggerated your concussion."

"You're joking."

"Not really, no."

"Don't you feel bad about lying?"

"Not remotely. I have no issue with it. It's just another tool."

"Just another tool?"

"Of course. Don't look like that. I bet you lie just as much and as often. About Luca, for instance, and about the timing. It was before you moved out but you said it was after; you didn't tell the truth about that. I lied to my wife for years. She knows that. She knew at the time, but she didn't want to spoil things and it would have spoiled things."

"What sort of lying?"

"Other women. Where I really was when I worked late."

"Ah. Ah, I see, I see."

He saw the look on her face. "My wife and I – we should never have got married. But when I find her, the woman I need...I'm looking for the person I'll be with when I'm very old, whose hand I'll be holding when I die."

Nina said, "Can I ask you a really straight, blunt question?"

"Fire away."

"Did you have a fling with Nurse Yannis? Was she one of the women you had an affair with?"

"Nurse Yannis?" It was his turn to look appalled. "Nurse Yannis. No."

"I'm sorry for asking."

"You don't need to be. Ask away."

"Your wife knew, and she didn't say anything."

"She left it to me to feel bad on my own, and eventually I did feel bad, and it was only when I felt bad that she left me. Life's a funny old game."

"Isn't it."

"Once the secret was out in the open, a whole load of secrets, they had to be dealt with and we couldn't go on as we had been. We were happy when I was a liar, and unhappy when we told the truth.... are you all right?"

"Could I have another small Metaxa?"

"Of course. I wish I could have one."

While he was gone Nina had cause to ask herself why she was going to tell him what she was about to tell him. Was it because she was saying goodbye and so it no longer mattered? Or was it because she wasn't saying goodbye, and needed to know how he'd react to hearing the worst?

When he came back, twenty minutes later and apologetic, Nurse Yannis had delivered the mail and Nina was reading a letter from her father. Now she was overseas he talked to her more than he'd done in years; the letters kept coming. This one was all about her garden. There was a list of things he thought she should plant, that would suit the conditions. He was going to weed out and clear most of the borders, he said, but had attached a sheet detailing the shrubs and perennials she might want to keep. He'd divided the page into a grid and filled each box with a drawing, captioned with both the common and Latin names.

"That looks interesting," Dr Christos said. "Have you told me yet – the thing you wanted to tell me? Not knowing what it is, it's hard to know."

"I'll get to it."

He could read her anxiety. "So what's come in the post?"

She showed him the beautiful sketches. "This is what my dad's like," she said. "He's relishing this. It's a project and he's good at projects. Better at projects than people."

"Was he a distant sort of father?"

"Not distant exactly. He took an interest in me and we had conversations, though his approach was usually quite purposeful. 'Let's talk about weather patterns, Nina. What do you know about how the weather works?' We didn't interrupt him in the study unless it was for a good reason. Dad's a euphoric workaholic, and lately I've seen that I could be the same. I've found myself wanting to disappear into it."

"What's his subject?"

"Modern British history. Right now, the First World War. He loves it, the work, everything about it. Mum explained it to me like that, that it was love."

"It wasn't love between your parents?"

"Absolutely it was. Until the bad year, the separation. They were devoted to one another. I thought that, at least. Everybody thought that."

"Were they wrong?"

"Who knows. People are revisionist about their feelings. They lose sight of how they felt, when they no longer feel whatever it is. Feelings are the hardest thing of all to remember, to put yourself back inside of. Don't you think?"

"What happened in the bad year?"

"There was a conversation they hadn't had before. They had a disagreement about what they'd do when I left home. And then my mother moved out. They separated, she moved into a flat in town, and then a year later she died. She was only my age."

"I'm sorry."

"I was the one who found her. She'd sent me out to get shopping. I came back with it and she was dead."

"That must have been a terrible shock." He looked shocked himself. "Poor Anna; poor, poor Anna."

Anna had been too tired to go out, but wanted to do something and decided she'd make a pear tart. Nina returned from her mission that drizzly, ordinary Tuesday with the ingredients it turned out Anna didn't have – the ground almonds, the vanilla extract – and found her mother stretched out on the sofa on her back, hands folded over her stomach, in perfect peace and symmetry. There was something disturbing about this implied acceptance. She couldn't think what to do: should she call the doctor, an ambulance, the police? What did you do first when someone died? She picked up the phone and dialled emergency services, and called her father and he came straight over. They stood looking at her together, Nina crying into her father's shoulder.

"That's not Anna any longer," he said. "Anna's gone; your mother's gone, Nina. She's passed over."

He'd used the language of his childhood, trying to comfort her, but neither of them really believed that Anna had passed anywhere. That *was* Anna. Anna was finished. Anna had come to an end. The whole labyrinthine question of life's origins, life's postscript, was the only issue that had brought Robert and the teenage Nina into alliance, and had caused Anna real sadness; Nina was determined about her atheism just at the time when Anna was devout. It was part of her small rebellion, that and dressing like a boy, not wanting to be a part of what her dad once called "the whole dismal culture of unsubtle self-advertisement" (the phrase had stuck in her head and cheered her, even now). As a student, she'd gone to charity shops and bought old tweed suits that smelled of wee, which was a common student thing back then, sometimes even wearing them with shirts and flamboyant ties. The mannish clothes upset Anna, as did Nina's apparent lack of interest in boys; Nina had only found out just before coming on holiday that her mother had wondered aloud if Nina might be gay. Robert had thought it was one reason Anna kept pushing her at the Romano boys, because she needed to know.

"Mum had been ill for months with this mysterious constant tiredness," Nina said. "She kept saying that she was on the mend but it was obvious that she wasn't. It transpired that one of her friends – Sheila Medlar – was saying privately to the others that her optimism was a big act and that really she was severely depressed. I hated her for that. Hated her."

Dr Christos looked dismayed by her hatred. "You don't think it was a kindness? Sheila telling the other friends that Anna was low?"

"That's how my dad sees it. He's unshakable that Sheila was devoted to her."

"You don't think so, though."

"It was vital to Mum that people did not know how low she was. Even me. I was also protected. It was only afterwards when I saw things she'd written that I knew how it had really been. She saw lying to me as protecting me, and her lying was a kind of love. She was determined to be thought to be coping and making the best of things, but Sheila insisted on seeing through it. I can't see that as a kindness." Nina looked again at her watch. "Mum never showed the truth to me, not once. That's the thing that upsets me now. She was always sunny, positive, a rock, but there's a cost when you're somebody's rock, isn't there? I thought that she was different to other people, that she had a knack for happiness. I still say so, when people ask about her, and ask how she was on her own, after the separation. I continue to be loyal. It's a kind of a loyalty to the view of her that she wanted me to have."

Anna hadn't known how ill she was. She lost faith in life and then in God, and thought that this double sense of let-down was enough to explain the trouble she was having climbing stairs. She returned to the village to see her doctor, and at first Alison was content to latch onto the obvious – recent depressing events – to explain her problems, and gave her drugs she didn't take. Anna made a dramatic exit from the church Bible group shortly after this, travelling back to the village again, so as to end her membership face to face. She told them, the assembled company, that she couldn't any longer believe in the goodness of a god who contemplated suffering as part of any kind of plan; when you stopped believing in God's goodness, she said, you seemed to have disproved the whole idea of God. They were convinced that the dissent was really to do with the breakdown of the marriage. Two women from the group visited her at the flat, to appeal to her to stay and to find love through fellowship, and then they went to see Robert when she died.

"Anna lost her faith, and I have never had any, and so you're wasting your time," Robert said to the women, both of them short-haired and in long loose dresses. "Worse, you are wasting my time." One had made the mistake of putting her hand on his shoulder, as if faith were a transferrable thing being transmitted through his collarbone, and he'd been very direct about his feelings after that. The women had fought back. Maria had come out of her house to see what all the commotion was about.

"Let me share something with you," this same woman had said, when visiting Anna and attempting the same manoeuvre. "Sometimes God makes our lives hard because that's what we need. Sometimes we need to have a harder life."

"You think my life with Robert was too easy?" Anna asked her. "What do you know about my life with Robert?"

Later, they'd recounted this conversation to her husband – for what purpose was anyone's guess; perhaps for moral education – and that's what had led to the shouting.

Nina had tried to explain all this to Paolo, and why it was that she couldn't – physically wasn't able – to get married in a church. He hadn't attempted to explain her reasons to his mother. Maria wasn't ever very interested in reasons, and in this case it was a position Paolo had some sympathy with. He was perfectly happy to think it was all rubbish and to appear to be devout when socially necessary. He didn't understand Anna's church, but nor could he grasp Nina's resistance to it; it was just church. In their teen years Paolo had gone to mass with his mother routinely, whereas Nina's only concession – as an act of loving hypocrisy – was to go with Anna to the midnight service on Christmas Eve. She'd found the experience infinitely depressing, all the mystery and beauty of the season reduced to a tedious travelogue of shepherds and inns. She wanted to hear about other things than that, about magic and paradox: how a virgin could be a mother, what or who the Holy Spirit was, and if God really did manipulate the movements of stars. What if the Big Bang that brewed up all our little accidental intelligences also made one freakishly vast one, a chemically induced god who found Himself alone, and also, to his own surprise, mortal? What if His person was physically contained in the expanding universe and had expanded too much, His lights dimming steadily over time?

Dr Christos said that his meeting had been postponed and that they should get some fresh air. Nina didn't look well, and there was time before Paolo arrived. Out in the garden, there wasn't yet any sign of the boat. Nina looked again at her watch; it was still only 2.45. When they got to the steps to the beach, the doctor took the crutches from her and balanced them against a table. "Lean on me," he said. "To give yourself a rest from those damn things. Put your arm around my neck."

"I'm okay resting against the barrier." She put both hands around the horizontal pole. It was interesting, this: her mind wanted to go forward into a relationship with him but her body didn't seem to agree. He might know this; he might want to discuss it as if it were a knot that could be unknotted. She needed to keep away from the whole question.

"What was it that you wanted to tell me?"

"I'm too tired." She kept it simple. She shouldn't even have flagged up the existence of the thing Paolo mustn't know. Off in the distance, on the beach beyond the harbour, the heat haze had rendered two figures insubstantial, even flimsy, as if they were only a trick of the light. Nina watched them under a sun-shading hand. "I know you don't believe in ghosts," she said, "but I used to see my mother when I was out shopping, ahead of me in the crowd and then gone."

"You don't see her any more?"

"I don't. But I did. I used to see her. That's what changed my mind about the spirits of the dead. I think they're real. I know they are. Where does that lead us?"

"You are wonderful," Dr Christos said, still facing the sea.

"I like you too." It was true, but what else did it mean? Perhaps only that they were in the same predicament. What was going on? She'd lost all faith in judging her feelings. Anna had given lots of good advice about keeping control, but she'd had her heart broken, nonetheless.

One day, out of the blue she'd asked Robert, in what was really only a conversational gambit at dinner, what he thought they should do when Nina left home. It was a light-hearted comment, whimsical, but he didn't seem to want to answer. He looked uncomfortable; he started to prevaricate, and so she began to press him – what did he mean, what was the matter? He said he thought that their life together was coming to an end. It had been wonderful, he said, but life was short and it should be about growth and change, when the appropriate time came. Anna couldn't react at first; she sat open-mouthed, having been absolutely wrong-footed. It had been a wonderful 21 years, he said, but now that Nina had left the family home he thought it would be better for both of them to pursue their lives in different ways. He was sure that if Anna thought about it she'd become as excited as he was about the possibility of a new life, of travel, of pursuing new interests.

"Of pursuing new women," Anna interjected.

"It's not about that," he said, in his practised tutorial fashion. "Why must you be so reductive?"

"You don't love me any more," Anna said, her voice breaking.

"No, I don't think that I do," Robert told her, looking pained. "I don't know why. I've felt this way for a while. I can't explain it. It's just something that's happened. I'm sorry this is happening now. I'm sorry, Nina, that you had to be here for this."

Nina had fled to her room, and Anna had gone after her, to comfort her.

Chapter Sixteen

Everything had been fine, or at least in some kind of balance, or at least in abeyance, until Francesca became ill. The illness was a shock to everybody, but wasn't at first regarded as a crisis, because it was thought that the cancer had been detected early. By mid-May in the year before she died she'd had surgery and chemo and seemed to be on the mend, and she and Luca went away to a swanky hotel to celebrate. The day they got back was also the day that Nina and Paolo went off to Rome for their annual visit; Nina accompanied him there on business every spring. Thanks to this overlap of away dates there hadn't been any contact with Luca for over a week, and so when she got into the car at the airport and turned her phone back on, Nina was surprised to find no messages waiting. Ordinarily there'd be a backlog of them in all formats: texts and emails and things written to her via social networks. Ordinarily the most recent would say, *Are you here yet? Talk to me. Tell me everything.* That was the normality, and the conversation would resume. Whenever she answered, even if it was hours later, Luca replied immediately, and if she didn't respond fast enough for him there'd be increasingly dramatic accusations it was impossible not to laugh at. He was always predictably direct. If she said, *Talk later,* he'd reply *Talk now. Can't wait. Medically urgent.* Even though Nina was absolutely staunch in her belief that it was harmless behaviour and harmlessly life-enhancing, this state of affairs could be tricky, domestically.

Paolo was tolerant, but tolerance had its limits. She had to limit the text exchanges while they were watching a film, for instance, even though (as she always argued) most television was more entertaining if you were also bantering with someone else at the time. (The net result was more happiness, so what was the issue?) If she replied at the dinner table to the question *What are you eating?* Paolo might pretend not to notice. Or he might say, "Nina, enough. He can wait. Turn it off."

Sometimes Nina was irritated by this. "It's just fun, Paolo. It's just Luca."

He'd wave at her from across the table. "Hello. Hello Nina. I am here. Perhaps you'd be more interested in me if I texted and tweeted you." Nina had to bite her lip because there was something in what he said. She and Luca had discussed this very thing: people did become more incisive, sharper, more lateral, when they were trained to be so by interacting online and by having to condense their experiences and thoughts; it was good synaptic exercise. Privately, she thought that Paolo could do with a bit of that intense verbal jousting and wordplay. But Paolo was disdainful about socialising on the internet; it had become a sore point and she'd learned not to challenge him on it.

When they got back from the airport Nina went looking for Luca in all the usual places – she'd never known him to have 24 hours of absence – but he hadn't updated his blog for nine days, nor been on Twitter, and nor had he posted photographs from his holiday. There hadn't been anything on Facebook, either, not since the two of them had competed one night, almost two weeks earlier, to find the better bits of old children's TV on YouTube. His last offering had featured Windy Miller of *Camberwick Green*, a show that was broadcast the year they were born, disappearing in the closing credits through the top of a music box in a slow rotation. That didn't seem like a good sign.

The silence continued. Nina sent a few messages about Italy, and looked at her phone throughout the first evening home, wondering why he wasn't communicating. Eventually she texted him. 'Are you dead?'

He didn't reply until the following day. *Too depressed for chatter. Hope Roma was fun.*

What's up?

Her phone pinged. *Meh.*

Okay, well if you want to say more you know where I am.

Thursday. Lunch. 2pm at our usual place.

The usual place was the same one as ever. It was tucked away down an otherwise commerce-free side street and then around a corner, and wasn't somewhere they ever ran into people they knew. Luca was late, this particular day, so Nina sat at their table in the corner and drank a glass of red wine and ate breadsticks and watched the door. Eventually he appeared, looking ill-shaven and wearing apparently new clothes, a long black overcoat, black jeans and a yellow sweater, a black cap, his usual bag slung across his body.

"Nina." He sat down, shrugged off his coat, put his cap in his bag and caught the eye of the waiter. "Vodka, please. Rocks, lime juice, no tonic."

"Yes, sir."

"It is fresh lime?"

"Of course."

He picked up the menu and studied it while Nina waited. He hadn't looked at her yet. "Have you ordered?"

"No. What's going on?"

"Onion soup, sea bass, chocolate tart. What say you?"

"That sounds good." He raised his hand and told the waiter, busy squeezing the lime at the bar, that they'd both have the menu du jour. "What's going on?" she asked again. "Did you have a nice weekend in Cumbria?"

He looked at her. "I want a divorce."

"What? Why? Has something happened?"

"Nothing ever does. That's the point." He raised his arms as if addressing a crowd, his voice like that of God in an old film. "We are sailing through identikit weeks towards death. Towards a flat-pack IKEA Valhalla." He put his arms down.

"You don't mean it; you're just freaking out again." She was confident that this was true. He could be a drama queen on occasion.

Luca said, "Cancer shouldn't be a reason for staying in a relationship."

"You sound like an arsehole." This was the ultimate sanction. They applied it to one another sparingly.

"I'm aware."

"She's going to be fine. She's going to be okay."

"You don't know that, and in any case whether she is or she isn't, our marriage has ground to a halt."

Nina frowned at him. "I thought you were going to shake things up a bit once she was past the treatment. I thought you were going to move house; go travelling; have time off."

"She wants to move, but it's only so she can remodel another flat. Not that she could fit that in, with the obligations and charities and lunches." He rolled his eyes. "She never sits still. My having time off from work would really just mean being an audience for Fran's mania. Let me tell you what happens when we go travelling… or rather when we go on holiday. We go on holiday; we don't go travelling." The waiter brought the vodka. "Thank you. When we were in Puglia for instance…"

"You had a lovely time." She balanced his excitability with stringent calm.

"No."

"Yes, you did. I saw the photographs." Her calm exhibited itself as a near monotone.

"That was the couple memory, not mine. The couple memory of any one thing is different to the individual one. Generally I subsume my own recollection of things to the Borg." He was doing the voice again. Such theatricality was usually to do with being severely rattled.

"The what?"

"It's in *Star Trek*. Cybernetic organisms, apparently individual but actually functioning as drones of a collective consciousness. Resistance is futile."

"Come on, Luca. You're hardly a drone. You tweeted pretty much constantly and there wasn't any sign of dissatisfaction at all, other than about having to come home. What went on in Cumbria? You've been very quiet. Twitter's been wondering if you're still alive. Has something happened?"

"I keep thinking about the road not travelled." He bit dolefully into a breadstick.

"Midlife crisis, much?" Did she look okay with the concept? Because she was absolutely the opposite. Rapidly, precipitately, he'd strayed into the intolerable.

"No." He drummed his fingers briefly against the table. "The time is coming to break out, I think." Horrified beyond words, Nina began to laugh. "You can laugh all you want," Luca said, "but I really think so. I need to get back to the man buried under 25 years of marriage, a man rendered unrecognisable by it." He crushed another breadstick against a plate.

She sat back and appraised. "Is that your first drink today? And what's with the stubble?"

He swigged thirstily at his glass, took a pause and then finished it in another long gulp, before signalling that he'd like another.

"It's one of the things I'm going to do, when I start again."

"What is?"

"I can have a beard if I damn well want one. I'm going to drink when I feel like it without having to be nagged. I can work all evening if the business is in trouble…"

She was startled. "The business is in trouble?"

"….without somebody sticking her head around the study door every five minutes and moaning that she's been on her own all day. I can spend money on bad art if I want. I should be able to go to Berlin on a stag do, without having to deal with the big puppy eyes. I can buy a stupid flash car if I want one. Fuck off, Francesca: I work my ass off and I don't have to clear everything with you. Plus, bliss, the quietness. I can have days when I don't have to talk, without the twenty questions about what's wrong with me and why I'm in a funny mood." He paused while two flat bowls of onion soup were delivered to them. Oniony steam rose and intertwined above the table. Luca loaded a crouton with rouille and set it floating, then loaded and launched another two.

"That's just what's needed," Nina told him as she began to do the same. "A crouton regatta. That'll help."

Luca put his spoon down. He opened his hands expressively. "I'm worn down by life, Nina. By living the wrong life."

"We all feel like that sometimes." She needed him to stop this, to recant, but how could she say so? He wouldn't have understood the reasons.

"My life's disappearing into weeks that are indistinguishable from one another."

She persisted in trying to normalise things. "But that's a normal feeling. You're just tired."

He was nodding. "I know. Thank you, my love. I like that dress, by the way. Nice colours, silky. I like."

"Thanks."

"Lately, Francesca wants us to go out every night. I don't want to go out every night. I'm deploying the full force of understatement here. Last night it was with her dull charity-organising friends to the theatre. I can't tell you how much I hate the fucking theatre. You wouldn't make me go to the theatre, would you?"

"Not if you didn't like it, no." What was she doing?

"You see. Exactly. Why go to the fucking theatre, home of the witless middle-class dullerati, and be menaced by ushers and shushers, and sit in a Ryanair chair with your knees jammed into the back of the passive aggressive git in front who turns to stare at you if you move, and have the best lines rendered inaudible by people eating bags of sweets, and pay £35 for the ticket and almost as much for bad wine in the interval… Wow, I'm on a roll now –"

"Yes you are."

"– when you could stay at home with a DVD and relax on your own sofa by your own fire with a plate of good cheese? She says she goes for social reasons. That's only inadvertently accurate. Social climbing and showing off."

Nina put her head to one side and sighed. "You really are in a filthy mood." There were two Ninas now. She saw the other one, sitting beside her, saying, *How is it possible to go blithely on to jest about the theatre, Luca, when you've just said that you are casting Francesca out?* That other Nina was gathering her things to leave.

Luca drank most of the second vodka and began to eat hungrily. He continued in the same vein. "Worse, the expectation that at the weekend I'll be happy to go shopping with her and sit with all the other whipped husbands at the changing-room entrance waiting to say what I like and don't like. That I'll pay; that I'll take her to lunch; that I'll agree to go to whatever she's organised without asking me. Sometimes a chap wants to do nothing. Sometimes a chap wants to go out in the car on his own, or sit outside a coffee shop and read and people-watch."

"Why can't Fran people-watch too?" The tone she was attempting was fond irritation. It was play-acting; territorially speaking it was absolutely new.

The rest of the vodka was downed. "She isn't you, Nina. She doesn't understand about silence. Ours is a house of death and hyperactivity and frankly I don't want to live with either. I don't. And I flat refuse to become middle-aged."

"We're all getting older." Her monotone was back again.

"No we're not." He took his big polo-neck sweater off, revealing a white T-shirt, and dropped it onto the adjoining seat. "I'm not. I'm not going to. She's become even worse since she got ill. She's become a tedious seize-the-day guru, constantly telling me to live each day like it was my last. That isn't always politically a good idea, when your husband is thinking of leaving you."

"Have you talked to her about any of this?" Her brow was furrowed, which was fine, but her mouth was getting out of her control: it was showing her real feelings.

"Are you all right? You have a weird expression." Nina couldn't answer. "Fran says she wants me to have my own life, my own friends, but then when I do she feels left out. Actually, what she wants is me at heel. But I might want to spend the day in bed, finding new music online and getting crumbs in the sheets, or go into the hills with the walking club and have a day of men and man talk: why not? Am I not entitled to live my life a bit the way I'd like to live it, without negotiating all the effing time? I am not going to a hypermarket in the car on a Saturday afternoon ever again. I'm not. Nor am I going in search of new lighting. The house doesn't need any more dressing. It doesn't. It's fine." They ate their soup in silence a few minutes. "I want to go back to the path I didn't follow."

"What path was that?" Nina smoothed hair back from her forehead. She was beginning to feel unwell. The room felt like it was ocean-going, like it had begun to float uncertainly forward.

"I don't know. I didn't go down it, the path. I fucking hate the fucking wine business. I married a woman I didn't really have anything in common with, because my mother would like her. Can I have some of your wine?"

"After two vodkas?" What was this? This wasn't usual.

"It's that kind of a day." He rested his elbows on the table and opened both hands in expiation.

Nina poured half her Shiraz into his water glass, and he drank it down. She sipped at her own wine; it disguised the set of her mouth. "What happened in Cumbria?"

"She wanted to do what we do here. She wants to go shopping, fundamentally. Acquisition is her life. Acquisition and a sun-lounger. Now she's pressing to go somewhere hot to recuperate; bloody Tenerife or somewhere. Tanning is another big interest."

She gave him a sidelong look. "Maybe you're just very boring."

She'd intended this to be the start of their making fun of one another, and of themselves, because really that was the only way out of this, but Luca wasn't so easily distracted. He leaned further forward and tried to get hold of her hands, but she put them on her lap. "I can't think how we got interrupted, you and me. I think I would have had a better life with you."

"No, you don't."

"I don't?"

"Not when you're sober. Did you drink before you got here?" She narrowed her eyes at him and he retreated, leaning his weight on the back of the chair. "I may have had a stiffener or two at the office."

"Aha."

He broke another breadstick into pieces with one hand, and corralled the shards into a heap. "That's the point, though. I had to be drunk to tell you how I feel."

"And how's that?"

He was still gathering the last of the cracker dust. "You know what I mean. It's been with us our whole lives. Our belonging together; our perfect fit."

"It wouldn't really have been different with me. We'd still have gone to the supermarket, sometimes even on a Saturday." This was the truth, in two sentences.

Now Luca sat forward again. "The thing with you and me is that we communicate. It doesn't sound like the most important thing in the world, but actually it is. I wouldn't mind being in a megastore with someone who also found it funny. You and me contra mundum."

"If we were together we'd be lonelier people." There it was, a third truth.

He put the glass down hard. "How do you figure that out?"

"Because it would all have gone wrong somehow, or off the boil, and we wouldn't have had anyone to go to." As she said this it was already out of date.

"That's a sad philosophy."

"Yeah, whatever."

"Yeah, whatever? Am I boring you?"

"You are a bit." She could say that to him. There wasn't anybody else she could say it to. That had always been the point.

Their main courses arrived, and Luca ordered more wine, and they ate and talked about other things. Nina steered the conversation elsewhere, into their respective trips and what they'd seen and eaten. But when the plates were taken, Luca reverted.

"Promise me one thing. If ever you decide you need a divorce, you think of me first." He thought he saw in her eyes that she took him seriously. What else could it be, that strange intense look in them? He went on, "But you're right, of course you're right. Our marriage is only perfect because it never happened. We haven't had to deal with dishwashers and bills and recycling and dull sex."

"Dull, is it? That's a shame." The back of her neck felt as if it was seizing up.

"Francesca lost interest years ago. Even before she got ill. The cancer has been a big sex drought, and now she's losing interest in me in general, I think."

"Oh I see, you're in need of a *cinq à sept*." It wasn't possible to smile. "On the way home from the office."

"I think the French are an enlightened nation. Shall we say five o'clock tomorrow? But I'm getting on a bit. I may not need two hours."

She hid her disappointment in him in checking her phone. "A quickie on the way home. Lovely."

"It's these little adjustments in life that make it tolerable."

"I'm glad I know that you're joking."

Luca could have joined her there. It might still all have been salvageable but instead he said, "We should get another bottle."

"No more for me." Nina was beginning to want to be brisk. "I'm already a bit drunk." She looked off to the side; she kept doing that, as if there was something off to the side that needed monitoring.

He raised his hand and ordered a single glass. "It's sad to drink alone, but it's a sadness I can bear."

"What did you mean, losing interest in you in general?" She had to return to this.

"Lately it's like she makes sure that we don't have time to be with one another. Fran's the busiest person without a job in the history of the world. Phone calls, press releases, campaigns going on in my kitchen. Miscellaneous women in and out, knitting blankets for Gaza. It's all about the world, now; she has to pay something back. Meanwhile I spend my free time alone."

"I thought you were just complaining that she didn't give you enough time on your own."

"It's a paradox."

"Things get dreary," Nina said. "That's the tendency. But things can be done."

"Are things dreary with you two?"

Nina took a moment. "Things are fine."

"In love, isn't fine another word for dreary?"

"Well. It would help if you didn't text me every five minutes." She meant it. Why hadn't she put a stop to it sooner?

Luca said, "So, I'll stop," but he didn't mean it.

He looked upset. She said, "Don't stop, but maybe not every five minutes; it gets on Paolo's nerves."

"Poor Paolo." He turned his mouth down. "He's never been playful though, has he?"

She turned it around. "Maybe you should play with Francesca."

"She's disturbingly literal about things."

"Didn't you know that when you married her?"

"I came to Casablanca for the waters."

"But you were misinformed." She couldn't help herself. It was instinctive.

"It's very simple. I've realised that. It's simple. I need a divorce. I need to have a different life. If it wasn't for Paolo... you know. I don't need to say any more. But Paolo. Why did you have to marry Paolo of all people?"

"You seemed keen at the time."

"Well, yes, of course. Because he worshipped you. More than you deserved."

"Thanks."

"He's the person I love most in the world." Now Luca looked and sounded unmistakably drunk.

"Even though you're constantly putting him down." She knew as she spoke that she'd only just got away with it, this frankness.

"But that's a joke. You know that, right? I couldn't ever do anything to hurt him. Not in a million years. Is he okay? I don't get the chance to talk to him enough."

This was practical now, and in the arena of made plans. She untensed her shoulders. "Perhaps while Francesca's so busy you should spend some time with your brother."

"That's a very good thought. We need some third thing, though; always have. Something to mediate: tennis, work, driving, running. Even then it's always been tricky, because you've always got in the way."

This – what was this? It came out of nowhere. "Got in the way how?"

He pointed at her. "You've always been the wedge between us."

The thing had hit home. Bam. Right in the heart. She said "This is beginning to sound like an accusation of something."

He stabbed at the table with the same finger. "It's just a fact. It's incontestable. You were always there in the photographs, right in the middle; one arm around each of our necks, right there in the middle."

"What are you saying?"

"It's just how it was. The girl next door we were both in love with, even when we were five years old. Besotted by the age of ten; in pain by the age of fifteen."

"We were friends, the best of friends, the three of us. Don't spoil that memory for me." She wanted to get up and leave. She couldn't leave; she needed to hear this.

"Don't get me wrong." Luca was aware he may have overstepped. "It was fantastic, until I kissed you. The highly erotic day of the splinter in the finger. It all went weird at that point, didn't it? It should never have happened. That's what kicked it all off." He looked towards the bar, the waiting barman. "I don't want pudding any more. Shall we get coffee?" Without waiting for her to answer, he raised his arm and ordered two espressos.

"Kicked what off?"

"The whole cycle. What if I hadn't kissed you? What if that hadn't made Paolo ill with jealousy, so much so that I had to back off? But what if Paolo hadn't been Paolo and failed to capitalise? I sent him to you over and over. I was in despair. He got you to the cinema and didn't follow through."

"What?" It seemed all aspirant, like a taken-in breath.

"What if Paolo hadn't given up and gone to work in London? And what if he hadn't said that it was okay for the two of us to get together? What if you hadn't laughed at me when I proposed? What if I hadn't told him that we had sex when Anna died?"

"What? What?"

Luca jabbed again at the table. "What if that hadn't made him cry? What if I hadn't gone to Italy to get out of the way?"

"Luca. Luca. Stop, I don't understand, what? What?" The words continued to be like breaths, and she had to swallow hard. "Jesus. I haven't heard about any of this. Paolo knows about the night Mum died? That's why you went to Italy?"

"Why would you have heard about it? It was between us." The

energy of the list-making, its sequential energy, had gone. He put his hands over his eyes and laughed privately at something he was thinking. He said, "I can't believe I'm telling you this."

"Tell me."

"You just have no idea. You've no idea, Nina. At all. None."

"Tell me, then."

"Take the engagement party. Our engagement party, as a for instance. I'd coached him on the phone, before he got on the train. Touch her arm when you speak to her. Think about how you feel when you talk to her – it'll show in your eyes. Hopeless, though. He's hopeless."

"Luca. I can't believe this." She couldn't look at him.

"I wonder sometimes what our lives would have been like, mine and Paolo's, if your parents hadn't bought that plot of land. If they'd stayed in the city."

"Well, thanks. Really." She spoke to the red and white table-cloth, the horrible clichéd cloth. She'd never liked this restaurant.

The coffee was delivered and Luca saw that she was upset, laboriously rubbing her face as she did when troubled, her fingertips working down from the brow, across to the ears and in again at the cheekbones, and then repeating the cycle, her eyes wide. "I'm sorry," Luca said. "I need to apologise. But you're my best friend and the only one I can tell, when I have trouble with women. It's just unfortunate that you're the woman I'm having trouble with."

"I can't believe this. Paolo knows about the night Mum died?" Luca reached forward and put his arms around her neck, dragging her towards him over the table. "Luca, that hurts. Hurts, stop."

He released her and slumped back. "I don't feel that well, actually."

"I'll call you a cab."

"Don't call me a cab. I'm a man, I'm not a cab. I'll walk; I need a walk." He looked at his watch. "Shit, I'm missing the sales meeting." He got his phone out of his pocket and looked at it. "Seven texts, three missed calls. I had it on silent." He began to text a reply. "I only have my phone in front of me all the time when I'm not with you. I have it constantly in sight in case you text me or email or call. What better definition of love is there?"

Nina couldn't say; she couldn't any longer talk to him. When they got out onto the street he put his arm through hers, and they walked hip to hip down narrow pavements and across cobbles, in the chilly, gusty May wind. She paused at the corner of his road and watched him walk to the door of his building, before turning in the direction of home, unable to answer his garbled farewell. Once there she ran a deep bath, as hot as she could bear, and lay in it for an hour and a half, barely moving, other than for refreshing the temperature. The day had been a disaster, and not only because of Luca's list, the way he'd described the workings of the triangle, though that was disturbing enough. What was really bothering her, what was keeping her submerged, only her head and her toes clear of the water, for 90 minutes in the silent bathroom, was that in breaking the rule, in stepping over the invisible line and saying the thing they never said about regret, he'd spoken in a way that could only make her think of her father. Luca seemed to be preparing to jettison his marriage. She'd been taken aback by the way he talked about Francesca, his judgement and the terms of his judgement. It wasn't any longer the playful criticism they indulged in, in Paolo and Francesca's absence. This was something else entirely. It was about an idea of love. Luca's idea of it was really only about himself and what might be given, what ought to be received. She had to interrupt her thoughts to censure herself: she had only herself to blame. Her thoughts became disordered and she went over it again. She had to take action, but what action? She'd have to be content with inaction, with a meaningful one, and it was going to have to be abrupt. Her shoulders began to shake because of the impossibility of cutting him off dead. But what choice was there? She wasn't going to be a party to this, an assumed accessory to Luca's decision. She was filled with revulsion. It was clear to her now. It had come to an end in the course of a lunch. She couldn't be Luca's confidante any longer. The way he spoke – it had brought it all back, the way her father behaved, his way of thinking. Her father had looked at the road ahead and had seen it as his own road, specifically his. It could have been Robert talking, lunching with a friend on a day 26 years before, sitting opposite a friend in a restaurant and saying that he saw no other option than to announce to Anna that he wanted a new life.

Francesca was at the door when Luca arrived home. "That was a long lunch," she said. "I tried to call you. The office rang and then Paolo, looking for you." She looked closer at him. "You look terrible. Perhaps cut down on the daytime drinking just a tad. Coffee. Come with me. I'm the one who knows how to use the coffee machine."

Luca followed her into the kitchen and put his arms around her from the back, and smelled her hair and then her neck, a deep inhalation. "Say you love me, Francesca."

"I love you."

"More sincerity would be nice."

She wriggled around to face him, returning his embrace, and they rocked together side to side. "You know I love you, but I'm busy and I haven't got much done this afternoon, wondering where you'd got to." She freed herself and fetched the milk.

"I told you. Lunch today, a Nina day."

"And so you've knackered yourself being über-Luca."

"I was tired before."

"You've sparkled and now you'll be grumpy. I know how this goes. Go and call Paolo and have a nap."

"Come to bed with me."

"I have things I need to do."

"Do you know how long it's been? You don't touch me any more. You don't kiss me on the mouth."

"I'm just preoccupied. I'm sorry. I'll make more time for snuggling."

"You want me in your life, still, don't you? Tell me you do."

Francesca put a hand on each side of his face, and held his gaze. "Luca. Stop this worrying. It's going to be fine, but right now what I need is for you to be the strong one. That's what I need. Can you help me?"

Luca had to scrunch up his eyes. "I'm sorry, I'm so sorry, but I'm so afraid. I'm so frightened."

Francesca put her face up next to his. "It's going to be all right."

"I love you so much," he said, grasping her and hugging her tightly. "Please, please. Promise me. Please don't die and leave me all alone."

Chapter Seventeen

Nurse Yannis came into the room and said, "Christos is with your husband."

Nina, who was lying down, had a physical reaction to the news, pushing off her hands and trying to sit up too suddenly, so that pain flooded into her limbs. The nurse came to her aid, making her turn onto her side, onto the uninjured side, and rubbing the small of her back. Throughout this process Nina asked for more details: where were they exactly, the two men, and why, and what were they saying? Nurse Yannis didn't know. All she knew was that Dr Christos's mission to the village was to meet Paolo off the ferry.

"It is a medical meeting only," she said, sensing Nina's distress. That was worrying. That was even worse, if anything.

"It didn't occur to me that he would do this," Nina said. Mistakenly she'd seen the hospital as a closed system, something hygienic into which Paolo would be admitted under laboratory conditions. She'd assumed that she'd be present at each Paolo–Christos interaction. The small world of island certainties, one she could hold in the palm of her hand, began to disintegrate and leak through her fingers.

Nurse Yannis didn't want her to, but Nina was insistent about going to see if she could see anything. She went on her crutches into the foyer, through the main door and into the car park, and looked up the road in both directions and saw nothing but the heat steaming off the tarmac; all was quiet. She went round the side of the building and into the garden, to the steps that led down to the beach, and looked along the pebbles and up along the harbourside. The sun was relentless, blinding, and she could feel the beginnings of agitation. Despite what Maria thought, Paolo was possessed of a natural authority, and Dr Christos might find himself trying to impress him with things that he knew and that he shouldn't know. She went back into the hospital and paced up and down the corridors.

At this moment, all the things said and given were regretted. Dr Christos didn't know the worst, the shameful truth about Francesca's death, nor what'd really happened on the day of the accident, but there were other things she should have kept to herself, and she was a fool: she knew this. Not that self-knowledge helped. Last night, aware that Paolo was in Athens on his stopover, and made jittery by the approach of today's reunion, she'd told Dr Christos about her lunch with Luca last May, and the crisis that followed in June. She'd told him about July, the annual Romano holiday, the controversial kiss. Telling him about May: what had she been thinking? The bistro, Luca's declarations, his insistence that he wanted to divorce, his secret opinions about his wife: she shouldn't have told him any of that.

Nurse Yannis came out of her office and said, "Do not worry. It is well. They have coffee and then they come."

Nina returned to lie on the bed and slowed her hammering heart, relaxing herself bone by bone, and began to feel better, but realised she'd placed her hands folded on her stomach, in Anna's death position, and moved them swiftly to her sides.

The June lunch, one that was to be unexpectedly memorable, had taken place on an ordinary Sunday, three weeks after Luca's drunken confessions; three weeks in which Nina tried to avoid having to talk to him or look at him when they were around one another; three weeks of abruptness in her texted and emailed replies. She'd tried ignoring him, a total cold turkey, and that had back-fired; he'd showered her with attention, with internet links and references to shared interests, with compliments and questions, and he did it publicly as well as digitally, so that she had no option but to respond. Open hostility wasn't possible. She knew better than to make an enemy of Luca; she'd seen, over the years, that the opponent always came off worst, and there's no worse enemy than an ex-confidante. What she needed, Nina realised, was to treat him as she'd always treated his wife, civilly but as if his being in the same room didn't matter, as if it didn't reorientate her mind. Luca, for his part, was just as ever; he was infuriatingly unaffected by her adoption of civility, or seemed to be, until the ordinary Sunday in question. It wasn't, in fact, an absolutely typical family event, even from the off, because it must have been obvious to all that Nina was being unusually distant with her brother-in-law. The other odd thing was that Francesca was conspicuously friendlier than ordinarily, greeting her warmly and kissing her cheek. Were the two things connected?

The two women had sat together, one at each end of Maria's formal couch, which was an uncomfortable object, oak-framed and firmly upholstered in broad blue and yellow stripes. Nina had been handed warm sherry in a little schooner designed for the purpose. Francesca was drinking warm tomato juice taken from one of the many cartons that (unaccountably) had been purchased and were stacked in the larder, having found a single ice cube in the freezer tray. They'd talked about the holiday that would begin on July 1st.

"It's such a pity you can't come for longer," Francesca said. "I understand why not. But you know, the thing to do is just relax. It doesn't matter. Focus on the rest of us. Focus on Paolo and not on you-know-who."

What was she saying? Did Francesca know what'd happened at the bistro, and was Luca you-know-who? But no – it was towards her mother-in-law that Francesca glanced; Maria was assumed to be the sticking point. Luckily Maria's attention was elsewhere: she was talking to her sister Emilia and she didn't hear. In any case Nina didn't need to worry about looking as if she was the prime holiday avoider, because Paolo didn't want to go to Elie either. He'd suffered too much Elie damage his whole childhood, he said. He didn't take much time off, and wanted to spend his nine days in Brittany with Nina. He'd been firm about this with his mother.

"Come down for a week," Francesca continued. "One that includes two weekends, and Paolo can join us for both of them at the top and tail. You can bring your work with you."

"I'll be too busy; I have deadlines around then," Nina said reasonably. "Deadline time needs too much concentration." This was a mistake. She should have opted for the wifely duties defence, the tired husband needing looking after.

She went into the kitchen and Francesca followed. "What does it cost you, really, what? To humour a woman in constant pain from arthritis, who has been widowed, who might be succumbing to dementia and who only has her two sons in her life? What does it cost you to put aside a few more days that in reality you could well afford?"

Luca came into the room. "Francesca, for fuck's sake," he said. He picked up the salt and pepper set and went out again.

"What?" she replied irritably. "Am I not allowed to disagree? Is that something else I'm not allowed to do?"

Nina got off the bed and went and stood in the corridor, balanced on one crutch, sighing at her Long John Silver reflection in the tempered glass of the wall, and stuck her head out into the garden and listened for a sign. Nothing. No stray word, no footfalls, no fragments carried from elsewhere. Why did time go so slowly? She returned to the bed, and lowered herself onto it and swung both legs into position so that she lay flat, and steered her mind back to Maria's house. Being there had always made her nervous; being around Francesca had always made her nervous, and nervousness had made her quiet, and quietness had been interpreted as aloofness, misinterpreted in the way that was classic of a noisy, demonstrative family. The gloom and formality of the interior hadn't ever helped with improving her mood; the décor of Maria's house hadn't changed much since she and Giulio were first married. Beige bamboo pattern wallpaper stretched across most of the downstairs, all across the hall and up the stairway, partnered by a carpet in one of those springy resilient wools, a design of pale-brown flowers on a green background. Through every room the dark Italian furniture was ubiquitous: a sequence of wood-carved cupboards, chairs, tables, and a massive sideboard with mausoleum columns.

Nina looked at her watch again. Time had slowed intolerably. She thought about how Francesca spoke to Paolo. Luca had said once that Francesca talked as if she and Luca were the royal line, and Paolo the king's brother. "Things are always hectic at work," she'd said to him, when he claimed to be too busy to spend longer in Elie. "Luca manages to take time off. You need to learn to delegate."

"No doubt." Paolo would never argue with Francesca, never had and never would, but the fact that he said no doubt to her so often might have been significant. He'd always insisted that he liked her, but had he really, or was it just another sort of loyalty to his brother? Unless there was a lot at stake, Paolo kept his thoughts about other people to himself. Nina and Luca, on the other hand, had always been completely frank with one another, about everything: no holds were ever barred. It wasn't just what they'd said but the frankness itself that had been seductive, and it was hard to feel as close to someone who was careful to be diplomatic. Had Paolo's diplomacy extended into their own bed, into their sex life? It was hard to know how far his courtesy reached. It was hard to know where the crossover point lay, between tact and self-delusion. He'd always insisted that his parents were happily married, for instance, that arguments were neither here nor there, and that their sleeping in different rooms meant nothing. There had been separate beds after Luca was born (it wasn't just about contraception; Maria didn't think sexual activity seemly with children in the house) – but Paolo had always maintained that their love was mutual and deeply felt. He denied that this was myth-making done collaboratively for Maria's sake, though the widowed Maria's reverence for Giulio had always seemed to Nina, and also to Luca, to be something quite specifically achieved in the remembrance.

It was the weekend that they'd argued about Maria's continuing to live alone. Luca would say afterwards that she was physically diminishing, that he was reminded of a wooden coat-hanger deprived of a heavy wool coat, and it was true that Maria's cheekbones had become prominent for the first time, though her hair, always raven black, petrol black, was still more black than grey. She'd been wearing a new dress, which was royal blue and cut like one of the Queen's, and was adorned with a spray of amethysts. Her boys had bought the brooch for her seventieth birthday, and she'd worn it every day since. That's right, it had been the Sunday without the meat. Aunt Emilia, a softer, rounder edition of her older sister, appeared in Paolo's line of sight and inclined her head as if he should follow, and so he did, going after her and into the kitchen. Emilia closed the door behind him. "There doesn't appear to be meat cooking."

Paolo crouched and opened the oven door and saw that within was cold and empty. "What on earth." He opened the fridge and looked in. "Here's the lamb, still here." He turned to Emilia. "What are we going to do?"

"There are sausages," Emilia said. "Get them out and I'll get the pan." She found the apron that once was Giulio's, a white apron embroidered with his name, that was hanging on the back

of the larder door, and put it on. "Oh and Paolo, about the vegetables. Look in the warmer." He handed over the waxed-paper
packet and returned to the stove, a great brown beast of a thing
as old as himself, and crouched, peering into the warming oven.

"Oh God," he said. "Have you seen these?"

"She said to me that the vegetables were done in good time and
left to keep."

"Carrots, cauliflower, potatoes. Carrots shrivelled, cauliflower
a mush."

"We had better do another batch, or else Luca will see it as
more evidence that she needs to go into care."

Right on cue, Luca came into the kitchen, looking quizzical,
and the situation was explained. He said, "We can't go on like
this, you know. Have you been in the bathroom? The bath is full
of old clothes."

"It isn't you who's having to go on like this or not go on like
this," Emilia told him. "It's just eccentricity. This – it's just vegetables. It seems to me to be a high price to pay, to have to give up
your home just for vegetables."

"Hear, hear," Paolo said, not looking at either of them, but
rummaging in the fridge.

Nina sat up in bed, pausing her breathing, and listened hard and
lay down again. It's fine, she told herself. The talkative Dr Christos
would be like a sun-parched beggar at an oasis. He longed for
outside contact, for an outside view, and another man's life would
have proved irresistible. It didn't have to be anything to do with
her. He'd be ordering a second coffee and keeping Paolo at bay.
He'd have looked at his watch and said it was hospital siesta time,
and that they needed to wait another half-hour. It was fine. It
would all be fine.

The conversation was resumed after lunch, as they stood on the
pavement between their parked cars. Paolo thought they should
get somebody in, a cleaner, someone who'd also be a friend and
keep an eye on things. Luca said that was just putting off the inevitable. Paolo said that if it were him he'd put off the inevitable as
long as possible. Nina said nothing. Nina had barely been present
all day. She'd followed her mind elsewhere. She'd thought about
work.

Francesca had been looking twitchy and now she spoke up. "I'm sorry, but I think that to have low expectations of an older person is patronising. Are we saying that's all she's capable of and so it's fine? She would want to know if the food wasn't good. She could improve it or she could say, 'Well, if that's how it is perhaps you boys should cook the lunch in future.' I, for one, would want that if it were me. I'd want to be treated like an intelligent adult."

"You seem to be arguing against a point I wasn't making," Paolo said.

"Come back to ours and have coffee," Luca said, "and we can talk some more there." He'd winked at Nina and she'd turned away.

She didn't want to go to Luca's. She said that she was tired, that she had a headache, but Paolo hadn't taken the hint; they'd followed Luca's car as it returned to the city and turned at a crawl into his street. Handsome deposits for the purchase of a home were gifted by Giulio and Maria at each of their sons' weddings, and the Romano brothers lived only a few roads apart, in flats within tall sandstone residences that were finished externally with artisanal stone-cutting and bay windows, that featured high ceilings and wooden floors, coal fireplaces and beautiful shutters. The only real difference between their two apartments was that Luca had bought a top-floor one with a substantial attic, and had overseen the construction of a maisonette at treetop level.

Aware that she was beginning to sweat, Nina got off the bed, went to the door and looked down the corridor. Nurse Yannis was there. "The boat is late," she said, holding her phone up illustratively. "It arrives now."

As far as it was possible to rush, Nina rushed into the garden, back to the steps to the beach, and looked towards the harbour, shielding her eyes with her hand from the sun. The ferry was there. Why hadn't it occurred to her before that the ferry wasn't there? She saw the captain of the boat – was that his name? It was a two-man operation. The skipper, perhaps. He was delivering grocery boxes and sacks of something unidentifiable, blue sacks onto the grey harbour wall. No passengers were any longer evident. So, they had gone for coffee, finally. She went back to her bed and looked at her face. She put on mascara and a coral coloured lipstick, and blotted most of the lipstick off again. She avoided her reflection because it asked her to confront something she didn't want to feel, but it was already too late: it was coming at her now, in waves, powerful, physical, like the coming of an illness, like something viral that Paolo had sent ahead of himself. Dr Christos was right when he said that it was just nostalgia, nostalgia mixing itself potently with fear of the unknown; she knew he must be right. To reinforce her resolve she flicked through text messages that'd come recently from her soon-to-be ex-husband, and found the one she wanted. *Need to move on to practical discussion about sale of flat and division of assets, so give it some thought.*

Maria had always liked what Nina had done with the flat; it was one of the few compliments she'd ever paid her. Nina's preference was for colour and warmth and books and pictures and rugs; she liked things, collections, a modicum of clutter. She liked light against the dark: set against the slate-coloured walls there were white-framed pictures, white crockery and candlesticks, white chairs, white fireplaces and strings of tiny pea lights. It was an environment that looked good at Christmas, with candles lit and all the reds and golds of the rugs and cushions glowing. Paolo hadn't wanted to be consulted; he had no idea about interiors, he said, and would make a hash of it. He just wanted homely comfort, he said; softness after a day of hard surfaces. Francesca, on the other hand, had to contend with a man who had a view on most things, and had reported back on every little plan, as if she were the designer and Luca the client. Luca was keen on business entertaining, and Francesca often cooked dinner for company guests. This was his showcase, his shop window, Luca said, and so it was important that the house was as orderly and impressive as possible. Sleek lines were the key thing, and open space: they'd taken out pieces of walls in the pursuit of flow, leaving half-walls, all of them white, which served as a backdrop to plain-coloured sofas and chairs that were stiff and severely modern, in dark shades of coffee and navy and aubergine. The kitchen that had been all wood and granite was now glossy red and bare. Lights were enormous and architectural. Bookcases were made of white cubes, and though some books were housed there among the Italian glass, they were big hardbacks on non-fiction themes, travel and art and photography; the paperbacks were kept upstairs on the landing, colour-coded like a rainbow. Large square footstools covered in cowhides turned out to have seats that were also lids, storage for the newspapers and remotes, the CDs and DVDs, the everyday items that otherwise would have spoiled the look and the line. Francesca had wanted a project and it had been a sad-looking flat when they bought it: the before-photographs were on display in the guest bathroom. The panelled doors had been covered with thin sheets of plywood. Wiring had been fixed with brass tacks along the bottom of the cornices, and someone – most probably the same someone – had glued a cushioned orange floor covering in a tile design to the bathroom walls. There had been a lot to do and Francesca had risen to the challenge spectacularly. She'd done not one but two refits. It had been the great achievement of her life, she said to visitors, watching for the nuances of their response.

The two couples were lucky in finding adjacent spots to park, over on the garden side of the road; Luca and Francesca were fortunate in having access to a lawned green space, furnished with trees and benches, that was collectively owned and only accessible through a locked gate.

"Luca has acquired a turntable," Francesca said, turning to Paolo as she unlocked the front door. "A stupidly expensive one and new speakers." The echoey white space smelled strongly of lilies: a vast bunch sat in front of the hall mirror. "Would you come and help me make the coffee, Paolo? Luca has some terrible music he wants to play to Nina."

"I don't want to hear it, to be honest," Nina said. She couldn't talk like this and had to check herself. "I'm sorry, I have a head-ache and I'm not in the mood."

"You don't have a choice, to be honest," Francesca told her. What was Francesca playing at? "He's rediscovering his old vinyl," she said to Paolo as he followed her into the kitchen. The Bee Gees were playing even before she'd filled the kettle.

"Oh no," Paolo said.

"Oh yes, indeed."

It was a thing of Luca's that he embraced the idea of bad taste, in music, in cinema and in art. He didn't apply the same aesthetic to food, nor to clothes, but he was a spokesperson, he said, for inconsistency, when it wasn't really inconsistency at all. Francesca sometimes felt the need to explain Luca's taste to people: the bad paintings in the flat, she advised, were purposely bad. She could sound a little defensive. Luca disliked her use of a value term. Naïve art, he insisted, was the right term. Art was art. You made things art by treating them as art and displaying them as art and calling them art; you made art by being an artist, and that was that. He liked to tease people by asking what they thought of the pictures in the hallway, their veering perspectives, the wonky buildings, the indeterminate animals, the human distortions, the paint-by-numbers green and brown landscapes that it turned out had been costly. It was his ice-breaker when new people came over. It had for a long time been a conversation-starter with his brother, also. Paolo had been heard to use the phrase "junk culture". He'd been known to make his brother show the whites of his eyes.

Paolo came into the room with the tray, and saw that Nina was off at the other end of the room, curled up on a sofa looking as if her thoughts were far away. He said "Darling – head still bad? I'll get you some Nurofen." He turned to Luca. "Can't we have something more serene than this crap? My nerves are still jangling from lunch."

"This too plebeian for you?" Luca asked him. "Do tell us why we shouldn't be listening."

Paolo went to the medicine cabinet and got pills. His voice said, "Much as I love you, Luca, sometimes I want to smash your face in."

"But crap how?" Luca called back to him. "How does Schubert feed my soul more than The Bee Gees? Tell me about the mechanism."

There was a pause and then Paolo came back into the room. "Luca, I don't want to play. Not now."

"Oh, go on. It's been such a boring day. I need something."

Paolo passed the painkillers to Nina, and a cup of coffee. "All right," he said.

"Uh oh," Francesca said. "Here we go."

"Let's consider what the music is for. What's it for? This is just for dancing. And also for sex."

"You sound like a 1950s American pastor," Luca said happily.

Nina was contemplating walking home alone. She wanted to bring him up short, bringing his smugness to an end. She wanted to stand up and ask the question. *Have you told Francesca yet?'* She had a sudden calamitous need to bring everything into the open.

"You didn't let me finish," Paolo said. "What do I want from music? What do I talk about when I talk about music? I don't have to want what you want, but you want me to say what it is that I want, so here it is, what I want. Poetry. Complexity. My brain engaged. Complicated feelings. All stuff I get from the Schubert and not from this. It's like reading; it needs to be worth reading. We shouldn't be afraid of discarding things." Nina felt a moment's alarm. "But I don't hate all modern music," he added.

"Yes, you do," Luca said. He looked towards Nina for endorsement but Nina was steadfast.

"Not so, not true," Paolo said good-humouredly. "I like a boogie round the kitchen just as much as the next man, don't I, Nina?"

"Oh my God," Francesca said.

"Paolo," Luca sounded like he'd got him by both lapels. "Do you have any music past 1950 on your iPod?"

"Not on my iPod, no, but –"

"He's going to get onto television next," Luca said, looking again at Nina. "That's going to invoke the offside rule."

"I think I'll go home." Nina spoke towards Paolo but he didn't hear.

Nor did Francesca seem to have. "Boys, stop," she said.

"There's a serious point to be made," Paolo said. "The big problem with cliché is that it distracts us from our real feelings."

"Nina!" Luca said, making her jump. "You are aware, I hope, that you married your father?"

"Oh, sod off," Nina told him, picking up a magazine. Francesca stifled rather artificial giggling.

Paolo was unwilling to let it go. "I think it would be interesting to raise a generation that didn't have a constant diet of mental chewing gum, and see how they turned out."

"They'd be just the same."

"I'm not so sure."

"Besides, it would be as inauthentic as the culture you object to. You can't impose this. It's evolutionary. You just don't like the point we're at in the cycle."

"We need to talk about Mum," Paolo said in reply.

"I won that round, in other words."

"You can think so. Be my guest."

"It's a no-brainer. She needs to go into a care home of some kind. A good one, obviously. The best we can find."

"I agree," Francesca said.

Paolo turned to her. "How do you agree suddenly? I thought you didn't agree."

"I talked to Luca about it in the car."

"Nina? Nina? Do you have an opinion?" Luca waved his arm as if bringing back someone hypnotised. "No, I thought not. Return to whatever it is that's more interesting than my mother."

Nina couldn't win. This is what would happen if she absented herself; she knew this. Life would quickly become impossible. She put the magazine back on the table.

Paolo said, "You know there isn't the cash for a care home."

Luca went to one of the cowhide footstools and took out a large white envelope. "I sent for this; it's a prospectus. It's not that far away and more like a hotel than anything."

"Great," Paolo said. "Who's going to pay?"

Francesca raised her hand slightly. "It's good value. She'd have a social life and keep-fit classes."

"You know the money's almost all gone," Paolo said, still talking to Luca.

Nina said, "Gone, what do you mean?"

"Ah, there we go!" Luca cried. "Now she's engaged; now the subject's come round to money."

Francesca was shaking her head. "They didn't tell you, then, that Maria's been subsidising the company for two years."

"She insisted," Paolo said. "And she'll get it back. The bank's been witless and reduced the overdraft." He looked intently at his linked hands, and Nina was aware that he was angry. "Perhaps she should move in with you two. Seeing as Francesca doesn't work and has the day to herself."

"I do work," Francesca said. "I work hard, actually. Just not for a salary."

"Perhaps she should move in with you two," Luca countered. "She likes your flat. She hates ours and Fran's not well enough to have a permanent guest."

"Nina already has a job."

"I'm sure Nina would cope fine. She's already shown herself to be an adept juggler." Nina stared at him, but Luca was looking at his brother. "I'm serious," he said. "I'm not having my mother living anywhere cruddy, being parked in heaven's waiting room and neglected. We can't afford a housekeeper, and in any case we all know she wouldn't tolerate a stranger in the house, in her kitchen. It wouldn't work."

"Okay, so maybe we need to think about other options in the family," Paolo told him.

"Who? There isn't anyone else. We can't burden any of the cousins."

"Well, I'm organising a home help." Paolo got to his feet. "We'll give it three months and convene again."

"Yes, boss," Luca said. "But you know that it's just delaying matters. Yesterday was a wake-up call."

"I know."

"What happened yesterday?" Nina asked Paolo.

It was Francesca who answered. "She got lost when she went to the newsagent's, and was found wandering."

"I'll get someone to start immediately," Paolo said. "Someone for the mornings, and they can walk to the shops with her, and we'll see how we go."

"She's not going to like it," Francesca told him.

"We'll discuss it again," Paolo said, standing up. "But for now I want to be at home and in a comfortable chair." He took Nina by the hand and led her to the door, with Francesca politely following.

"I'm sorry, Nina," Luca called after them. "I just don't think that we have any choice."

Chapter Eighteen

In the interim, between the fraught Sunday lunch and going to Elie, Nina barely communicated with Luca. She framed her silence as a work pile-up, as the necessity of dealing with a backlog that needed to be cleared before the holidays. To ratify the excuse she'd also announced her absence online, citing a need for manuscript leave, and then she'd needed to honour that and stay away. Luca's texts continued unabated and were answered perfunctorily. He must have known that she was angry with him, and why. How could he not? It was a relief, in a way, that apparently there was something obvious and concrete – his outrageous suggestion about Maria – at the back of her displeasure, like a false bottom in a Chinese box, diverting everyone around them from its real causes.

Nina had hoped, for the first 24 hours afterwards, that Luca's suggestion was a prank, and that he was about to backtrack. *Gotcha*, he'd say, in a one-word text message. She waited for the message all day, but it didn't come. She thought it had, seeing his name on an email, but all that he'd written there was that he was coming round with cake. *Sorry, can't*, she replied. 'Too busy and in too bad a mood'. (She was cross with herself for conceding this. He shouldn't need prompting to apologise.) She had to put two kisses after her name, because that was the norm, and anything less than that would have risked starting a war she couldn't win. She had to say that she was looking forward to seeing him in Elie. This was the kind of lying that now needed to be done. She toyed with the idea of adding a comment about Maria, asking for clarification, but didn't. He needed to bring it up first.

By Monday evening it was clear that it wasn't remotely a prank. Paolo returned from the office looking like the bearer of bad news, and with a very expensive bottle from the company cellar. He mentioned, while pouring two glasses of this sensational twelve-year-old red, that Luca had brought up the subject of Mum again. Luca had been persuasive, he said; he'd made the point that they probably wouldn't see that much of her, other than at mealtimes; they could get the biggest spare room fitted out with an ensuite and a sofa and TV. It was something to think about.

"I don't need to think about it," Nina told him firmly.

"Are you sure?" He was grinning over the rim of his glass.

Oh God – he was attempting a tease. "You don't agree with Luca? You sounded as if you were trying to persuade me."

His smile grew wider. Jesus, he thought it was funny. "He's right about the money though," he said. This was instantly sobering. "We need to start working on her to sell the family house. After that she'd have all the options in the world." He saw her relief. "I told Luca that was how we needed to play it, and that moving in with us wasn't ever going to happen."

"I don't want to go to Elie," she said to him. "I would do almost anything not to have to go."

"I feel similarly," he said. "It's always a nightmare. But we don't have any choice. Don't worry: you worry too much. It's going to be fine."

The Romanos had gone to the same seaside village every July since Paolo was small, north across the Forth Road Bridge and east onto the coast road, through a landscape of gently rolling farmland, of barley fields and old hedges and polytunnel strawberry growing. Elie's photogenic low-slung cottages, some of them with outer stone stairs, were mixed in with handsome merchant villas, stretching in a row along a main street from which narrow lanes led down to a crab-shaped bay. When, rarely, conditions were sunny, warm and windless (the full triple was a near impossibility) it was a magnificent place to be on holiday, but as Luca was often heard to say, in 40 years there'd been only four sweater-free summers, and once a decade was a pretty bad average.

"Why can't we go to Italy next year?" he'd say to his mother, as they cowered in blowy summer rain beside the pier. "If we book well ahead the air fares will be much cheaper than you think." But Luca knew why not. It was because his dad had loved Elie, and things that Giulio loved had become commemorations that verged on imperatives. Luca didn't like to contradict his mother's memory of his father's memory, but what he remembered most was boredom, and also arguments. What he remembered most, he said, was it hardly ever being the right weather for swimming.

They always stayed in the same rented place, which was booked ahead on a permanent basis, a three-storey double-fronted stone house with a long green garden behind. There were six bedrooms and Maria always had the best, the one with the window seat and telescope and the harbour view, despite protesting every year that she didn't need it, not now she was widowed. Francesca and Luca took the second-best room, which was next door, though its view was impeded by the jutting-out of Maria's window. Nina and Paolo had technically the biggest room, one that overlooked the lawn at the back, and Emilia and Mick had the other garden-view room beside it. Up the second set of stairs were the two small bedrooms and lavish bathroom that made up the separate little kingdom enjoyed by Emilia's no-nonsense, frizzy-haired daughter Janine, her husband Dan (both of them wearers of jeans and plaid flannel shirts) and their nine- and eleven-year-old boys who, as Janine often said, had been coming here since before they were born. The annual decamping to the house was a ritual that looked never to end, but this visit would turn out to be the final one. At the time, nobody but Luca had an inkling that it was going to be Francesca's last summer, but nonetheless the cancer had been a rallying call. The family had rallied, and on the long weekend that Nina and Paolo visited – one that had become six days, lasting from Thursday to Tuesday – the numbers were boosted by other short-term visitors. Sophia, Janine's younger sister, was there with her baby, insisting that the sofabed was fine, in fact the sofabed was ideal as she could watch television while feeding in the night, and had easy access to the kitchen. Two very elderly great-aunts, younger sisters of Giulio's Scottish mother, were there the same week, and had been secured a ground-floor room at the hotel 200 yards along the high street.

When Nina and Paolo arrived, dinner was being made cooperatively under Luca's direction; he was supervising the chopping-up and oiling of vegetables for roasting, and so Nina and Paolo walked into the kitchen through a door that opened onto activity and noise. Francesca approached holding Sophia's baby, a small wrap of pink wool with tiny pinker feet sticking out of the bottom of the shawl, a bundle that she was balancing expertly over her shoulder with one arm while holding out a corkscrew with the other.

"Paolo – brilliant timing; could you open the wine? We're all gagging for a drink. The last game of Pictionary got really out of hand."

"She's not kidding," Luca said, pushing a cleaver through a butternut squash.

The baby was crying, and Francesca began pacing up and down, rhythmically patting her back and singing a lullaby. Nina dropped her handbag and coat on a chair and went and helped Paolo, taking glasses out of the dishwasher. "They'll be too hot for white wine," Francesca said, interrupting her song. "You'll need to run them under the cold tap."

Sophia was lying on the kitchen sofa with her eyes closed. "Thank God for Francesca," she said. "This evening colic is beginning to wear me down."

The fire was almost out and it was chilly, so once she'd dealt with the glasses Nina went and fed the woodburner in the corner with knobbly bits of kindling, setting a big log on top of them. She sat on the bench seat in front of the stove, facing its window, watching to see if it would catch or dampen, and Luca came and sat by her.

"Hello, friend." He tugged at the elbow of her sleeve. "Everything good with you?"

"Same old same old." It was all she could manage.

"Wish it was just you and me here, so we could have a proper talk." There was something about his voice, and when she looked at him she saw that there wasn't any doubt that he was unhappy. She had to remind herself that unhappiness was at the heart of this, that Luca wasn't himself. Perhaps she'd been too hard on him. Glancing around the room, she saw that everyone was absorbed in other tasks and that Paolo had his back to them, in conversation with Dan. Francesca had left the room with the baby, still singing. The travel cot was lodged upstairs till bedtime.

She said, "Is there something wrong?"

He put his arm around her shoulder and drew her closer. "Things a bit tricky at home."

"Have you said anything?" The softest whisper possible.

"Anything about what?" He loosened his grip. "Also… I have to apologise about the Maria thing. And about being an arse in general. I'm not myself. Normal Luca will be resumed."

"It's okay," she said, although it really wasn't.

"Aunt Nina!"

They turned to look behind them and found that the boys were there with a kite, one standing at its diamond-shaped head and the other holding the end of its ribbon tail. "Aunt Francesca made this with us today."

"It flies brilliantly."

"Can you show it to me in action tomorrow?" she said. "If the wind's blowing."

"When is the wind not blowing?" Luca got to his feet. "Where's Fran?"

Dan answered him. "She's gone to try and get the baby down." Sophia was asleep and snoring quietly.

Luca went to the table, to where Paolo and Dan were seated beside chopping boards. "We need to get this dish in the oven. Is it ready?" He peered into the tray. "A tad more oil stirred in. I'll get the duck breasts organised."

When Francesca came down again, looking pleased and holding a white plastic baby monitor, Nina was reading and marking up a manuscript on the sofa, curled up on the end cushion by Sophia's feet.

"Did you have to bring work with you?" Francesca asked her.

"There's always work," Nina said, not looking up. "I'm just doing an hour before dinner and then I'll put it away."

"What are you going to do now?" Luca asked his wife. "You're going to watch television. You think that's more worthwhile?" He didn't say it unkindly and Francesca wasn't offended.

"Probably not," she said. "But it's about togetherness, isn't it?"

"Togetherness is vital," Luca said, and his eyes went to Nina. Francesca looked at her too. Nina didn't look up from her work.

The next morning when Nina went down, Francesca was already out with the boys. She came in with them just as Luca was serving up pancakes, bringing a blast of cool air, the smell of drying seaweed and a cold brine tang. "That kite is indeed a brilliant flyer," she said, cheeks pink with health.

"You're just a big kid," Dan said. "But thank you for the lie-in. What bliss. I can't tell you."

"I love it," Francesca told him. "Probably because fundamentally I'm still a child myself." She looked it, just for that moment, standing in cut-off jeans and flipflops and a shirt of Luca's that she'd tied at the waist. "Where's Janine, still in bed? And where's Sophia? And where's my…" She looked into the pram. "Ah, there she is."

"Janine's having a bath. Sophia's in the conservatory with Nina. They've already had breakfast."

"Have you tasted her ravioli, the one stuffed with pumpkin puree?" Sophia was asking just then, as they sat on long cane chairs side by side. She was talking admiringly of Francesca. "She even makes the puree herself. She's our Nigella, isn't she? Even looks like her a bit, don't you think?" Petite and girlish, with a high brown pony-tail and in exercise clothes, Sophia had a paperback opened and flattened on her stomach, but was finding it hard to concentrate. "Sorry for gabbling but it's just so seldom I have an adult to talk to. Stephen is on the road so much. He's in the Czech Republic this week. But needs must."

"Must be tough with a baby," Nina said, putting the pencil down on the manuscript.

Sophia was aware of the situation, childlessness-wise, and in Nina and Francesca's company was always quick to correct any idea that she might need sympathy. "Don't listen to me. I moan far too much. Stephen's always saying so. I got a text from him this morning. *Hope you're okay*, it said, *my beautiful little moaner*."

Nina had just got back to work when her phone buzzed and it was a text from Luca. "F back, mad on endorphins, and is heading your way. Love you piglet."

She couldn't not respond. She texted back. *Pigtails. The nickname is PIGTAILS.*

Her phone buzzed seconds later. *I saw how much pavlova you ate last night.*

Francesca came into the conservatory holding Sophia's baby. "Soph – she's going to need another feed before we go to the beach. Nina, I'm going to get the picnic organised, so could you give me a hand with that?"

"I'll give you a hand happily," Janine said, coming into the room with a towel around her head. "What are the boys doing?"

"They're making a banner for the talent contest," Francesca told her. "And don't worry. You go dry your hair. Nina will help."

It was a given on the annual holiday that the family went to the beach every day, unless conditions were judged to be too atrocious. Rain wasn't necessarily a deterrent in itself; if they'd stayed in because the weather was mediocre they'd have stayed in a lot of the time. If it was just a tepid drizzle, wet-weather gear would be donned and the boys would be taken out beachcombing, with a promise of a visit to the sweetshop on the way back. Paolo and Luca weren't deterred even by heavy downpours. They ran along the beach together first thing no matter what, once they'd compared running-gear brands and trainers, and made the breakfast together afterwards, exuding self-satisfaction over plates of toast and eggs.

"Right," Francesca said, as Nina followed her into the kitchen. "Luca's popped out to the bakery to get the fruit tarts. He was going to make a pie but the apples weren't up to scratch. Maria and Emilia have already done the rolls, but to be honest they're pretty deadly, so I thought we'd make salads to take down in Tupperware."

"Shall I do couscous?"

"Lovely, but don't put sultanas in it this time, as Luca has a bit of a one-man campaign against. Maybe a coleslaw. The celeriac could go in that too; Luca found one yesterday at the shop. I'll do a tomato mozzarella and get some greens organised."

"We're going to need cutlery, then," Nina said.

"Obviously," Francesca said. Then, realising this was abrupt, added, "Quite right. Which is a pain, but Luca's been grumpy about not getting enough vegetables." She looked inside the dishwasher. "This wasn't properly stacked, again, so some of the soup bowls will need rewashing. I'll get Mick onto it." Nina was looking out of the kitchen window, and saw Mick standing mournfully by the pond with a cigarette. He had a slight stoop, and lots of silver hair that flowed untidily from a receded hairline, and was clad in a leather coat cut like a suit jacket. "Between you and me and the gatepost, Mick's not massively a team player this year," Francesca continued. "He's spent most of the last two weeks at the bottom of the garden, looking at the fish and smoking. I've had to speak to him about throwing in the stubs." She went out through the garden door and instructed Mick, and then she was back. "It's damp and blowy, so could you get Paolo off the computer and onto coat gathering?"

After they'd got the lunch organised Francesca went to get the aunts. She'd shown in previous summers that she had a knack for mothering them, so people tended to leave her to it. The old ladies had differing infirmities: Virginia was mobile but was often confused – *dotty* was the family word – and Joy was sharp-witted but couldn't walk far. Francesca took charge. It was Francesca who picked them up and took them home again when they were tired; it was Francesca who spoke to the hotel manager about the room temperature not being right. She seemed not remotely burdened by the role, in fact, quite the reverse. If the aunts had problems she could solve she seemed positively buoyed.

It didn't rain that day, or at least not explicitly, but the breeze across the beach was persistent. Paolo and Luca arranged the double windbreak, an L-shape of striped red and white protection, and Francesca sent the boys to find the usual rocks (which were nearby, in yesterday's location), so as to weigh down the picnic rug, a vast rubber-backed cloth in Black Watch tartan.

Once it was in place Nina sat on it, with her knees up, resting her book against them. She'd barely finished the first page when someone landed behind her, seating himself right behind her, his back coming into contact with hers and a voice telling her to rest her weight against him. Luca. She and Luca had always done this on the beach and it hadn't ever bothered her before. What to do? There were a few moments of mental tussle before she let herself relax against him. She didn't want to comply, but wanted even less to have a public conversation with Luca about why not. Paolo, too, was reading, a few yards away, lying on his front on his beach towel as he preferred to, looking away from them and towards the sea, and Francesca was on his other side. The boys had brought their ghetto blaster with them, and were playing a rap CD, not overly noisily but loud enough to mask what Luca was saying, turning his head to the side and away from the others.

"Francesca's driving me nuts. She never stops. Constantly on, on show, on form. Comes a time when you just want to relax." Nina didn't reply. She was going to have to move. She'd take her towel and go and sit by Paolo. How was Luca going to object to that? "I keep thinking about our summers," Luca continued. "Lazy unfocused days in the garden with you. Books, the radio, making daisy chains. Lovely sleepy aimless chat. That was the last time I got to relax on holiday."

Now the boys were standing in front of them, imploringly. "Uncle Luca, will you come swimming?"

"Sorry, boys. I have to read this very important book." He picked up the novel he'd brought and looked at it, and the boys went over to Francesca, and asked her.

"I'm not feeling that well today," Francesca said. "But I'm sure Aunt Nina will go with you."

Back they came. "Aunt Nina, will you come?"

"Okay," Nina said, "but not for very long because it's freezing." She stood up, discarding her Aran cardigan, and pulled her jersey dress over her head, and there was quietness, a hush, as people paid discreet attention to her disrobing. She had long smooth limbs, her skin apparently poreless, and hip bones that jutted against the red swimsuit. Luca watched her go, and then Paolo looked up from his book.

"Jesus, you're thin," Francesca said to her back. She turned to Luca. "Shall the rest of us have a sedentary game of cricket?" She waited. "Luca? Hello? Can you stop pretending you can't hear me?"

"I was taken right back," Luca said. "Just then. Looking at the three of them. I could see Paolo and Nina and me, swimming here when the Findlays came for weekends."

"Even in the rain," Paolo added.

"It was me and Nina who swam far out, though," Luca reminded him. "You didn't like the deep water."

After lunch they took the equipment back to the house. Once Francesca had organised the men to tidy up, she installed herself in the conservatory to read, and everybody took their cue from this and found their own corners. It had begun to rain steadily. Luca produced a bag of DVDs, absolute classics he said, and announced around the house that he was putting on a black and white Chinese film that was a lot more fun than it sounded.

"There's exactly 90 minutes till tearoom time," he shouted, "so I'm putting it on right now if you want to join."

He'd stopped at the shop on the way home to get the newspapers, and handed them now to Paolo, who settled himself in an armchair, half to read and half to watch. They bought a selection of papers every day, though Luca refused point blank to get his mother's usual *Daily Mail*, saying it would be good for her to have a holiday from indignation. Luca was doing the hard-sell on the Chinese film to sceptical-looking boys, when Nina said she was going for a siesta. She picked up the manuscript and went upstairs.

At four o'clock they reassembled. Luca used an old car horn to signal that it was time, one from the 1920s that was left in the house for the purpose and which made a phenomenal noise. It could be heard everywhere in the village, he said, pointing its nose out of a window towards the sea, and bringing the boys running. Nina, lying on her front on the top quilt of the bed, was woken by its sudden alarming bellowing, emerging too suddenly out of sleep. She'd been swimming across a lake towards an island, its single house showing its chimney pots above the treeline. Now, as she felt herself coming to, she was aware that Luca was in the room: he was getting on top of her and putting his face into the crook of her neck and shoulder. They used to lie like this while listening to music. Nina realised she was chilled; she should have got under the duvet, but no sooner had she realised it than Luca was warming her.

"You look half frozen," he said, kissing her neck. "White as a sheet." He forced his arms under her stomach.

"Luca, get off."

"All we need now is Pink Floyd," Luca said, getting up. "I miss those days. Why did we let those days end?"

At the tearoom, which was run by an imperious elderly woman Luca always referred to as the Countess, with the aid of timid student helpers, the Romanos squeezed in around three wooden tables they'd pre-reserved for a month. There was no consultation of menus because they always had the same, delivered on multiple formal cakestands and in scalding-hot metal teapots.

"We shouldn't do this," Luca said, speaking to Nina, who was across the table from him. "It spoils everybody's appetite."

"After a day on the beach and just a sandwich, we need something at four o'clock, though," Francesca said, getting sticker books out of a bag. "The boys need something, and the aunts. You don't feed us till after eight."

"Nina agrees with me, though, don't you?" Luca said.

"Nina doesn't; Nina likes cake," Nina said, rubbing her tummy.

"As if," Francesca said, reaching for a meringue.

Nina turned to her. "As if?"

"You're not fooling me that you eat cake. Look at you. That is not a carb-eating body."

"It is, you know," Nina said affably. "It's genetic probably. Genes, inherited metabolism. It's just luck. My mum was a great cook but she was the same size when she died as when she married and could still fit into the dress."

"How do you know that?" Francesca asked, cutting the cream meringue in half and putting the other bit on Luca's plate. "Did she try it on again, at some point, to show you?"

"She didn't, but she was the same size."

"I am afraid I never believe in metabolism or genes as a reason people are skinny," Francesca told her. "If women are skinny it's because they don't eat or because they exercise a lot. I think it's a bit of both with you, isn't it?"

"I run, but it's because I love running," Nina said. "I spend my working life on my behind."

"Why don't you run with Luca in the mornings, then?"

"Luca and Paolo run too fast. They make my gentle jogging look like it's under-achieving."

"That's because it is," Luca said.

After dinner there was television, and board games, though TV was a risky business with Maria in the room; if it wasn't a quiz or talent show or a costume drama she found little to approve of. Films were a particular issue: they couldn't be higher in age classification than a twelve, and even a twelve was risky. Paolo went through the DVDs in the cupboard on their second night and didn't find anything he knew she'd like aside from *The Sound of Music*, which they watched every year.

"They don't make certificate U films any more," he said. "It's a real problem. And even then, even if it's a U rating I sweat buckets. Even animations are too racy for my mother, or too vulgar. It was a really bad idea, putting on *Shrek* last night."

"Ogre sex," Nina said.

"And farts and bogeys," Luca added. He grabbed hold of Nina around the waist and tried to do a sort of polka, spinning around the chairs. She couldn't stand it. She felt almost violent. She pushed him away. "Stop! Stop it!"

"You're in such a bad mood," Luca said. "You really hate being here, don't you?"

"I brought a few things for her," Francesca said. "Your mother. They're in the canvas bag. *Ladies In Lavender*, maybe, and then something for us once she's gone to bed. She loves anything with Maggie Smith in it."

When *Ladies in Lavender* started up Luca said he had things to do in the kitchen, pizzas to organise for tomorrow and bread for morning. He asked Nina, who was putting the manuscript away, if she'd come through and do the pizza toppings, and because she hadn't contributed much to the domestic day she agreed and followed him out. If Luca had wanted a private conversation it was not to be, because the boys were in the kitchen, playing with the table football. Nina sat opposite Luca, and did the slicing-up of vegetables and deseeding of chillis, and asked if she could help with the dough. "Kneading is a one-man job," he said. "Much as I'd like to get your hands in here with mine."

"Gross," a small voice said from the direction of the soccer table. "Get a room."

Francesca was standing at the open door. "I'm not thrilled with you two," she said. "I have gone to all the trouble of scouring the city for Maggie Smith films, even though I'm ill and tired, and the least you could do is stay put and make it a family occasion, but no! What do you do, the minute I put the DVD in the player? You make a swift exit. I'm sorry if I'm over-sensitive but I think it's bloody rude."

"I'm making a cake for afterwards, and rolls for breakfast," Luca said. "I judge that to be a better use of my time."

"I'll leave you to it," Nina said, returning to the others.

Luca brought a pot of tea through once the film was over, and flapjacks that were still warm.

"So what are we watching now?" he said, perching on his mother's chair arm.

"Telly's going off," Francesca said. "Boys need to get to bed. Who's for charades?" The boys hated parlour games so this was a well-judged move. They went up compliantly, with Game Boy consoles that Francesca had gifted, deflecting Janine's protests by saying they were early birthday presents.

Nina was sitting away from the group, at the other end of the long room, looking at the manuscript. The natural light was dimming and so she moved the armchair around, turning its back to the window. It was only a coincidence that she'd placed it right next to the other chair in so doing. It perhaps didn't look like one, when Luca went and sat beside her.

"What are we reading?" he said. She handed over the first page and he speed-read it. "Oh, bigamy, lovely." He handed it back. "And how topical."

"Your three other wives will speak up eventually," Nina told him.

"They don't speak English," Luca said. "And nobody will ever think to look in Livingston."

"These two, they never change, do they?" Emilia said, inclining her head in their direction. "They've always been the same."

The following night when Luca pulled his chair up to Nina's, Emilia was less well disposed to their breakaway conversation. "What are you two up to down there?" she demanded. "What are you plotting about now?"

"Talent contest secrets," Luca said, tapping his nose.

"Doesn't sound like that to me," Emilia said, casting her eye around the room as if sharing her suspicions.

Paolo patted the cushion next to him on the sofa. "Come and sit by me, Nina. It's much warmer over here by the fire. Aren't you chilly up there? Don't you want to see this film? Maggie Smith's in it."

"I'm fine," Nina said, putting down the manuscript and picking up *Middlemarch*. She pulled a blanket down from the back of the chair and tucked her feet up into it. "I'm enjoying my book. I've only got 40 pages left."

"Nina has a higher mind," Francesca said.

"Francesca," Luca warned.

"No, I'm an admirer," Francesca said. "I can't concentrate on books. Too much else going on in my head." She looked around at the others, before fixing on Janine's face. "And really, isn't there way too much fiction published, and not enough of the interesting stuff?"

"I like a good story," Janine said. "But biographies are my favourite."

"Exactly," Francesca said. "What could be more interesting than another person's life? There's a point to that."

Nina didn't want to sit next to him. She moved her chair back to its original position, beside a standard lamp, and turned it on and settled herself once more to read. Luca looked up from his laptop and from chatting on Twitter – he was tweeting amusingly about his family holiday, garnering many approving replies – and met Nina's eyes. He made a subtle kissing motion, a discreet spasm of lips, and moved his own gaze to her phone, which was sitting on the chair arm. Her attention was directed to its blinking red light, signalling receipt of a message. He'd sent her a message on Twitter. Paolo didn't have an account there, and nor did Francesca, so it was a safe place to communicate things too difficult to say in other ways. It didn't beep like a text message would have, but arrived silently as a thought sent through the air, sending its small bluebird emissary.

Sorry, it said. *Sometimes I want to stab her with a fork.*

The next day after the picnic lunch Nina said she was going to take some pictures, and would stay on a while. The new tide had brought fresh shells and driftwood.

"Suit yourself," Francesca said. Nina made her way along the beach with her bag, her camera. "We'll do the clearing up," Francesca called after her. "Don't you worry about us."

It was one of those bright and yet cloudy Scottish summer days, the sun lighting up the sky as if through milky-grey glass. Nina took photos of the headland and of the lighthouse, and her heart was heavy. She decided to walk along to the shop, and when she'd acquired a chocolate bar and a can of Coke, went and sat by the war memorial. It was a Galaxy bar, sweet and pappy, and pieces melted into sauce on her tongue. Luca would have disapproved of such a low-cocoa "so-called chocolate". She could hear his voice. (He would have had an apoplexy about the Coke. She'd already had to pretend that she'd never been in a McDonalds.) The war memorial was unusual in listing not just the names but also the trades of the lost, and many of these jobs were themselves long gone. There were ploughmen and an apparently disproportionate number of chauffeurs, mysterious numbers until you took into account the many landed estates in the vicinity. The local aristo-cracy had figured large in the history of the place. There was still a small tower by the bay, roofless now and having lost its glazing, that was built for Lady Anstruther to use as a changing room when she fancied a bathe, and that even had its own fireplace. Nina had taken lots of photographs of it over the years. On this visit she'd come across a newly published booklet about the village, and had read bits out the previous evening while Luca was cooking.

"Listen to this. A servant rang a bell while Lady Anstruther was swimming, to alert the villagers to stay away."

"We knew that," Francesca said. "Giulio told me that the first time I came here, long, long ago." Maria rewarded her with a devoted look.

Nina took pictures of the inscriptions on the memorial, and then someone poked her in the ribs and she turned to find the boys were there. Sandy-haired like their father, they were each wearing knee-length shiny black shorts and football sweatshirts.

"Boys. Hello. What are you up to?"

"We're going crabbing. Will you come?"

"What do I have to do?"

"You put the bacon on the hooks and you wait for the crabs to arrive," Jules (Giulio Jr) said.

"It isn't difficult even for old people," Gregory added.

Nina laughed. "Okay, well in that case I'm in. Bet I catch more than you do."

The surprising thing was that she did. She caught three, and Jules caught one, while his brother caught nothing. When they got back to the house, the whole family were gathered in the kitchen and so Nina had the widest possible audience for her glory. Both Paolo and Luca were watching when Gregory described how Nina had caught three crabs on her first go. Nina stood smiling, in her white shorts and her Breton blue jumper, her skin beginning to tan, her hair wild with salt. She was aware of the gazes of both her husband and his brother.

"Four crabs for dinner, that's fantastic," Luca said. "I was going to go out for fish but these will be ideal for soufflés."

"Ideal for soufflés," Paolo repeated.

"You won't laugh when you've tried one," Luca said gruffly.

Nina dispatched the crabs, driving a kebab skewer swiftly into the hole under the flap in the shell, as her mother had taught her, and put them in a pan to boil.

"You're really cool, Aunt Nina," Gregory said.

"Norwegians are taught this at school, the art of killing,"

Francesca said. And then, putting up both hands, "Joke!"

When Nina went up to her bedroom to change into trousers, Luca followed her there and shut the door. "What are you doing, what do you want?" she asked him, sounding more threatened than she'd meant to.

"You're so on edge," he said, sitting on the bed. "But despite that you're looking incredibly beautiful." She wasn't going to thank him. "I'm in the way. I'll go. I wanted to apologise again for Fran."

"It's fine." She busied herself with the clothes in the wardrobe. "Can you excuse me, please – I want to get changed."

"I can tell that there's something really wrong," he said. "I just wanted to add that I'm here for you, always and at any time."

Despite herself, Nina was touched by this. "That's good to know. My legs are cold. I'll have a hot shower."

"I've seen you in your underwear before, don't forget," he said, getting up and leaving her. She locked the door after him.

On the morning of Nina and Paolo's last day the world outside the door was puddly and chill. Nevertheless the family equipped themselves and proceeded to the beach, though it was clear soon after arriving that there was little appetite for transcending the weather conditions. People seemed tired. The beach cricket was short-lived, abandoned because nobody was really in the mood, their play lethargic. They huddled over an early lunch. Emilia found sand in her cheese roll, and after this ate as if she'd found glass in it – which in a way she had, sort of, as Jules pointed out.

"Emilia, it's hardly anybody's fault if sand blows into the food," Mick said, his Glaswegian accent suiting chastisement.

"Why do we have these stupid picnics every day, even when it's horrible weather?" Luca asked rhetorically. "Let's pack up and go to the pub. Fresh scampi. A bottle of Sancerre."

"No one drinks Italian any more," Paolo said.

"I can't face another ham sandwich." Luca sounded genuinely under strain.

"Luca, there's salad," Francesca said. "Have some of this one. Nina made it; you'll like it."

"There's egg and cress," Emilia said, rummaging in the bag.

"Hard-boiled eggs are disgusting," Luca said. "They won't be anything but crumbly in a sandwich unless you cement them with mayo, and that makes the cress go slimy. Cheese and tomato is the work of the devil."

"Are we going to get the complete list of demon sandwiches with annotations?" Paolo asked him.

Luca decided he was going to visit the seafood shack, the hut run by the fishermen, so as to buy more crabs, the ready-prepared kind, and asked for a show of hands. He did a count and then he was off, striding across the hard sand in red bermudas, boylike from the rear, his brown feet pink underneath. Nina watched him going, his bag bouncing against his hip and his wavy hair ruffled by the wind. It could have been the teenage Luca. She could see herself, the teenage Nina, running after him and jumping on his back.

"He's really out of sorts, isn't he?" Paolo said to no one in particular.

"I'm worried about him," Francesca told him. "He's been very low." She seemed to be looking at Nina as she spoke.

"What's up?" Paolo asked.

"Apart from work? He's worried about me, my health, among other things. He may need to have some proper time off."

Nina walked back to the house feeling bad about her campaign of indifference. Luca was depressed and that explained almost everything. She had to be kinder.

On the last night that everyone was there, a talent contest was held, as was customary. Dan and the boys had prepared the main sitting room, shifting sofas and armchairs into a line at one end and creating a stage out of rugs at the other, with the banner strung across the wall. Paolo refused point blank to take part – this happened every summer – though he was happy to be the manager, with the list, and in charge of lighting and music. Maria opened proceedings by singing a sentimental Italian song with Francesca. Luca did magic tricks half remembered from his youth, getting some of them wrong and making the boys scream with happiness. His wife was his sidekick, in a cocktail dress and heels of Sophia's that she'd brought in the hopes of nightlife. Emilia recited a poem she'd learned at school and could still recall perfectly: Keats' *Ode to a Nightingale*, which – Nina was astonished to see – brought Luca to the brink of tears. Mick told jokes, not all of them suitable for Maria. Sophia was excused on the grounds of breastfeeding having turned her brain to mush. Janine and Dan did a jive to a 1950s medley. Nina, who'd been surprised to find that the house piano was more or less in tune, played Chopin nocturnes that her mother had taught her. Maria adored Chopin, and Nina was embraced for her trouble. ("You brown-nose," Francesca said). The boys enacted a scene from a Harry Potter book, pretending to be Harry and Ron. There'd been a protracted debate in the kitchen about who should be Harry, sorted out by use of cheese straws, one of Luca's talent show snacks, one straw shorter than the other. At the end the judging was done by paper ballot. Maria and Francesca's duet was declared the winner, though the boys, not yet knowing much about tact, went ahead and voted for themselves. When they'd finished, Luca put the jive medley on the CD player again, and attempted to get Nina to dance with him. "We can show Dan and Janine how it's really done," he said. Nina said she was too tired, but Luca wasn't at first deterred. He chased her around the room. People didn't take her protests seriously, nor her calls for him to stop.

Afterwards, when everyone had turned in, Nina climbed into bed without her nightwear, waiting while Paolo sent his last email. He undressed and put his clothes away and found his pyjamas, but once readied, he didn't even look at her; he crawled in over the mattress on his front and rolled under the duvet so that he was turned away from her, and was rapidly asleep. Nina lay awake, and then at 2am she rose and put her dress back on, not bothering with underwear, and went down to the kitchen to make chamomile tea. Luca was there, on his laptop, on twitter, regaling his followers with talent show stories, though Nina didn't realise he was doing that until she looked at her own phone, while waiting for the teabag to steep, and saw that she'd received an alert. Someone had mentioned her there; the alert was automatic. Luca had included her name in his posts, as if his satirical portrayals were from both of them. She sent him a reply. *Good effort, but bring a bunny next time and a top hat.*

He looked up from his laptop and grinned. "Come here."

She went across, thinking he was going to show her something on the screen. They often shared internet finds, things silly and profound, and funny YouTube animal clips. They'd always taken a similar delight in skateboarding bulldogs. But it wasn't that.

Luca swivelled out of the kitchen chair and looked up at her, in the dimness of a room lit by a solitary night-time bulb, and put his hands onto her waist, and ran them down over her bottom and onto her thighs. "No knickers," he said. "Jesus, that's so exciting. And no bra either. Come here." She pulled away and folded her arms over her breasts, looking down on him chidingly. "You seem really alive to me," he said. "You've always seemed to me to be the only other person who was as alive as I was."

"Thank you."

"I love you, Nina Olsen Findlay Romano," he said. "Give me a kiss."

"And so – so what?" Dr Christos had said, somewhat wearily, when she told him about it. "You kissed him; big deal." It was clear he was becoming bored.

"We didn't. We didn't even kiss. I said no, and he said, 'Please, just one kiss; life's so hard and a kiss would make it better.' I didn't have the courage to refuse. The explanations would have been long and he wouldn't have stopped; he would have kept at it; he would have found a way to get the whole family involved. That was my instinct. I was – it sounds weird but I was slightly afraid of him. So I leaned forward to give him the kiss on the mouth, and Francesca walked in. He saw her before I did; she came from behind me. I was leaning forward and down to kiss him when his eyes widened and he jumped back, pushing the chair back, scraping it along the stone floor. The timing was really unfortunate and so was his guiltiness. I don't think she heard his invitation; she just saw me leaning in."

"So what happened?"

"Francesca said, 'Here you both are', with a disastrous kind of tone to her voice. I didn't look at Luca. I went past Francesca and up the stairs without saying anything to either of them."

"Why didn't you say something?"

"Like what? Like whining, 'It wasn't me; it was Luca; he started it'? It was best to say nothing. In any case I relied on Luca. I'd always relied on Luca to cast me in the best light."

"But he didn't?"

"I don't know what was said. But Paolo had a visit from Francesca, to tell him about the kiss, and about my initiating it. Paolo has come to use the word initiate a lot. So you see, when she died and I was so unhappy and withdrawn, Paolo was sure of what was coming. He thought Luca and I were having an affair. He didn't believe me, when I said that we weren't. He didn't believe me. That's how I came to say to him that I didn't think we were any longer in love."

Nina heard them now, the two pairs of shoes on the hard tiles of the hospital corridor. Paolo and Dr Christos were approaching together.

Chapter Nineteen

The footsteps paused and she could hear them, Paolo and the doctor, making their polite farewells.

"Here we go." Nina had to say it to herself aloud.

At the centre of her anxiety, beyond the surface worry about shouting and slammed doors and becoming a bit of a hospital laughing stock, was the possibility that the man who was about to come into the room would turn out to be a stranger. Paolo wasn't the same man she had lived with and had left six months earlier – she wasn't the same, so how could he be? So much that was essentially unknowable had washed through the situation since they'd parted, and she couldn't really guess at the sort of structures he'd built around himself, his defences and his certainties; the way he now imagined his life; the way he narrated the past. Quite apart from the way a sexual and possibly also loving relationship with Karen might have affected him, there might also be new friends, new advisors, new interests, new thoughts: he was becoming the person he had begun to be without her. She knew there had been a series of conversations with Luca. Perhaps, in talking to his brother, Paolo had revealed something of himself that had always gone unsaid. His secret heart: the question had begun to preoccupy Nina very much. Paolo's secret heart wasn't something she felt she'd ever known. They'd lived together, for the most part perfectly contentedly, but Paolo had never really been revealed, and to that there was now added a further layer of mystery, in everything that had happened, that had been said and decided since she'd left.

He was here. He knocked twice and put his head around the door and now he was here. It was very, very strange that he was here. It joined everything up in a way that was necessary but also regrettable; not only difficult, but just plain odd. The island didn't really feel as if it was fully in the world, not the old one of the old life. It felt more like somewhere that had been stepped aside into. To have someone from the past walk into it was like time travel, like past and present being bridged by science in a hitherto impossible manner.

"There you are," he said, as if he'd been searching, coming into the room and smiling towards the window as if she were there. "So how's the invalid?"

"I'm okay, I think. Much better in many ways." She was pleased with this response. It covered everything and gave nothing away.

"You look very well." He'd only glanced briefly at her; he went straight to the vertical blind that covered the French window, and pulled it to one side. "Do you mind?"

"If you like, though my nurse might tell you off as it's theoretically still siesta time."

"We need light, I think." She'd never seen him so self-conscious, and it was contagious.

He stood looking out at the garden.

"So how are you, how was the journey?" she asked his back, aware that she was beginning to fidget.

He turned from the window. "So let's have a look at this troublesome leg," he said, sounding for all the world like the consultant at Main Hospital. He stood over her shin with his unsteady hand extended. "May I?"

"Go ahead."

He was already folding up her trouser hem. "No cast? I expected a cast."

"They don't do it for this kind of injury. I told you on the phone."

He brushed the fabric down again, and pulled the blue chair across. "How's the brain progressing? Cussed or concussed?"

"What did Dr Christos think?"

"He says you're more cussed every day." He looked down at his hands, his thumbs rotating one another. The moment had come, the silence after the pleasantries. But what moment? Was she supposed to embark on explaining herself again? What about his parting words as she'd gone through Security?

Nina wasn't going to initiate. She'd spent her whole married life initiating. All she could do was retreat into formality. "You look tired. I'm sure we could rustle up some coffee, if you'd like some. The doctor has an Italian machine."

"Coffee would be good."

He looked weary, his clothes creased from travelling, their fabric wrinkled at the elbow and behind the knee. There was newsprint on his pale summer jacket and a dribble of coffee on his blue shirt. His hair stood up in a shock; he saw her notice it and smoothed it through. "I'd forgotten how difficult it is to get here. It was a voyage of many parts. Taxi to the airport, flight to Athens, overnight stay —"

"How was it, the overnighter?" She wanted more detail about unimportant things.

"Procedural. Then the connecting flight, the bus to the ferry port, the boat across here. Dr Christos met me at the harbour and walked me over. He said I could stay with him if I wanted and save paying for a hotel. He has a spare room and the evenings are usually solitary, and what did I say."

This was alarming. "What did you say?"

"I said thanks but no thanks. I'm already booked into the taverna. I couldn't let Vasilios down."

"Why did you change your flight and come early?" It'd been bothering her.

"I needed a rest."

Perhaps that was really all it was. "You'll enjoy the weather," she told him. "The weather's been faultless." There was nothing for it but to treat the momentous as trivial and vice versa. Wasn't that how catastrophe was put in its place? The one-liners had always been reserved for the big things, the non-births, the deaths and betrayals. It was likely as not going to be the only way of managing their new status with one another, the post-marital world.

Perhaps Paolo saw that they had drifted too far into the banal. "Look," he said. "I didn't come here to yell at you. I'm hoping that now we have some distance we can be constructive, and make plans. We need to go through the boring details. I've been to a solicitor, as you asked me to – I found a new one so that you can use Graham." Graham Pye, a friend of her father's, had always done their legal work.

"Okay." He was clear of it all now. He was free. He was recovered. It was, in its own way, devastating. She tried to locate a teasing sort of tone in herself, something frivolous. "You've had a long chat with the doctor, I hear. Village spies have been keeping me informed."

Paolo deflected in his usual oblique way. "I didn't want to stay at his house, but I liked him. We had a cup of coffee until siesta time was over."

"Although he knows I don't keep the siesta."

"He told me you have grown fond of one another."

"What?" He was smiling. "You're kidding. Tell me you're joking."

"That was the gist of it."

She couldn't help herself. "So what else did you talk about?"

"We talked about the leg, which I'm assured is going to be better than the other one. We talked about the accident, how you bashed your brain on the road and whether it's safe for you to fly."

"And is it?"

"It has been for a while, I gather."

"I feel fine."

"Before we say any more, I've something to tell you."

"What – what is it?"

"Nothing terrible. Mum had a TIA – that's a small stroke – sorry, I can see that you knew that's what it means – and she's been in hospital. She's going to be fine, but she's high maintenance and Luca's not been finding trips into the ward easy. It's only been six months, no, nearer eight. Christ. Eight months since he lost Francesca. And even though she died at home... you know. It's still the hospital."

Dr Christos appeared at the door. "Ah, you found her then," he said, nonsensically. "I hope you're pleased with how she's looking."

"Better." Paolo turned to look at him.

"Indeed, yes. Well. I must be off. Rounds to do, but see you later, I hope." A moment later his face came around the door. "I'll send some coffee in."

When he'd gone Paolo reached into the top pouch of his rucksack. "I almost forgot; I bring figs. They were selling them at a stall at the ferry port." He handed over a brown paper bag, heavy with fruit, its juice staining wet through the paper. "There were more but I thought I should test one. Then I thought I should test four, to be sure." His mood had noticeably improved.

Nina peered into the bag. "Look at them. They smell heavenly."

She ate one, and she and Paolo looked at one another. She saw his feelings, his indecision, travelling over his face. Evidently he'd seen the same in her. He said, "You look so nervous."

She evicted a hard stump of fig stalk onto her cupped palm. "That's because I am."

"It's okay. We've talked it through. Expensive phone calls."

"So that's that."

"And now we're all set for having the friendliest possible dismantling, as long as – a small proviso – we steer clear of certain subjects for the rest of our lives." There was something prepared-speech about this. *Dismantling?*

"Can I say –"

"No, you can't." He cut her off, his voice growing louder, and this made sense to her. He'd been angry all along, and it was like trying to keep something ducked under water that was determined to breathe. His geniality was a rationed thing that might run out. "Sorry, but there's no need to keep going over things. Honestly. It's a beautiful day. It's raining and blowy at home and I'm on a Greek island. I want to get some sun." He got to his feet. "We're over the worst; let's not keep rehashing it. You were under his spell; you've always been under his spell, and he was at a low ebb. We talked again. He's very clear that he initiated."

"But why's initiating so important?"

"It was kindness and comfort; it followed on from kindness, he said. I understand that impulse."

"You do? You understand that impulse?"

"Of course."

"You – you're still seeing Karen?"

"What, since yesterday? Will there be need of daily reports? It's stuffy in here." He got up and opened the French door, said, "Whoah, it's hot," and closed it again.

"It's your life, Paolo." Her mouth had dried so that she could hardly speak. He must hear it, her cotton mouth.

He was facing away again. He said, "Luca was such a mess after Francesca died. I've never seen anyone so..."

"Broken."

"Yes." He returned to the chair, sat down heavily in it and stretched his back, arching it and extending his legs, all the while making small animal noises of bodily easing. "Too much sitting." He sat up straighter and rubbed his face. "It took us all by surprise, how the whole construction, the public Luca, fell apart."

"The whole construction?" These weren't Paolo-style words.

"It was something Luca said. He talked a bit about the public Luca. We had a proper talk in the end. We didn't part on the best of terms, though."

"What else did he say?" There it was, the thing she wasn't ever going to ask.

Paolo didn't address the question. He said, "I suppose that what still nags at me is that there was... a second source of grief."

"What do you mean?"

"I wondered if he'd assumed that you'd step in, in some way. Somehow. After his wife was gone. And was disappointed. He's really not good at living alone."

"It wasn't that."

Nurse Yannis came in with a tray of coffee and almond thins, set it down and was gone again.

Paolo handed Nina a cup, and ate one of the biscuits. "Dr Christos seems a very easy person to confide in, from what little I've seen."

She felt in need of a bracing thoroughness. "You want to know what I've told him? He knows the basics. Not everything. The basics only, of what happened. The material facts."

Paolo remained cool-headed. "I'm glad you've had someone to talk to. You said when you moved out that you didn't seem to know yourself very well. It sounded like you were saying that you hadn't faced up to something – your feelings for someone else."

"That wasn't what I meant."

"Having Luca living with us brought those feelings to the fore."

"It wasn't like that."

"To be honest I've been worried that the falling-out was fake, so as to create an honourable pause before you moved in together."

She had to shut her eyes. She found she'd raised her hands. "No. No. You've got it all wrong."

"Tell me, then. Make a stab at it. In fact, you can stab it as well. Good idea."

This made her smile. They smiled at one another. Dr Christos had said that when he saw his ex-wife now he thought, *How could I ever have been in love with her?* Nina wasn't thinking that. The relief at seeing Paolo, here in this faraway village encircled by the sea, the sense of rescue, was absolute. She felt the full force of it and then the inappropriateness of it.

He said, "In any case I'd better go and check in. I'm staying in your old room. In our old room, it turns out. I didn't book it that way." He looked at a message that had beeped its arrival on his phone and looked glad about it.

"Who was that?" She couldn't help it.

"Just Karen, asking if I got here and how many people my Greek has offended so far."

"You speak Greek? Since when?"

"She spent time on the coast of the mainland in her gap year as an au pair and picked some up. She taught me a few phrases." He put his phone away. "I'm going now but I'll be back."

An hour after he'd left Nina's phone buzzed. *Expensive text message! Bouncing to UK satellite and back again! So wil b shrt. Having swim, but back visit u after. P.*

When he came back he was accompanied by Nurse Yannis, who'd brought fresh mint tea and fruit and yoghurt cake, the tray that was produced for VIPs. Their flow had been interrupted, so Nina asked more about Maria's illness and Paolo described it at length, the symptoms, the stroke, the hospital dash and the hopes of a full recovery.

"Which reminds me, I need to call Luca and find out if she went home. She was supposed to go home today. He's taking her to his place to sleep." He went outside, through the opened door, into the freshness of the early evening, and paced up and down while talking, like he did at home, and came back in again looking the same. Nothing had occurred that was transformative. "As we suspected would happen, she flatly refused. She's at home and Luca's there."

"Did you say anything to him about what we've talked about?"

"No. Are you going to ask me what was said every time I speak to him?"

"There is a risk of that, yes. Till it wears off."

"When's that likely to be?"

"You will tell me, won't you, if Luca says anything new, or if you have new thoughts. Don't bury this, not until it's properly dead."

"It isn't properly dead, then?"

"I didn't mean feelings. I meant last talks about feelings. Last feelings about the last talks. And so on."

"I get it."

"It's a slowing ripple effect in a pond."

"You left me, Nina. It doesn't matter. You can love my brother if you want." No self-pity was evident. He began to pace again.

"Look. Look. Listen to me." This was becoming exasperating. "You've got it all backwards. I've fallen out even of like with your brother."

"You said when you left that you hated him. Hated him. I have to tell you – that was hard to get my head around. He says it was about territory. Was that all it was – territorial? He needed us, you know. It made a big difference to him, being allowed to take care of us. Why couldn't you be kind?" He went a few steps to the left and then a few steps to the right.

"I can't talk to you about this," she told him.

"Show me some respect, Nina." He sounded on the verge of anger again.

"Respect? What are you talking about?"

"You and Luca – you're doing what you always do. You pretend not to be one organism any more but you're still behaving like one. I've been lied to. I know that. I need to know, right now, the whole truth of what happened."

"I was ill, Paolo."

"I know you were unwell." He could be heard restraining his temper. "But what I still don't understand is how you got from first, resenting him, to second, sleeping with him, and then from there to never wanting to see him again." He used his hands placed together, cutting through the air to suggest the three stages. "It's a baffling ABC, that. He says there was a reconciliation, and that it was the reconciliation that led to sleeping together. He can't explain why you fell out again, after that, except to be clear that it was you who initiated the rift. Was that… It wasn't anything to do with how he'd behaved?"

"We were both all over the place."

Finally he sat down. "You can see what I'm getting at, though."

"Not really."

"He can be… I hear things about him." He'd heard – what had he heard? "It doesn't matter. It was difficult, when you left, leaving just the two of us. He was cast very low; he was really down about your having gone, which made it worse. It helped with not wanting you back. I needed you to apologise."

"You've made me afraid of saying sorry."

"You shouldn't be. Say it. But you don't need to say it. Water, bridge, under; it's all water-bridge now. You left me, Nina. You've moved on. I've moved on. Life goes on. You're moving to Greece. Your doctor is apparently infatuated with you."

"What makes you say that?" She couldn't help but be flattered. It meant there was still an option. She told herself that she needed to take Dr Christos seriously. It was that or loneliness.

"The truth is…" Paolo got back to his feet. "The truth is, I don't have the energy to be at war with anyone. I never have had the energy. You understand what I'm saying. I just want us to be able to communicate." He went and opened the door again, stepped outside and took audible breaths. "It's wonderful out here. We should be out here."

"We can go out if you like, and sit at the table by the steps." She began to get off the bed.

"In a little while." He came back into the room. "It's just as well he's going to Rome. He knows it and I know it." He leaned against the door jamb. "It's stalemate now, with Luca. Our closeness is pretty much defunct."

"Don't say that."

"It's just a fact. We won't get back to how we were." He checked his phone again. "Please try and see it from my side." He scrolled through his messages, while talking and while readjusting the collar of his shirt. Couldn't he have brought T-shirts? "The timing of it – Luca had become free and then you told me you didn't think we were in love." He looked up from reading. "What would you have thought, in that situation? What would you have concluded?"

She wanted to say, *Please, for God's sake, don't use words like concluded!* Instead she said, "I asked if you thought we were still in love and you didn't say yes. You couldn't look me in the eye and say yes, or even 'of course'. It seemed important. It seemed final."

He put his phone away in his bag and rearranged things in there. "Nina. Asking someone if they think the two of you are still in love is the same as announcing that you're not in love."

"I thought we weren't going to go over this again."

"We can make this the last time, if that's what you want."

She knew that she should tell him everything, the whole story, but even if you confessed and were absolved, how did you believe you were really forgiven; how did you avert someone's secret hatred? Secret hatred was the worst, the thing that scared her most. "I thought it was you who wanted to stop going over it."

"You're right," Paolo said. And then, "I'll tell you what it is that I have trouble with. Love as opposed to 'in love', and how time isn't always taken into account. How friendship and loyalty aren't taken into account."

What could she say to that? He wouldn't have believed her if she'd agreed. "I'm sorry. I'm truly sorry."

Saying sorry made things worse. This had always been the pattern.

"I'm going back to the hotel," he said, picking up his jacket and bag. "I'll have a nap, a shower, dinner, and then I'll be back." Pausing at the door, he added "I don't think we should talk about this any more, do you? We're beginning to regress."

Nina couldn't think what to say to him.

A few minutes later Dr Christos came into the room wearing a white coat and a stethoscope. She'd never seen him wearing a white coat, nor a stethoscope around his neck, and it occurred to her that they might be for Paolo's benefit. "Hello, hello. Just on my evening rounds. How are things? How is the conversation going?"

She found she didn't want to answer. It didn't seem possible to answer. "It's fine," she said. "We're talking."

"I'll be back after dinner with a bottle of something and you can tell me everything. I want the play by play."

"Actually, Paolo is coming back then."

"Okay. Well. I guess I'll see you tomorrow."

He went out of the room, and then returned. "I just wanted to add – forgive me, please, for any apparent ebbing and flowing. I don't want to confuse things, or get in the way while Paolo's here, and as you can imagine I have certain professional obligations." He looked towards the open door. "But I want you to know that you've become important to me in a short time."

At 8.35pm Paolo returned, with apricots, chocolate and a paper bag of salted nuts. "There she is," he said, coming into the room.

"Here I am. Still here in my monastic cell."

"Not a bad view from your monastery."

"The best." It was hard to smile.

"It's dark out there already. I'd forgotten how early it comes. It was pretty much dark by seven. And I'd forgotten how many mosquitoes there are." He scratched at his wrist. "I should have eaten the Marmite."

"What Marmite?"

"Karen says if you eat plenty of Marmite before coming over, they can smell it in your blood and stay away."

"Karen seems to know these things."

"She's done a lot of travelling."

"That's nice. So how was your swim, your dinner?"

Paolo brought the chair right up close to the bed, folded his arms onto the sheet and rested his head on them, his eyes closed. He said, "I'm so tired, Nina." She had to stop herself from smoothing his hair with her hand. "You are still coming home with me, I assume. To your place, I mean. To your home. What's the plan?"

"The plan is that I'll stay with Dad and put the cottage on the market, and put most of my stuff in store, and then I'm coming back here for the winter."

"You're not going to live at the cottage while making these plans?" He lifted his head, the better to hear.

"I'm not going to spend another night there. Don't give me a hard time about it."

"It's your call." His head went back onto the bed.

She knew she must never engage with its consciousness again. She must be separate and brief, a visitor. She must pack up and disengage, and do all of this as quickly as possible, turning the key on it, never to return. "I don't know what I'll do after that. Once Easter comes."

His eyes sleepily opened and closed. "You look anxious. Don't be anxious. We're going to get through this. It will – what's that word – normalise. Things will normalise."

"But in what way?"

"At the risk of sounding trite, I think that if you've really given Luca up, anything could be normal that we wanted it to be. We can be exceptionally civilised about this whole process."

"The dismantling."

"Indeed."

"Why do you say 'if'? You know I don't want Luca."

"You always did, though, didn't you?"

"I just wanted to be near him. I just wanted to keep talking."

"You were in love, Nina." He'd closed his eyes.

"It wasn't that."

"You say that now."

"But it's only now that matters, surely."

"I don't think you think that's true."

"The chain is broken between Luca and me."

He sat up again and rubbed his face. "I'm exhausted. So how do you feel about him going to Rome?"

"How do I feel about it? I'm fine. I hope it works out."

"He was going to go earlier, but then Mum got ill. He's going to live near Francesca's brother. It's all arranged. The brother arranged it."

"Last wishes. She wanted him to move far away."

"Mum's moving there, too. He's coming back for her once she's well enough. Meanwhile we've got the carer on full-time hours."

"Maria's going too. Wow. I wasn't expecting that. Are you okay with all this?"

"Absolutely I am. It's wonderful for her. I haven't seen her so happy for a long time. All she talks about now is how much she is going to love living near the relatives that she's forgotten she fights tooth and nail with."

Paolo was fine. He was well on the way to being recovered. He could make jokes about his mother in the middle of the conversation.

Dr Christos came in holding a bottle and three upside-down glasses, their stems between his fingers.

"Oh," Nina said. "Hello again."

Paolo stood up. "Good evening."

It was Paolo he spoke to. "I thought you might like to try a glass of island wine."

"That would be wonderful."

"As you're a wine expert."

"I'd be very interested."

"It's not a marketing exercise; don't worry. They don't make enough to export it." He gestured with the bottle hand. "We could go outside. I've had the anti-bug lamps lit for a while."

"Sounds very good to me," Paolo said. It wasn't clear if Nina was invited, but she went anyway.

Once they were seated and extra candles had been found – there was a box of matches in the doctor's pocket – and the wine was poured, and Paolo had declared it good and unusual, Dr Christos said, "Did Nina tell you that she's moving here?"

"Naturally," Paolo said, as if it was a stupid question.

"I have good news on that subject, in fact." He turned his attention from Paolo. "I'll show it to you tomorrow, Nina. I'll drive you up there. It's a very nice house, up on the hill."

"How long is it available for?" Paolo asked him.

"Until the spring, when the holiday lets start again."

"It's available at a low cost?"

"Very low, if Nina wants it."

"Then I think Nina does."

"Hold on a minute," Nina said.

"As long as it's okay for other members of her family to come and stay."

"Of course, of course," the doctor said, looking miserable.

"I will come too, to see the villa, if that's all right."

"Of course. The more the merrier."

Paolo began to ask questions about the wine. Nina excused herself, saying her leg was aching and she needed to rest, and left the two men sitting at the outdoor table in the dark. She could hear what they were saying, as she fought to stay awake. They were still talking about the old world and the new, although only in wine-making terms.

Chapter Twenty

Nina opened her eyes and Dr Christos was there wishing her a good morning. He looked at her chart and she watched his face for signs.

"Pain all gone?"

"I feel fine again. Thank you." She'd had a severe headache in the night and there had been a well-disguised concern. "What time is it?" It wasn't yet light.

"Just after five."

"Why are you here?"

"I'm your guardian angel; didn't you know that?"

"Nice thought."

"So what brought it on, the headache? It can't have been the wine. You only had a sip." Evidently he wasn't going to mention other sources of stress.

"Bad dreams." She realised, but only when her grip tightened involuntarily around it, that she was still holding her mother's diary. When she let go of it and looked at her clammy palm, she saw that blue biro had transferred from its cover, and that the doodles around the spine were smudged.

"What is that?" His curiosity was undisguised.

"It's not something I could bear to lose." She put it on the bedside table and closed her eyes. "I'm going back to sleep now." She wanted to tell him the worst about herself, to blurt it. She'd start with the ghost in the cottage, and how she'd known that it was Francesca.

Dr Christos said, "Anyway, I must get home to my dog. I'm on duty at seven."

She half opened her eyes. "You have a dog? I thought your dog died."

"I have a new dog. An inherited dog."

"You didn't tell me; what's the story?"

"No story. I don't tell you everything." And then, "There isn't much to tell. It's a mutt. Its owner died."

When he'd gone, Nina found that she wasn't sleeping, but merely telling herself to sleep, and so after a while she gave up and picked up Anna's journal and read sections of it again. It had a smell, not a maternal one especially but of the house and of childhood: a scent with a hundred obscure unnameable strands. When she'd read it the first time the sorrow had been overwhelming, but now: now was different. She'd found a way of knowing and accepting its sadness. Memories could be retrieved and reinterpreted, like books that read quite differently when you picked them up again, years later after life had taken its bite out of you, but having gone through that process Nina felt able to reinhabit the original version of the past. She'd never destroy it, the diary, but she was going to put it at the bottom of a box, just as Anna had done. Perhaps fear was addictive, like lots of other things had proven to be. The key thing was this: practising forgiveness of the staunchly unforgivable had made everything better. Even Sheila Medlar could be pardoned for her small but savage infringements, though the fact that Sheila had known for so long about the events recorded in the diary, the fact that it was Sheila who had authorised its handing over, still rankled and was probably always going to.

Robert had been nagging Nina to pay a call on the Medlars since the day she moved into the cottage, so three days before leaving for Greece she'd surrendered to the inevitable and gone to visit them. It didn't need to be a big visit, he said, but they'd love to see her. It was amazing, he said, that Nina hadn't run into Sheila and Gerald in the street – not knowing that Nina had gone to special effort so as not to. She knew that the Medlars were creatures of habit; she knew the habitual schedule of their shop and bank and library visits and did her shopping at lunchtime, which was a Medlar-free zone of the day. Their house was down a long private track at the other side of the village and was still called the Farm, even though it hadn't been one for a long time. It was ugly and grey-harled, an L-shaped botch of two centuries' additions that had once presided over 40 acres of fields, land that was now under housing, other than for a two-acre paddock that had come under Gerald's cultivation. Nina decided to go the high street way so that she could stop off to get sherbet. Once, Luca had instigated a #1970sSweets hashtag on Twitter, and he'd said then that sherbet was the hard stuff: sherbet went directly into the central nervous system. She felt the need for a hit of something – another something, strictly speaking, as she'd already drained last night's bottle of Shiraz, swigging down the glassful that remained.

Walking into the mini supermarket, Nina felt like her vision was divided into a split screen, half blandly modernised, kitted out with shelves and plastics, and half the hardware shop it had been when she was young. There had been dark mahogany fittings, a counter the length of the room, and Gus McInnes in his brown-paper-coloured coat, his square face set in concentration as he tried to solve somebody's plumbing issue, offering gadgets and advice and wrapping both in brown paper. In 1971, when they'd moved in, the shops were already wartime survivors, and Anna had found the old-fashionedness disconcerting. Since she'd died there'd been rapid change. McInnes was long gone, and so was Rudolfo – real name Roger – at the hair salon, which was now the village deli, its pavement blackboard promising local cheeses and ice creams, its windows decorated with jars of fruits steeped in alcohol and oatcakes tied in cellophane like gifts. Haig the fishmonger and Rossiter the butcher were gone too. The village had become huge, formless, part of the city, its once-green lanes lined with modern housing. Ribbon development was too misleadingly beautiful a term.

Nina got to the track and found that there were children there in front of her, two girls and a boy, all of them aged about twelve and in tracksuits. They could have been the young Nina and Becky and Andy – the three of them had been thrown together in the week between the Romanos going off to Elie and the departure for Norway – though this young Nina was a darker blonde than she had been, her plaits half fallen out. All three turned to look at who was coming towards them. The boy wasn't as tall and broad as her old friend Andy Stevenson, who'd been square-faced and had rosy cheeks and a springy thatch of brown hair. Sometimes, thanks to brutal hairdressing, Becky Winter was mistaken for a boy; the Winter children all had the same haphazard kitchen-executed hacked-off style, but Becky also had the reddest mouth, a true red that was startling against her paleness, and the most beautiful grey eyes, silver grey outlined in slate. Nina dreamed about Becky from time to time, and wondered where she was now. She'd failed to find her on Facebook or Twitter. Becky probably had a different name these days.

The threesome stood aside to let her pass, and after walking on a little way Nina went to the fence, and found that the boulder Luca had put there 35 years ago was still in place. She could see over the top and into the garden, which looked smaller but otherwise just as she remembered it, with its fruit trees, tidy rows of vege-tables, greenhouses, bantam pens and shed. Sheila had babysat Nina (had insisted on babysitting) and had described herself as an aunt, and the Medlars' bikes had often been parked at the Findlay house in the late afternoon. Sheila always brought home-baking, pitting Scottish buns against Norwegian ones, insisting on their particular Scottishness; Scottishness was a constant preoccupa-tion, and even cake a kind of patriotism. She had one of those symmetrical, expressionless snub-nosed faces, short-nosed with a long upper lip, and wore, as a kind of uniform, circle skirts she'd made herself that reached mid-calf and billowed as she cycled by. She'd worn her long brown hair up in a high bun; Nina had seen her once with it down, in her garden early in the morning, feeding the fish in the pond, and it had stretched right down her back. Gerald Medlar had been hugely tall with long skinny legs and a full dark beard; he'd worn jackets with many pockets, and always a hat, and looked like a Victorian naturalist.

The children were standing behind her. "This is a dead end," the boy said. "And that's private property." He was grumpier, sourer-faced than Andy had been. Andy was apple-cheeked and good-humoured and had found almost everything funny. Later on he'd had a fine line in cynicism. It'd been Andy that Luca spent time with as a teenager, once he and Paolo didn't hang out any more.

"I used to live here when I was your age," Nina said. "I went to your school." The children weren't interested in that. "The Medlars, who own this garden, have lived here since then." She looked at the grass for sign of hazards, getting down carefully from the rock.

"They're old people," the Becky-lookalike said.

Nina moved towards her. "Are you a Winter, is your name Winter?" The girl shrank back.

"Don't tell her anything," the boy said. "Go home and tell your dad."

Nina walked onwards. When had she last seen Sheila – other

than in the street, waving and saying "how are you?" while dashing past? The last time they'd had a proper talk must have been after Anna's funeral, at the wake that had progressed, as these things often did, from polite teatime chat over ham sandwiches to late-night booze and brutal tribal honesty (though not on Robert's part; Robert had remained dignified). A lot of whisky had been drunk, and a lot of maudlin platitudes had been exchanged, and then Sheila had made her anti-papal remark, and Maria had taken offence. These spats weren't anything new; no love had ever been lost between the two of them, not even at the beginning. Maria had been resentful of Sheila's taking on the role of spare parent to Nina, when Maria was right there, next door, and yet was seldom asked to step in. She wasn't asked by Anna because she was... Maria. Other people's children didn't like her. Nina hadn't. Perhaps it was because it was clear to them that Maria was incapable of childishness, her default setting set at an unbending authority; it was Giulio that their sons went to in times of trouble. Maria could only be authoritarian in their company, and if they were noisy or irritating she'd withdraw to the adults-only sitting room, the one the boys weren't allowed into other than for special occasions, and she'd smoke and listen to old Italian records and watch television there. Sheila, on the other hand, would get down on her knees and have big conversations with children about their small worlds, and had done so often with the young Romano boys. It wasn't an experience they remembered fondly. Maria had told Anna once that everybody – far from being complicated – could be described in three words and that Sheila was wet, manipulative and a fanatic.

At just before 7am Dr Christos came back into the room. "Still awake? What is it that's keeping you awake?"

"I don't know." The more accurate answer would've been, *There's a long, long list.*

"We can talk about it over breakfast." From across the hospital grounds came the sounds of the kitchen being opened, the electric metal shutters going up. The sun was rising at the same time. "I'll go get us something." He kissed her on the cheek on leaving and said he always looked forward to getting back to her, and Nina had a momentary sense of rightness. The past was gone and over, and she had to be forward-looking now. People said you should trust your feelings, but sometimes that was bad advice. Feelings are conservative things, and reactionary, and bogged down in the past. It didn't matter what reservations had inked themselves onto the list. Allowing this interesting-looking, complicated man to woo her might be the right decision, nonetheless. The new feelings would come, they would follow, coming in like a new tide as the old tide receded. As her mother had said, it was important to think about the actual experience, the life she'd have, the decades to come and the hour-to-hour. Nina was confident that the hour-to-hour would be entertaining, and that she'd be loved. What better basis was there? If it was set alongside the prospect of Miss Plowman's life, it had to be preferable.

Dr Christos prepared a plate of food for her, spooning on a little of everything. He passed it over and poured the orange juice. "Headache all gone?"

"I'm fine. It was thinking about Becky Winter that brought it on. An old schoolfriend. I'd never felt guilty about her before, but then suddenly I did."

"What did you have to be guilty about?" He took a peach from the tray and sat on the end of her bed.

"We dropped her. The rest of us went to a private high school and we dropped her. We had new friends who looked down on the Winters, and we lost touch. That's how it goes."

"I wish we lost touch here. The same arseholes at every wedding that were arseholes when they were seven and are still arseholes." She raised her eyebrows at him. "No, I know," he said. "I'm not sure that sort of language is becoming from my mouth, either." He aimed the stone at the bin and threw and scored. "Listen, don't go wasting any energy at all on feeling guilty about anything. Life is seriously way, way too short. I'm not going to get pretentious about a doctor's perspective, but you know – we see things. In any case I'm sure nothing you've ever done has been a cause for proper guilt, not outside the normal parameters of human error." He seemed to want to convince her and she loved that he spoke like this. He opened the French window and let the morning air in. "Seriously. Don't be guilty about anything. It's over. It's done. You're a good person and always meant well and that's basically all that counts."

As she approached over the cattle grid, seeing the house in front of her, Nina was nervous about seeing Sheila, though social encounters had all proved manageable thus far. When Nina had to, she upped her game. It was one of the problems. It made telling anyone how she was really feeling impossible. But as Anna had remarked once, when Nina was upset about Luca, a fiction of coping facilitated coping.

"Smile at the world," she'd said. "Even if you don't feel it. Even your own body will be fooled by your pretending and you'll feel much better."

Nina hadn't been to the house for three decades, but nothing seemed to have changed. The door and window frames were still painted grass green; the bicycle stand was still there, and so were the bicycles, apparently the same. They were the kind you don't see any more: butcher's bikes, her father had called them, upright and skinny with bells and baskets, their metal bits solid and black. Nina walked past them and into a porch framed in honeysuckle, the door left ajar. Before she could press the bell the door opened further and Gerald Medlar was standing in front of her, as lanky as ever, youthful-bodied and upright, though his beard was now white and his eyebrows pale and wild. Above blue cords, gardening trousers gone to holes, there was a checked blue and yellow shirt worn over a thin white polo-neck. He was holding a tray of seedlings. He almost dropped it when he saw Nina standing there.

"Nina Findlay," he said, retreating a step and smiling at her as if it were somehow ironic that she stood in front of him.

"Hello."

"We heard you were back, that you'd bought Miss Plowman's cottage. How very good to see you. Sheila will be delighted." He half turned and bellowed his wife's name into the hallway. A voice from upstairs said, "Gerald? What is it?"

He angled his head away to answer. "Come here! There's a nice surprise at the door!" When he turned back to Nina she could see that he was afraid. He was going to have to talk to her until Sheila got there. Anna had said once that she thought embarrassment was the reason Gerald bought a house with such a huge garden and tended it so obsessively, that gardening was his refuge from other people, and sure enough as soon as Sheila appeared he made his excuses, striding off across the grass towards the greenhouses. "Back in a tick," he said over his shoulder. "I just need to deal with these or they'll dry out. Put the kettle on, Sheila."

"Let me look at you." Sheila hugged Nina lightly and then stepped back to scrutinise. "Well, just look at you, same as ever," she said. Sheila too looked only marginally different. She'd been Nina's teacher in her last year at the primary school and by Nina's rapid calculation must have been at least 65, but although she'd filled out a little, around the belly and the throat, which had grown a little bullfroggish, and her hair, still worn the same, was now more salt and pepper than brown, the effect was rather as if a woman of 30 had been aged for a role; there was something unconvincing about it. She was wearing a blue skirt and matching blouse that were almost certainly home-made, that looked just the same as the clothes of decades earlier, that probably *were* the clothes of decades earlier. She took Nina into the kitchen and told her please to make herself absolutely comfortable, providing a William Morris cushion for one of the sturdy pine chairs. Nina sat as instructed, looking around the room, which was unchanged, still lined in yellow-painted tongue and groove, from a table covered with an oil-cloth printed with apples and blossom. Sheila sat opposite and reached over and took her hand, and Nina had to concentrate hard so as not to cry. Pity was the worst. Sometimes pity seemed like a low trick.

"You'll have heard all about it, then." Nina was aware that her eyes were filling and was furious with herself.

"There are never any secrets in villages. Or rather there are, of course, but everybody knows them." Sheila laughed, a short pealing laugh. She'd always believed that laughter was the best medicine. It's what she'd said to Robert when Anna left him. Now she put her hand to her forehead. "Tea. I was meant to put the kettle on." Nina was aware she'd been given time to master herself. "But you're all right and that's the main thing," Sheila's back said as she lit the old stove.

"I'm all right and that's the main thing," Nina said. Was this it? Was this all? She was filled with gratitude. "Tell me all your news."

"Nothing much to tell. We're both retired now. Gerald lives in his garden, and I read a lot, and paint and do this and that, and we go away four times a year. Quarterly. Religiously, as it were. Not usually overseas. We're about to go to Norfolk, in fact."

"Lovely." Nina managed to say the word but was awash with melancholy. This was the parallel marriage to that of her parents, the one that had survived, and it was hard to face up to their differing fates. This was the counterpart pairing, offering a glimpse of how Anna and Robert might have been if still together, and Nina couldn't help but suffer a deep unwanted envy of the Medlars and their undramatic continuing. They'd not had children – Gerald hadn't wanted them, being concerned about population control – and so there was no child who would have escaped being devastated by a separation; there was no child who could have revelled in this, their amiable togetherness in early old age, safe in this farmhouse kitchen, with parents who looked to be immortal. She felt the unfairness of it. She looked across the table and saw her parents sitting there. She aged her mother to keep pace with the softness and elegance of Sheila's own ageing.

"I still see your dad," Sheila was saying. "As you know he comes over once a week for a cup of something, a glass of something if it's the evening."

"I didn't know. He doesn't tell me these things."

"He'll never change. He was here last night. He's so happy you're back in the village. He was talking about your mother and I told him that I still miss her, every day. He said he felt the same." *It's easy to miss her now she's dead*, Nina thought. Sheila had begun to miss Anna even before she was dead. She said, her back to Nina, at the sink, "I tell him that your mother is with God, but you can imagine how he feels about that."

Nina looked at her own hands, as if critically, and had to pay attention to her mouth, which was tensing up and gathering, her tongue hard against its roof. "Thank you," she said eventually.

Sheila brought the tray to the table. "Have you spoken to your dad today?"

"I'm going there after this." Nina looked at her watch. "So I can't stay very long."

"You haven't spoken, then. Today. Look what I've done, I've poured without the strainer. Honestly sometimes I think I am losing my marbles." She returned the poured tea to the pot.

"Is there something – is Dad okay?" Nina was visited by something ominous.

"Your dad is fine. I made scones this morning so we should eat them; they don't keep." She found the strainer and returned with a tin that had once been for toffees. "Heaven knows where Gerald's got to. He's probably forgotten you're here."

"Dad – he isn't ill?"

"Oh darling, no, not ill at all. Hale and hearty."

"I can't stay very long I'm afraid."

Sheila's shoulders sagged, and her face. "Oh. Oh well. As ever, love goes with you." She was prone to saying this sort of thing.

"You're very kind," Nina said, as always she did. She didn't have to mean it.

"Your dad told me you've been low, and have seen a professional, a therapist, and I said I thought that was natural, and a good thing. The end of a marriage is a huge event in a person's life, a person of heart and soul, I mean, and you have always been that." She cleared spittle from the corners of her lips with her fingers. "Like your mother. Wonderful Anna."

"Thank you. You're very kind."

Gerald came into the room and went straight to the sink, where he washed his hands thoroughly, rubbing between his fingers and over his knuckles, before picking up and using a nail brush with vigorous strokes until he was satisfied. He sat and sighed happily, and downed his tea and crunched up two biscuits while pouring a second. "So. All well with you, Nina?" He was looking at the post, squinting at the fronts of envelopes and then opening them with a paper knife. "Drink up," he said, draining his own cup. "Dying to show you what I've done with the garden. There's some spectacular stuff coming in for the autumn show."

Sheila said, "Gerald, I'm just going to give Nina the tour first." She patted the table. "Come on. Quick tour. I'll show you my work before you're submerged in dahlias."

Nina followed her out of the kitchen and back into the hall, over the nut-brown carpet, and saw, through doors left ajar into sitting and dining rooms, that it was all exactly as always. The look of the house had been fixed 30, 40 years earlier, and it was still furnished with the sort of flat-faced, wood-grainy sideboards and cupboards that spent a decade being disdained in junk shops but are now classified as period in sales rooms. They went up the stairs, where Sheila's watercolours had been hung in a staggered row: daffodils and roses and snowdrops, things grown and brought in from the garden that had died on the page before wilting; irises flattened like a boned chicken. They went briskly around the three bedrooms, one stylised pretty wallpaper succeeding the next, a

Sanderson transition of dusky pinks and greens.

"But it's a perfect tip in here," Sheila said when they reached her and Gerald's bedroom, picking up a pair of black socks and a towel, which were all that disturbed the pristine neatness. Nina had never been in there before. There was more of the same sort of furniture, and hatboxes that served as bedside tables, piled high with early Penguin editions, their whites yellowing and front covers curled. There were more botanical watercolours: Sheila said that she'd begun to sell them at agricultural fairs. She asked Nina to say which she liked best, and Nina picked an unconvincing cherry tree, and Sheila took it from the wall, looking at the sticker on the back, and said she could do it for £35, which was chum rate, and Nina could pay her next time. She took a marbled gift wrap out of a drawer, wrapped it up and handed it over.

"Cake," Gerald said, as they reappeared in the kitchen. He was ticking items off on a bank statement. "Cake, Nina. Come and sit down. Can you make a fresh pot, Sheila? This one's stewed. Made by my own fair hands, Nina. Fruit cake. My special recipe. A smallish slice? Good girl. I'll give you the recipe if you want. It's the easiest cake in the world: you soak the raisins overnight in cold tea, melt the butter and stir everything in a pan before baking. I can't be doing with any of that rubbing-in malarkey. Or creaming. Creaming's even worse."

Sheila reboiled the kettle and the others watched her. "Miss Plowman's house," she said as she was spooning more leaves.

Gerald had been prompted. "That's quite a project," he said. "Would you mind if I came and had a look at the garden? I've been itching to see it properly for a long time."

"Of course you can." (No, no!)

"I hope you're steeling yourself for a lot of man-hours. Woman-hours."

"I don't want to change much. I like it overgrown. It has a 'garden of goodness and evil' sort of look." Sheila frowned at the description.

"You must put the health of the garden first, though," Gerald said. "It would be absolutely immoral to let it decay past the point of saving."

"I think Nina's garden morality is probably her own affair," Sheila said evenly.

"I think Nina knows that I'm only trying to help," Gerald replied, equally flatly.

"Nina does and Nina is grateful," Nina said. "I hear you are going to Norfolk. I've never been. I have always fancied a slow boat, a slow week on a boat, I mean."

"That's exactly what we're doing!" Gerald exclaimed. "On the Broads. Hiring bikes there so we don't have to take ours on the train."

"We still don't have a car," Sheila said.

"Never had a lesson," Gerald added.

"It amuses him," Sheila said. "How fashionable the way we live's becoming, again; the way the world turns."

"Amused is hardly the word," Gerald chided. "The fact is that the earth is in crisis. I don't actually know if it can be saved now, but we can delay things by making radical changes to consumption patterns."

Sheila brought the tray to the table. "Nina doesn't want to talk about consumption patterns."

Gerald changed tack. "Do you recognise this shirt, Nina? Sheila's the queen of make do and mend. I've had this shirt for twenty years at least! I'm proud of that, how little we spend. We grow almost all our own food, now we're vegetarian."

"Except on holiday; we eat meat then," Sheila added. "Vegetarian food in pubs is always terrible."

"We go mad on the pub meals and the beer and we have a lovely time, don't we?" Gerald said, beaming.

"Sounds really fun," Nina said. She looked at her watch. "And now I must go. Dad was expecting me five minutes ago." She stood up, her chair scraping back on the stone floor. "So I had better go. But it was good to see you."

"What, no time for the garden?" Gerald said, disappointed.

"Next time," Sheila told him. "She can't keep Robert waiting."

"Well, I'll say goodbye to you then, Nina," Gerald said, with such unfriendliness that Nina blushed.

"Don't sulk, Gerald," Sheila said, guiding Nina back through the hall to the porch. She watched her putting on her boots. "Happiness, it isn't difficult really, you know," she said. "It's just about being grateful for what you have. Truly grateful, every day, and showing your gratitude to one another."

How dare you, Nina said, though only to herself, as she rose from zipping and delivered her smiling farewell. "Lovely to see you."

"Forgiveness is important, dear," Sheila called after her. "Forgiveness may be the most important of all the virtues."

Nina waved as she rounded the corner. She realised that she'd left the watercolour behind.

When she got to her father's house Robert was standing inside his opened front door, as if she was expected, one of his fingers marking the spot he'd got to in one of the reference volumes. He looked anxious. "Sheila's just called me," he said, before Nina could speak. "She was worried she'd said too much."

"What's going on?"

"It's about your mother. Her diary."

"Diary – what diary?"

He turned and walked towards the study and Nina followed, saying, "Dad, what about a diary? Dad. Stop. What diary?"

When he came out again he was holding an A5 book, a fat journal dense with paper, gilt-edged, its once pale cover much drawn on in blue. "When we were in the attic, clearing out some old boxes last week –"

"Who's we?" Nina interrupted.

"We didn't know it was there. A box of your mother's things we hadn't known about."

"Who's we?"

"Sheila came and helped me sift through it."

"I bet she did."

"Nina, Sheila has been kind to me. She said she'd deal with the box and I was to leave it to her. She put the diary in the rubbish bag, but then I checked to make sure nothing we wanted had found its way in there. Sheila didn't want me to read it. She said she'd look at it first, so I knew there was something."

Nina held out her hand. "Please, Dad." Robert gave it to her, though he looked reluctant. "What is it that I should know?"

"Your mother. I think you should know your mother."

"I knew my mother better than you did." She felt it again, the old resentment. "You've read Mum's diary? Without telling me?"

"I'm telling you now."

"You shouldn't have done that." Why was so she so upset, so

threatened? Later it would seem that there was only one answer.

"I didn't know what to do for the best." He looked genuinely troubled. "You've been so unwell and I thought it was best not to tell you, but Sheila insisted. She's usually right about these things and she thought you had a right to know the truth."

Chapter Twenty-One

It was Paolo who brought the mid-morning coffee in. "I came in to say goodnight but you were fast asleep," he said, vaguely accusingly. There were responses Nina could have made (*Are you saying that I use sleep as an avoidance of you? Because that's pretty ironic*) but she confined herself to apologising.

He asked if she had spare postcards, and she said she did, but it turned out she didn't have any new ones left: the paper bag was empty. Nina's eyes went over to the window, to the shelf beneath it and the letter-writing folder, a soft zipped thing constructed from satisfyingly weathered brown leather. Paolo mustn't open the folder and go foraging and find the card she'd written on the hill. She'd used one of the cards she'd bought 25 years ago and hadn't used, left-overs that'd sat undisturbed inside the folder ever since. It was a sort of time capsule, this old-fashioned artefact; it had been her dad's once, when he was young, and he'd gifted it just before the wedding, for the writing of thank-you notes. He'd assumed it was empty but when she'd first opened it Nina had found scraps of old letters and old stamps, and she'd hung onto them. She'd brought the writing set with her on honeymoon, and had taken the surplus cards home again, and hadn't looked inside it in the intervening years; it had gone into a drawer and had been forgotten, until, in the unusual state of mind she'd fallen into when packing for this holiday, she'd wanted the folder, and had found it and put it into her suitcase.

Paolo passed the folder over, and she unzipped it and took out the five cards that had remained unused. Paolo didn't notice that they were old postcards, but there wasn't any reason why he would have done. They'd been in the folder and out of the light and hadn't really aged; the shop still sold the same ones now, the same old images, the same out-of-date typeface.

"I'll go and write them at the café and send them off," he said. "I'll have a bit of sun and a swim and come back after lunch."

"You're not staying to come with me to see this villa? Sorry,

I thought you wanted to."

"Sorry, I should have said. I saw the doctor on my way in. He's got meetings and has postponed. Not that I'm surprised."

"Why aren't you surprised?"

He was looking at his phone. "Bugger," he said. "Bugger, bugger."

"What's the matter?"

He was already leaving the room. "Sorry, got to make a call!"

They said sorry a lot to one another now.

When he'd gone Nina took out the postcard that she'd written to him just before the accident. She'd taken it out of her handbag and put it back in the folder with the others, after her things were brought from the hotel. What she'd written there shocked her. Who was this woman, who'd written these mad things? The madness stretched right across the space, leaving no room for an address, but that was okay, as the card had been sold with an envelope. She didn't recognise herself – although the simplicity of her opening words, what she had to say about regret, was undeniably moving: she was moved by her own heartfelt directness. She folded the card in half, and folded again, then tore it into shreds and put the pieces into the inner zipped pocket of the bag, ready to dispose of elsewhere. She imagined herself swimming far out underwater, using only her hips and her legs together, the postcard held tight across her chest as she took it to its hidden cavern. She was going to have to take it home with her. She couldn't put it in the bin. Dr Christos wasn't a bad person, of that she was sure, but he was the sovereign of this small world and might feel that everything was under his dominion. He might have a very clear agenda, one he might think was also in Nina's best interests.

Just as she was thinking this, the doctor came into the room and said it was time for a walk.

"I'm too tired," she told him. "I'll do it later."

"They all say that. Come on; let's take a turn around the grounds, as Jane Austen might say."

"You read Jane Austen?"

"I do, I read her when I'm feeling low. *Persuasion* is my favourite."

"*Persuasion* is my favourite too. You're the only person I've ever met who chooses *Persuasion*." She thought, *This man has been granted to me.* She got off the bed and onto the crutches. She could hear her mother saying, 'Wake up! Take this chance! Chances don't come often!' She'd said once that Nina should be brutal about opportunity; it hadn't meant much to Nina at the time.

They went around the hospital perimeter, along its smoothed-out paths. It was growing hot, and the doctor held a Chinese parasol over her head throughout, a lacquered red and white umbrella that was embellished with flowers and smelled of old glue. He said that he was having an early lunch because of a meeting, and had asked for Nina's to be delivered at the same time so they could eat together. When they got back to the room Nurse Yannis was there with the tray, which she put on the table with a little more force than was needed. "It is not fair to the cook," she said, looking at the doctor. "Think of other people." Nina was embarrassed about this selfishness by association. The point had been made in her own language.

"Don't look like that," Dr Christos said when she'd gone. "I often eat early and it isn't an issue. She is becoming absurd."

The plates held two great mounds of moussaka, its thick slices of aubergine protruding from a brown-tinged bechamel sauce that was scattered with chopped herbs. "Hilariously, for a Greek, I don't really like lamb." He looked mournfully at his lunch. "I don't really like sauces either, if we're going to entertain ourselves with a list. You mentioned that you and Luca used to make lists. I'm not keen on spice, spicy things, are you? Celery. I'm not keen on celery. Nor walnuts. Can't stand sponge cake. Or marmalade. London was constant sponge cake and marmalade. Do you have any aversions?"

"Not really. Only liver. And I don't really like rice and especially not risotto, which has been tricky on occasion."

They ate for a while in silence and then he said, "Changing the subject, have you thought any more about what you might do? I've been thinking about your bed and breakfast idea. I can see how it could work. We could do that half the year and go south for the winter."

"We?" She smiled, trying to make light of it.

"We what?" He seemed puzzled.

"Nothing."

He hadn't meant "we". He hadn't meant that. His phone rang

and he sighed and answered it. "Okay," he said into the receiver, once and then a further five times at intervals, before pressing the button to end the call. "And so I have to go. Again."

Shortly after this she heard him talking to Nurse Yannis, their voices raised. It was in Greek so impossible to know what was said, though it was clear there was vexation on both sides.

She didn't see him again until after five. In the quiet of the hospital siesta Nina thought she heard somebody crying, a woman, and when Dr Christos came back the weeping was explained.

"I'm just going home," he said, coming into the room. "Heavy day. We lost one of the old ladies. Agatha. Upset us all. Upset poor Nurse Yannis very much."

"Oh no. Agatha. I'm so sorry."

Agatha was the old lady in the long pink dressing gown, who'd tried to talk to her in the garden. They hadn't been able to communicate, but Agatha had smiled at her in a way few people did, with radiant sincerity, as if she recognised Nina and as if she loved her. Nina had returned the smiles in the same way, and it had felt like something real had passed between the two of them. Nina had looked forward to seeing Agatha and exchanging these reassurances.

"She died in her sleep this afternoon. It's very sad. Life seems very sad today. I'm going home to cook. Cooking relaxes me." He looked worn out.

"What are you going to cook? I'm sorry about Agatha."

"She was old and ill and didn't know it was coming. I'm not sure if that's a good thing or not, but anyway. Thank you. An omelette with capsicum. Peppers. I grow peppers at the back of the house, and aubergines. I eat a lot of peppers and aubergines." He seemed reluctant to leave her. "Would you like some tea? It'd be nice to have a cup of tea before I go. I wish I could take you with me. In fact, do you want to come? You could, you know. I'll bring you back again afterwards. I'm the one who authorises the signing out."

"I'd better not. But thank you. I'd love some tea."

When he came back and had settled himself he said, "Do you mind if I make a sort of a speech?"

"What is it?"

He pushed the mint-leaves further into his glass with a teaspoon.

Nina waited. "I've been wondering if maybe it's best to be direct. In the circumstances it might be best to be really direct. Despite how I look and sound, like shit no doubt, I am feeling, what's the word... the only word for it is alive. Alive, like I'm coming alive again."

"Dr Christos –"

"I know. Timing. Timing is almost everything. I won't say any more. I should go home. I'm sorry, I'm emotional and strung out today." He put the tea down and slouched in the chair. "So we need to change the subject now. Tell me a story, would you. I'm frazzled."

"What kind of a story?"

"Tell me more about the psychiatrist. What did she ask you? I'm interested. If you don't mind, that is."

"I don't mind in the least."

The hospital was enclosed by a high stone wall and tall gates, and was converted from a sinister Victorian house, one with ugly single-storey prefab additions. Outpatients was usually held in one of these, but the heavy rain of August had caused its flat roof to leak, and so the clinic had been moved temporarily into the main building. The receptionist directed Nina through double doors and to the empty waiting room, where she sat down opposite a print that was of two ducks with bow ties going down a country road with picnic baskets held in their wings. The psychiatrist came in, a young woman, brown-haired, faultlessly and sexlessly slender, wearing a brown dress, a brown cardigan, round-toed buckled shoes that were unscuffed, and one of those complicated braids that weave down the back of the head: a neat person and practitioner of order. Nina followed her down a corridor and through another set of doors, and as she did so from somewhere not far off there was a sudden loud kerfuffle, two people shouting, a shrill scream. The doctor said, "I'm sorry; just go into Room 7 there," and disappeared around the corner at a trot. Nina tried the door of Room 7 but it was locked. She didn't know what to do, and stood in the gloom becoming aware of a soup of aromas: dust, bleach, an institutional lunch cooking, new carpeting and old trouble. Two people came out of the television room and stood looking at her: a man who looked old at first glance, but at second glance probably wasn't, and a woman far younger, wearing a red sweater with a polar bear on it and tartan pyjama bottoms, who came and stood in front of Nina and asked her name. The man looked left and right and at his watch, and left and right again, his face betraying a mild impatience and fret, like a spy waiting for a contact on a bridge, one who's already late and has never been late before.

"So what did you talk about?" Dr Christos seemed bored with scene-setting.

At first she'd wanted to know about the separation, which seemed the obvious cause of the recent unravelling. Nina wasn't able to tell her about what'd happened with Luca, or rather not willing, but something had to be offered up, so she chose childlessness and its griefs as her theme, painting it as a bottled-up conflict that had unbottled itself under other marital pressures. Among the fibs and exaggerations there were truths. She explained about the miscarriage and the phobia of pregnancy that had followed, a situation Maria had been sceptical about.

"My husband's free now to find someone fertile. I think he'll remarry quickly. I think he'll find someone quite a bit younger than him. Than me."

"I see."

"He wants five. He always wanted five. He had names for them, five girl names and five for boys."

This was true. Paolo had listed them in his diary, at the back. After the baby died he'd go and stand in his room (they'd known it was a boy), one the Romano extended family had over-equipped, and look at the furnishings and the cowboy wallpaper, the map of Italy, the painted blue furniture, the wardrobe with the tiny masculine clothes and shoes.

"It frightened me," Nina told Dr Christos. "Not the talk to the psychiatrist, but the hospital itself, the patients, the way they were. The way they'd changed. I kept trying to guide the conversation back to the people I'd met in the corridor, what it was they'd been before and how they'd descended. It frightened me that the descent might be easy, that I might be at the beginning of it."

"What did she say?"

"She couldn't talk about the others. Of course she couldn't. Patient confidentiality."

"So what else did you talk about?"

"She wanted to know more about the marriage. I found myself telling her about Luca's wedding, what my dad said and why it was that I couldn't marry Luca. I told her about seeing Paolo standing alone at the reception, and having the epiphany, and how I'd never regretted it. Which was true, though Paolo doesn't think so."

"What do you mean, after what your dad said?"

"He didn't like Luca. Doesn't like him." This was true, but it wasn't the point. "And we talked about my mother. I said to her that I became my mother when my mother died, and she fixed on that."

"You told me about the day after. The day after she died. Putting on her clothes."

"The other thing is that I stopped talking. It was Anna who began to speak. My old way of talking... I said that it disappeared like the sea into itself at Corryvreckan. That's a whirlpool, off the Scottish coast; it's like the plug has been pulled in the sea. I'm not sure the psychiatrist was convinced that healthy minds can operate in metaphors."

"It was Anna who began to speak?"

"I was just thinking earlier how different it would have been, if it had been Mum who was here with the broken leg."

"How would it have been different?"

"She'd have befriended everyone, the whole island; they'd all have been here visiting. She'd have told stories and enchanted you, evaded all your serious questions, turned your questions on their head and given silly answers. She'd have talked in parables and then made you divulge. She wouldn't have let you anywhere near her."

Dr Christos frowned at her. "Nina, have you undergone – how can I put this – a disillusionment about your mother?"

"Not that. I see her differently now, I suppose. Isn't that true of all people once they're at a distance?

"Usually it's the other way around and people idealise."

"When Francesca got ill it began to be hard work. I began to be more like Nina, the old Nina, and of course Paolo didn't like her. He'd never really liked her. It was always Anna he wanted. Then, when I found out..." As she said this she realised that she could hear his feet, his shoes, his way of walking, and only had the chance to say, "He's here," before Paolo came into the room.

"Aha," he said, and then, "More tea, is it. Always tea. Tea and sympathy." Nina stared at him. "I'm interrupting; I'll leave you to it." He swept past them and out into the garden. "I'm having a cigarette with George."

Dr Christos went and stood inside the opened French window. "It's lovely out here now," he said to the two men. "I'm just going home. Rough day."

She could hear Paolo's voice saying, "Hope you have a good evening."

When the doctor had gone she went out into the garden and found that George was no longer there. She said, sitting down, "Well, that was rude."

"What was rude? I didn't want to interrupt. And I just wished the man a good evening."

"The man? Paolo, what's got into you?"

"Do you want to come back to the hotel with me and have dinner?"

"I can't walk that far."

"Of course you can. Have you tried?"

"The crutches have bruised my underarms."

"You're going to have to leave the hospital eventually."

"Of course. Why wouldn't I want to leave the hospital? I can't wait to leave."

"I'm beginning to understand the attraction."

"What do you mean?"

"The bubble. The being waited on hand and foot by a devoted servant. The man who wants you to talk about yourself all day."

She was hurt. "That's really unkind of you."

"Unkind but accurate. Look, I'm going to have to go. I have calls to make. I'll see you tomorrow." He looked at his phone as he was leaving, clicking through messages and raising his arm in a generalised wave. Nina was irritated by the constant overriding presence of the phone, its third mouth, its multiverse brain and all-seeing eye. She wanted to take it and throw it into the sea, but was simultaneously aware of the irony.

When dusk began to fall she went out into the garden. Standing by the steps to the beach, she saw Dr Christos walking along the shore with his back to her. He came up onto the road and reached the harbour and walked along its wall, along its edge as if it were a dare, swinging his left leg out and over the water repetitively.

He was having to concentrate on his feet and on the way ahead, barely even glancing at the sea; he looked like a man with a lot on his mind. When he got to the other side he turned around and might have been able to see her watching, so she retreated to her room, unaware that Nurse Yannis was waiting for her there. She gave Nina a fright, sitting there so very still. Nina didn't see her until she sank down onto the bed.

"Shit! Oh! You frightened me, sorry."

"Why you watch Christos?" Nurse Yannis asked her.

"I wasn't watching. I went out to look at the sunset."

"He is in love," Nurse Yannis said, beginning to correct an overgrown cuticle on her thumb.

"We're just friends," Nina told her.

Now Nurse Yannis bit at the nail as if it were urgent work. "So I tell him not to come any more to sit here."

"You are going to, or you have?"

"Tomorrow I tell him." She put the lamp on and closed the French window, opened the smaller window and put the mosquito screen in place, observing the evening ritual. "He tells the same. Friends, only friends. But I know this. I see this another time." She looked at Nina as if expecting her to speak. "He tells me what you say about God," she added, sounding disapproving. "But it is God who saves you on the mountain." Nina wasn't going to get into this. The nurse made a dismissive clicking with her tongue. "You believe in God when you are in the accident. You ask God to help you, in the car."

"What car?"

"Christos, he sits with you in the car when you go to the hospital."

"What? No. It wasn't Dr Christos in the car with me." She was trying and failing to see the face of the man in the ambulance.

"Yes. Christos in the car."

If Nurse Yannis said it was Dr Christos, then there wasn't any doubt. Of course it was. Why wouldn't it be the island doctor, sitting monitoring her in the back of the ambulance? Who else would it have been? She'd thought Dr Christos was Paolo: she'd hallucinated Paolo into the car, a man with only the most basic physical similarity. She couldn't remember what she'd said but remembered wanting to say everything. She'd been sure she was going to die, and it had seemed vital that she set the record straight.

That being the case, it was possible he already knew what she'd done, and was keeping quiet. This restraint was admirable, not hypocritical but an enhancement.

Nurse Yannis said goodnight, giving her a parting stern look, and Nina turned out her light and looked at the moon outside the window. Why didn't she have the courage to be an atheist? She remembered reciting the Lord's Prayer on the plane when the turbulence was at its worst, and afterwards feeling too ashamed to meet her own eye in the airport bathroom. She reached over for her earphones and iPod and listened to Allegri's *Miserere mei, Deus*, which she'd always found soothing. Its being religious music, written for the papacy, was neither here nor there; it had been a favourite of Giulio's and that was its meaning for her. "Gregorio Allegri, 1582–1652," she said aloud. She spoke her memory of facts, dates, at every opportunity now: it was a thing she did to reassure herself she didn't have brain damage. She closed her eyes and thought about churches she'd been into in Italy and art she'd seen there, reassuring herself that it was all still intact, the memory of Italy. She thought about virgins in blue cloaks, chubby-thighed cherubs, the gilding used by painter monks. She hoped to dream herself into a benign medieval world, but when eventually she slept she found herself in an aeroplane crash, on a Greek hill in the dark. Dr Christos was looking down at her and bending to kiss her on the mouth.

She heard him saying, "Nina, Nina, are you awake?" and opened her eyes and there he was, standing in her room.

"Dr Christos. What is it?" The bedside clock's illuminated hands reported that it was only 11.45pm.

"I'm just going home. I wanted to say goodnight."

"Night night. I'm asleep."

"I'll see you tomorrow. We got interrupted in the talk about your mother. Was there something you were about to say? It seemed like you were going to tell me something."

It was dark. She was only half conscious. It was an ideal time. "I found out before I came here that she had an affair." Her voice sounded thick and fuggy. "Just before my parents separated."

"She was having an affair? Anna was having an affair. Who, who with?"

"My dad found a diary, one that maybe she'd left for him to read."

"It's the one you brought with you." Nina didn't respond. "She was having an affair. I wasn't expecting that. So, who was it?"

"Too tired," Nina told him, her voice distorted. When he asked her further questions she pretended to have gone back to sleep.

He was back just after breakfast, while Nina was writing to her father. She expected him to burst in looking eager for more details about Anna's fling, but he was grey-faced and darker grey under the eyes. The death of Agatha had caused this, she assumed. She asked him if he was okay and he closed the door and said, "There's something I need to tell you."

"Uh oh." She thought it was a joke. "What've you done?"

"Behaved really badly. And stupidly. I was stupid."

"What kind of stupid?" She put the pen down on the letter.

"I wasn't going to tell you this."

"What stupid thing have you recklessly done?" She was reckless herself. She was still confident.

"I slept with Doris last night. My ex."

"Oh. Oh God." The shock was beyond concealment. "What happened? I mean, how did that come about?"

"We were both stressed out, and I was feeling down about not being able to save Agatha, and then Doris called, worried about her dad, so I went over to have a look at him."

"What's wrong with her dad?" Nina managed to say.

"He has dementia. He has bad days. He thinks that Doris and I are still married and that we have young children and he frets that he never sees them. He talks to little girls in the village thinking they are his granddaughters. He tries to grab hold of them. It can be difficult. We had a drink, a few drinks; we got a bit drunk once we'd got him to bed, and one thing led to another."

"These things happen."

"You disapprove."

"It's not up to me," she said. "I'm happy for you if you're happy."

"I'm not, that's the point. What makes you think that I'm happy about it?" He was openly impatient. "But now, now I'm in trouble, because Doris might think we're getting back together. We did it once before and got back together and it was a big mistake."

"I see."

"The point I'm not making very well – sorry – is that I don't want Doris. But it's risky, wanting someone new, wanting something new…" He looked at her and she realised he was talking about her, making his declaration right now, in the middle of confessing. "It's so risky, so dangerous, and I admit, I don't mind admitting this: I can feel the pull of returning to the past. Being pulled back to safety. Everything I say to you that you mustn't do." Nina didn't appear any longer to be listening. She stared at the letter, at her handwriting. "The thing, a second thing, is that I'm worrying now. I worry that you think of me as the kind of man who has affairs."

"You're saying you're not."

"I'm just lonely, Nina."

"I understand that." She continued to look at the letter.

"I'm sorry."

"You don't need to be." She was as serious-faced as he was.

"No, I do, I need to apologise. I really am at a low ebb. I'm tired and Agatha trusted me to make her better and I couldn't, and I'm just really tired. I shouldn't have talked about sleeping with Doris. Certainly not in those terms."

"It's okay."

"Phone calls today, and an inspection, so I'll be in the office." The change of focus was abrupt. "You know the drill. I'll see you later. Get some exercise." He jabbed towards her with his index finger as he made the point about exercise. Nina looked at this hand that was never going to hold hers, never going to touch her. It was over. She went into the bathroom, shedding her clothes and fitting the plastic protector over the injured leg, and stood in the shower for a long time, in tepid water, holding onto the safety rail, utterly bereft. What was she going to do now? She was stranded, and nowhere, and there was no obvious path. She'd been idiotic to think that the universe had provided. The universe couldn't have cared less. The universe didn't know what caring was; it didn't even know about knowing. It was time to let go. There had seemed to be only turnings, pauses, changes of direction, from one man to the other and back, as if that were the only decision that needed making. It was depressingly familiar, this pattern, this context of two possible men. She'd been caught in a closed loop, and now it was time to let go and to step outside of the whole situation.

Chapter Twenty-Two

It was hard to know what the other diaries were like because they hadn't survived. Why had Anna kept this one and not burned it with the others on the garden bonfire, the day Robert said he was no longer in love with her? It could only have been because she wanted him to find it. The fire had been small but its offerings wide-ranging. The notebooks and journals, plus paperbacks of an apparently random kind – no doubt not random in the least – and some clothes went onto the fire one by one, and Anna had stood in front of it expressionlessly. Nina had watched from her window; it was astounding to see her mother burning books. This, a two-hour lapse from optimism, had been Anna's only period of accusation, counter-accusation. It was a silent one. Nothing further was ever said between them about the separation or its causes, and she'd moved out the next morning. Robert rang every Sunday to check she was well, and they'd chatted a few minutes about the week they'd each had, as if they were friends. Sometimes Nina had been with her mother during these phone calls, and had seen how civil and friendly Anna was to him, and how hard she was hit afterwards. It was hard to know if Robert had any insight at all into the overlap between kindness and cruelty.

Once she had possession, Nina carried the diary around with her, though she slotted it into the kitchen bookcase when she was packing for Greece, among her mother's Norwegian-language novels, the ones she'd read when she was homesick. Taking it to Greece would be a haunted, compulsive thing to do: she knew this. Nonetheless, when the alarm woke her in the early morning she went straight to the shelf and picked the diary up and stuffed it down the side of clothes in her suitcase. By then she'd read it so many times that she had it virtually by heart. It was the diary from the year Anna and Robert separated, and it was the opening pages Nina kept returning to, the ones preceding the Easter disaster.

It all started innocuously enough. After an ordinary New Year week of scribbled arrangements, planning last outings and last meals, the day arrived for Nina's return to university, for her second spring term. The date of her departure, January 7th, was marked by three words, Nina Goes Back, written in large print and enclosed in a double rectangle. She'd shaded the space between the two so that it looked like a plaque.

Took Nina to the train. It's hard to know how to go on with this, Anna had written, returning from the railway station alone.

January 8th: *Cathartic house clean, baking, thank-you cards, phone calls. Feel better.*

January 9th: *Looked at premises for my shop. The house is so quiet that all I can hear is my own mind talking. It's absolutely intolerable. Sounds like exaggeration. Isn't exaggeration.*

Nina traced her fingertip over her mother's handwriting, following its upswings and downward flourishes, the neat angular precision of the middle register. She'd used a fountain pen and blue cartridges. There's something immediate in ink and also something everlasting.

January 10th: *Cinema. Walk afterwards. Heavy heart. All my life has been about looking after people. As a daughter it was all about being pleasing. That's how I cared for Mormor, in being pleasing. Then seamlessly I was passed on to Robert, and Robert was easy at first, until Nina arrived and he was so jealous.* Underneath this it said, *It is Nina who has been the great love of my life.* This last line was added later in a different, darker ink. Had it been written during the separation? Was it a message from the grave?

January 11th: *Missing Nina so much today that I can barely breathe. Need distraction. Tried Sheila's recipe for apple crumble. Half and half, rolled oats as well as flour. That is the real Scottish way I'm told. There's a real Scottish way for everything.* And then, added in pencil, *Sheila insists on custard and not cream, but custard is barbaric stuff. Egg sauce with apples. Disgusting.*

Later: *Missing Nina so much. Crossing off the days.* More than one instance of this. Multiple instances of others. *Tried to call Nina but had to leave a message.* Nina felt bad, remembering not wanting to return her mother's calls. She'd been embarrassed by getting the daily evening call from home.

The mood changed when Nina came back in February for a weekend for her father's birthday.

Such a good day today. Counting my blessings. Why do I forget to count my blessings? Anna had noted down the things they'd done, the funny moments. *We misread misled as my-zuld in the crossword and couldn't think what it meant.* Personal snippets. *Nina looks more and more beautiful and has no idea at all.* Shortcuts to things now lost. *Joke about the sheepdog and the island.* Hearts were drawn in the margin. And then Nina went back to Glasgow.

I'm aware that sadness is making me ugly, her mother had written on March 17th. *I'm aware that this is noticed.*

And then the following day: *I always had an inkling that it would matter. And lo, it matters. Has it mattered all along? It's hard to say. At first, there was gratitude that overwhelmed everything else. He said so. He called me his angel. He said he was still amazed that I'd said yes. He watched me if I was in a room. That is all over now.*

There was also this: *Out in the garden, a single tree is showing its colours. Spring seems counter-intuitive this year. Something in me that was open has closed. In some ways it's better to be closed. It's what I want to say to Nina, but don't know how to. Better only to be open in certain ways, but to know how to give all the signs of being open. Better to adopt the hard shell, but make it a beautiful one. An exotic beetle shell with enamelled jewel colours.* Something had been added afterwards in that second shade of blue. *He thinks having a child was the end of us, but actually it was what made us survive. He has no idea. Why else would I have stayed?* Among all this, in the pages leading up to April, there were eight instances in which a date was circled and the words *The Boy* were written next to the circled number. That was all. Nothing else was written or hinted at, until the eighth entry.

At first Nina had been too afraid to talk to Robert about what it might mean. She'd let him talk to the answerphone. She'd avoided him for 24 hours, and then she'd had an absolute turnaround. She'd run all the way there, across the field to his house, and demanded to know everything he knew, and he'd yielded to pressure and had told her. The day after that she'd gone to him again, invited to eat with him. The text message said, *Come round for supper. It'll save on the shopping and washing up, and you'll have been busy cleaning.*

It hadn't occurred to Nina that there would be cleaning, but it made sense. Her father had always cleaned the family house top to bottom before they went away. He'd take charge, redoing the rooms and surfaces that Anna insisted she'd already done. He couldn't bear to come home to squalor, he'd say. He'd tire himself out with it and become so grumpy that Anna would sit in the back seat of the car with Nina and not with him, and the two of them would play travel versions of board games. Nina felt deeply resentful of having to clean the cottage, but on the other hand it wasn't possible to leave it in this state, strewn with newspapers, used teacups and pizza boxes, because judgement was inevitable. Her dad had a key and he'd come in to water the plants, to close and open curtains so as to outwit burglars and to pick up the mail from the doormat. Housework was unavoidable, but just as she was starting, dear God, no, there was someone at the door, at the window, tapping on it with an unconvincing smile: Gerald Medlar, asking if he could look at the garden. She'd pleaded busy-ness and being behind schedule – ideas he had a natural respect for – and left him to do his survey alone. It was hard to talk to him because she was having trouble breathing, felt as if she'd held her breath for weeks, and the strain of it, of not breathing out and needing very soon to breathe out, was becoming too much to manage. She could hold out until Greece, and then she would allow herself to be ill. She'd be ill and then she'd be well again. She longed to be in a hotel room, all of her life and history shrunk into one suitcase. She could see that she was going into a period of silence, and needed to be somewhere she'd be allowed to be quiet. The silence seemed to originate in her belly, like a tumour. She needed to hold it there, at bay. Once silence got into the liver there was nothing to be done.

Robert seemed to have forgotten that she was coming. This wasn't unusual. There was no answer to the doorbell, nor to her shouted hello, opening the front door to the sweet zigzag drama of Mozart's violin concerto. She found him in his study, surrounded by books; he was always happiest surrounded by books, which validated and rewarded him in two ways: he felt the keenness of the challenge and knew he was up to the challenge. In a life that had presented him, in some key areas, with failure, the things that he was better at than most people had become more and more vital; over and over he sought out the drug of intellectual excellence, and scored. Nina stood looking at her father working, his back to her, and remembered other days she'd stood there, waiting till he noticed she was watching. Sometimes it was like he was brought up too fast from deep water, like he was at risk of the bends. Today there was a laptop on the desk, a new acquisition, although he still did most of the initial work longhand, on pads of narrow-ruled paper in a spiky miniature script that made Nina think of an army of tiny beetles with sharp small antennae. The laptop was sitting semi-alertly, functional enough to deliver the Mozart, while work continued by hand. Beside it a book in grimy brown cloth sat open, kept flat with a ninettenth-century gadget Anna had bought him, an iron bar with movable enclosing arms that had probably been intended for bibles. The work in progress attempted better to clarify the period from 1910 leading up to the outbreak of war. He'd been asked to send a sample, the first three chapters and a detailed synopsis to a publisher, but wasn't yet happy enough with the chapters to send them. He hadn't been happy enough with them for years. The further he got down the road with the project, the more the opening chapters had to change, and the beginning was the last thing he was going to be able to write.

It had seemed obvious to Nina that when she saw Dr Christos again things would be tricky between them, but the awkwardness was entirely one-sided. He came in with coffee and with the mail and seemed more relaxed than earlier. Perhaps confessing having slept with Doris was a burden he'd unburdened. Whatever the case, it wasn't referred to.

"So tell me, tell me," he said, sitting down. "Tell me what happened next. Who was the Boy? Was it Paolo?" Clearly he was relishing all this.

"It wasn't."

"It wasn't? It wasn't Luca?"

"It wasn't. It wasn't Luca and it wasn't Paolo. It was another boy entirely. Someone else." She had to remind herself to be normal. She couldn't take it out on him, her horrible confusion. That wasn't going to work. It'd make her unattractive, for one thing. She wasn't going to be whiney and needy. She needed to keep things absolutely open and possible while she was digesting the situation, the Doris situation and her own. Nothing was clear yet. There were ups and downs, but that was normal, no doubt, in the case of second relationships, when both of you were divorced and weary and used up and compromised.

"Are you all right?" he asked her.

"I'm fine. I'm just tired." How often it was used, this line, the *fine but tired* line, when transparency needed to be avoided.

"So how old was he, this boy?"

"Twenty. He was twenty."

His eyes went to the diary on the bedside table. "Can I have a look at it?"

"No. Sorry."

"Why not?" He looked quite put out.

"I'd rather you didn't." It was a reasonable reaction, surely, but now she began to feel as if perhaps it wasn't. It would have been a marker of an increasing intimacy, perhaps, to have shown him.

"Just a second." He answered a text message, and while he was doing so, Nina picked up the letter he'd brought and opened it.

He found this distracting. "Who's the letter from?" He was still texting.

"From my dad. He's had a breakthrough on the thing he's writing." She turned the page over, a single piece of paper. "And yes, that's basically all. It's all about work." She looked again at the envelope. "Judging by the date, seems it's been lost in the post."

"He sounds like the kind of man who won't ever retire."

"Officially he's retired, but he keeps going. He still goes into the university, dressed up in his nice old suit, and potters about the department and tries to be of use, but basically they want him to shut up and stop interfering."

Or so Nina had heard, via Gerald Medlar, whose younger brother was on the faculty. "I hope I'm not speaking out of turn," he'd said, when he came to see the garden. He poked his pointed tongue out onto his lower lip when he thought he was being wicked. "Of course your dad will always be valued, but it's important to know when to retire from the field. In this case the academic field."

"You have something of your father, too," Dr Christos said. "As well as your mother. Your enjoyment of words and your thoroughness. You must have these qualities I imagine, to be an editor."

"I'm very like my father. The irony is that my mother and I weren't really alike. She wasn't a reader, barely read at all, other than for the self-improvement books. Even then she'd get bored and abandon them halfway through; she'd want to be doing things. She was a remorseless doer of things. My dad's idea of bliss is a library and being left alone in it. But it's too easy to divide them like that."

One thing Nina found was that people were surprised when it turned out she was bookish and reserved, and had a tendency to fret. They said that she didn't look the type. Paolo had been as surprised as anyone. For a long time, Nina had thought that she was a mixture of both parents, that it was a divide, two extremes that had blended together, that beneath Scandinavian cover of lightness and sun, her father's darker Scottish soul, shaped by centuries of dour Hebridean ancestors, had worked its way in and made its pathways. People made assumptions and Nina had done it herself, associating Anna's blondeness, her easy-tanning skin, her energy and her sky-blue eyes with summer. But of course it wasn't anything like that simple.

Nina and Robert had sat in the garden, after their roast beef and potatoes, and the conversation was at first just about the holiday, the garden, the keys. Nina knew that she was going to have to initiate, or they could discuss putting evening lamps onto timers for quite a while yet. She said, "I want to talk to you a bit more about Mum." Robert said he'd like more coffee, and would she like one? She let him go to the kitchen and have his thinking time. When he returned he was ready.

"Your mother made you into her very best and closest friend," he said, pushing down the plunger slowly in the cafetiere. "Which was wonderful in its way. Her focus on you. Her extreme focus." He glanced at her to see how she was taking his use of *extreme*. "She was never more awake and never happier than when she was focused on you." He poured the coffee . "But think for a minute how that made me feel. You see, from my standpoint it could sometimes look as if Anna was making a point. She was alive with you in a way she wasn't any longer with me."

"Oh, Dad."

"Sometimes it seemed as if it was a way of keeping you to herself and keeping me away from you. The two of you developed that shorthand way of talking, those in-jokes." He got up, rubbing at his lower back, and began to pull dandelion leaves out of the rockery. "Little blighters are inextinguishable," he said, pulling and heaping.

"I always thought that's how you wanted it. I would have loved to spend more time with you."

"Really? Is that really true?"

"Of course. What do you mean? Of course it is."

"I had to over-compensate, bring balance. That's how I felt about it. It always felt as if I had to hold up the flag for an intellectual life." In his own reckoning his detachment during Nina's childhood had been not deprivation, but a gift. "You never got enough time to be bored. You never got enough thinking time. Your mother was there day and night, wanting your attention."

"She was the one giving me the attention."

He took handfuls of dandelions to the wheelbarrow. "I didn't see it that way, I'm afraid. You loved your mother, you still love your mother and I wouldn't want it any other way. Of course not. But she was the neediest person I have ever met."

Now he went into the house and began clearing plates and Nina saw that he would prefer to be alone. She said she had better get going.

"Have you lots still to do?"

"I haven't packed yet."

"You'd better get off then." He began to run the hot water into the sink. "I'll miss you when you're away."

"I'll miss you too, Dad." She put her arms around him and her cheek against his back, while Robert stood helplessly with his arms raised, holding the washing-up brush. "I must go and get organised. But first I need a pee."

As she went into the downstairs bathroom she heard him saying, "For heaven's sake, Nina, *pee* is so vulgar."

"Sorry," she called back. "I just need to micturate." It was one of their old jokes. From the loo she could see the stencilling she and her mother had done, the stems of mistletoe that arched around the window frame, the one wonky one from when the mylar film had slipped. When she came out she called out

that she was popping into Mum's room to get something, and
headed up the stairs. They both called it "Mum's room" now.
It was cold in there even in warm weather, the special chill of a
room that's unvisited, as if human interaction were important
for buildings to stay alive, as if they feed somehow off our alive-
ness. Sometimes, on the pretext of needing to find something,
she went and looked through the boxes; she'd rearrange things
and weed out a few more things for throwing away. As the years
passed, throwing things out and donating them became easier.
There were always objects at the outer margins of sentimentality,
that detached from posterity as time went on and the demands of
posterity shrank smaller. Some things could be ditched, and some
others – a very few things – were put into daily use again. Last
time, she'd retrieved the recipe book, which for a long time, in all
that interval, had been too poignant a thing to take possession of.
Its silk ribbon was still at the last recipe, the page for the pear and
almond tart, its instructions neatly amended (one more egg yolk,
50g more of ground almonds), the page smeared in butter. Anna's
old Smith Corona was also there, on top of a jewellery box. The
typewriter had always seemed too personal to give away, but now
it was moving to the margin and beginning to detach itself. Its
charity shop time was imminent.

When Nina emerged again, putting a summer dress of her
mother's into her bag, Robert was standing by the coat-hooks
holding her jacket. He opened the front door and peered out.
"Please go the road way. It's getting dark."

"I'll be fine. I like the field. I have my phone. Don't worry."

"And you have your keys, I hope."

"Of course." She felt for them through her coat pocket. Keys
weren't just for door-opening. The summer before high school
he'd coached her in what to do if grabbed or attacked by a man,
and a key in the eye had been part of it. Anna hadn't approved of
the coaching. She wanted Nina to go out into the world trusting
people and expecting the best of everyone, she said, and not
anticipating danger from strangers.

Robert's answer to this was always swift. "Remind us how
many unlocked bicycles you've had stolen from outside the shop,
because you prefer to trust people."

Nina made her way across the field, following the line of horse chestnut trees. The last of the evening light was horizontal and chilly and intensely yellow. She noticed that she had cow-shit on her boot; how could the shit of a grass-eater be so unpleasant? She and Luca had discussed this once online and had concluded that it could only be a kind of weaponry. She wasn't going to think about Luca. She noticed how red her skirt was against the dark green of the evening grass, and how auburn her coat, as red-brown as a conker. This alertness might herald an onset of mania. She noticed that she was breathing quickly. She registered that the earth smelled of autumn, which had crashed in a month early. There was mist sitting over the stile at the far end, and there was damp, and the smell of emergent mushrooms. Her jacket had angora in it and was delicately hairy, like the new winter coat of a wild pony.

As she got to the middle of the field she saw the cows. They were not the usual cows, the placid and elderly milkers, but bullocks, their eyes full of curiosity, their muzzles like wet plastic and their breath visible. They'd been bunched static and invisible to the right, but were now approaching her at a canter. The thing to do was not to run away but to turn and face them – it was counter-intuitive – so she raised her hands and shouted, "Yarr, yarr!" and rushed a few steps forward. The two at the front jumped back, splaying their front legs like playful dogs, and the ones at the back barged into the ones at the front and then there was a group of seven beginning to spread out around her, while another half-dozen walked unhurriedly up to join in. They were young but already getting heavy. They were already marked for death, with blue numbers inked on their shoulders and a yellow ticket attached to one ear. Nina had to tell herself not to begin to have these thoughts. One of them, a pretty cream colour with a curly topknot of hair, came forward, waggling his head and snorting, his nose running, and she began to walk briskly onwards. Three of them, the cream one and two others, trotted past, overtaking her effortlessly, and she could hear the rest of them approaching at the same speed. She remembered her mother saying to her once that if horses stampede, what you should do is lie on the ground. She'd made a rhyme of it: "If horses charge you, lie on the ground; they won't trample you, they'll go around." Nina lay down on the wet grass, on her side, slightly curled, and the bullocks stopped moving, standing looking at her with interest. One of them came forward and snuffled at her hair – she could smell his warm animal self – and then he moved away and began to graze, and the rest of the herd followed.

At this point Nina's phone rang out in her pocket, and it was Paolo.

She answered it while sitting up. "Hello?"

"Just checking up on you. What are you doing?"

"I've just left Dad's and I'm walking home."

"The road way, I hope."

"Hold on a minute." She got to her feet and went forward, brushing mud and grass from her clothes as she went. The bullocks let her pass as if they hadn't noticed her. They'd had their fun.

"Just to say that the offer's still open, if you need a lift to the airport."

"Thanks. I have a taxi booked, but thank you." She could be normal. She could be so normal that nobody would ever know. It was just down to – what was that word Fran had used about Luca, when she went to see Paolo? Compartmentalising. It had seemed patronising, at the time.

"Also I wanted to say…" Nina waited. "…something about Francesca."

She was startled by their synchronicity. "What about her?"

"I know you've been worrying. About Francesca's illness. About your making her ill." Christ. What had brought this on?

"People can't give other people cancer," she told him. Now she was the sensible one.

"That's exactly my point. They can't."

"I appreciate it."

"She didn't mind. Francesca. About you and Luca. I mean, obviously the kiss bothered her."

"There wasn't a kiss." Nina glanced around to make sure the cows weren't following. "Hang on a minute." She fumbled over the fence and onto the pavement. She was absolutely filthy and smelled bad and cowpat had got onto her jacket.

"Most of the time Francesca didn't really take it seriously," Paolo said. "She had the measure of the situation, you know."

She was walking past houses with lit windows, and lowered her voice. "What measure?"

"She said to me once that she was glad he got so much attention

from you, because otherwise he might have screwed his secretary.
And mine."

"Luca wasn't like that."

"Yes, Nina. He was. He is." Even as she'd defended him she
knew that she was wrong. It was the oddest thing; it was something she didn't know until she was told it, and then she knew that
she'd always known. A little piece of it was already buried there,
in the depth of herself, and had acknowledged its parent with a
cold hand. She thought about smashing the phone on the ground.

"You've always made this mistake," Paolo said. "Just because
he was playful with you. Because he appeared to confide. Wrong,
Nina. And I say this as someone who loves him unconditionally.
Nina. Hello? Are you still there?"

"I'm here, but I'm going now. I'm almost at my door." She
wasn't, but she didn't want to hear it.

"I love my brother," Paolo's voice said. "You know how much
I love my brother. His behaviour is another matter and we have
to separate the two things. He sleeps around. He sleeps around,
Nina, and always has. The truth is, he has screwed his secretary,
and he's made numerous passes at Karen. That's Luca, I'm afraid."

"So ...." Dr Christos said. "You're basically okay. You didn't look
very happy, when I came into the room."

Was she supposed to flatter him? Did he want to hear that she
was confused, her feelings all over the place?

"Ach," she said, dismissively of herself. "Brooding. Brooding
again. I go round and round with things that can't be solved and
that need to be forgotten." She'd taken care to add that last bit so
as to be clear that it wasn't Doris on her mind, but Paolo and Luca
and the past.

"Well," Dr Christos said. "You're going to have to be brave and
cut the rope."

"Paolo's good at that," she said. "At cutting the rope. When I
left him, my dad was sure that I'd return home in a day or two.
And I think there was a window. I needed Paolo to come to my
door in the rain, but he didn't. He got on with things. He accepted
the new situation in a way that made me sure he wanted it; he'd
wanted it and he was relieved."

"Of course. Or he would have fought for you."

"His ability to adjust offended me. I needed him to be more

upset about the separation and he wasn't. He got up in the morning and got on with things."

All reports agreed that Paolo was fine, seeing other women and getting on with life. He got on with his life. Was that impressive or a terrible indictment? To get on with life after your wife has left you: to function, to go to work, to manage to have ordinary conversations, to laugh at people's bad jokes, to cook for yourself, to socialise, to read the paper and understand it, to go to bed and sleep well: these were all among the things that Paolo did in the days immediately following Nina's exodus. They were all things that Nina failed to do. Paolo was immensely brave, her father said. Nina wondered if that was it, or whether it showed a certain lack, some missing filter, or perhaps an overly evolved one.

"And so, the time has come again for the doctor to do some doctoring." Dr Christos made as if to leave the room and then didn't. "I want you to know something. We haven't talked any more about it, about what I said to you earlier, and you might not want to talk about it again – I'd understand if you didn't – but Doris has emailed, and she says she wants us to reunite. As I thought might happen. I'm going to turn her down. I thought you should know." He came closer. "The truth is that you can never go back. Once something is broken, it can be repaired but it will never be the same as before it was broken. Like a teacup. It can be glued together, but it isn't the same. You can't drink tea out of it any more."

Nina was vaguely provoked. "Are you very subtly trying to tell me something about my marriage?"

In turn Dr Christos was perturbed. "You're not going to reunite with him this week, I hope. There isn't going to be a big reunion scene in my hospital, I hope."

"Why would you hope that? Don't you want me to be happy?"

"Of course, but I don't think going back to Paolo will make you happy."

"You hardly know me."

"On the contrary, I know you quite well. I've heard it in your own words."

A few minutes later Nina heard a blazing row between doctor and nurse, each of them shouting accusations she couldn't understand, followed by intemperate door-banging and then a long, deep silence as if the whole fabric of the hospital was sulking. She picked up a book, but immediately she'd found the page Nurse Yannis came into the room and sat in the chair. She appeared to be calming herself. She had one palm placed across the other at right angles in her lap, her fingers taut, and slowly rotated her hands.

"Is everything all right?" Nina asked her.

"I must talk about Christos. Christos is an angry person."

"We're all angry sometimes," Nina said. The nurse waited. "What are you saying? He is violent, abusive? He hits people?"

"No; he hates with his mouth only."

"You have been fighting. I hear you arguing. I'm sorry you don't get on well."

"He is not the person he is here," the nurse said. "Here with you, this is happy Christos. Always control."

"I think he is under a lot of stress at the moment," Nina said blandly. She wasn't going to take sides.

Nurse Yannis couldn't reply because Paolo had come into the room. "Who's under a lot of stress?" He dropped his rucksack onto the bed and asked Nurse Yannis if he could speak to Nina.

"There's something I need to talk to you about," he said when she'd gone, closing the door after her. "About Christos, who is apparently rather stressed at present."

"Doctor Christos," she corrected. "What about him?"

"Is there really something going on between you? Something that might be serious?"

The possibility had to be defended. "What's it to you? You're going out with Karen."

"You're quite right. Do what you like."

"What's going on?"

"I don't like him, Nina. I'm worrying about you."

"What don't you like about him?"

"I hear things. I don't want to say more because gossip is gossip, and I don't like gossip." He opened the bag and handed over yesterday's English newspaper. It had sand on it and was dribbled with chocolate ice cream, and was wrinkled from where it had been dampened by seawater and had dried.

"He isn't perfect. But I'm fond of him, warts and all." She heard this come out of her mouth as if somebody else had said it.

"He has warts?" Paolo asked, looking distressed. "Where are they? You have to watch out for warts."

"You're very funny. Now shut up."

He shrugged it off. "I worry about what you're getting into, that's all."

She needed to take things down a notch. She said, "To be honest, I'm not getting into anything." Why did she need to do this? What business was it of his? "I appreciate your worrying," she added.

"Okay then." He seemed reassured. Jesus – it was hard work, keeping everything possible and unresolved, and keeping everyone at bay. The plates were spinning on their high precarious poles.

"You don't need to worry," she said, emphatically, sincerely. "I know about his reputation. It's been discussed. The conversation hasn't only been one way."

"You know about Doris."

"I know about Doris."

"You do?"

"Of course."

"Oh. You don't know about Doris."

"What are you talking about? Of course I do."

"It doesn't matter. We'll talk about it another time."

"Please – please don't do that doesn't-matter-talk-about-it-later thing. Is there something you know that I should know?"

"As you say, you know all about Doris."

"What? What are you saying now? Is that sarcasm?"

"Not at all. You know about Doris or you don't, and as you say, you do. But I think we should change the subject, as walls have ears."

Chapter Twenty-Three

The next day Nina was woken by a row, one that began in the corridor and adjourned to an office, where it continued in a muffled form. She didn't see Dr Christos, nor Nurse Yannis, all morning; an auxiliary came round with the trolley and to do the tidying, and the other doctor, the one Dr Christos said looked after the geriatric patients, a white-haired, white-coated man called Dr Argyros, came in to look at the chart on the end of the bed, but didn't speak to her; didn't even look at her.

It was time for physiotherapy, so she went along to the treatment room at the other end of the hospital. It was at the furthest end of the other spur of the C-shape, and she could have gone out of her room and across the paving and in through their garden door, but she liked to go along the corridors, wishing other people *kalimera* and being *kalimera*'d back. Aside from the elderly residents there was a young woman who'd had a baby, and three post-surgical recuperators who'd returned from Main hospital, including a lively boy of twelve who'd had his appendix out and was routinely in trouble for ramming people's ankles with his remote-control car. In addition there was George, who seemed to come and go. George, she could see, through the long windows that faced into the courtyard, was at his usual table with his newspaper, and Nurse Yannis was sitting with him. When Nina got to the physio room, her single white plimsoll squeaking on the grey rubber floor, her crutches tick-tocking in rhythm, she found a note on the door in two languages saying that Mirella would be fifteen minutes late, so she sat down on the hard chair just outside her office. The blind was across the door to the garden, but the door had been propped open, and she heard Nurse Yannis saying her name.

"Christos has never been able to resist a pretty face," George said in reply. He had a native English accent, quite nasal and flat. He sounded as if he came from the Midlands. "Her looks are already beginning to go," George added, consolingly.

Somebody called the nurse's name; Dr Christos calling from inside the hospital, through a window pushed open. "Yannis!" Once she'd left, Nina pulled the blind to one side and went out into the garden, and sat at the next table to George, positioned so she could see Mirella arriving.

Looking towards him, she said, "Hello there."

"Hello," George said.

"You're English; I didn't realise."

George seemed unconcerned, lighting up a cigarette. She waited for him to say something else, but he took no further notice of her, returning to his Greek crossword. Nina's phone beeped and it was a text from Paolo. *When physio done, fancy walking to village to meet me at café? Physio been delayed,* she replied. *Enjoy the sun and come by later.* She picked up her crutches and went to the steps to the beach, and looked up at the deserted bus stop, and went down the side path to the front entrance. The road was empty, and the hill empty even of goats. Back in the foyer she heard the noise of a vehicle pulling up, and saw Mirella arriving in her little electric car. Going past Dr Christos's office, Nina heard his voice, sounding as if he was talking to someone in distress, with soothing repetitive reassurances. Was it Nurse Yannis in there? What on earth was going on? She made her way back across the garden and saw that George was watching her. "Is everything all right?" she asked him. George just shrugged. It didn't seem to bother him that language-wise the game was up.

When she came out of physio and back into the sun, Dr Christos was there, with a tray of coffee and three cups. He paused at George's table and asked if he'd like one, and George said, "No, thank you," in English without looking up from his paper.

"Getting back to the Boy," Dr Christos said, sitting down. "To be honest I thought it was possible you were lying to me and that in fact it was Paolo. It wasn't really Paolo?"

Nina joined him. "It wasn't Paolo. Nor Luca."

"I didn't suspect Luca. Luca likes to be in control."

"It was Andy. My childhood friend Andy Stevenson."

"Your childhood friend?"

"Andy from the village gang."

"Andy! Really? Andy with the rosy cheeks and thatch of hair. Luca's friend."

"Though the thatch of hair is grey now. He's still got the rosy cheeks. He still looks like a farmer."

"You've seen him?"

"I have."

"So he was twenty and your mother was, what, 45?"

George made a disgusted noise, stubbing out his cigarette with energy. He got up from the table and walked away as fast as he could, which wasn't fast. He had a bad hip, a stick, and took his time to leave the garden. Nina watched him go. "George is English. You didn't mention that."

"I'm sure I did. How else were you going to tell him you needed to phone me?"

"What's he doing here?"

"Oh – George is a local now. He's lived here a long time. He comes for his treatment and then he goes home."

"But he smokes."

"We can only advise. So how did Sheila know what the diary entries meant, when all it said was The Boy?"

"She'd seen them, the two of them, together. She already knew."

"What happened?"

"She didn't knock on our door any more. She just went in."

There was a hierarchy of door behaviour in the neighbourhood back then. Acquaintances and strangers knocked and waited. Friends knocked as they came into your house; not really asking, just announcing. Sheila had elevated herself still further, even though they didn't really like each other; there were things they did instead of liking one another. Signs of intimacy instead of intimacy.

"And there they were, presumably."

"She went rushing in to tell Mum something, and the sofa is straight ahead of the door. All Mum wrote in the diary was *Sheila came over at a bad time*. That was it: one corroborating line. Sheila told Dad that she saw Andy lying on top of my mother, and that they were kissing. He had his legs together and hers were around him. They had their clothes on, but his shirt was out of his trousers and my mother's hands were inside it, on his back. She was clear about that particular detail."

"Have you spoken to Sheila?"

"No. It's all been relayed through Dad. I've avoided Sheila. I'll continue to avoid her."

"And she'd seen the diary, before it was found?"

"No. She saw the year embossed on the front, when they found it in the box, and knew what must be in there, and made sure she got to look at it first. She tried to put it in a rubbish bag. She'd kept what she knew from my dad for all those years. Decades."

"He didn't know. And you didn't know?"

"I was at university when all this happened. I had no idea at all."

"So what did Sheila do, when she saw them together?"

"Apparently she ran out of the house, and didn't talk to my mother again for almost a week, and then she arrived at the house one afternoon, saying they had to clear the air. That was their last conversation."

"Do we know what was said?"

This time, Sheila rang the doorbell and waited, which was significant in itself. That was an unsubtle adjustment.

"She told Mum she didn't feel she could be her friend any more. Which shocks me. It shocks me even more that Dad says he can understand why Sheila had to cut Mum off. He was relieved, in a way, about the diary, when it surfaced. I could see it in him, the relief. It let him off the hook, finally. It explains everything to him now, why he began to feel differently about her."

"So Sheila and Anna, what happened after that?"

"Mutual avoidance. They wouldn't tell their husbands what they'd fought about. Sheila shunned Mum, afterwards. She didn't visit her at the flat, not once. I can't forgive her that; that's the unforgivable thing, to me. Anyway. It occurred to me that she might have been misrepresenting what she saw – for whatever reason – and I had to know, so I spoke to Andy. He said Sheila's story was accurate."

"You tracked Andy down?"

"He didn't need tracking; he still lives in the village. He works at the garden centre with his father. I've seen him twice, the first time when I was buying plants. He helped me choose. The second time the conversation was a bit different. I marched in there. I was very straightforward. Makes me smile to remember it."

"So, do you know if they…" Dr Christos trailed off.

"Andy says not. Kissing only, he says. Not that it makes any difference. It doesn't make any difference to Sheila or my father. It's immaterial to them, whether it was just kissing or not."

"I understand that point of view."

"The thing is, Sheila had always disliked my mother."

"Surely not. She was just easily shocked and worried about associating with a scarlet woman."

"Sheila and Gerald had convinced themselves they were my parents' best friends. They were always there, always there, and then Mum moved out and they dropped her like a rock. Off the end of a pier."

"There you go. It was about their own respectability, no doubt."

It wasn't just that, though. Sheila had always disliked her. Nina had spent her whole childhood aware of it. Sheila would often have a go at Anna, frequent little laughing teasing goes at her: digs about Anna not having to work, for instance, though actually she would've loved a job. The self-help books; Anna's quoting the self-help books was not popular with Sheila, and of course Robert joined in with that. He was glad to have an ally. Nina watched and learned: she saw that Sheila picked up on things Robert disagreed with Anna about, and began to have the same opinions. Music. Art. Politics. Food. Anything and everything.

"It was a very odd friendship – from Sheila's side, pretty much about constant friendly belittling. She'd ridicule Gerald, too, in front of my parents, about his low status. Dad had done some television, a history programme, and Gerald was a science teacher at an unruly school and smelled of chemicals."

"That lab smell. I have such a strong memory, now, of the labs at the school in Athens."

"You went to school in Athens?"

"High school, yes, a boarder. I got a scholarship and off I went. My father saw it as some kind of class betrayal. But let's not dwell on that. Sheila would have thought your dad very respectable, being a professor and having come from a church background. Presumably a Protestant church."

"It was clear she thought Dad had married beneath him. I remember one day over tea she asked about Mum's past, and Mum told her that she had been raised by her grandparents because her mother was a drug addict and died young; I hadn't known that, so I was as surprised as anyone. She told Sheila that her grandfather worked in a factory, and that they lived in a rented flat, and Sheila drew her own conclusions."

"It sounds almost like she was teasing Sheila."

"I'm sure she was."

It had seemed to the young Nina that it was her father Sheila really came to see, and visits were usually timed so that he was also at home, on the pretext of Gerald having another man to talk to. She had a thing for Robert. How else to explain her and Gerald's constant visits, two, three times a week? There every Saturday teatime with cake in the bicycle basket, drinking cup after cup of Lapsang and hanging around, and being sniffy about offers of Romano wine, which wasn't as wholesome as their elderflower. Her being infatuated with Robert was well known and gossiped about in the village and obvious to everyone but her husband. Or maybe he did know and didn't mind. Maybe he came along so he could keep an eye on her. Maybe he got a kick out of it. There was something about Gerald that had always made Nina wary. She shrank away when he tried to hug her, and had done so even when she was small. The look on his face, his keenness to hug, his constantly trying to get the young Nina to sit on his lap. In his presence on the doorstep she'd felt the old shiver across the back of her neck.

"Was there something going on there, between the two of them, Sheila and your dad, an affair?"

"No. He says not and I believe him. Dad's so conventional and Sheila even more so. But I remember seeing them once, at our summer party, when I was about fourteen, fifteen. Everybody else was in the garden and the two of them were in the sitting room, unaware that I was up on the landing watching. She was standing right in front of him holding a glass of wine, too close for a friend of his wife. She said, 'She doesn't deserve you, Robert', and put her hand onto one of his jacket lapels, and got hold of its edge and ran along the length of it slowly with her fingers. It was like she was staking her claim."

"Maybe it was one-sided. You can hardly blame your father for that."

"Later that night, when people had gone home, he said that Sheila Medlar was well named, as she was a meddler, and that she'd been unkind about Maria. Then he added that he wished that Sheila would stop fussing over him. He overdid it, the protesting."

She smiled, despite herself.

"What's funny?"

"Luca always said that he thought Gerald and Sheila were secretly swingers."

"Maybe they were."

"Sheila was always calling Mum a hippy; once I heard her say there'd been too much drug use, but Mum never took drugs. Unless... it's just occurred to me that she might have been talking about the antidepressants."

"There were antidepressants?"

"It makes a lot more sense now, now I know about the Boy. It makes everything fall into place. How guilty my mother was. She thought it must have been her fault, somehow, that Dad didn't love her."

"Who else's fault can it have been? We fall out of love for a reason."

"Sheila waged a long-standing and low-key campaign over years and years. I think it was Sheila who sowed the seeds of my father's decision. He says not. He calls it support. Sheila supports him. Sheila has always supported him, he says. It's a useful personal verb, isn't it? I've always thought Sheila was the reason they separated. It was a subtle, unusual thing: she talked my father out of being in love."

"Nina, Anna was having an affair with a twenty-year-old boy."

"But he didn't know that! She was only having the stupid fling because Dad lost interest in her. She said there had been signs, in retrospect. His not wanting to talk to her. His loss of interest in how she'd spent the day. His lack of interest in her shop plan. Things she didn't seem to be able to do anything about. She needed so much to be admired and my father had stopped admiring her. It made her ill. It made her make odd decisions."

"I have to tell him how ill you're feeling," Nina had told her mother, sitting with her in the window seat of the flat, looking out over the botanical gardens. Her hair was taken out of its plaits, combed through by Anna's fingers and re-plaited.

"I'm fine."

"Dad asks how you are and I can't lie to him and say you're fine."

"I'm just tired," Anna insisted. "It will pass."

"You shouldn't lie to him either, on the phone."

"He'd feel like it was his fault, and it isn't his fault that I'm ill," Anna said. "It must be my fault. We each carry with us the power to be well and whole, and it's a choice, whether to keep that power or to give it away. It's a fault in me somehow. I have failed to be well."

"You're not making sense. Sometimes it's just bad luck."

"Please don't tell your father. I hate to think of his suffering."

"Of his suffering! Of his suffering? Come on!" Nina was finding it difficult not to hate her father.

"I love him. Just because he doesn't love me, that doesn't stop me loving him as I always have. That's never going to change." Anna began to stroke Nina's head. "I want him to be happy. That's all I ever wanted. And if this makes him happier, this living separately – then I'm glad. I'm perfectly fine on my own. I have good friends, lots to do. I love living in town. I have plenty of money. And you. I have so many blessings."

"The shock of my father wanting a divorce was terrible," Nina told Dr Christos. "Really. Utter, utter shock. She didn't get over it. That's the point, for me. What it did to her. The affair's irrelevant."

"You're still defending her absolutely, aren't you, even though you know what the diary was trying to tell you."

"It tells you something different than it tells me. What it tells me is the same thing I already knew, that it was my father who killed her."

"It wasn't. It wasn't."

"I don't know how else to see it. People, they can hurt other people so much that they cause them to die. That's just a fact. That's something I have to live with."

"But she was having an affair. We both know what that means. She didn't love him any more, either."

"She'd always been good at being happy, but then when she was desperate she gave me no clue. I look back on the phase in which I know she was desperate, and see no difference in her. She was just the same with me as she'd ever been. When I first read the diary, and when I looked back, I began to feel…"

"Unsure. I see. Unsure how real her happy self ever was."

"Being told by someone you love that they no longer love you – I was never ever going to let that happen to me."

"Nina –"

"Never, never." She began to get up. "I have to go to the bathroom." When she'd got to her feet she said, "I'm sorry, I don't want to talk about it any more."

It hadn't ever been possible to confide in anyone about the way that her mother's death had changed everything, other than in the practitioner of order, the woman in the brown dress at the psychiatric hospital. Nina had gone to the final appointment determined not to tell, and had told everything. It wasn't the death itself, but what Robert said afterwards that changed the trajectory of Nina's life.

When Nina rang her father to say that her mother had died, he seemed to know even by the way she said "Dad" that there was catastrophic news.

"What is it, what's happened?"

When she'd told him, she'd heard him sit down hard into his chair. She could imagine him in his study, at the desk, staring unblinking out of the window at the rockery, the alpine plants, the bird table, the rose bushes. Her mouth was distorted in the effort not to be heard weeping.

"I'm so very sorry to hear that," he'd said. "I can't tell you how sorry."

After the funeral directors had been they'd driven back to the village in silence, and little was said over scrambled eggs on toast and tea. Robert put the television on, which he did routinely now when Nina was there, because of all the things they couldn't say to one another, all the unresolvables. Nina was willing to go along with this, but only on the assumption that he was working up to something, a statement of loss and sorrow. Even the merest hint of guilt and regret would have done; even if it had been bogus and artificial, he needed to do that, to honour Anna, to be kind to Nina. But Robert didn't. Nina, eyeing the clock on the mantel, decided she would wait till 9pm, and then she was going to have to say something. When the clock reached 9.05 she put down her book and looked across at his chair. He was watching the news for a third time that evening, apparently engrossed.

She said, "How can you love someone and then quite suddenly not love them?"

Without looking away from the screen he said, "This isn't the time."

"Yes. This is the only time. I need to know." She reached for the remote and turned the TV off.

Robert looked around the room as if the answer might lie there. "I don't know. I can't honestly tell you because I don't know." He looked at her, his brow furrowed with sincerity. "I'm sorry. That's all I can say."

"There has to be more to say than that."

He took his glasses off and put them in their case, and put the case on the lamp table. "It crept up on me slowly. Over six months or so. And then over a few weeks it became much more intense and certain. It began to feel as if it would overwhelm me if I didn't speak up."

"That it would overwhelm you? But what was it? What was the it?"

"Don't raise your voice, please. I don't know. They were feelings, not reasons. Feelings can change."

"But surely feelings about people are based on something?" She could hear her voice beginning to be unstable.

"It's a difficult thing to say, about romantic love. You're very young. You have all this to come. It's not like the love between parents and children. It shouldn't even be the same word."

"But that's the trouble. I'm as baffled by this, I'm as offended by this as if you'd stopped loving me."

"I'll never stop loving you. That isn't possible."

"You say that but how do you really know? Feelings change."

"Some feelings don't."

"But you see, you see. That was the kind I thought you had for Mum; the kind that doesn't."

"Don't get angry with me, Nina."

"Who should I be angry with, then?"

"With death. You're angry with death." He put his palms over his eyes, resting his chin on the heels of his hands. "There are things you don't understand when you're twenty, but you think you know everything, then. You think it's all so simple."

"Some things are simple," Nina told him. "They should be."

"Should is another matter entirely."

"I still can't believe it," Nina said. "That she didn't tell me she was so ill. That she told you."

Anna had discovered that she had a heart problem, and had begun a course of medication.

He smoothed over his eyebrows, once, twice, firmly with his fingertips. "She only told me on Sunday, and only because I asked."

"And why do you think it was her heart that failed?" The accusation was obvious.

"How dare you," Robert said quietly.

Nina felt the blood rising in her face. She stood up. "I'm sorry." She sat down again.

"Your mother was coping fine. I spoke to her once a week. I still cared about her, Nina."

"Coping fine? Coping fine?"

"Yes, coping fine. She was always doing something, going somewhere, rediscovering her old friends. She said it was lovely to be back in the city and to see the gardens from her window. She sounded happy."

"Jesus, Dad."

"Jesus Dad what?"

"I just don't think you knew her at all. I just don't think you knew anything about her." Nina stood up again. "I'm going to spend the night there, at Mum's flat."

"Nina. Please."

"It's what I want to do tonight. I want to be there. I'll talk to you tomorrow."

When Luca rang to express his sorrow, and to ask if Nina wanted company, Robert told him that she was alone at Anna's, and that he'd appreciate it if Luca could go round and be with her. He'd done so, with cheesecake and fizz, and they'd lain together in the spare bed. But at 2am she'd offended Luca in a way that could never be put right. At 2am when he'd asked her to marry him, she'd said that he had to be joking.

Chapter Twenty-Four

Just after lunch, Paolo came into the room looking round-shouldered and exhausted.

Nina was writing in her notebook, and the first thing he said was "What are you writing about?"

She'd seen that look on his face before. He'd always seemed threatened by her journal-keeping, as if the things she said there must be critiques of her life, and as if inevitably he must be one of the things criticised.

"It's just about the day. It's always about the day, and things I want to remember." Paolo knew what a diary was. Why did she always feel as if he was trying to catch her out by asking?

He sat down heavily in the chair and turned his shoes up and looked at them. "Don't you think sometimes that maybe you should live life more, instead of endlessly scrutinising it?"

She was still writing. "Absolutely. I'm sure I do. Most people do."

"Most people." He sounded fed up. "I couldn't give a damn about most people."

She put her pen down. "What's the matter, Paolo? You've been here two minutes and you're already bored."

"I'm not bored, I'm just tired. But thanks for pointing that out."

"I wasn't having a go at you."

"It sounded like you were."

"All I'm saying is, don't feel an obligation to come and sit with me."

"You think I'm here because of obligation?"

"I was perfectly fine for almost three weeks. I managed pretty well on my own."

"Perhaps I should go, then."

"Don't go. Please stay."

"I have other things I ought to be doing. I came to bring you fruit and a magazine someone left at the taverna. Seeing as you're lacking in things to read." He put a brown paper bag on the table, and a copy of *Woman & Home* that had a ripped cover.

"Thank you." She should have left it at that, but couldn't. "You know, that was a perfect little example of a thing that we've always done, that's always been an issue with us."

"What's that?" He picked up the magazine and flicked through it.

"The way we escalate something that's really nothing, that's really only banter."

"You do that. It's something you do."

"We do it together. I say you look bored, and you say, 'Well, I'm sorry if I bore you', and are offended, and then I'm offended that you thought I was saying that you bore me, and whoosh whoosh, up it goes in a blue flame."

He put the magazine back on the table. "It was supposed to be a general topic. I've had a similar conversation with Luca, about over-thinking, his over-thinking."

"What does he over-think?" Instantly she was nervous.

"In his case it's more to do with his virtual life. He's reading again now and doing more, but he disappeared into the internet for a while. He stopped leaving his flat, pretty much, when he was on leave. He recognises it's an issue. I think it's the main reason he's going to Rome. He's intending to be more of a physical being there, he says – to go out in the evenings, socialise, travel a bit." He gave her a searching look. "Is it okay for me to talk like this?"

"Of course." She looked out of the window at the sunshine.

"You're over-sensitive sometimes. As well. I need to add as well, because I mean as well as me. I can be over-sensitive. But all I was asking, when I came into the room, was a friendly question about what you were writing about. I could see it was one of your notebooks. It was a conversational opener, not paranoia."

"But you can see that it's my journal. It's to do with private thoughts by definition."

"It was only banter, Nina. You could have made a joke of it and said it was about how I'm getting fat. You could've claimed that it was a love poem to a rugged Greek doctor with a stubbly chin. What's a good rhyme for rugged, I wonder..."

"I'm sorry if I'm humourless." She was aware that she didn't sound sorry. "I haven't had much to laugh about recently."

"Oh lord." He put his hands one to each side of his forehead in mock horror. "The self-pity continues apace."

"Self-pity? Self-pity?"

"Don't shout. The whole hospital is listening."

She quietened her voice. "Escalation. My point exactly."

Paolo folded his arms. "While we're having a heart-to-heart, can I say that it's always pissed me off, how you and Luca treat me as if I'm not as intelligent as the two of you. Not so intellectually lithe. Luca's lovely phrase. It was something he admitted to, when he was too unhappy to edit himself."

Nina began to feel cold. What other unedited things had Luca told him? It was her turn to be affronted. "We have never done that."

"As if my brain is less evolved. Which is my own phrase, and not one of Luca's, as it happens. I can use language too."

"Who's self-pitying now?"

"As if I'm unsubtle and blundering, and as if I'm a bit slow in contrast to you two titans of repartee." He saw her shaking her head. "Oh yes you do. It's something I don't miss about having you around. The divorce is absolutely the right thing, isn't it? It's good to be reminded of that."

"Well, that's charming."

"You and Luca, your self-congratulatory superiority, that's been the number one problem. You think it was banter that was the problem? Escalation? Why do you think it was so easy for banter to escalate? What lay behind that?"

"Nothing lay behind it. You can't keep blaming Luca for all of our problems, Paolo. It's too easy to blame Luca."

"You're so critical, you know. You are the most critical, intolerant person. You say Francesca was, but really you were just as bad, only it was never in public, and never with Luca, but always with me behind closed doors. It was as if I paid the price for it."

"Super charming. Well, I imagine it's all a lot more soothing to your soul now, now you have Karen in your bed, who thinks everything you say might have been misattributed to Oscar Wilde."

The argument had brought Nurse Yannis and Dr Christos to the door. Separate doors. Nina could see part of Nurse Yannis's leg in the corridor, and the doctor's right hand at the edge of the French window.

"There we go. Zing. You never used to talk to me like that.

Luca's been a terrible influence, appalling."

Nina wanted to cry and to be forgiven, but instead she said, "Maybe you should go."

Paolo didn't need telling twice. He gathered up his things and left, saying good morning as he skirted around the nurse. She heard the swish of the electronic glass door in the foyer, its double swish as Paolo left the hospital.

Dr Christos came into the room shortly after. "May I come in? The auditors are in my office and it's getting too hot out there." He settled himself in the chair with his usual work bag, his glasses on and a pen behind his ear. Nina opened the novel she'd been reading and stared at the text, and a misspelled word leapt out at her. She folded the page corner down. She could email them when she got home.

He said, "Well that was a difficult one."

Nina was still furious. "Forgive me if I'm not yet ready to make it into an anecdote."

"That's fine." It seemed to be. He took a sheaf of paperwork out and assumed the note-making position, one leg balanced on the other, resting his folders on his raised thigh.

"I'm sorry," Nina said. "That was rude. I'm nothing but rude today. I don't know what's wrong with me."

"It's difficult having Paolo here." It was a catch-all diagnosis, pronounced while reading an invoice. "I must admit, I have trouble not rushing to your aid when I hear him yelling at you."

"We were yelling at each other. It was 50-50. And necessary, probably."

"Be wary – it can be dangerous, the post-mortem." He put the files down and opened his laptop. "It's easy to think the big row has arrived, the one that clears the air. Big row, make-up sex, vow renewal on the beach. Believe me, I've been there."

"You and Doris? You renewed your vows on the beach?"

"It's all recriminations in the end. A clean slate is basically impossible." He looked at her, diagnostically. "Do you want me to have a word with him, to say you want him to go home early?"

"No. But thanks."

"My advice is, stop explaining yourself – why should you have to keep on explaining yourself? Draw a line in the sand, Nina, Cut the rope."

"You're right. I know you're right."

"Imagine being with someone new," he said, squinting at the screen as if that's where his concentration lay, as if what he was saying wasn't something important. "Someone you have no bad memories with. No self-delusion. No doubts. No past arguments. No awful days you have to pretend didn't happen. No papering over cracks and hoping for the best and suspecting the paper won't hold. None of that. Zero. No shadows." He began to type vigorously.

Nina felt it, the upswing, and had to dismiss it. She wasn't going to be carried along by the hypothetical future. She said, "I know, I know." She picked the book up and Dr Christos kept working.

After a while she said, "My mum said to me once, you think that your suffering is also someone else's suffering, but the truth is that you're the only person who's suffering, so take a decision to stop suffering and let it go: just let it go and never think about it again. Not ever."

"Was she talking about your father, the separation?"

"No, she was trying to get me out of brooding about Luca. I was young. He wasn't talking to me and it seemed like the end of the world."

"Your mother spoke a lot of sense."

Nina turned onto her good side and away from the chair, and watched the open door, its narrow window into the hospital corridor. She saw the old man go by, the one who wore a smoking jacket and velvet monogrammed slippers, limping past very slowly on his walker. She needed to think. One thing at least was very clear: Dr Christos thought there was going to be something between the two of them. He thought that the thing had already begun. Was there still possibility here? She'd decided there wasn't, but there was a chance this was just her own intolerance at work. Susie had talked to her about this recently (she was online dating), about middle-aged people being far too prescriptive and having far too limited a wish-list. "Love can grow out of apparently rocky ground," Susie said. "I know of examples."

Nina knew Paolo was right; she was intolerant and critical; she was too hard on people; she always had been. Too hard on some, too generous to others. How did you fix that in yourself? And how did you know if a decision to pursue a relationship, despite your (perhaps over-stringent) qualms, was actually going against good instincts, just a desperate hanging-on to a once-lovely idea, as if tenaciousness might be enough? She'd told herself multiple times that it was over, the possibility of Dr Christos and her island life, but it had been necessary to keep telling herself, because something stubborn in her held stubbornly on.

She heard Dr Christos's voice say, "You seem unhappy."

"I'm fine. Just tired." There it was again, the fine-tired line.

"Yesterday you were happy about seeing Paolo, and today fighting with him has made you unhappy." She didn't answer. "He's a powerful force in your life, isn't he?"

She turned so she was flatter and could see him. "In what way?"

"I think you'd have a lot more objectivity about things if Paolo hadn't come here."

"Objectivity. How does that apply to relationships?" She laughed, hoping they could laugh at the absurdity together, but instead he looked almost bitter. "You're not going to do a stupid thing and renew your vows on the beach, I hope," he said. "Like lots of other idiots have done."

She rearranged her pillows, one lengthwise and one at right angles, and as she was doing so her phone made its text-arrival noise. *Tring*. He waited while she looked at it. "Paolo," she said. Paolo had written to apologise. *Seems I can be critical and intolerant too. Am not titan, but maybe titanic.* She couldn't help smiling.

"I think you're going to have to work harder at cutting that rope." Dr Christos closed the laptop lid decisively. "Facts need to be faced. You weren't happy, which is why you slept with Luca. I wasn't happy with Doris, or I wouldn't have slept around either."

"I didn't sleep around."

"The numbers aren't relevant."

"I think they are, actually."

"Kissing, sex, what's the difference? It's all adultery. Even this thing of ours is really adultery of a kind."

"What do you mean?"

"You know what I mean. Men don't have close friendships with women, not really. You and Luca – you were always really only about sex. It was always foreplay, wasn't it?"

"No. No, it wasn't." She wasn't going to smile, not in that concessionary way that women did, that meant *I might not really mean this*, and *I don't have any opinions I hold more strongly than that I need you to adore me.*

Nina's phone rang out, interrupting them.

"Paolo. Where are you?" It was an odd question, but she hardly knew what she was saying.

"Stuck at the taverna waiting for a Skype call. How's it going?" Evidently no mention was to be made of earlier, or of text messages.

Dr Christos mouthed "I'll go" and Nina said goodbye. She stuck two fingers up at the door when he'd gone and – tragically – felt much better.

"So what have you and your doctor been talking about today?"

Nina sighed, saying "Oh" at the same time. "I can't. I can't have any more big conversations. This is turning into a ridiculous day and I'm just not able to."

"What's going on?"

She was doing it again; being frank about the wrong things. "It's nothing. I'm fine. I'm just tired. I'm not sleeping well."

"Me neither." She could hear him drawing on a cigarette. "I'll pop up after the call. If you want to see me."

"I do." She needed to say more. "I do," she said again. She had to close her eyes on her own ineptitude.

"Have things got ridiculous with the doctor?"

"No, no." Yes, yes. "In fact we were talking about Sheila Medlar. Dad and Sheila Medlar." Even now, she hated to bracket the two names together.

"The dreaded meddler," Paolo said. She could hear him relaxing. "It was a bit of an error on Robert's part, letting her mother him. I have a vivid memory of the shirt. The shirt day."

"What was that?"

"Your dad let Sheila alter his shirt when he complained that it was too baggy for his suit jacket. Ignoring your mother chipping in saying she would do it."

"I remember."

"Sheila was a marvel, wasn't she? That was his word. She's one of those women who take pride in not having time to relax. She worked full time and also managed to have a cleaner house. They bonded over time-saving gadgets; a particularly dismal mushroom cleaner comes to mind. All those colour supplement wonders. Anna was more focused on playing and making a mess. I loved that about her."

She needed to tell him. "I found stuff out about Mum and Dad, before I came here, that I didn't tell you."

"What kind of stuff?"

And yet, she wasn't yet ready. "We found an old diary. She'd written about being unhappy when I left home."

It had been sufficient, the generalising. "My mother went round to comfort her, the day you moved to Glasgow. I think she struggled after that." She could hear it in his voice, the tact, the understatement.

"It was my going to university that started it." She said, this and there was a powerful sense of release. Perhaps it would only ever have been possible in this peculiar way, on the phone and in the same Greek village.

"Don't feel guilty."

"I do. I always have. I always will."

"She was unhappy even before you left school. We've never talked about this, but I think her flirting with me was another symptom. Even before you went to Glasgow."

"Don't."

She heard him light another cigarette. Why was he smoking so much? "Don't be guilty. It's not your fault, Nina. It's not your fault she wasn't happy."

This set Nina off; not only the words but the way that he said them. He heard it happening and let her cry. She had to dry her face with the back of her hand. She said "I discovered just before I came away that she was on antidepressants." He was quiet. "Paolo?"

"I knew about that."

"Did you visit her, at the flat?" Dread flickered deep in her stomach.

"Why do you say it like that?"

Nina cleared her throat. "How often did you visit?"

"I was the one who took round the wine. I took the boxes of wine round there that Dad sent. He sent wine and he sent flowers. The box of pills was on the kitchen counter. The antidepressants. Jesus, maybe they were tranquillisers. Jesus. What year was this again? Anyway, she saw me notice them and put them in a drawer, and thanked me for the wine and ushered me out. That's what happened every time I made a delivery: hello and thank you and how-are-you that wasn't a question, not listening to the reply. She'd lost interest in me by then." He dragged deep on his cigarette. "We should be having this conversation face to face. I'll come over."

"First can I say something else? I've always wanted to tell you. The flirting bothered me. It's always bothered me."

"Whose – Anna's?"

"No, yours. With my mother. It really bothered me."

"Her flirting with me, Nina. It wasn't my flirting with her. Constant flirting with me, when I was, what, eighteen, nineteen? In front of my mother, in front of my dad? It was absolutely bloody mortifying."

"No, no, no," Nina said placidly. "You can't rewrite that particular bit of history, Paolo Romano. You were flattered." She felt almost drunk. Perhaps they could say anything, everything; maybe even standing in the same room.

"Flattered? You're joking. My mother was upset by it, which really bothered me."

"I have to tell you, you looked pretty happy at the time."

"She chaperoned you so much. Always there, always with you. You were joined at the hip. Nobody could get anywhere near you. You were with Luca and me or with your mother."

"Er... this is a bit off point, isn't it?"

"It was also about keeping the boys away. Apart from me; she felt in control of things if it was me. It wasn't just me that she flirted with, you know. Luca. Andy Stevenson. Boys at the tennis club."

"Why do you mention Andy?"

"They played tennis together."

"Did they? I didn't know that."

"And then if we sat in your garden she'd be in and out, trying to join in, eavesdropping."

"She approved of you. She was the one who urged me to go out with you. You remember, when you came and took me to the cinema that night? My mum in her yellow dress?"

"When you came into the kitchen, she'd just put her hand against my lower back, actually almost onto my arse, when she was leaning on me to pick up a hairslide that had fallen out."

Nina began to feel shivery, imagining a cold sheen breaking out on her face. "You were the one who kept landing on her, acciden-tally on purpose, at the concert for Maria's birthday."

"Not on purpose at all. Not at all. She stroked my hand. She put her hands on top of my head and it didn't feel as if she was going to let go again. My mother was really upset, in the car on the way home. You must remember, Nina, how Anna flirted with my dad at all those get-togethers."

"She liked your dad."

There was a pause, a muttered expletive. He seemed to be talking to someone else away from the receiver.

"Is someone else there with you?"

"It's Skype. It's kicking in. Sorry to cut you off, but I'm going to have to go. I'm supposed to be in a conference call. I'll be in later."

"Work to do, even here? Can't you leave it behind even for a few days?"

"You sound like Francesca. And no, sadly not. There's a big deal going down, which I will tell you about when I see you. Plus I haven't called Karen today. So I'm signing off. I'll see you soon."

Nina looked out of the window and saw Dr Christos there, sitting at a table working. Perhaps he wasn't really working. Perhaps he'd positioned himself so he could listen in. Perhaps he was on Twitter. Perhaps he was emailing a friend and discussing her, perhaps only her body. Perhaps he was having a conversation with Doris that belied everything. Though there wasn't any evidence of any of that, nothing at all. Nina realised that she'd become someone who was quick to lose faith in people; it had come swift on the heels of losing faith in herself. Instances of loss of faith made attempts to be instantaneous and sweeping and had to be manually corrected. She wished she had the other notebooks with her, the dozens she'd filled at the cottage. She felt the strongest urge to read through them and annotate them with a sharp red pencil. She'd put lines through whole sections.

Chapter Twenty-Five

When he came looking for her the next morning, Dr Christos found that Nina had gone out onto the terrace and was standing by the steps to the beach. He had hospital paperwork with him and his glasses on his head, and looked harassed.

"Nina, about the house-hunting. I'm sorry it kept getting postponed; it's been one thing after another, but I've fenced off tomorrow after lunch. Is that okay?" He was already seating himself at the table beside her, the one furthest away from eavesdroppers, dropping a heap of files onto the table and pulling his chair into the shade of the big rectangular umbrella. Nina sat down opposite him. "So, your last day tomorrow. How are you feeling about going home?"

"Nervous."

He looked up from working. "It'll be all right. You'll be back here before you know it. A Greek spring to look forward to."

Nina turned her head to check no one else was in the garden. "You haven't told Paolo anything, have you? Things I've told you."

"Things you've confided to me? Absolutely not. I am as the tomb when it comes to secrets." He tapped at his breastbone.

"Can I tell you the thing that Paolo mustn't know?"

"Of course." He put his pen down, his phone, his glasses. Now she had his full attention.

"You know I said I changed the date of the thing with Luca." She couldn't call it anything but "the thing".

"Yes."

"I said it was earlier in April. That wasn't true, either. It wasn't how it happened."

"What happened really?" He leaned forward and rested on his elbows.

Something occurred to her. "Isn't it your day off?"

"It is. Theoretically."

"So what are you doing here?"

"I wanted to see you." He said it like it ought to be obvious.

"It happened before Francesca died, and not afterwards. While Francesca was very ill." The shock that she'd anticipated wasn't forthcoming. She had to say it again. "It was before Francesca died, and not afterwards."

"So, you made love while Francesca was ill." He wasn't shocked in the least. "It doesn't change anything, you know."

"And then she died. Did you know this already?"

"I didn't."

"I was sure you knew this already. I thought I'd told you in the ambulance." Now at last he looked surprised. "I know you were with me. Nurse Yannis told me."

"I'm sorry – I waited for you to recognise me, but then you didn't and it seemed too late to tell you."

"I didn't tell you about Francesca?"

"No. Well, you may have done. It wasn't that you didn't talk; you talked all the way there. You called me Paolo. You thought I was Paolo – but you see, that also meant you assumed I knew what you were talking about, and I hadn't a clue. None of the names and dates meant much. Plus, people with concussion very often free associate. They say all sorts of things. I'm afraid we sort of tune out. We let people talk."

"I didn't even ask myself how Paolo could have got there."

"You were talking to another man and you thought I was him. We stopped in traffic for a minute outside the town hall, and there was a cat on the steps. You started to talk about a cat you'd seen at home, and then you got hold of my hand and told me you were more sorry than it was possible to say."

"I remember that."

"We drove up to the hospital. You were still talking about time and forgiveness. It moved me very much. You started to tell Andros the same things, repeating yourself as we were getting you out of the car. You were injured and dusty, covered head to toe in pale dust, and making this earnest, urgent speech about love. That's when you got hold of his wrist. You made a big impression on him. He thought you'd fallen from the sky or came from the sea and had become human. He doesn't believe in any of that stuff, obviously, but he was actually slightly freaked out."

The doctor's phone rang and he answered it, dealing with queries, his profile serious and intent, and Nina watched him talking. He had to be told the worst. He had to be made to see that it wasn't possible to love her.

When he'd finished the call she said, "Francesca was two weeks from the end of her life. Two weeks."

He took it well. His reply wasn't hesitant. "Which has made you very guilty."

Guilty wasn't enough of a word. Its black hole wasn't deep and dark enough. "Beyond guilty. Beyond all other guilt."

"But it's retrospective, this guilt," he told her. "You weren't to know that's what would happen."

"We didn't. We didn't know. She was fine until the holiday. She thought she saw us kissing, Luca and me, and after that she thought everything Luca had told her about me was a lie."

"How do you know?"

"Luca told me. He told me later. But even at the time I saw the effects on her. It started that autumn with depression, with fatigue, and then they found another lump, and it had spread, and nothing could be done."

"It wasn't your fault."

"In February, when she died, she was supposed to have another six months at least. At least six; six months to a year, they said. But you see, after Luca and I... there was a very sudden deterioration after that. She only lived for two weeks after that."

"Coincidence. She would have deteriorated anyway, Nina."

"Luca told her. About the sex." She covered her face with her hands. "Did I tell you that? He told her what we'd done, and then she was sure about the kiss."

Now he looked surprised. "Why did Luca tell her?"

"Luca can't bear to look at me any more."

"Because of the guilt, Nina." He looked saddened. He shared a little in her desolation.

"He moved in with us so he could torture me."

"You asked for forgiveness in the ambulance. I didn't know what I was forgiving you for, but I gave it to you anyway, for what it's worth. Perhaps not much." She looked at him, her face brighter. She felt better for telling. He'd heard it, the terrible thing, and showed no sign of liking her any the less. He said, "We don't have to believe in God to absolve one another."

She said, "You're a good man." It was true: a good man, and interesting, and wasn't everybody flawed in some way or other?

The night Luca came to Nina was one of a fierce dry cold, so cold that it hurt even to breathe. It was an evening that he knew Paolo would be out: Paolo was at the AGM and was staying on for the drinks afterwards; a man who'd worked closely with Giulio was about to retire. Luca had been excused both events, because Francesca was ill, but then Maria turned up at the flat, and was sitting with her chatting and knitting. "You're going to be fine," she kept saying, a mantra that interrupted whatever they were talking about, at intervals; a punctuating chorus. Maria was still sure that Francesca would recover. She was knitting her a sweater. Knowing that his mother would prefer to have Francesca to herself, Luca had been busy on his laptop, until at just after nine he closed the lid and got up and stretched and said that if Fran didn't mind he'd pop in on Bob Gillespie's leaving do. If that was all right, he said again. Francesca said that of course he must go, and that Maria would look after her. She lay on her dark-brown sofa, propped up by silk cushions, wearing one of the beautiful dresses that she'd bought when the cancer returned. This one was green silk with billowing sleeves and a wide sash; she wore it with white stockings and white kid slippers, her hair up and fixed with diamante-headed pins, her face serious but not unsmiling, her eye contact soft and direct. She looked like a painting by Sargent or Whistler.

Nina had visited that afternoon, when the winter light had been dim and silvery, and a log fire had crackled in the grate and all had been calm. Francesca had been into town that morning and had exhausted herself: she'd had to call Luca from the middle of John Lewis, in the middle of shopping, unable to walk further. It was entirely her own fault, she said. She'd been warned not to over-do things after the second bout of chemotherapy, and lo and behold had over-done things. She rolled her own eyes at herself. She was brave, making light of it, but she was also observably weak, having trouble getting to the bathroom. Seeing this, Nina had failed to know how to act or what to say; they'd never been friends and being natural was proving impossible. She'd taken refuge in being of practical use. She'd gone for groceries and made tea. She'd taken the crockery to the kitchen afterwards and busied herself there, and then she'd said that she had to go to a dental appointment, an invented one, hugging Francesca's face to hers in leaving. Francesca had returned the embrace and Nina had burst into tears. It risked being offensive, Nina's own irrelevant upset, but it had counted for something, that hug; she'd cherish that hug later, when the self-examination began in detail, spooling out of her unstoppably. It was the last time she'd see Francesca.

When Nina got home she found that Luca had texted her. *Thanks for coming. Know it's just chemo that's made her ill, but it's frightening. Grateful that you're always there.*

She texted back. *I'm here for you. You know that. Always and at any time.*

When Luca turned up at her door, Nina had been drinking wine and watching a recorded episode of *CSI*. Detective shows had become a habit, amassing on her television on series-record. It had been a cold winter and she went for the ones that had sunshine, that had backdrops of sunny climates – *CSI*'s Miami, *The Mentalist*'s California. The day had troubled her and she'd had too much to drink; she was opening the second bottle when the bell rang. She went to the intercom bad-temperedly and asked who it was and buzzed Luca into the building, watching from the banister as he began to come up the stairs at a run. Something had to be the matter. She called down the stairwell. "Is everything all right?"

"Just visiting," he called back, running up two, three stairs at a time.

She returned nervously to standing in her doorway, wondering how to handle this. Her policy with Luca, one she'd maintained for nine months, one of rigorous detachment, had been thrown into disarray since it became clear that Francesca's condition was terminal. It wasn't any longer possible to treat him with such coolness. Francesca's being so very ill had made detachment look like something else, something that was really about her and not about him. It had subverted the whole situation. So she stood nervously, wondering what the urgency was, and was taken completely by surprise when Luca ran at her. He didn't speak but came right at her, banging the door behind him with one arm and moving fluidly to encircle her waist, still moving forward, so that she was lifted, almost lifted off her feet, struggling to keep contact with the floor as she was pushed backwards. He almost knocked her over; he was still pushing forward and almost lost his balance and she began to lose her own balance, tipping back, but then before they could fall she hit the wall hard and came to rest against it, and pushed herself upright again. Before she could move away from him Luca was in front of her, opening his legs and pressing himself into her, and then he was kissing her, hungry and certain.

"And you – you kissed him back?" Dr Christos looked appropriately disappointed. That was good. She needed him to be horrified.

"We kissed. Well, he did the kissing and I did the being-kissed part."

"Oh, come on. There isn't any being-kissed part."

"We had very brief sex. Our clothes still mostly on. Against the wall. It wasn't really a two-way thing." She looked intently at his face, waiting.

"I get that completely," he said. He saw the look on Nina's face but didn't understand it. "What's the matter?"

"He and Francesca hadn't had sex in a long time," she continued. "Paolo and I weren't having sex, either, and of course Luca had probably told her that. Luca had probably told her every confidential thing I told him when we had lunch."

"You and Paolo weren't any longer making love?"

"We did from time to time, but it was more like a necessary release than anything. It was like eating when you're tired."

"I know what you mean." He looked around to check they were alone. "It was like that with us. When we made love it was almost embarrassing. It made it obvious how separate we'd become."

"The more the sex dwindled, over the years, the more Luca and I were physical with one another. That's chicken and egg, right there. I'm aware of that. But even before the dwindling, Paolo had handed me the initiative. He didn't initiate."

"He'd lost confidence."

"It wasn't just about sex. He made me dictate how things were, how we communicated, what we did, how we lived, and then on the day we split up he said that my dictating had got him down. I couldn't win."

"You were right to tell him you weren't any longer in love. That was brave."

"Luca and I could always risk being low with one another and this was the ultimate low. Francesca was dying. Paolo and I weren't communicating. Luca and me... we had the ultimate sympathetic conversation, one without talking."

"Exactly, exactly," Dr Christos enthused. "I mean, sex is just sex, right? We bring our bodies together and it feels good, and all the additional material – it's really just mythologising. It's not emotional. It's not betrayal. You hit the nail on the head there. The ultimate sympathetic conversation." His phone was ringing again and Nina watched him talking. Even without Greek she could tell that he was saying he'd call back.

"That's the line, anyway. The one I used on the psychiatrist at first."

"What do you mean, line?" He put his phone away. "What sort of a line?"

"I told her about Luca, the sex, Francesca, but I was managing the divulging very tightly. I gave her the line I just gave you, the healthy line about ultimate sympathy. Like it was nothing. A part of our friendship and one we knew we mustn't pursue, but essentially without consequences. Although, I added, Luca had wanted consequences. He'd wanted to be with me and I'd said no. She swallowed it all, just like you did."

"Because he didn't want to be with you."

"No."

"I'm sorry."

"Don't be sorry. It's not the right thing to be sorry about."

"I don't understand."

"Have you ever had someone kiss you so hard that you can't move, holding your face still, clamped still with the back of your head pressed against a wall? Forcing their tongue into your mouth? Has that ever happened to you?"

There had been urgent coupling – sex that was all about Luca's rapid climaxing and not at all about hers. She could only hint at this with Dr Christos. She would never tell him how it really was, her initial refusal and Luca begging her, still holding her face, *Please Nina, please Nina, I love you Nina, please Nina I need this so much*, and her consent and his going at her so fast and so hard that it hurt. The reason she couldn't tell was a simple one; it was because she was too ashamed. It was also a complicated one: she was ashamed of being ashamed. She'd consented, after all.

Instead she repeated herself. "It was over quickly. It wasn't really sex at all." He had a second chance to wonder, but didn't, for a second time. But then why would he?

Afterwards she and Luca sat in silence on her sofa together, his hand on her thigh. Luca had his own reasons for keeping quiet, and Nina didn't trust herself to speak. The pressure of the unshed tears was almost unbearable and she didn't know how long she could delay. The well of her tears was filling and filling; there was already wild sobbing, though it was confined inaudibly to her head. Luca, unaware of (or perhaps unconcerned about) her despair, rested his head on the sofa-back, his eyes closed and face blank. He'd absented himself; she could see that. After a few minutes, a token few minutes, he'd patted her leg and stood up, and he'd said, "We should do this in another 25 years. Actually it's been 26, hasn't it? 26 years." She hadn't said anything, just stared at him. He'd reached for his shoes, saying, "I'd rather not go, but needs must," a claim that was very evidently fake. Nina had watched as he adjusted the laces and tied them tight with a double knot. He'd reached for his jacket and looked at his watch. He'd said, "In fact what I'll do is go to the drinks for Bob, just for one. I ought to say goodbye to him. I said I'd be there." He'd taken his phone out of his pocket and pressed two buttons and held it to his ear, his eye already on the exit. "Fran. Me. Assume you're asleep. I'll be home by 12. See you later. Bye, darling. Bye. Bye." The last word was softer, a whisper. As he'd gone out of the door, without turning to look at her, he'd said, "I'll ring you tomorrow." And then, devastatingly, "Take care."

He didn't ring. He didn't text, even when she prompted him late the following afternoon. Why did she text him? She knew she really mustn't, but she had to. Despite knowing she hadn't done anything wrong, she needed to be told that she hadn't. She needed that, more than that, and even prompting him to deliver it was a kind of humiliation. But something had to be done. She'd begun clock-watching. She'd lost concentration on the manuscript that was already late.

Hey. Said you'd call me. Hope Fran's more comfortable today. Let me know if she wants me there.

Luca didn't answer, so the next day she sent another one, and then another, and they too went unanswered, so she stopped messaging. She couldn't believe that she hadn't heard from him. There hadn't been a word, a call; no acknowledgment at all of her sacrifice. Worse, there was the possibility that it hadn't even

occurred to him that what had happened would have consequences. Sacrifice wasn't too grandiose a word. At the very least it
was her own peace of mind that was in jeopardy. It was something
important, a cherished thing that she'd allowed him, and at the
very least – was this a peculiar way of looking at it? – there ought
to be thanks. Thanks and moronic little emoticons, at the least,
and a little bit of open-hearted, well-judged self-loathing on his
side, for what he'd asked of her. Friendship and text kisses at the
least. But there was nothing. Silence that was brought to an end
only by a death. Nina got the message: the vivid, unmistakable
one that was passed back from him, his not replying. In effect it
was Francesca who was punished, because Nina stayed away.

Francesca died in her sleep fifteen days later, on a day that sparkled white with frost. She'd died in the mid-morning, having said
she was too tired to get up and would have a lie-in. When Luca
discovered her he phoned Paolo at the office, and Paolo went
straight over there and made the calls that needed to be made.
Luca wouldn't let him call Nina, not until the arrangements had
been put in place. Once Nina had been telephoned, Luca pleaded
to be taken out of the flat and to anywhere there was alcohol,
and so when she arrived she found only neighbours there, holding
the fort. Paolo texted to say that he was on his way to collect
Maria, and that Luca was walking back alone from the pub, but
then Luca didn't turn up, and when Paolo and Maria arrived he
was still missing, though other people were arriving in a steady
stream. Francesca had left explicit instructions and cases of a very
good wine for just this occasion, which meant that people who
hadn't seen each other for a while couldn't help themselves from
becoming lively; when Luca arrived, ringing the intercom because
he couldn't find his key, Paolo went down the stairs to intercept
him, to warn him that the wake was already in progress. Luca said
he wasn't coming up. He was going to climb a hill, he said, and
look at a view, and didn't want anyone's company. Nina could
hear the two men talking, their words soaring upwards from the
opened door. She waited, looking down over successive banisters
and steps that curled away in a spiral like a shell, but it was only
Paolo who appeared.

"I'm going back to the office to tell the staff," he said, his
face tipped up and his voice amplified by the tunnel effect of the

stairwell. "They don't know yet and I need to tell them what's happened."

Nina went back into Luca's flat and stood in the kitchen, unsure what to do. It occurred to her that Francesca might still be there, up in the bedroom. Nobody had mentioned this, but maybe she was still there, in state in her bed upstairs, what remained of her – remains was a terrible word – with people gathered round addressing last remarks. Nina went to the stairs and stood on the bottom step and listened, but couldn't see or hear any activity. She returned to the kitchen and opened more wine for the mourners, and found peanuts and crisps, and took a tray into the sitting room. Maria was there, seated on one of the hard upright couches with the angled metal legs, being comforted by Emilia, and as Nina was about to go in, around the half-wall from the kitchen, she heard Maria saying, "I don't want atheists in the house, depriving my loved ones of their heaven." She went in and put the tray down on the coffee table and picked up her coat and went home, and had just shed her shoes, kicking them aggressively towards the hall table, when her mobile rang and it was Paolo, saying that he was leaving the office and going to the hill to find his brother. "He's gone to Arthur's Seat. Francesca made him promise to climb it when she died. Something else he was supposed to do there, I didn't catch it all."

"Oh God."

"She said she'd be there too if it was possible to be. She believed there'd be a short window in which she could communicate, before her spirit passed on." His voice began to break. "I'm going to return to work afterwards if that's all right."

"Of course it's all right. If you're sure. I'll see you later."

Ten minutes after this, Luca texted to say that he was parked outside. Nina left her door open and ran down the stairs to the ground floor, and found him sitting in a black cab, its engine running. He hadn't arrived there, but was merely in pause, the driver sitting staring ahead awaiting orders. Luca, too, was staring ahead, as if mimicking the cabbie's vacancy. His face was greyed over and his eyes hooded, his mouth turned down, his hair unwashed and his collar askew inside his sweater. She got in and sat turned towards him. She took his hand; he was cold to the touch. His coat was too thin for the weather and he'd lost his gloves and hat. He didn't seem to want to meet her eyes. What on earth could she say that would match the gravity of the situation? In the circumstances all she could do was be sorry.

She said, "I'm so sorry, Luca," and he nodded, looking ahead. "Do you want me to come back to the house with you? I won't come if you'd rather I didn't." Why had she said that, giving credence to her imagined culpability? Speaking his disdain for him?

Luca put his hands over his nose as if in prayer. "I need to get back," he said. "And thanks. It'd be better if you didn't come with me."

Chapter Twenty-Six

Nina's phone buzzed and it was a text from Paolo, asking what time he was expected. Dr Christos asked her who it was on the phone, and she told him. She put Paolo off, writing, *Get some sun and I'll see you later.* Dr Christos asked what she'd said in reply and she told him. He looked relieved.

"So, over the next week Luca continued to be silent," she said, "and the reason for it wasn't embarrassment, but something else."

"What?"

"He worried that I had material. I had a weapon, this thing that we'd done that I had up my sleeve, and that I could take to Paolo at any time. That's the kind of person Luca thought I was."

"Surely not."

"After the funeral he was in a bad way. He was on leave from the office and Paolo found him one afternoon in his pyjamas, watching daytime television and monosyllabic. Paolo rang me; he wanted to invite Luca to stay with us. There wasn't any way of saying no."

Luca was grateful; he'd been hugely relieved when Paolo suggested it. It transpired that Paolo had already suggested it and asking Nina was just a formality. So, Luca moved in with them, theoretically only temporarily.

"Luca was living with us and the secret was also living with us. The strain was terrible. I thought Luca would find it difficult to be around us after everything that'd happened, but it didn't seem difficult at all; he treated me like a stranger." It was as if Nina were a distant relative or an old friend from college who'd come to stay, and it were Luca and Paolo's flat. "Luca was on compassionate leave and he threw himself into being a perfect housekeeper. I found him one afternoon in our bedroom, Paolo's and my bedroom, tidying up the books on the bedside tables and insisting it wasn't any trouble." There wasn't any escaping him, even at night. Luca was in the spare room, right next to theirs. They had to whisper in bed and sex wasn't possible.

"I hope you told him straight that it had to stop."

"I didn't. I had become afraid of him. He took over the shopping and cooking. He took over in general, and it wasn't possible to tell him to stop because there wasn't any doubt that it was helpful, and he'd just lost his wife. There wasn't an evening without him there, in the kitchen, making bread, making delicious meals that Paolo waxed rhapsodical about."

Meanwhile Nina was working stupidly long hours and taking on more projects, to avoid having to be around the two of them. That was a mistake. When she gave ground, Luca took more ground.

"It must have put you under so much strain. How did Paolo react? He must have seen what was happening."

"At first he genuinely didn't seem to notice it – the silence, the atmosphere. He was tired, doing Luca's job as well as his own, and Luca was odd, anyway, grieving, in other ways unlike his usual self, so it didn't strike Paolo as inexplicable that Luca only spoke to me to ask if I wanted more salad, or if I had any washing that needed doing, or could I turn off the radio because he was finding it annoying."

"It was an invasion."

"You don't want to hear the whole saga, I'm sure, but eventually when Luca was provoked it was clear that he didn't love me. Worse, that he disliked me, that he blamed me."

"People don't always use words in the same way."

"Well, that's the problem – it's not a thing, it's not cheese or a thing we all agree on, like wet or dry, or cloudy or sunny – words we all agree on. People could feel the same thing and call it by different names. People must use the same word and mean entirely different things."

"Love, infatuation, obsession, resentment – they all blur into one another. I've had experience of this."

"In what way?"

"A nurse at the last hospital. She ended things after a month and I was knocked flat. It's still hard to know what to call it. I say love, you say infatuation, my wife says obsession: all of them are ways of describing the same thing, the way I reacted."

"How did you react?"

"I became depressed. Doris quit her job and then I quit mine, and we came home, we came back here. It wasn't because of my dad dying and my mother getting ill." He worried at his lip with his teeth. "And now you know the worst. We know the worst about one another."

What could she do? She reached across and pressed his hand.

"Luca said that he'd never loved me, not even at the beginning, not even when he proposed. He said proposing had been a mistake. He was swept along by the emotion. First sexual experience. My mother's death. Everything was heightened." Nina shifted her weight in the chair. "I'm uncomfortable again. Do you mind if we go inside?"

She went slowly into her room and lay on the bed, denying gravity to the leg and enacting the long exhale of gratitude.

"He was aware, saying love one day and not-love the next, that I couldn't challenge his feelings. Feelings aren't things anyone can argue with. He exploited that; it was easy to say it wasn't ever love. He used one of the conventions. He'd never loved me. It shut the conversation down."

"Yes."

"Two months. We had two whole months of Luca living with us, the same day after day. It got so I'd be afraid to go into the kitchen. He'd made camp there with his technology all spread out." His computers and his iPad and his phone and his chargers and all the cables, his miniature TV and his music system. His retro music pumping. His magazines and his work files and printouts; his printer set up on the butcher's block. His recipe books, his kitchen gadgets he couldn't live without; his own better coffee machine, his juicer and his better knives.

"It really was an invasion."

"He'd glare at me when I went in there. He wouldn't reply if I spoke to him. I'd hear him talking quietly on the phone to other people and I began to be paranoid. I started hiding in my room."

"That's not good."

She'd sit on her bed, having claimed she preferred to work in bed, her heart beating hard. He'd come in sometimes, without knocking, with a tray, a cup of tea, some fantastic leaf tea he got sent in the post, the specialist items arriving in constant packages. He'd bring leaf tea in on a tray and his warm lavender shortbread.

"By this time I was ignoring him and it was mutual, so I didn't thank him any more for tea-trays, which meant I didn't say thank you for coq au vin or the oven cleaning either, and of course Paolo noticed *that*." Nina went up onto her elbows so she could see the doctor. "I was the first to crack. I cracked. It was as if Luca was waiting for me to apologise. What was I supposed to be guilty of? I couldn't take it any more, the silence in the flat like fog, this damp and deadening fog. I was beginning to be ill."

"And Paolo didn't see?"

"Paolo thought my behaviour was unaccountable. That was his word. You see, when Paolo appeared, Luca was sweetness and light and talkative. It was just like when we were young, except this time it was Paolo he allied himself with, and me who was ignored. Luca adjusted himself to talk like Paolo likes to talk. The two of them had nice evenings together, sitting for hours over Luca's elaborate meals, the endless bottles of wine." She gathered her thoughts. "So – one day I asked Luca if he wanted to walk with me to the park. He didn't want to – that was his first reaction, to say no, but then something made him change his mind and off we went." They went down the hill from the city to the Botanics, saying nothing to one another, walking alongside one another and saying nothing at all. They reached the big circular pond that's at the centre of the gardens, and stood looking at the fish and it was now or never. "I was so nervous. I said, 'I don't know why you're being so weird with me, but I just wanted to say that I love you. I love you, you know.' He was supposed to say he loved me too. He was supposed to explain himself. He said I was sweet. Sweet: it's a dagger in the heart."

"Is it?"

"Oh God, yes."

He said he was tired and that he was going back, and off he went, leaving Nina standing at the pond. When she got home, not long afterwards, she could hear that he was cooking, singing along to The Rolling Stones, so she went into her bedroom and wrote him an email, one that was quasi-hysterical. What had she done? How did she deserve this treatment? She couldn't take any more, she said. She was at the end of her tether.

Five minutes later, a text message arrived. *We need to talk.*

Nina didn't get it. She thought he was saying that they needed a proper talk. They weren't together, so how could it be the other sort of *we need to talk*, the one that heralds the breakup? It didn't even occur to her that Luca was breaking up with her.

She was heartened. *I'd like that very much.*

He texted again. *Nina, I'm not in love with you. Please stop this.*

Nina was stunned. What did he mean? When Paolo got home she was still writing the answering email, a long email, and this was the point at which it all got very complicated. Not because she wanted Luca, but because she was offended. She wasn't having him saying he didn't love her. She reminded him of how it had been between the two of them since childhood. She cited examples, one after the other; irrefutable things.

His reply was one line. *How much did you have to drink when you wrote this?!*

Nina got into a sitting position. "Francesca had given him advice, in the letter to be opened after she died. Advice for a second marriage. Live somewhere far away from Nina, that was the gist of it. Like it was my fault. As if I initiated and he was helpless to resist me. I was so upset by it. He'd always initiated, always always, and at the time, whenever it was happening, our double act, everybody but his mother pretended to be amused. Everybody. Sometimes even Francesca."

"Francesca was brave."

Nina sat up straighter. "One thing I've learned: some men have affairs, intimate friendships, whatever, as a prelude to leaving their wives, and some men do it so they don't have to."

A reception was held that night, the night of the long email, a presentation of medals for service at one of Francesca's charities. Francesca had been awarded one posthumously. Luca went to accept it on her behalf and wanted the whole family to be there. He made a speech and was in tears at the end, paying tribute to her and fighting his tears. Nina said to the president of the charity at the drinks afterwards that she didn't feel she'd achieved anything. She hadn't had children. She'd worked on not very great novels, nothing particularly great, her whole working life, and would leave no lasting mark. She'd lived a small life. He said that a small life was fine as long as you were happy in it, and didn't impede or hurt others. Nina thought, *Jesus, how smug can you get?* But, then that night she couldn't sleep.

Everyone went back to Luca's after the ceremony. Paolo made omelettes, and Nina was reprimanded by Maria for playing hostess. It was as if she'd dishonoured Francesca and was flaunting the fact. Paolo was mystified by his mother's hostility and told her off: what was she talking about? Somebody had to put the plates and glasses out. Luca sat motionlessly at the dining table resting his chin on his hands, and didn't seem any longer to know where things were kept. Nina conceded directorship of the laying of the table to Maria, but then of course Maria didn't know where the plates were kept either. She apologised. She said she was upset and Nina said it was fine. Luca didn't react to this at all, not to any of it.

After this there was a sort of reconciliation, though it turned out to be temporary.

The following morning, once Paolo had gone to the office, Nina went nervously into the kitchen to get breakfast and found that Luca was already there, on Twitter, typing madly and smiling at the screen. He spent his days mooching about in the flat, in and out of rooms and up and down the hall, and Nina stayed in her bedroom, but it wasn't possible to stay out of the kitchen entirely. She was standing at the toaster feeling miserable, looking at the bread in the slot as if it mattered, and heard his voice saying, "Look" and then "Nina." She turned to face him and he said, "I'm really sorry." He made a sorry face. Nina sat down in the chair across from him and said, "It's okay." It had to be okay. It couldn't be anything but okay, because Francesca had died. Peace had to be made, and quickly.

He said, "I don't really know what came over me. It's not that it wasn't wonderful sex. I'll never forget it. I'll cherish the memory always." He seemed to be serious, but he must have known it wasn't wonderful – at least not for Nina. It hadn't even been something they'd shared. It'd been something done to her. She'd permitted it, his rapid unromantic release, but she'd barely even participated. If he was prepared to lie so blithely about that, what else might he lie about? The other thing was that he seemed to have forgotten entirely that he'd cut her dead afterwards, after the wonderful and cherished sex. He hadn't made any reference, since the event in question, to *kindness and comfort*, the words he was going to use later, in his letter to Nina; the words he'd use later when he discussed it with Paolo, as if Paolo should be proud of Nina for having sex with his brother.

It was all the wrong way round. She wasn't having this going on the record, not even their own personal record. She said the words she was thinking out loud. "Actually it wasn't wonderful. It wasn't really even sex. It was more like something that was done to me."

Luca took grave and instant exception to this. He jumped up, his eyes bulging, his muscles all clenched. He came storming round to her side of the table, shouting, "What did you say?", roaring like a mad person, like an angry father who's been disrespected. Nina got out of her chair as quickly as she could, pushing it towards him as a barrier and moving swiftly backwards and away. He kept coming. He pushed her backwards with the flat of his hand.

He said, "Are you suggesting that you were raped?"

She was shaken. "Of course not."

"Because you need to be very careful with your insinuations." He was literally trembling with rage, his fists all gathered up. He left the flat – he grabbed his coat and his laptop, his phone, and off he went, slamming the door. Then he came rampaging back in, coming intimidatingly close to her again, and pointing at her, jabbing the air. "You should've said no. You should've refused, the night I came over."

"What?" She was absolutely thrown by this. "What?"

"You fucking slut."

She couldn't believe it. She gasped. "*What* did you call me?"

The look on his face was as if he'd eaten something foul and rotten. He said, "I'm wasting my time here," and off he went.

Nina didn't think he'd come back to the flat, other than to move out his stuff, but no. It turned out he'd gone straight to the office and announced that he felt ready to resume work.

Paolo brought Luca home with him at seven o'clock, all smiles, both of them in a notably good mood. They went and ensconced themselves in the kitchen, opening the first bottle and talking through the day's events, and Luca made dinner, and things continued in that same vein, following the same pattern, for another six days. Luca had long conversations with Paolo deep into the night, ones Nina wasn't welcome to join. He needed Paolo now. He claimed Paolo back, and of course Paolo couldn't help but be flattered by that, by being needed; he couldn't help but be a little bit flattered by being preferred.

"The night I left, Luca had gone home – but it was only so he could get more of his stuff. That was the last straw. I went and stood in front of Paolo, who was reading, and said, 'Paolo, do you think you and I are any longer in love?' Suddenly that seemed to be the point. It seemed like that was the real problem."

"Paolo didn't see that Luca had put himself between you?"

At first, Paolo thought Nina's saying she was moving out was just flouncing. He thought it was childish. Luca was cheered up by looking after them, and he was making a big effort to help around the house. It was kindness, and it wasn't possible to object to kindness, not in those circumstances, not without looking like a monster.

"All Paolo saw was me behaving badly. It even occurred to me that Luca was going to tell Paolo about the sex, in order to get me to move out, so he could have Paolo to himself."

"He wouldn't have done that."

"That wasn't the worst thing. The worst thing was yet to come."

Nina had arrived weeping at her father's house that night in a taxi. He didn't take her moving out seriously, either. The two of them had a conversation about Anna, and then Robert went up for an early night. Nina watched television and drank some more of his whisky, and then at about 11.30pm the phone rang. Luca had called her so late because he'd waited till Paolo had gone to bed.

"Luca was furious. What the hell was I playing at? He'd got back to the flat and found that I'd gone. I'd yelled at poor Paolo and stormed off. How could I be such a total coward? How could I do that to Paolo?"

"Understandable. In a way."

"He said, 'Do you want to hear what I really think? I've never liked the way you've treated my brother.' I was so upset. I was shaking violently; I could hardly speak. I said, 'The way you treated him, you mean.' He said, 'No Nina, it wasn't me who was married to Paolo and who failed to love and cherish him.' I couldn't believe my ears. I kept saying, 'What? What?' I had chest pain. My breath was short. I couldn't breathe. I thought I was going to die."

She said, "I don't understand," though that wasn't true. She understood everything. Nonetheless like an idiot she started making more lists. "Why were you constantly trying to be with me, and touching me; why did you roll me across the floor, and throw me in the sea so you could put your hands under my thighs, and why did you constantly bitch about Francesca?" He said he remembered it differently.

"Then he said, 'There's something else you need to know.' He'd told Francesca about the sex. She'd known about it since the day after it happened. That was completely shattering. I hadn't seen her again; I'd kept away. Luca was blanking me so I stayed away. I should have gone to see her anyway. I know that. I'm not proud of that. I missed two family Sunday lunches with an invented flu bug. Francesca knew, all that time, that I'd had sex with her husband. She didn't call me. She didn't say anything."

"Oh, Nina."

There wasn't even the remotest possibility that Luca had hinted how it really was. He would have painted quite a different picture. Though perhaps no picture was painted. Perhaps the brutal, informative *Nina and I had sex last night* was enough for his wife. Francesca may well have closed her ears against more details.

"It had a big impact on me. I was worthless, a worthless person. It still makes me sweat to think how betrayed she must have felt."

"What a mess." Dr Christos was shaking his head.

"I told Luca I was never going to speak to him again, and he hung up the phone and that was that. I haven't spoken to him. I haven't seen him. I sent him a chirpy postcard when I first got here, about the island food; just about the food. I have no idea why I did that. It makes me laugh, actually, to think of him receiving it and being puzzled." She laughed bleakly. "I suppose in time we might have to make our peace, not a real peace, but maybe a token one. Maybe I just won't see him again. I hope not. But if we did and if, sometime in the future, he was ever to refer again to our supposedly golden time, the summer we were eighteen – he was always harking back to it – I'd have to tell him the truth, that most of the time it wasn't how he remembers it. For most of the time we were both supremely bored."

"Yes. You should tell him that." Dr Christos had to leave her, to go home and walk his dog, who'd been locked in on his own all day. He said he'd be back later, after Paolo had been to visit, to see how she was. He kissed Nina on the cheek before he left.

Once he'd gone she dozed a while, and had dinner, which was a spinach filo pastry pie with pine nuts and unexpectedly good, and watched Greek television, looking at the pictures but thinking about Luca, and then Paolo was there, cursory in his greeting and fishing a packet out of his bag.

"Here. I brought more figs. And also, red wine." He produced the bottle. His expression was grim.

"Are you okay?"

"Things on my mind."

"What kind of things?"

"Work. Work which has followed me to Greece. And also, Christos. Christos is always here. I swear he has a lookout who warns him I'm walking down the road; he always seems to be leaving your room as I come through the main door."

"He doesn't really have enough to do."

"And that's why he's hired the locum."

"He hasn't hired anyone. There isn't any money."

"You haven't met him? Dr Argyros? He's Doris's uncle. He's come out of retirement temporarily. He seems very nice."

"Dr Argyros? He came in once and looked at the chart, but he didn't even say hello. You've met him?"

"We had a brief chat earlier. I thought he was very personable."

"It must have been for his sake, for Dr Argyros's sake, to give him a job before the funding runs out."

"Look," Paolo said. "Speaking of money running out, there's something you need to know. It's about the business. It's being sold. Hence long phone calls, and emailing from Vasilios's bar, and bad nights."

"What? Oh no, why?"

"Hence also, I'm afraid to say, Mum's stroke."

"Paolo, I'm so sorry. This is terrible news. Can't it be sorted out? Is there still time to sort something out?"

"It can't be stopped now, not now the bank's got wind of the trouble we're in. It's started raining so they've taken their umbrella back. But there's a buyer and a good offer – finally the right offer, we hope, after a lot of messing us about."

"You're not going to be Romano & Sons any more?"

"They're keeping the name, the brand, and they're keeping

the sons, at least for now. I told them I wanted to go part time, maybe become a consultant, depending on the money. I think the time has come to change my life."

Chapter Twenty-Seven

On their last day Paolo texted to say that he'd hired a car from Andros and was going to Main Island for the morning, and did she want to come? Nina didn't feel up to it, but said she hoped to see him later.

Back at 1.30 to take you to lunch, he replied. *Be ready. Also, at 4.50 precisely we're going for a drink.* A second text followed on its heels: *That's today's schedule, so rest up and no excuses.*

She was waiting in the foyer when he arrived, roaring up in a tiny car. It was too small for someone with a broken leg, he said, getting out and locking it up, and in any case he didn't fancy going to the café again. The taverna was out, too. Both tavernas.

"Because of the eavesdropping?"

"Because of the world-class eavesdropping; correct." He held up a bulging carrier bag. "Picnic. I've been to the market. The town was hooching and I had trouble parking, but it's beautiful over there, the main square, the planting, the shopping, the church. I'd live over there if I were you. Anyway. Picnic. Come on – can you walk 200 yards, along to the next bench? It's hot but there's that big tree. I noticed there's shade creeping over the seat, so it should be good timing."

They went slowly, at Nina's pace, along hot tarmac, past arid verges that smelled of summer, and sat on the bench, and looked at the twin headlands that framed the bay, and at the far shore of Main Island, whose outlines were gauzy and drifting. Nina glanced at her watch. The bus would already have been through on its lunchtime run. She was wearing a big hat and sunglasses, hoping to be incognito, but the crutches were a giveaway and various islanders came over to wish her well. "Here comes another one," Paolo kept saying, as they were approached again by a concerned and smiling face. "It might be time to learn how to say that you're feeling much better." In between halting conversations they ate stuffed vine leaves, an oily aubergine salad and a pale bitter cheese that was good with the fruit that emerged from a series of paper bags. They talked about the food and the view and locals they'd met, and what living there in the winter might be like.

Afterwards, Paolo delivered Nina back to her room and said he'd be back in two hours precisely. He said she should be ready to go out for a late-afternoon jaunt.

"What kind of a jaunt?"

"All will be revealed. Bring a cardigan, hat, suncream, the usual kit. Camera. Don't forget your camera. I've got some phone calls to make first, but I'll come back for you."

The picnic had made her tired and sweaty, so Nina changed out of trousers and into a loose floral dress without sleeves, and lay on the bed to rest. She'd just got off to sleep when Dr Christos came in, wearing jeans and a white shirt, a red embroidered waistcoat, the Aviators tucked into his collar. "So here we go: time to go and look at the villa. I ran into Paolo outside and he said he'd have to miss it." He looked at his watch. "We have one hour 45, so we'd better get going. Dr Argyros is covering. Are you ready? My car's outside."

Dr Christos's car was a small silver hatchback, immaculately clean, its interior smell suggestive of air conditioning and recent valeting. The passenger seat had been moved back to its furthest setting, and he helped Nina manoeuvre herself into it, pulling the strap of the seatbelt across her and fixing the buckle. "We don't have much time," he said, "so I'm only going to show you the house that's in the top village today, but I can send you lots of pictures of another one, which is across the water, and a link to their website." He reversed the car and turned out of the car park, letting tourist bicycles go by first, cycling raggedly in a bunch. Nina was reminded of her childhood village, the gang on their bikes. There was safety here, and a society and hopefulness.

"That sounds good," she said, absent-mindedly.

"I also know of several good places to buy, which I'll send you details about. You can have a look at them in November when you get back." They went along the coast road, and as they got to the turnoff he slowed down. "First, do you want to go along and have a quick look at my place and have some coffee there?"

"Maybe if we have time afterwards."

"Okay, let's get straight to it." He put his foot down and turned up the hill, taking its initial steep slope at quite a clip. Round two

soft bends they went, and then a third, and as they approached the
site of the accident Nina could feel the beginnings of panic. Her
breath quickened and shortened and she found that she'd clamped
both hands onto the dashboard. Dr Christos glanced at her once,
twice, as he was driving. "You all right?"

"I'm fine." It was interesting; now that they were out of the
hospital grounds her first inclination was to lie.

"You're finding the hill very interesting." Nina had her head
turned to the right, grateful to be on that side of the car. "Are you
okay?"

"I just want to get past here."

The car slowed almost to a halt. "Do you want to stop and take
photographs?" He took his hands off the steering wheel, looking
out over the valley.

"No, thanks," Nina said firmly. "Can we just press on?" They
drove around the tight corner and another softer one, and saw the
roofline of the hamlet ahead, and then the canopies of trees that
lined the small square. "I took photographs there before," she
added, less severely. "I was taking pictures when Andros almost
ran me over."

He glanced at the camera in her lap. "That's right, we picked
it up off the road. You've used it at the hospital, so it still works."

"It does. Amazingly."

"Have you looked at the pictures since the accident?" he asked
her, slowing for goats.

"I deleted them all."

"Sunsets are difficult things to capture on film."

They drove at low speed through the village, circling around a
sleeping dog and pausing so that children who were playing football could get out of the way. They stopped by the gate into the
allotments, and Nina saw, through the loose hedge of fig trees,
that there were long rows of plants, some at ground level, some on
canes and wires, a vivid red of peppers and tomatoes, the purple-
black of aubergines, racks of foliage and hidden hanging beans,
and women bending to the task, in their black patterned dresses
and dark headscarves. She felt a surge of optimism. Perhaps she
too could have a garden. Perhaps there'd be nowhere better in the
world to be a woman who lived alone than here. There might not
be friendship of a straightforward kind, but that mightn't be a
bad thing. There'd be community, and perhaps that'd be enough.

Perhaps it was what she needed, a kind of embracing and protected seclusion, something at once loyal and incurious.

Dr Christos drove on, taking the dirt road to the left after the final house, bouncing gently along through the accumulated dust of a long and rainless summer, and Nina saw the side wall of the villa sitting ahead of them. The track curved first to the left, closer to the edge of the cliff, and then curved round to the right so that the front of the building came into view. The afternoon light shone against it, spangling off the glass, and she realised that she'd seen its white face, its blue shutters, many times from down on the shore. They parked to the right, under a high shed with open sides, and came out into a small side garden, in which agave and other succulents rose solidly, architecturally, out of terracotta pots. There was also a mosaic made of beach pebbles, of a whale encircled by fishes. Stretched across the wall in front of them, above the ground-floor windows, was a vast red bougain-villea that teemed extravagantly with blooms.

Dr Christos led the way round to the front door, to a terrace with a wooden table and chairs, all painted in a peeling grey green. "It's not completely ugly, is it?" he said.

"Oh my God, look at this."

It was like looking out from the top of the world. The hill descended in bursts, rocky and dotted with tussocks of pale grass and wild flowers; beneath it she could see the pastel colours of the shore, the wide blue of the bay. Stepping further forward, a narrow strip of the lower village became visible, the houses stretching along the coast road. Main Island seemed huge, close at hand, and smaller more distant islands appeared as blue smudges on the horizon line.

"In fact, you can see my place from here." He took the crutch from her good side and led her by the hand, further into the garden, past pots of cacti and between stumpy olive trees that had ropes of fairy lights twisted into them.

Inside the villa, one big opened-out room was subdivided by open-backed bookcases into a sitting end and a kitchen end, whose units were built of breeze blocks coated in plaster and painted white, its worktops made of coloured tiles. The floor was a warm brown ceramic, the chairs big and soft around a blue enamel stove, the void around it filled up with a tightly squeezed-in pattern of the cut ends of logs, and the basket beside it full of knobbly vine faggots that served as kindling.

"She imported the wood at vast expense, the owner," Dr Christos said. "Mostly because she loved the smell."

"Whose is it, the house?"

"It belonged to Doris's family. Still does, but it isn't a family home any more. They keep it for letting now."

"It's Doris's house?" She glanced nervously around. What if Doris was about to walk through the door? What if – she hadn't thought of this – she was one of the women at the bus stop, one of the gardeners?

"It's her father's, technically. He did the conversion and put in the ensuite bathrooms himself, before he got ill. Doris doesn't want to live here."

"Why not?"

"She's fallen out with the family. It's mostly one extended family up here, spread between the houses. Mostly they're related to me, in fact. You'll like Olympia's sister particularly – she's a cultured and well-travelled person. They'd like you to live up here. You're a celebrity now. They'd see it as a victory over the other place."

Nina went slowly up the stairs and Dr Christos followed closely behind. They stood in the three bright bedrooms, one after the other, looking at white walls and old beds and reproduction icon paintings, and opened and closed cupboards. They went in and out of the tiny but nicely done bathrooms, and looked out from the room that would be hers, out at the spectacular view.

"So what do you think?" he said eventually. "Can you imagine living here?"

"This is the kind of place I can imagine writing the book."

"Writing one? You're going to write one?"

"I'm going to have a go. I always wanted to. This might be the time. I can imagine working here, here and in Norway."

"You'll probably find it's harder than it looks." She didn't have anything to say to that. "Probably best to stick at what you're good at," he added. "That's something I've also had to learn. So what do you think – it's a wonderful house, isn't it?"

"It really is. Thank you for showing it to me."

"So is the deal done?" He looked and sounded hopeful.

"I'll think about it and let you know."

"But you're coming to Greece? That part is for definite, isn't it?"

"I haven't decided yet."

"Oh, come on, Nina." He put his hands on the sill and leaned his head against the window and closed his eyes. "This is just the usual backtracking." She thought she saw a glimpse of it, the reputed temper, just as it was being reined in.

"The usual?"

"You're afraid of drawing the line and stepping over it. Just do it. Live your life forwards for once. Go forwards! Don't think about jumping; just jump!"

She couldn't look at him. She worked uselessly at the window mechanism. "I can't get it to open."

He was still talking. "Listen to the things you told me in your own words. Have what you want for once. What you want. There is a wonderful life here, laid out and waiting for you. It's all waiting." He moved forward and put his hand on her arm. "Stop that a minute. Listen to me. Don't do it. Please. I understand why you might backtrack; I've done it with Doris and I've always regretted it."

"You don't really know me," she said. It was true, despite everything, despite the stories, despite all the disencumbering.

"Of course I do."

"No." She made a last heroic push and the window opened onto a rush of warmth, the aromas of air and ocean, plant-life and heated-up gravel and stone. She could see the women at the allotments if she leaned out far enough.

He was standing right beside her now, trying to meet her gaze, but she wouldn't look at him. "And this is your way of telling me you are returning to Paolo."

"I'm not saying that. I'm just saying that when things get fixed, when you say them, they're not always true for very long. It's all continually evolving. Sometimes it feels like the things that can be spoken aloud are all the wrong ones. Like they're stand-ins for what's really going on."

"Nina. Nina. Look at me." When she turned to him he put his hands at the sides of her neck and moved them slowly along to the ends of her shoulders. "We need to give this a shot. We do. You know we do. We need to find out one way or another." He bent and kissed her gently on the lips, and she looked at his mouth and knew it was the wrong one. Perhaps there wouldn't be a right mouth again; not ever. Was she ever going to acclimatise to the idea? "Can I make a suggestion?" he asked.

"Suggest away,"she said, but she was ill at ease.

"Come back to my house, and go to bed with me."

"So direct." It was all she could manage to say. She turned back to the view, leaning out of the window as if compelled, and it occurred to her that she was physically blocking him.

"I like directness." He sounded playful; playfulness was an impossibility. He might have thought her cryptic, even coquettish. That wouldn't do.

"What is that going to teach us, if sex is just sex?" She seemed to be asking the question of the garden and its miniature orchard. What would it look like here at night?

"Nina. Please talk to me. Look at me." She withdrew and turned to face him again. "It would mark the start of things for us, something ready to resume for when you come back. Don't you think?" He put his fingers over hers. She looked down at them, and registered the feel of them, and knew without any doubt that it was the wrong hand, and had to move hers away.

"I'm sorry," she said. "I don't want to. I'm sorry."

He took a step back. "That isn't the impression that you've given."

She frowned at him. "What impression is that?"

"My turn to be sorry," he said. "I didn't mean to imply there was any kind of a promise. I was just surprised. You're not attracted to me?"

"Things work differently for me than that. Physically." What was she saying? She had no idea any more.

"Oh, I see. Do we have to be engaged first?"

He smiled at her and she smiled back. This felt easier now. "I may have only had sex with three people, my whole life. But when it's happened it's something we've arrived at; we've arrived at it. It hasn't been like – like –"

"Like what?"

"Like an audition."

"All dates are an audition though, aren't they, when you come right down to it." She was struggling to get the window to close properly, and he stepped in and did it for her. "I'm not going to see you for a while and we've been granted this small time together.

I want to be closer to you." He bent and kissed her again, very softly, a few seconds of soft pressure, removing himself very slowly again. "Warm skin against skin."

She said, "I'm meeting Paolo after this."

"We have time." He dipped his chin and looked charmed, as if she were an innocent and her objections endearing.

"It isn't that."

"I understand; I'll take you back to the hospital. Come on." They went down the stairs together, Dr Christos going ahead in case Nina stumbled forward. He said, "You haven't looked in the kitchen cupboards. You should probably look at the kitchen a bit more closely, if you're to make a decision from home. I noticed you didn't try the water pressure in the bathroom."

Nina obediently opened doors. "There isn't a dishwasher; that's a pity."

"It will only be you, though, and me sometimes, I hope, and I'll do the washing-up."

Nina followed him out onto the garden. "It is incredibly beautiful." She could hear in her voice that this was a plus point, being voiced in fairness to a longer list of negatives. There was an audible sense of regret in it, one that she knew he'd also heard.

They got back into the car and Dr Christos said, "Can I ask you one thing?"

"Fire away." She put her seatbelt on.

"What did you and Paolo talk about at lunch?"

"What did we talk about?"

"I wondered if I'd missed part of the story." He started the car. "Bring me up to speed."

"It was just chat." She found she didn't want to tell him about the picnic. There'd been something about it that was inexplicably private.

"What was the chat about?"

"You want me to tell you what we chatted about."

"Please."

"When you were married to Doris, were you constantly asking her what she was thinking, and what was said and what texts she'd received?"

"Of course."

"I can't tell if you're joking."

"I'm not joking. I would never have let her have a close friend-ship with another man."

"Let her? You wouldn't have let her?"

"No."

"Not all other men are rivals, though."

"Of course they are." They bumped and juddered back down the pot-holey dust track. "In fact, let's stop at Olympia's sister's house. She would like to meet you and this might be a good time."

"Do you mind if we don't? I'm really tired. Lunch was tiring."

"Well, never mind. What shall we do instead, with the time we have left? Let's go to my place. I'd like you to see it." They came out onto the road. "Don't worry – you look so worried! I'm not going to corner you there. Tell you what – we won't even go in. You can sit on the veranda and I'll make us some tea. What do you say?"

"If you want to."

"If I want to?"

"That'd be nice, thank you."

They drove back through the village, skirting around the same sleeping dog and slowing for the same football game. The same goats were standing at the side of the road.

"Are you afraid that you'll grow bored here? Because I have family over there" – he nodded towards Main Island – "where perhaps you would be happier."

"I don't think my dream of living here was very realistic," Nina said. "But thank you."

"What was unrealistic about it?"

"I feel a little bit of panic at the idea of living here."

"Marooned."

"Yes, sort of that." They went round the sharpest bend and past the accident spot, and Nina made herself look at it, catching a glimpse of the ledge down beneath the new barrier. She said, "Do you think you will move away?" He needed to see it, the obvious thing. She needed to know that he'd understood.

"I don't know." His disappointment in her was obvious. "I feel responsible to the hospital in a way I wish I didn't. And also, the fact is I wasn't happy in London or in the States. I seem to have allowed myself to become a man with no country. When I'm away I feel Greek and I'm homesick as hell, and when I come back I hate the place. There doesn't seem to be an answer."

They'd reached the junction and turned right in the direction of Blue Bay.

"I can see how that might happen," Nina said. She felt terrible. "To be honest I feel a bit the same way myself."

They were quiet until they got to the house. "I'm sorry I rushed you," he said. "I'm just eager to know you. I'm happy to take things slowly. Let's go and drink tea and sit on my veranda like an old married couple."

Standing there with him, only yards from the shore, Nina could see the whole panorama of the life she was turning down. The shuttle ferry was in its dock and the great whale's-back shape of Main Island lay ahead; seabirds decorated the undisturbed blue and the sun was deliciously warm on her face.

She said, "You're so lucky to have all this."

He unlocked the door. "Snowing at home," he said, going in. "Snowing in October." A few moments later his face reappeared. "Sit yourself down. I don't recommend the one with the cushion. It's unstable and might have teeth. The rocker is too rocky for someone with a broken leg. I'd go for the basket chair if I were you."

Nina sat down, keeping her sore leg extended and lowering herself as she'd learned to. A tabby cat blinked at her from the cushion, its front paws tucked under its chest, sphinx-like in pose and ecstatically relaxed. How would it be, for this to be home and for this to be an ordinary afternoon in her life? She knew that all she needed to do was follow him into the house and close the door and kiss him, and she'd leave Greece with her future assured. It would have been impossible to exaggerate, even to herself, how deep and persuasive the enticement was, the internal monologue in support of making that wrong decision. She also knew she wasn't going to do it, though this knowledge arrived with its sense of loss already in place. This could have been her life. There was Dr Christos, making mint tea after a day at the hospital, coming to sit with her on the veranda, and there he was picking vegetables in the back yard for dinner; she'd pour the wine and he'd barbecue the fish, threaded in chunks onto skewers with their garden onions and courgettes. On warm evenings they could cross the deserted road and go and swim. They could do it naked and in the middle of the night.

"Would you like cake?" a disembodied voice called out. "I have some that Doris gave me, but it may be a little stale."

After they got back to the hospital and were about to get out of the car, Dr Christos said, "Just one more question. Three, you said. Who was the third?"

"The third?"

"The third lover. You mentioned there've been three."

"Haven't you guessed?"

"No. Was I supposed to guess?"

"Andy. Andy Stevenson." She opened the door and had to wait.

Dr Christos got out of his side in a rush and pulled the crutches from the back seat. "Andy Stevenson. My God. Was this before he made love with your mother?"

"He didn't."

"I don't believe that, though – do you?"

"Course. He said so." Her statements were becoming shorter.

"Nah," Dr Christos said. "But even assuming not... was this before he had that famously chaste kiss on the sofa with your mother?" His voice was different now, when he spoke to her. Perhaps she'd liberated him from the burdens of a constant and wearying kindness.

"No, it was after she'd died."

The doctor slapped the car roof as if vindicated. "He was the boy who wasn't a Romano, with the wrong kind of hands! The one you were supposed to take to the wedding and who sent you scurrying to Paolo!"

She waved at him. "I'm going in now, so bye."

"You slept with him on the first date" Dr Christos said disdainfully. "Andy. On your only date, even though you didn't like him."

What could she say? She hadn't known how to stop it, once it started. It had been awkward, embarrassing, and Andy had been insistent. She said, "These things happen."

"You slut," he said, as if it was a joke.

When Nina went into her room she found Paolo sitting there. "You're early," he said, "And our outing has been delayed."

She sank onto the bed with a grateful long sigh, and lay flat on her back with her arms open.

"So how was it?" he said, looking up from yesterday's *Times*.

"Lovely, it's really lovely."

"So are you going for it? Deal done?"

"I'm not sure. Not because it isn't lovely, and not because I wouldn't be welcome, I hasten to add." She heard Paolo laugh, a short laugh, and raised her head briefly at the neck to look at him. "What is it?"

"I don't know anybody else who'd say *I hasten to add*. I've missed *I hasten to add*."

"Ha."

"I go to the art gallery now and look at the pictures you used to go and look at, and I go to the museum."

"When do you get time?"

"I've been reading books that you gave me at Christmas but that I've never read, and some of the books that you've worked on, that you left behind."

What was this, and what was she supposed to make of it, and how was she supposed to answer? "You've been reading books I've worked on?"

"I see you in them sometimes, especially in that one you more or less rewrote. The sentence structure of it."

"That terrible murder thing set in the hotel?"

He was still looking at his paper. "It's not terrible. You made it less so." He shuffled down further in the chair and raised the pages higher, so now she couldn't see his eyes. "I like the idea of walking in your footsteps and seeing things with you, even though you're not there. It feels like togetherness in a way."

Not a phrase came to her. Her vocabulary, her articulacy, her ability to think on her feet: all of it had vanished.

Nurse Yannis came into the room and took the clipboard from the end of the bed. "It is the end of the chart for you. No more chart."

Paolo put his newspaper down. "Thank you so much for all you've done."

Nurse Yannis turned to the patient. "You go home tomorrow, Christos says. You are not here for the winter, I hope. I say because it is cold here. People are surprised. It is cold and it is closed."

"Not as cold as at home."

"And also it is windy, at the top, and the heating is not good there. Also, nobody has English."

"Except for Olympia's sister."

"That is true. And now I must attend." She left them alone.

Paolo went and shut the door after her, and when he'd returned to his seat, said, There's something I need to tell you. Nina was still looking at the ceiling, and so when he went on, "Forgive me if I'm wrong, but I'm not sure you're aware that Nurse Yannis's Christian name is Doris," she was able to be shocked and embarrassed without looking him in the face. The effects on her system were immediate, surging in. It was like standing in the shallows and being hit from behind by a wave. She was having some kind of physical crisis, perhaps a cardiac one: blood swept into the top of her head and back out of her fingers and she began to feel cold, her hands tingling and feet numbing.

"I knew that," she said, rubbing laboriously at her eyes with icy finger-ends.

"You did?"

"Of course." She pressed her lips together, sucking them into her mouth, and rubbed at her chin and then at her nose.

"What's the matter?"

"Just itchy." Her heart was pounding, beating hard at her chest wall, and pains were shooting across the side of her head. She looked critically at her hands, at her fingernails, noting the tremor there. Paolo must be able to see it. She wanted to run. She began radically to slow everything down that was herself and that was still within reach. She said, "I must go to the loo before we go out," and began to rise into a sitting position, still facing away from him. Matters were delayed while she rubbed at her lower back. She said, "I'm stiff today." The walls seemed to be rising, the bed rising as if inching upwards in a lift.

Paolo's voice sounded far off. "You knew that it was Christos's wife looking after you?"

"Course. Why don't you go and have a smoke with George?" How had she said these ordinary words?

She couldn't look at him openly, but turned her head enough to see that he was looking at his watch and patting at his pockets for his cigarettes. She waited until he'd gone into the garden, and then she got to her feet, and made it to the bathroom by holding onto things, and sat there for a few minutes, and then after flushing the unused loo she went to the French window and said, "I'll be back in a tick," already turning away as Paolo opened his mouth to respond. She went along the corridor to Dr Christos's office, and

found it empty, and went straight to the cabinet and found her file.
ROMANO. Nina.

It was all in Greek. Of course it was; why wouldn't it be? She took the top sheet and put the other pages back, the daily charts with their ups and downs. She pushed the cabinet door noisily closed again, and went out into the corridor just in time to see George going into Nurse Yannis's office, Doris's office. She knocked on the glass upper section of the door and was invited in, their two faces looking up at her expectantly.

"What does it say?" She gave the sheet to George. "The bit at the top in red ink, with the asterisks around it."

George looked at it and said, "You'll need Christos's permission for this."

Nurse Yannis leaned forward and took it off him, turning it the right way round, and said something to George that made him raise both hands in surrender. "Okay, okay." He turned to Nina. "Suicide risk. It says suicide risk."

"What?" Nina cried. "That's just ridiculous. That's ridiculous."

She heard someone sounding a car horn outside. She heard Paolo shouting, "Nina, where are you? Come on – it's time to go."

Chapter Twenty-Eight

It wasn't about being unhappy. This was something Nina knew she would struggle to make anyone understand. It wasn't that. It was about feeling nothing, and no longer being able to think, and realising that things had come to a close, because the non-feeling and non-thinking weren't going to end. The holiday had shown her that. There wasn't any meaning to the repetition of the days. Waking at the taverna on the eighth morning she knew that something had changed. It had all changed, her self, the system of herself. New things were spawning and multiplying in her brain; it had started in her brain, like a package that appeared in a locked room, and was unwrapping itself and activating. It was colonising her, imposing itself on her, this new and alien Nina. Thoughts that weren't hers flooded into her mind, preoccupations that she tried to put aside, to master with her usual thinking, but it wasn't any good; they kept coming. It started with maths: at breakfast she tried to devise equations, bent over her notebook, trying to remember how they went and how they were solved, longing for a dog-eared school maths book. She began to think about engineering, about weight-bearing, about bridges and how they might work, and made drawings. When she closed her eyes she saw old aeroplanes in the sky.

She became convinced that an underwater swim would help, that water in her ears was going to be the remedy, and set off towards the beach leaving her breakfast half eaten. A tune came into her head and she began to beat out its syllables against her thigh as she walked along, using three fingers to tap it out and finding it fitted exactly. It was three-divisible. The syllables of all songs could probably be divided into three. Other tunes began to present themselves, and the first two she tried conformed, but then a third one didn't fit the theory. She tried another, and a fifth, and there were ragged ends to most of them, in fact; anxiously, she couldn't find another three-divisible tune. She sat down on the harbour wall, ignoring the fishermen, and got her notebook out and began to count out the beats of more songs. The survey showed that some were fours and some were fives; she began to make a list of all the songs she could think of, written under three columns, but it was difficult because her eyesight was going blurry. She was tired, so tired, going into a stage beyond tired, slipping beneath a creeping exhaustion. She knew she wasn't going to make it to the beach. She looked back in the direction she'd come in; she had to go back to bed and sleep, and it was urgent that she get there as soon as possible. She began to make her way back to the taverna, the heat thick as soup. She was slow and everything else was speeded up: the traffic, the way people spoke, the birds overhead – all of it was going at a rush and flashing by. She went in through the taverna's main door and into the bar, to the foot of the stairs, and paused wondering if she might need an injection, or a pill: she could see herself in a curtained booth in Accident and Emergency – another three – and her smiling face saying, "It's such a relief to find there are all sorts of numbers." That, of course, was a twelve, which was really a three in disguise. She'd been intending to go up to her room but stood on the bottom step and looked up and couldn't hear anything. It was dangerous up there. Francesca was there with a white cat.

"Nina?" She turned and saw Vasilios and he said, "Are you okay?"

She scanned his face and couldn't think of his name. In any case it didn't matter now. All she could do was retrieve what she could, in armfuls, and retreat and wait it out, though waiting might not be enough. It might get worse. What would happen next? She needed help. It was going to get worse. Her towns and villages would be overrun, her institutions closed down; the vast dark forest was full of little fires. Panic began its ascending, a whole load of miniature panics, starting in her knees and climbing up her sinews with sharp claws like bats. She had to get help.

"Nina? What's the matter? Can I do anything?"

She looked at Vasilios blankly, aware that she was standing very still. She couldn't answer him; her mouth wouldn't open. Everything in her was seizing up and deadening. She had to get medical help. She dropped her swimming bag on the floor and turned from him, going out of the taverna and onto the road, aware that he was following her.

"Nina, are you all right?" Hearing Vasilios's voice, she turned to look at him – he was standing on the top outer step of the hotel – and raised her hands, her fingers splayed and palms towards him, pushing him with air.

There was a boat about to go and so she ran towards the ferry dock, shouting for it to wait, and boarded it just as it was untying. The twenty-minute journey was all about slowing her breathing, the slowest possible, and marshalling old pieces of memory, remembered bits of Eliot and Larkin, the words staunching the unravelling like a tourniquet; it would do until she got to the hospital. She'd meant to go to the hospital on the town bus, but instead when it stopped at the market she got off with everyone else and wandered round the stalls, pretending to look at bunches of herbs and bottles of oil, handling things as if she was going to buy them and putting them down again. She felt physically unwell, her knees weak, and decided that what she needed was something to read and a glass of white wine, and to sit watching market day from somewhere close by. There was a second-hand English bookstall, the front of its two trestle tables hung with Union jack bunting, and so she bought an old hardback and took it to the terrace of a nearby bar, and read until the threes receded. In their place there came a decision, one that was sweet and obvious. When she went back on the afternoon boat she felt almost elated.

Walking up the hill, Nina was focused only on picking the right location. There were no sentimental thoughts, no doubts, no pangs about last walks or last anythings; sensible decisions needed to be made. She couldn't, for example, go up too far and risk being seen by the women in their allotments. The hill ascended in stages, rising and then flattening out, and for most of the way it was the same off the side of the road, following the same undulating pattern into the valley. Climbing further, she saw that the village was like a model beneath her, a toy, something scoopable in two cupped palms as if from a basin, and when she paused to look at the view she realised that she'd arrived. There was a short descent to a flattened-out area, a wide brief apron of land that jutted out, where she could be alone and write a letter, and beyond that a sheer drop, which was freefall and joy and an ending. It was a marker of how unwell she was that she didn't imagine how it might feel, this ending, or what the experience would be like for those who found her. It was all more abstract than that in her mind, like a switch about to be switched off. She knew that she could take this power and use it. She would walk off the edge of the world and then there would be nothing, and no other days would have to be endured.

First, though, the letter had to be written, a short one – it could only be a short one – that was lucid and unambiguous. Above all it was important to ensure that Paolo knew that none of this was anything to do with him. That at least was what she intended. Cautiously she descended from the road and onto the ledge, holding the grey dress closer and guiding herself against the wall of the slope with the other hand. It was a soft and easy scramble down. Now there was need of somewhere to write, but there was nowhere good to sit, no boulders, and having inspected the sandy loose surface she saw that there were ants, hundreds of teeming busy ants; the ledge was alive with them. She climbed back up onto the road and went and sat on a squared-off rock in the shade of the hill. How was she to begin? Onto the old postcard, one bought 25 years earlier, she wrote, *I should have loved you, Paolo. I wish I'd loved you. I wish I'd let myself. We could have had a wonderful life.* Then she wrote, *If I could do it all over again I'd do it all differently.* That was all she could say about it because there were other things to add. The message had to be brief because otherwise, given a pad of writing paper, there might have been twenty pages and still not an obvious end to it. Who, given unlimited pages, would have felt that twenty were enough?

She'd meant to write about the couple at the market, the English couple who ran the bookstall, but it wasn't possible to do them justice and in any case nobody else would have seen why they were important. She'd watched them, transfixed, from the bar as the argument escalated. He'd said something to her that had shocked her, his wife, so that she stood staring at him, stopped dead in her tracks, and then she'd fled him, threading through the market-place in tears, crying noisily so that everyone else who was there paused what they were doing to watch. He'd shouted after her, "You've always been a toxic bitch!" Not just toxic, but always. Nina had watched the man to see what he'd do next. He'd packed up the piles of stock into his car, boxing some and then throwing the rest in after, one by one, so that pages creased and snapped and covers twisted and exploded, and he'd slammed the boot lid down and he'd driven away. Nina had gone forward to the last section of the book she'd bought from him, a published edition of a writer's diary. She already knew what happened at the end. The writer had seen the dark wood ahead of her. She'd known what it meant and where it led. She'd chosen to make her own exit, wading into a river with stones in her pockets. Nina threw the book away in one of the market bins, on the way back to the boat.

When the postcard was written, she left her bag sitting by the rock and went back down the slope, slipping her way down for the last bit, and walked along the ledge, which stretched for 30 feet or so if you included its tapering-off. She stood looking out over the village, the tavernas, the shore and the sea, as the dusk grew deep, dun to sepia and sepia to pink; the sun was ripening and rosy, illuminating wisps of cloud with golden auras. She'd said to Paolo on the postcard that she wasn't sad, that it was all completed. Her last thoughts, she said, were of how beautiful the world was. She realised that she wanted to illustrate this idea by leaving photographs for him of the view from the hill, the village below her so nestled and safe, the loveliness of the sky and the sea so tranquil and silvery. It was a perfect little world and she couldn't make herself belong in it. She looked around for her camera and realised that it was still sitting in the handbag, which had been left beside the rock as a marker. There was nothing for it but to scramble back up the slope, and so she did so, and stood on the deserted road with her camera to her eye. The song had come to her, the one in Spanish that was about Luca and Francesca. She'd been taking photographs and singing the song when, having turned the viewfinder from landscape to portrait and back again, she became aware that something huge and white had appeared at her right side.

On the morning of the day that Paolo first arrived from Athens, Nina had begun to talk to people about the accident again. She'd said to Dr Christos that this would be an ideal day to see Andros, who'd sent a message asking if he could visit. The timing was significant: talking to Andros was a way of preparing for Paolo coming, rehearsing what she'd say to him about the accident. She needed to have her story straight. Dr Christos understood that Nina needed to prepare. He understood why. He'd been the first at the scene, driven there by Dr Argyros. Dr Argyros had stayed to attend to the bus passengers, and so it was Dr Christos who'd found the postcard when he looked in her bag for ID. It had been convoluted but her intentions had been clear and he'd taken her intentions seriously; he'd had to; this wasn't something he was able to keep to himself. He'd shared his knowledge, his fears with the hospital on Main Island, and once he'd done that, had to fight to get them to release Nina into his care. He'd had to share his anxieties with Doris, who'd be looking after her; he'd had no choice about that either. When Nina arrived he said to the staff and to George that he didn't feel he could leave her alone in her room for long, that everyone was as casually as possible to keep watch. He'd been anxious about her mental state, when he heard she was being sent back to him, so he was relieved to find her talkative and coherent. It was more than relief. It was almost overwhelming. He'd assumed, that night on the hill, that it was transitory, his being so drawn to her, that it was just about beauty, but walking into her hospital room that first morning, the uninvited inescapable thing was there again and stronger than ever, the attraction he'd felt first at the scene of the accident, and even more decisively in the ambulance, the unfathomable, inexplicable sense of belonging. Unsuspected by all who knew him, Dr Christos was a deeply romantic soul.

He was still helping her to rehearse when Andros arrived. He was saying, "It must have been surprising when you saw the minibus coming at you so fast."

"It was beyond surprising," Nina said. "It was like standing on the beach and a killer whale shooting out of the surf with its mouth open. It was like looking up and seeing a satellite about to land on you. It bypassed the whole idea of fast."

As she spoke a face came round the door, a disembodied head simultaneously with a double rap of knuckles. Startled, Nina knocked her notebook off the side of the bed. Her first thought was that it was Paolo arriving four hours early: Andros was a similar height and breadth, and his dark hair wasn't dissimilar, but the man who said, "I will get it," and came to the bed and bent to pick the notebook up – he wasn't Paolo. She saw, as he stooped, a pink shiny bald patch, and noticed, as he straightened himself and handed it to her, that his eyes were small and his nose Roman: he was a man of about 60, his face crumpled into wrinkles and furrows. He wasn't wearing his usual baseball cap, his usual sweatshirt, but grey suit trousers, shiny black shoes, a blue blazer with gold buttons, and he was holding a leather bush hat.

"I am Andros," he said. "I have the bus." He made a steering-wheel-turning motion with the hat.

"Andros! I'm sorry, I didn't recognise you. Please sit down. I wanted to see you before I went home so I'm very glad you came. Do I talk too fast?"

"A little." He tilted his flattened hand side to side in approximation.

"Your face was the first thing I saw when I woke up on the road," she told him, talking more slowly. Andros sat awkwardly on the edge of the chair. "Thank you so much for everything that day. I'm glad I can tell you in person how sorry I am for causing so much trouble."

Perhaps Andros had been expecting to do the apologising. He didn't seem to know what to say, and so Dr Christos launched into the story of how instrumental he'd been in getting the hospital built, and how he'd worked on Michael Ithika at an EU reception they'd been to in Athens, adding, "He is a good man, Michael Ithika, despite being so stupidly rich." He turned to Andros. "Though I am not going to introduce Nina to him."

"The old bus was a bastard," Andros said, changing the subject. "My new one is here and so I am happy." Dr Christos was trying to hide a smile and Nina remembered that Andros was well known as a collector of foreign-language swear-words.

"Every cloud has a silver lining," she told him. "Well, some clouds do. It might be rash to be too sweeping and include all clouds." Andros looked puzzled. "It's a saying. Good things can come out of bad. You got your new bus, at least, and everybody's okay."

"Everybody is okay," Andros said, putting both thumbs up. "And I have no more nightmares. Not now I have a new bus."

"You've had nightmares?"

"A little bit. But okay now."

In fact Andros was still having bad dreams. Olympia, who'd become attuned to his restlessness at night, woke him up when the twitches and mutterings began, because the key thing was to prevent his reaching the point at which the bus began to tip and he knew for certain that not only was he about to die horribly, but that everyone in his bus was going with him, over the edge of the cliff. He'd begin to whimper and to shout and she'd wake him by putting her face close to his and saying his name progressively louder. She'd go and get him a Metaxa and sit watching him drink it. Andros would rather have had a beer from the refrigerator but Olympia's faith in the restorative powers of brandy was deeply ingrained. There was no medicinal tradition of administering lager to the afflicted.

"They put the fence up now. For years I ask about the fence and they say no, but now the fence!" He reached down into the plastic bag at his feet and brought out Ouzo and two shot glasses.

The day of the crash was as ordinary as any other day. After the post-breakfast run, taking the women up the hill to their gardens, Andros spent the morning at the bike hire shack, where he had an extended conversation with three Australians, looking with them at the island map on the wall. After he'd done the lunchtime trip that brought the tourists back from the beach and brought the women down again, he had a sandwich and a short siesta and did some paperwork at home, and then it was time to take the women back up to the allotments. He returned to the bike shack for its afternoon hours, and as he was about to leave for the final run of the day, the one that brought the gardeners back in time to cook dinner, he'd got oil on his hands and had wiped his palms against the hips of his trousers, thinking he was wearing the apron. That was what had made him late. Not that it mattered; the women never seemed to mind his going off the schedule as long as he turned up eventually.

After he'd put the oily trousers in the washing machine, he'd taken a bowl of white beans and a piece of cold mutton from the fridge to warm a little for later, and a stubby loaf out of the freezer, throwing a teacloth over it because of the cat. He'd taken the bus down to the harbour and had collected his single passenger, a frail old man returning home with his shopping. He'd trundled through the village, passing Olympia's shop, raising his hand mechanically in greeting, and turned up the hill road, feeling the old bus straining in its effort to keep climbing, particularly at the sharper turn, where he'd had to change gear to make that last push. He hadn't seen Nina: Nina had been down on the ledge. When he got into the hamlet's tiny square, with its white war memorial, its copper drinking fountain, now verdigris green, its tree shade and purple oleanders, the women were standing waiting in a chattering cluster at the yellow bench. They were talking over each other as he pulled up, and kept talking as they climbed in through the sliding door, continuing their debate without acknowledging him. "Yes, and I said to her, even before her son left home, that he would marry a girl who didn't want to return here to live; what would an Athenian girl want with a life here, other than for a summer house; a summer house perhaps..." He left them to board while he took the old man into his house, and then he popped over the road to Olympia's sister's, owner of some of the goats, to get the cheese and yoghurt she'd put aside for him. It had been hard to keep the visit short. She was lonely and liked to talk, and this too had caused a delay. If his timings had been usual, he'd have seen Nina on his journey up, making her way up the hill, and on his journey down again he'd have seen her writing a postcard at the side of the road.

Andros left Nina and began walking home again, out of the hospital foyer through the front entrance and past the big stone tub full of flowering thyme, turning onto the road and plodding off on foot, the Ouzo bottle clanking gently against the glasses, the pale dust coating his dark shoes. When he reached the house, stepping out of the heat and into its twilit coolness, he put the carrier bag onto the kitchen table and opened the shutters a little. He changed out of his church clothes, hanging them up in the wardrobe, and went out through the back door, returning into sunshine, into his hillside patch of garden, one that he'd terraced and shaded and irrigated for 40 years. He picked tomatoes and peppers and two knobbly courgettes. He'd asked Nina, just before he said goodbye, what had gone through her mind when she saw the minibus coming at her. "I didn't think anything; it was too sudden," she said. She'd used the practised imagery about satellites and killer whales. "Though when I was lying on the ground, and you were looking down at me, I did think to myself, 'Oh no, my camera is probably broken and it was really expensive.' What did you think about?"

Andros was sure that he was going to die, but even so, despite the finality of the situation, his last thought as the bus tipped and flipped and executed its perfect circle was "The yoghurts and the cheese are falling out of the box."

Chapter Twenty-Nine

Nina came out into the corridor and saw that Paolo was standing outside her room. The horn beeped a second time. He said, "Here we go. That's Andros. Our transport."

"I'll just be a minute," she told him. "Two minutes. I'll see you out there."

"I'll get your bag." He disappeared inside, and after taking a steadying breath she went back into the office, closing the door behind her. Nurse Yannis and George looked as if they expected her return.

"Nina," the nurse said tolerantly.

There wasn't time for pussyfooting. "I'm so sorry, Nurse Yannis. I didn't know; you should've told me."

George thought she meant the diagnosis. "She couldn't tell you what it said in the file."

"Not that. About being Mrs Christos. I didn't know and I need to apologise." She stopped herself from repeating that Nurse Yannis should have told her, because it was supposed to be an apology. She could see through the glass upper of the door that Paolo was waiting in the corridor with the bag over his shoulder, and said, "I have to go but I'm sorry." She thought, *I am constantly apologising; I have to find different words.*

Mercifully Paolo gave no hint of having overheard anything of what had taken place. She asked him where they were going.

"Andros has organised a boat trip."

"Oh no. What? I can't."

"I knew you'd say that, which is why I didn't tell you before."

"But I can't. My leg. I can't get into and out of a boat."

"He's thought of that. Come on. You can't let them all down."

"All? Who's all? Oh God, do I have to?"

"It's just a few people who wanted to give you a send-off. We're going round to the back of the island. A few drinks and a send-off. People have been making cakes. You have to come."

"Are Dr Christos and Doris coming?" She tried to sound normal, though the trying was obvious.

"They're on duty, but we're invited to dinner with them later. Here in the courtyard. Christos asked if we'd like that and I said yes. Are you all right? You don't look well. Perhaps I should cancel."

"Please don't," she said, beginning to go towards the foyer. "I can't let everybody down."

The boat was decorated with strings of Greek flags, and another string of squares of white card, each one marked with a letter in blue paint that spelled out GOODBY NINA, a banner that'd been hung across the outside of the cabin. Paolo saw that Nina had noticed the missing E and said, "Don't you dare." Andros had put out a pair of sturdy boards that were used for the elderly, leaning them against the boat and using the main rope to keep the boat tight against the dock, but the angle was difficult on crutches, so he and Paolo took an elbow each and lifted Nina from the harbour-side. Beneath the banner, a chair awaited her and an upturned crate for resting her leg. When everything was set and she'd given the thumbs-up to say she was comfortable, Andros cast off the lines and fired the engine into a low rumble. They chugged off at a stately pace towards Blue Bay, hugging the shore and slicing through the inertness of the afternoon sea, and Nina, having been confined, was attentive to it all, every detail: the way the water moved, the rise and sturdiness of the hill and its colours, the shape of the village and its human bustle, the low autumn sun that cast strong shadows. Slowly they made their way round towards the rockier side of the island. Paolo was quiet, but his face suggested enjoyment, a quiet pleasure in things without need of talking, so Nina pulled her hat down closer and stood and leaned over the side, peering into the deeps. She needed time to think about Nurse Yannis, to remember talks they'd had and consider them in the light of the new reality. She searched her memory for pieces of film about Dr Christos, finding quotations from him about his marriage, the things he'd said about Doris, the things he'd said quite separately about the nurse. Did it all fit together? She had to make it fit. She'd become afraid of things that didn't fit.

Perhaps he'd noticed the outward signs. Paolo said, "It's so beautiful here." He shifted his weight so that his arm touched hers, and nudged her lightly. "Incredibly," she said.

"Look up there," he told her, and she looked up, holding onto her sunhat with one hand across its crown. A herd of goats had reacted to their passing by running for safety in an untidy group, bleating, their bells jingling. Nina lifted her camera to her eye. The faded sands and ochres of the hillside were dotted with blue greens that were themselves peppered with flowers, and striped with the khaki, the mint-green and metallic-leaf glint of olive groves, and beyond were the vineyards, whose terracing was like something to do with ancient gods, like carved-out steps leading up to a temple. The boat went on further, until the island was end-on and narrowed. It was a perfect merging point, offering a view to one side of a pink and toffee-coloured pebble beach, and to the other, as Blue Bay receded, of its final strip of pale-yellow sand, the white houses looking down like sentries from the slopes above. The boat rounded the corner, which was dramatically rocky, a jumble of fallen boulders, the sea eddying as it was pulled in all directions, and then they were past the furthest point, the sea calm again. The shoreline was only intermittently accessible here, through the wall of rocks, and few people visited other than to swim from their yachts in its privacy. The boat chugged on past two small coves, through a patch of turquoise water that was undisturbed by weed, and then into navy blue, over a deeper section, before cruising over a shallower jewel green. Now that Nina had decided never to return, this was paradise again.

Finally they sailed into the shelter of a more deeply cut bay and the shade of the hill, and the lowering of the anchor was the cue for a sudden busyness. Vasilios brought out folding tables and the women began to bring out the cakes: lemon and almond, berry and yoghurt, placing them down alongside sticky foil trays of baklava. Andros and George saw to the coffee, brewing it up freshly in a pan, and Olympia, immaculately dressed as ever in a cream dress and jacket, her reddish-blonde hair swept back into a pleat, produced floral tea-plates, small silver forks and blue and white checked napkins.

George pointed to a screening row of tall cypresses, dense and darkly green, that had been planted in a rectangle on a lower, flatter part of the hill 200 yards or so further along. "That's Ithika's property," he said. "He owns the next bay and he's built a big modern villa there. He's made a swimming lagoon, partially enclosed; he's put ladders down into it from the rocks, and he's installed a big pontoon to swim out to and sunbathe on."

"Can we go and see?" she asked him.

"No, there's an agreement not to. There's a security guard in the cottage. He keeps watch, and we keep our word."

"But doesn't the road go in between, in front of the house?"

"He had the road moved."

Vasilios put a small table beside Nina's chair, put two tiny white cups on it and returned to the cabin. When Nina took up her crutches so as to return to her seat, Paolo brought his face closer to her ear and said, "I hear you and Christos are going out for dinner, when you come back in November."

She'd forgotten that she'd agreed to this; the conversation felt as if it'd happened long ago. Even the house visit earlier that afternoon felt mysteriously distant. Paolo didn't know – how could he know – what momentousness the day had brought. He couldn't know what trespass the day had brought and where it had taken her, the idea of trespass. Nina went to her chair feeling utterly depleted and spent. She wanted to lie down on the deck and curl up and be lulled into sleep. She wanted a thick mattress on the floor of the boat and a night full of stars. What could she say to Paolo about this projected future dinner date? It was hard to know, particularly as Andros was standing beside her, pouring coffee for both of them from the pot, the dark liquid arcing and aromatic.

"It's all right," Paolo said. "He knows all about it. Everybody knows all about it. Doris made sure of that."

Vasilios, standing to one side with his wife, laughed and waggled a finger. "That is true, my friend," he said. His wife smiled widely. She reminded Nina of Maria, except for the generous wide smile.

"He asked me if it was okay to ask you, and I said that of course it was." Paolo looked out over the sea, frowning at it, the cup in his hands. "Then he confessed that he'd asked already."

"You know that you two are having dinner with the two of them tonight," George said. "Andros and I are helping out. Personally I wouldn't miss it for the world."

"She fights hard," Vasilios said. "That is what I must say about Doris. She fights."

"I admire that in her," Paolo said.

Love can't be said to be an event. Things that happen quickly can unhappen just as fast; falling can be offset by unfalling, by getting up and carrying on as if falling never happened. But even though all this is true, and wariness natural, and even though Nina had known Paolo all of her life, something occurred as he said these five words – *I admire that in her* – looking earnestly at Vasilios; it was something that seemed to happen as if it were an event. Nina looked at him, at the cup in his hand, at the hand itself, at his wrist, at the set of his shoulder, at the set of his jaw, at his eyes, crinkled and dark with amiability, and found she was having a physical reaction to him, one that felt new. It was something beyond the reckoning: the good memories, the list, the many things she could have listed as good in him. She was aware of the force of his mind, and his kindness, and saw them illustrated in his face. There had been some shift. She was aware of his physical self, the outline and musculature, the gently rounded belly, the hint of a second chin: she could take possession of them and felt as if she were beginning to. In her mind, there was something she was being asked permission to allow to happen. It would happen if she gave consent. It was something she let go, a sort of release, as if in slow-motion through a trapdoor. She let go of it and was aware of it, the falling, a soft descent from somewhere to somewhere else. She gave the falling permission to fall further. She said yes to it and her heart swelled with incomprehensible non-thoughts, with warmth. Ideas were feelings and vice versa and all the usual categories were running into one another and being superseded. She looked at his face – he was still talking to Vasilios – and looked away again. What to do? She thought about going over the side of the boat and swimming for land. She couldn't stay here: the geography of this gathering was all wrong, its past context of heartbreak, its convivial impending divorce, its apparent emergent relationship with the wrong man. She wanted to stand up and make a speech. "You've got it all wrong," she'd tell them. "I was stupid for a long time, and then for a brief time unhinged." She realised that she might have spoken some of these words aloud. Everyone was looking at her; Andros and Vasilios, waiting for her next move, blinked at her with their long eyelashes like two bullocks.

All that could be done about this embryonic and unstable complexity was to keep it uncontaminated by explanations. She, said, "Could I have some more coffee?" and rubbed at her upper arms as if she was cold. Still talking to Vasilios and without breaking off, Paolo reached down and picked up Nina's jacket and put it around her shoulders. They were talking about business, the two of them, about long hours and thankless tasks and low rewards and whether it was all worth it. They were interested in one another. It was almost as if she was with Paolo for the first time; with him and not just in his company. Something had fallen away, an old adopted context. What would life be like if it was genuinely one to one? She looked at Paolo's mouth as he spoke, at the strong lines of his top lip, his hand on the cup, at the way his chin tilted up when he laughed. She wanted to touch him, to run her hand down his spine to where the flesh became convex and muscly. Did he still sleep on his front, now that he lived alone? She wanted to see his face on the next pillow, the half face turned towards her in sleep, and to see his eye open and to see its delight in her. When had she last seen it, that unclouded confidence? The truth was that she hadn't ever seen it. She wanted to move under his arm and put it diagonally across her body and to adhere, to find and enforce points of physical adhesion. If there was a moment, this was the moment. It would stay with her always.

Paolo noticed the change in her expression. "What is it?"

"Nothing, really." She couldn't look at him while having these thoughts, afraid he'd read them and even more afraid of witnessing his feeling otherwise. A sudden sweeping grief came over her and she thought she'd cry out with the melancholy of it. Twenty-five years, and so much of it had been lived only as if life had been postponed. It was how she had been while life was in a state of postponement. Why hadn't she understood what it was that she had let go by so unmemorialised? She could have had a genius for living and done everything and been diverse and fulfilled: she could have cooked well and painted and been a better friend and done all the million things. Why hadn't she done the million things? Phrases came to her from the books her mother had read: *the nurturing of proper joy, the cultivation of the authentic voice. You mustn't become ill again*, her mother's voice said in her mind. *I know, I know*, she answered. *It's all still waiting for you*, her mother's voice said. It was okay. It wasn't really Anna's voice, but her own.

"Nina? Are you all right?" Paolo put his hand in hers and she gripped it tightly and he squeezed hers in return. She forced herself to pay attention to what was being talked about.

"Of course Doris must be there," Vasilios was saying to George. "She knows that she must stop them being alone on this last night."

"There is danger of madness on a last night on a Greek island," George said, taking the stopper out of a bottle of beer and swigging from it. "And believe me, I know. I fell for it myself. Became emotional about leaving, went to look at a house... and there wasn't even a woman involved."

"Olympia's sister still waits for you," Vasilios said, roaring with laughter, which everybody but Olympia joined in with. "You better do it soon, George, or she will die a virgin." Olympia was not amused.

"I am, as ever, only too glad to entertain you," George said.

Andros produced a bottle of Ouzo. "Perhaps this?"

Vasilios went and got a crate of tall glasses from the cabin, ready filled with crushed ice, and added the Ouzo to each, the liquid filling milky white in its contact with the meltwater. Nina stood and drank hers down in three long gulps.

"Steady there, Tiger," Paolo told her. "Are you okay?" He looped his arm around her shoulder from behind and she put her hand onto it; he put his mouth to her ear so that only she could hear. "I know you didn't know about Doris." All she could do was squeeze his arm. "I hope it wasn't too shocking. I hope it doesn't spoil your plans."

"I don't have plans."

"But you're still coming back here to spend the winter."

"No."

"Ah... I wondered."

"I'm not coming back."

"Well, I have to say I'm relieved."

"You are?"

"You might find yourself in the middle of something."

"I'm still reeling. About Doris. All that time and he... Why didn't he tell me, why didn't she tell me?"

"I imagine they have their reasons."

Vasilios had been listening, none too subtly, and stepped

forward now. "It's not a good idea to stay here, Nina," he said. "It's not over, Christos and Doris."

"Isn't it?" Paolo looked surprised. "He gives the impression that they're about to divorce."

"This is the third time," Vasilios told him.

"That's true," George said. "The third time she has left him. She went back twice. Generally they reunite in the winter when the tourists are gone. But I don't know about this winter."

"I'm not coming back," Nina said, addressing them all. "I love it here but I won't be back."

"That's a good decision," George said. "As for Doris, I think that she is learning finally that it's hopeless."

"But Vasilios said" – Nina turned to look at him – "Vasilios, you said that Doris fights hard."

"Yes."

"She tries to keep women away from him," George said. "He has flings, but they never last. He's in love with her, you see, although he'd deny it if you asked him. The last one was the Irishwoman. She lasted a week and a half at the villa."

"What happened?"

"She had food poisoning, seafood she'd eaten in the port." George inclined his head towards Main Island. "She was only hospitalised for 48 hours, but stayed on afterwards and she and Christos had a big romance. This was when he and Doris were apart the second time. The woman told him all about her past, her alcoholic ex-husband, and she moved into Doris's house, the house you've looked at. Then, a week and a half later the husband turned up. The tavernas were full and so she said he could stay. She swore there wasn't more to it than that. But that wasn't good enough. Christos asked her to leave."

"I'm not sure the situation was completely his fault," Nina said.

"It's always his fault," George said. "You'll find if you live here that most of the island sees things from Doris's point of view."

"Except up at the top village."

"Even there, though their blood loyalty decrees otherwise. They remember hearing about the affairs in America when his daughters were small, and Doris's anguish. They're good people, but they're slow to forgive."

The light was failing fast as they chugged back round the rocky point, making a wider circle this time, and as the harbour came into view. Vasilios switched on the boat lights and the village began to illuminate itself, window by window as if in reply. The street lights came on, and mosquito candles began to be lit on verandas, and scooters began to be visible each as a single firefly light on the coast road. There was a unanimous quiet as they sailed back to the mooring, the sun beginning its setting, deep dun and sepia pink, and nor did Nina and Paolo speak to one another as they made their way back to the hospital, Nina swinging along more slowly than usual on her crutches. She was dog tired. Paolo came into her room and stood by the door with his hands in his pockets, watching as Nina poured water and drank. She sat on the edge of the bed and longed for quietness, and to be solitary. She was too tired to have feelings, or to practise the avoidance of them, so when Paolo said that they had half an hour till dinner she told him that she'd rest for a while. She turned herself to lie flat and closed her eyes and dared to rest her palms over her belly, drifting into sleep and aware that Paolo had got his laptop out. It seemed only to be for a minute that she was gone from there, a tiny scoop of sleep, but the next thing she knew he was saying her name and that it'd been half an hour and she needed to wake.

"I'll change my dress," she said, sitting up.

"I'll leave you in peace a few minutes." Paolo went out into the corridor. Evidently Dr Christos was there: she heard him ask if he could have a word with Nina alone, and heard Paolo say, "Well, that's up to Nina, isn't it?" and then the doctor knocked on the door and was invited in. He was dressed in a black suit, a black T-shirt, grey and white Converse sneakers. He smelled good when he kissed her on the cheek.

"Paolo thinks you're married to Nurse Yannis," Nina said without hesitation.

He was prepared. He looked as if he'd expected it. "I am, I'm married to Nurse Yannis."

"Dr Christos." Words failed her.

"We don't share it because it makes things complicated here, and my wife prefers to be private."

"She keeps her maiden name, then. Doris Yannis."

"No, it's my name. I am Yannis also. Christos is a first name in Greek. It is like Christopher. My surname is Yannis."

"Why did you pretend to be Dr Christos?"

"I don't pretend. It's my name."

"Why did you keep all this from me, all this time? All those conversations."

"At first it was for the children who come to the clinic, and then the old ladies liked it, and so it stuck. Plus Doris wanted us to be separate at work. I think that's fair enough." He shrugged.

"You didn't tell me. No secrets from one another, you said. Why didn't you tell me? Your wife told Paolo ten minutes after meeting him."

"I have always failed to have control of my wife."

"Christos. Can I call you Christos?"

"Of course."

"You were keen for me to be here over the winter."

"I still am. I would love it."

"You were interested in me."

"I am interested in you." Now he looked as if he'd had a new thought. "But I see what's happened. You have been subject to island propaganda. I thought this would happen when you went off on the boat trip. These people, Nina, they have small minds."

"It's not that."

Christos didn't seem to have heard. "I've told you already that I was unhappy in my marriage."

"That isn't it, though."

"I'm sure there are things Andros and Vasilios and George told you that made your hair stand on end, but there are also things they didn't tell you. They left out the part, I'm sure, in which they were instrumental in making my romances fail. This island, it's a very conservative place. Until I'm divorced no one here is going to allow me to find love. Even then, they are going to take a long time to welcome someone new. Even though it was Doris who left, they will always see me as the bad guy."

"I'm sorry," she said. She couldn't think what else to add.

"I won't get the chance to talk to you again," he said. "So I just want to say something to you. Which is this: that no matter what you think, or hear, or decide later, it was real to me, this love."

Dinner was held in the hospital courtyard, in candlelight. Nurse Yannis looked pretty, in a black lace cocktail dress and a dark-red shawl and lipstick that matched it. The atmosphere was at first subdued.

"I'm sorry we have to eat at the hospital," Christos said, breaking the silence. "Technically we're on duty. Though it's a quiet night, or should be, medically speaking."

George and Andros, in black trousers and white shirts, served the tomato and feta salad, and then the *kakkavi*, a seafood stew that Olympia had made, and Paolo began to steer the conversation. "So," he said. "Is food very different between different islands, and is it markedly different on the mainland?" Nina realised that he'd given some thought to this, to what they might talk about. He had a mental list, and chaired the discussion, leading them from Greek food to Greek tourism, from Greek history into Greek art, and from there, via the controversy surrounding the Elgin marbles, to the museums and expense of London. Luca would have been scornful of him for this, and Luca would have been wrong.

"That is a lovely evening," Doris said at the end, squeezing Nina's wrist. "And I am sorry I am secret."

When Nina said goodnight and went to bed, Paolo followed her through the French window and into her room. "Nina." She turned to face him; only half of his face was illuminated, in the dark-blue light that came in from outside. He came close to her. "When we get back... I think we should live apart and see what happens."

"What's likely to happen?" Her voice matched his for softness.

"It'll start with dinner. A restaurant."

"You're asking me out to dinner?"

"I'm only going to ask if you're going to say yes. Are you going to say yes?"

"What are we going to talk about?"

"All the things."

"What things?"

"All the things we never talk about."

"And what about Karen?"

"I might have exaggerated a bit there. Or invented. One of those. I apologise."

She sat down on the edge of the bed. "But what about the broken teacup?"

"The what?"

"Once it's broken it's never any use again, no matter what."

"Well, that's crap, isn't it?" He went and sat on the blue chair.

"Why is it crap?"

"Who compares love to a teacup?"

"It's just a metaphor."

"Who says it's a teacup? Why isn't it a rainbow and all a beautiful illusion? Why isn't it a watch, an old-fashioned watch with tiny gold workings? That's very fixable."

"It's a metaphor for fragility."

"Whose metaphor? Oh, don't tell me." He dipped his head into his hands and rubbed the back of his head as if relieving tension there. "I've been talking to someone. A therapist."

"A therapist? Really?"

"It was useful in getting me thinking. One of the obvious decisions was to have a break from the 60-hour week. Twenty-five years of that is probably enough." He got to his feet. "Lots to say on that topic and on others, but now I must bid you goodnight. I'm getting too tired to avoid being sentimental. Goodnight, love. I'll be here in the morning at nine."

In fact he was at the hospital by 8am, with his pinstripe rucksack and the pale summer jacket that was still soiled from the flight over. They went out into the garden together, to eat bread and jam and drink coffee there, at the table by the steps to the beach, and to feel the early sun on their faces for the last time. Hearing a characteristic tone and pattern of group chatter, Nina went to the furthest corner with her camera and looked up towards the road, and took pictures of the women at the bus stop, and saw the minibus arrive for them and watched them board. She took a last batch of photographs of the view. Out in the bay there was a windsurfer, working the light breeze and having to make do with slow progress.

Paolo came and stood beside her. "Have you missed me?"

"Truthfully, not at all."

"I haven't missed you either," he said. "That's reassuring."

"It is, isn't it?" she agreed. "It's good that we feel the same."

He picked a sprig of mint and sniffed at it. "I know I haven't been the most engaged companion, Nina."

Nina picked her own sprig and rolled its oils between her

palms. "It was both of us."

"About you and Luca. Tell me one last time what your thoughts are. What your thoughts are today. I won't ask again."

"Whatever it was, it's gone, Paolo. It's gone and over with."

"I've been afraid to ask you this. Has the texting started again, the emailing – has it all started again? Are you in touch? Are the two of you about to start to build another wall?"

"It hasn't and there won't be any more of any of that. There won't be emailing. There won't be contact. Not because there mustn't be; because I don't want there to be. But I don't want his name to be a name we can't ever mention. I hope that you'll pass along news of him, when there's news to tell."

"Smell this rosemary." He handed her a sprig of it. He said, "Well." The pause seemed very long. "Faced with a choice between safety, walking away, or trying again and maybe failing, I'd choose failure. I would." He rolled another rosemary sprig between his palms and inhaled. "But I do think we should live apart, at least at first."

"It's what I want, too," she told him. "I'll rent something, once the cottage is sold. Near the Botanics, as a base. Six months of that, and then we'll see."

"You might come to Greece."

"I won't be in Greece but I might be in Norway."

"We can be friends, at the least. Don't you think? I don't want my life to be without you, cut off from you. I can't think of anything I want less. Anything beyond that… It might not work. It's going to be obvious if it doesn't."

"Is it? Is it going to be obvious?"

"You've got to get past this, Nina. This thing between your parents. Yes, it's going to be obvious. I promise you. I need you to make the same promise."

"Just some paperwork to sign." They turned to see Dr Christos holding up a sheet of paper, and followed him back into Nina's room. "Rats," he said. "I've brought the wrong form; I'll send Doris in with it."

A few minutes later Nurse Yannis came in. "For signing, here and here, and also the address, please."

She turned to Paolo. "Can you be in the office? There is the letter for the next doctor. I forget." Paolo followed her out, and when they'd gone a little way she said to him, "Christos, he comes to the airport."

Paolo thanked her and went further down the corridor and walked straight into Dr Christos's room without knocking. The doctor stood up so quickly when he saw who'd come in that his chair tipped over.

"If you have anything to say to Nina, you say it right now," Paolo told him. "Go to her now and say it and I will wait here."

"I will write to her," the doctor said.

"You will not write to her. You write to her and there is going to be a fight. I will be back and I will find you."

"It isn't up to you." Dr Christos raised his voice. "She is only returning to you because she's afraid of life. You know this and I know this."

"You don't really know anything at all about us," Paolo told him.

"I know more than you think."

"You think you do, but really you know nothing."

"You're wrong; I know absolutely everything."

"No doubt she's told you the whole story. It may be the whole story, but it isn't the real story."

"In what way not real?"

"You have no idea how unbreakable we are. We are unbreakable."

"You are separated," Christos reminded him. "Until a week ago you were all set to divorce. So don't give me that unbreakable shit."

"If she divorced me and married you I'd be closer to her than ever; far closer to her than you could ever be," Paolo said. "I'd be her Luca, you see. It'd be my turn to be Luca."

He saw that Christos had recognised the truth of this. It registered in a changed expression in his eyes.

They could hear that the taxi had arrived, its engine idling and then coming to a halt. Paolo said, "I wish you well," and stretched his hand out to shake, and Christos, ignoring the offer, turned his attention once more to his email inbox. He said, "I imagine you can see yourself out."

Paolo returned to Nina's room and was followed in by Andros, his face pink with heat. "You are ready, I hope," he said.

"I am, I'm ready," Nina told him, beginning to gather her

things. Paolo picked up the bags and led the way out into the foyer and through the sliding door, the sun blazing. Nina followed, glancing behind and expecting Christos to appear, but he didn't.

The car was black, but with TAXI painted on both of its front doors in white. Andros stowed the luggage, and Doris came out and kissed Nina on the cheek and said a solemn goodbye, and then she returned to stand in the shade of the porch, waiting to wave them off. As Nina got into the car she saw that Christos had appeared at the entrance and was looking at them through the glass. Doris turned and said something to him, and he pressed the button for the door to open and came out to stand beside her. He raised his arm in farewell and didn't seem to want to come closer. Nina looked at him through the car window, frowning at him and enacting little waves, but he didn't come closer. He raised his arm again as they drove off, remaining blank-faced, before turning and going back into the building with his wife. Nina tried to turn in her seat, constrained by the seatbelt.

"What's the matter?" Paolo asked her. "Have you forgotten something?"

"Christos didn't say goodbye."

"I'm sure he did," Paolo soothed.

"What bad thing have I done? To be treated like that?"

"I'm sure you didn't do anything." He half turned from the front seat to look at her. "But you are going home with me. And he was standing next to Doris. So perhaps he couldn't say what he wanted to. He asked for your email address." He returned to facing forward.

"There isn't going to be email."

"You know, you can have friendships with whomsoever you like," Paolo said, turning again. "I hope you liked my use of whomsoever in that sentence. You don't need my permission to have friends."

"I know. But not this one."

Andros drove them along the coast road, slowly through the village – last looks, last looks – and into a queue of three cars already waiting for the morning ferry. Once they'd parked, Paolo said, speaking to the windscreen, "So what are you going to do over the winter?"

"You asked me that. I already told you."

"Tell me again."

Andros looked at Nina in the driving mirror.

"I'm going to find a rental near the Botanics," she said. "I'll live there until the spring, and then see. I've been thinking a lot about Norway. I'd like to spend next summer in Norway, at the lake house."

"Those are good ideas." Paolo reached his hand around the back of his seat and found hers, and then he let go again and got out of the car and came and sat beside her in the back. He said, "Dinner on Saturday, maybe. That is, if you're free."

Nina said she thought she was.

Andrea Gillies won both The Wellcome Prize 2009 and The Orwell Prize 2010 for her first book, *Keeper*, which was prompted by living with someone with Alzheimer's. *The Enlightenment of Nina Findlay* is her second novel. *The White Lie*, about a landed Scottish family determined to keep a dark secret, was published to critical acclaim in 2012. Find out more about the books at www.andreagillies.com, and follow her on Twitter, @andreagillies.